KU-335-490

MARY HIGGINS CLARK

A CRY IN THE NIGHT

POCKET
BOOKS

LONDON • SYDNEY • NEW YORK • TORONTO

First published in Great Britain by Collins, 1983
First published by Pocket Books, 1997
This edition published by Pocket Books, 2004
An imprint of Simon & Schuster UK Ltd
A Viacom Company

3 5 7 9 10 8 6 4 2

Simon & Schuster UK Ltd
Africa House
64–78 Kingsway
London WC2B 6AH

Simon & Schuster Australia
Sydney

www.simonsays.co.uk

A CIP catalogue record for this book is available from
the British Library

ISBN 0 7434 8435 5

Printed and bound in Great Britain by
Cox & Wyman Ltd, Reading, Berkshire

In happy memory of my parents and brothers,
Luke, Nora, Joseph and John Higgins,
who did, indeed, give joy to my youth

Acknowledgment

My very special thanks to Dr. John T. Kelly, M.D., M.P.H., Professor of Psychiatry and Professor and Associate Head of the Department of Family Practice and Community Health, University of Minnesota Medical School, for his generous and expert assistance in helping me design and interpret the psychopathic personalities found in this book and in *The Cradle Will Fall*.

A CRY IN THE NIGHT

Prologue

Jenny began looking for the cabin at dawn. All night she had lain motionless in the massive four-poster bed, unable to sleep, the stillness of the house oppressive and clutching.

Even after weeks of knowing it would not come, her ears were still tuned for the baby's hungry cry. Her breasts still filled, ready to welcome the tiny, eager lips.

Finally she switched on the lamp at the bedside table. The room brightened and the leaded crystal bowl on the dresser top caught and reflected the light. The small cakes of pine soap that filled the bowl cast an eerie green tint on the antique silver mirror and brushes.

She got out of bed and began to dress, choosing the long underwear and nylon Windbreaker that she wore under her ski suit. She had turned on the radio at four o'clock. The weather report was unchanged for the area of Granite Place, Minnesota; the temperature was twelve degrees Fahrenheit. The winds were blowing at an average of twenty-five miles per hour. The windchill factor was twenty-four below zero.

It didn't matter. Nothing mattered. If she froze to death in the search she would try to find the cabin. Somewhere in that forest of maples and oaks and evergreens and Norwegian pines and overgrown brush it was there. In those sleepless hours she had devised a plan. Erich could walk three paces to her one. His naturally long stride had always made him unconsciously walk too fast for her. They used to joke about it. "Hey, wait up for a city girl," she'd protest.

Once he had forgotten his key when he went to the cabin and immediately returned to the house for it. He'd been gone forty minutes. That meant that for him the cabin was usually about a twenty-minute walk from the edge of the woods.

He had never ᴛaken her there. "Please understand, Jenny," he'd begged. "Every artist needs a place to be totally alone."

She had never tried to find it before. The help on the farm was absolutely forbidden to go into the woods. Even Clyde, who'd been the farm manager for thirty years, claimed he didn't know where the cabin was.

The heavy, crusted snow would have erased any path, but the snow also made it possible for her to try the search on cross-country skis. She'd have to be careful not to get lost. With the dense underbrush and her own miserable sense of direction, she could easily go around in circles.

Jenny had thought about that, and decided to take a compass, a hammer, tacks and pieces of cloth. She could nail the cloth to trees to help her find her way back.

Her ski suit was downstairs in the closet off the kitchen. While water boiled for coffee, she zipped it on. The coffee helped to bring her mind into focus. During the night she had considered going to Sheriff

Gunderson. But he would surely refuse help and would simply stare at her with that familiar look of speculative disdain.

She would carry a thermos of coffee with her. She didn't have a key to the cabin, but she could break a window with the hammer.

Even though Elsa had not been in for over two weeks, the huge old house still glistened and shone with visible proof of her rigid standards of cleanliness. Her habit as she left was to tear off the current day from the daily calendar over the wall phone. Jenny had joked about that to Erich. "She not only cleans what was never dirty, she eliminates every weekday evening."

Now Jenny tore off Friday, February 14, crumpled the page in her hand and stared at the blank sheet under the bold lettering, Saturday, February 15. She shivered. It was nearly fourteen months since that day in the gallery when she'd met Erich. No that couldn't be. It was a lifetime ago. She rubbed her hand across her forehead.

Her chestnut-brown hair had darkened to near-black during the pregnancy. It felt drab and lifeless as she stuffed it under the woolen ski cap. The shell-edged mirror to the left of the kitchen door was an incongruous touch in the massive, oak-beamed kitchen. She stared into it now. Her eyes were heavily shadowed. Normally a shade somewhere between aqua and blue, they reflected back at her wide-pupiled and expressionless. Her cheeks were drawn. The weight loss since the birth had left her too thin. The pulse in her neck throbbed as she zipped the ski suit to the top. Twenty-seven years old. It seemed to her that she looked at least ten years older, and felt a century older. If only the numbness would go away. If only the house weren't so quiet, so fearfully, frighteningly quiet.

She looked at the cast-iron stove at the east wall of the kitchen. The cradle, filled with wood, was beside it again, its usefulness restored.

Deliberately she studied the cradle, made herself absorb the constant shock of its presence in the kitchen, then turned her back on it and reached for the thermos bottle. She poured coffee into it, then collected the compass, hammer and tacks and strips of cloth. Thrusting them into a canvas knapsack she pulled a scarf over her face, put on her cross-country ski shoes, yanked thick, fur-lined mittens on her hands and opened the door.

The sharp, biting wind made a mockery of the face scarf. The muffled lowing of the cows in the dairy barn reminded her of the exhausted sobs of deep mourning. The sun was coming up, dazzling against the snow, harsh in its golden-red beauty, a far-off god that could not affect the bitter cold.

By now Clyde would be inspecting the dairy barn. Other hands would be pitching hay in the polebarns to feed the scores of black Angus cattle, which were unable to graze beneath the hard-packed snow and would habitually head there for food and shelter. A half-dozen men working on this enormous farm, yet there was no one near the house—all of them were small figures, seen like silhouettes, against the horizon. . . .

Her cross-country skis were outside the kitchen door. Jenny carried them down the six steps from the porch, tossed them on the ground, stepped into them and snapped them on. Thank God she'd learned to ski well last year.

It was a little after seven o'clock when she began looking for the cabin. She limited herself to skiing no more than thirty minutes in any direction. She started at the point where Erich always disappeared into the woods. The overhead branches were so entangled that

4

the sun barely penetrated through them. After she'd skied in as straight a line as possible, she turned right, covered about one hundred feet more, turned right again and started back to the edge of the forest. The wind covered her tracks almost as soon as she passed any spot but at every turning point she hammered a piece of cloth into the tree.

At eleven o'clock she returned to the house, heated soup, changed into dry socks, forced herself to ignore the tingling pain in her forehead and hands, and set out again.

At five o'clock, half frozen, the slanting rays of the sun almost vanishing, she was about to give up for the day when she decided to go over one more hilly mound. It was then she came upon it, the small, bark-roofed log cabin that had been built by Erich's great-grandfather in 1869. She stared at it, biting her lips as savage disappointment sliced her with the physical impact of a stiletto.

The shades were drawn; the house had a shuttered look as though it had not been open for a time. The chimney was snow-covered; no lights shone from within.

Had she really dared to hope that when she came upon it, that chimney would be smoking, lamps would glow through the curtains, that she'd be able to go up to the door and open it?

There was a metal shingle nailed to the door. The letters were faded but still readable: ABSOLUTELY NO ADMITTANCE. VIOLATORS WILL BE PROSECUTED. It was signed Erich Fritz Krueger and dated 1903.

There was a pump house to the left of the cabin, an outhouse discreetly half-hidden by full-branched pines. She tried to picture the young Erich coming here with his mother. "Caroline loved the cabin just as it was," Erich had told her. "My father wanted to modernize the old place but she wouldn't hear of it."

5

No longer aware of the cold, Jenny skied over to the nearest window. Reaching into the knapsack, she pulled out the hammer, raised it and smashed the pane. Flying glass grazed her cheek. She was unaware of the trickle of blood that froze as it ran down her face. Careful to avoid the jagged peaks, she reached in, unfastened the latch and shoved the window up.

Kicking off her skis, she climbed over the low sill, pushed aside the shade and stepped into the cabin.

The cabin consisted of a single room about twenty feet square. A Franklin stove on the north wall had wood piled neatly next to it. A faded Oriental rug covered most of the white pine flooring. A wide-armed, high-backed velour couch and matching chairs were clustered around the stove. A long oak table and benches were near the front windows. A spinning wheel looked as though it might still be functional. A massive oak sideboard held willowware china and oil lamps. A steep stairway led to the left. Next to it, rows of file baskets held stacks of unframed canvases.

The walls were white pine, unknotted, silk-smooth and covered with paintings. Numbly Jenny walked from one to the other of them. The cabin was a museum. Even the dim light could not hide the exquisite beauty of the oils and watercolors, the charcoals and pen-and-ink drawings. Erich had not even begun to show his best work yet. How would the critics react when they saw these masterpieces? she wondered.

Some of the paintings on the walls were already framed. These must be the next ones he planned to exhibit. The pole-barn in a winter storm. What was so different about it? The doe, head poised, listening, about to flee into the woods. The calf reaching up to its mother. The fields of alfalfa, blue-flowered, ready for harvest. The Congregational Church with worshipers hurrying toward it. The main street of Granite Place suggesting timeless serenity.

Even in her desolation, the sensitive beauty of the collection gave Jenny a momentary sense of quietude and peace.

Finally she bent over the unframed canvases in the nearest rack. Again admiration suffused her being. The incredible dimensions of Erich's talent, his ability to paint landscapes, people and animals with equal authority; the playfulness of the summer garden with the old-fashioned baby carriage, the . . .

And then she saw it. Not understanding, she began to race through the other paintings and sketches in the files.

She ran to the wall from one canvas to the next. Her eyes widened in disbelief. Not knowing what she was doing, she stumbled toward the staircase leading to the loft and rushed up the stairs.

The loft sloped with the pitch of the roof and Jenny had to bend forward at the top stair before she stepped into the room.

As she straightened up, a nightmarish blaze of color from the back wall assaulted her vision. Shocked, she stared at her own image. A mirror?

No. The painted face did not move as she approached it. The dusky light from the slitlike window played on the canvas, shading it in streaks, like a ghostly finger pointing.

For minutes she stared at the canvas, unable to wrench her eyes from it, absorbing every grotesque detail, feeling her mouth slacken in hopeless anguish, hearing the keening sound that was coming from her own throat.

Finally she forced her numbed, reluctant fingers to grasp the canvas and yank it from the wall.

Seconds later, the painting under her arm, she was

skiing away from the cabin. The wind, stronger now, gagged her, robbed her of breath, muffled her frantic cry.

"Help me," she was screaming. "Somebody, please, please help me."

The wind whipped the cry from her lips and scattered it through the darkening wood.

1

It was obvious that the exhibition of paintings by Erich Krueger, the newly discovered Midwest artist, was a stunning success. The reception for critics and specially invited guests began at four, but all day long browsers had filled the gallery, drawn by *Memory of Caroline,* the magnificent oil in the showcase window.

Deftly Jenny went from critic to critic, introducing Erich, chatting with collectors, watching that the caterers kept passing fresh trays of hors d'oeuvres and refilling champagne glasses.

From the moment she'd opened her eyes this morning, it had been a difficult day. Beth, usually so pliable, had resisted leaving for the day-care center. Tina, teething with two-year molars, awakened a half-dozen times during the night, crying fretfully. The New Year's Day blizzard had left New York a nightmare of snarled traffic and curbsides covered with mounds of slippery, sooty snow. By the time she'd left the children at the center and made her way across town she was nearly an hour late for work. Mr. Hartley had been frantic.

"Everything is going wrong, Jenny. Nothing is ready. I warn you. I need someone I can count on."

"I'm so sorry." Jenny tossed her coat in the closet. "What time is Mr. Krueger due?"

"About one. Can you believe three of the paintings weren't delivered until a few minutes ago?"

It always seemed to Jenny that the small, sixtyish man reverted to being about seven years old when he was upset. He was frowning now and his mouth was trembling. "They're all here, aren't they?" she asked soothingly.

"Yes, yes, but when Mr. Krueger phoned last night I asked if he'd sent those three. He was terribly angry at the prospect they'd been lost. And he insists that the one of his mother be exhibited in the window even though it's not for sale. Jenny, I'm telling you. You could have posed for that painting."

"Well, I didn't." Jenny resisted the impulse to pat Mr. Hartley on the shoulder. "We've got everything. Let's get on with hanging them."

Swiftly she helped with the arrangement, grouping the oils, the watercolors, the pen-and-ink sketches, the charcoals.

"You've got a good eye, Jenny," Mr. Hartley said, visibly brightening as the last canvas was placed. "I knew we'd make it."

Sure you did! she thought, trying not to sigh.

The gallery opened at eleven. By five of eleven the featured painting was in place, the handsomely lettered, velvet-framed announcement beside it: FIRST NEW YORK SHOWING, ERICH KRUEGER. The painting immediately began to attract the passersby on Fifty-seventh Street. From her desk, Jenny watched as people stopped to study it. Many of them came into

10

the gallery to see the rest of the exhibit. Not a few of them asked her, "Were you the model for that painting in the window?"

Jenny handed out brochures with Erich Krueger's bio:

Two years ago, Erich Krueger achieved instant prominence in the art world. A native of Granite Place, Minnesota, he has painted as an avocation since he was fifteen years old. His home is a fourth-generation family farm where he breeds prize cattle. He is also president of the Krueger Limestone Works. A Minneapolis art dealer was the first to discover his talent. Since then he has exhibited in Minneapolis, Chicago, Washington, D.C., and San Francisco. Mr. Krueger is thirty-four years old and is unmarried.

Jenny studied his picture on the cover of the brochure. And he's also marvelous-looking, she thought.

At eleven-thirty, Mr. Hartley came over to her. His anxious fretful look had almost disappeared. "Everything's all right?"

"Everything's fine," she assured him. Anticipating his next question she said, "I reconfirmed the caterer. *The Times, The New Yorker, Newsweek, Time* and *Art News* critics are definitely coming. We can expect at least eight at the reception, and allowing for gate-crashers about one hundred. We'll close to the public at three o'clock. That will give the caterer plenty of time to set up."

"You're a good girl, Jenny." Now that everything was in order, Mr. Hartley was relaxed and benign. Wait till she told him that she couldn't stay till the end of the reception! "Lee just got in," Jenny continued, referring to her part-time assistant, "so we're in good shape." She grinned at him. "Now please stop worrying."

"I'll try. Tell Lee I'll be back before one to have lunch with Mr. Krueger. You go out and get yourself something to eat now, Jenny."

She watched him march briskly out the door. For the moment there was a lull in the number of new arrivals. She wanted to study the painting in the window. Without bothering to put on a coat, she slipped outside. To get perspective on the work she backed up a few feet from the glass. Passersby on the street, glancing at her and the picture, obligingly walked around her.

The young woman in the painting was sitting in a swing on a porch, facing the setting sun. The light was oblique, shades of red and purple and mauve. The slender figure was wrapped in a dark green cape. Tiny tendrils of blue-black hair blew around her face, which was already half-shadowed. I see what Mr. Hartley means, Jenny thought. The high forehead, thick brows, wide eyes, slim, straight nose and generous mouth were very like her own features. The wooden porch was painted white with a slender corner column. The brick wall of the house behind it was barely suggested in the background. A small boy, silhouetted by the sun, was running across a field toward the woman. Crusted snow suggested the penetrating cold of the oncoming night. The figure in the swing was motionless, her gaze riveted on the sunset.

Despite the eagerly approaching child, the solidity of the house, the sweeping sense of space, it seemed to Jenny that there was something peculiarly isolated about the figure. Why? Perhaps because the expression in the woman's eyes was so sad. Or was it just that the entire painting suggested biting cold? Why would anyone sit outside in that cold? Why not watch the sunset from a window inside the house?

Jenny shivered. Her turtleneck sweater had been a Christmas gift from her ex-husband Kevin. He had arrived at the apartment unexpectedly on Christmas Eve with the sweater for her and dolls for the girls. Not one word about the fact that he never sent support payments and in fact owed her over two hundred dollars in "loans." The sweater was cheap, its claim to warmth feeble. But at least it was new and the turquoise color was a good background for Nana's gold chain and locket. Of course one asset of the art world was that people dressed to please themselves and her too-long wool skirt and too-wide boots were not necessarily an admission of poverty. Still she'd better get inside. The last thing she needed was to catch the flu that was making the rounds in New York.

She stared again at the painting, admiring the skill with which the artist directed the gaze of the viewer from the figure on the porch to the child to the sunset. "Beautiful," she murmured, "absolutely beautiful." Unconsciously she backed up as she spoke, skidded on the slick pavement and felt herself bump into someone. Strong hands gripped her elbows and steadied her.

"Do you always stand outside in this weather without a coat and talk to yourself?" The tone of voice combined annoyance and amusement.

Jenny spun around. Confused, she stammered, "I'm so sorry. Please excuse me. Did I hurt you?" She pulled back and as she did realized that the face she was looking at was the one depicted on the brochure she'd been passing out all morning. Good God, she thought, of all people I have to go slamming into Erich Krueger!

She watched as his face paled; his eyes widened, his

lips tightened. He's angry, she thought, dismayed. I practically knocked him down. Contritely she held out her hand. "I'm so sorry, Mr. Krueger. Please forgive me. I was so lost in admiring the painting of your mother. It's . . . It's indescribable. Oh, do come in. I'm Jenny MacPartland. I work in the gallery."

For a long moment his gaze remained on her face as he studied it feature by feature. Not knowing what to do, she stood silently. Gradually his expression softened.

"Jenny." He smiled and repeated, *"Jenny."* Then he added, "I wouldn't have been surprised if you told me . . . Well, never mind."

The smile brightened his appearance immeasurably. They were practically eye to eye and her boots had three-inch heels so she judged him to be about five nine. His classically handsome face was dominated by deep-set blue eyes. Thick, well-shaped brows kept his forehead from seeming too broad. Bronze-gold hair, sprinkled with touches of silver, curled around his head, reminding her of the image on an old Roman coin. He had the same slender nostrils and sensitive mouth as the woman in the painting. He was wearing a camel's hair cashmere coat, a silk scarf at his throat. What had she expected? she wondered. The minute she'd heard the word *farm,* she had had a mental image of the artist coming into the gallery in a denim jacket and muddy boots. The thought made her smile and snapped her back to reality. This was ludicrous. She was standing here shivering. "Mr. Krueger . . ."

He interrupted her. "Jenny, you're cold. I'm so terribly sorry." His hand was under her arm. He was propelling her toward the gallery door, opening it for her.

He immediately began to study the placement of his paintings, remarking how fortunate it was that the last

14

three had arrived. "Fortunate for the shipper," he added, smiling.

Jenny followed him around as he made a meticulous inspection, stopping twice to straighten canvases that were hanging a hairbreadth off-center. When he was finished, he nodded, seemingly satisfied. "Why did you put *Spring Plowing* next to *Harvest?*" he asked.

"It's the same field, isn't it?" Jenny asked. "I felt a continuity between plowing the ground and then seeing the harvest. I just wish there was a summer scene as well."

"There *is,*" he told her. "I didn't choose to send it."

Jenny glanced at the clock over the door. It was nearly noon. "Mr. Krueger, if you don't mind, I'm going to settle you in Mr. Hartley's private office. Mr. Hartley's made a luncheon reservation for you and him at the Russian Tea Room for one o'clock. He'll be along soon and I'm going to go out now for a quick sandwich."

Erich Krueger helped her on with her coat. "Mr. Hartley is going to have to eat alone today," he said. "I'm very hungry and I intend to go to lunch with you. Unless, of course, you're meeting someone?"

"No, I'm going to get something fast at the drugstore."

"We'll try the Tea Room. I imagine they'll find room for us."

She went under protest, knowing Mr. Hartley would be furious, knowing that her hold on her job was becoming increasingly more precarious. She was late much too often. She'd had to stay home two days last week because Tina had croup. But she realized she wasn't being given a choice.

In the restaurant he brushed aside the fact they had no reservation and succeeded in being placed at the corner table he wanted. Jenny turned down the suggestion of wine. "I'd be drowsy in fifteen minutes. I was a bit short on sleep last night. Perrier for me, please."

They ordered club sandwiches, then he leaned across the table. "Tell me about yourself, Jenny MacPartland."

She tried not to laugh. "Did you ever take the Dale Carnegie course?"

"No, I didn't. Why?"

"That's the kind of question they teach you to ask on a first meeting. Be interested in the other fellow. I *want* to *know* about *you.*"

"But it happens that I do want to know about you."

The drinks came and they sipped as she told him: "I am the head of what the modern world calls 'the single parent family.' I have two little girls. Beth is three and Tina just turned two. We live in an apartment in a brownstone on East Thirty-seventh Street. A grand piano, if I had one, would just about take up the whole place. I've worked for Mr. Hartley for four years."

"How could you work for him four years with such young children?"

"I took a couple of weeks off when they were born."

"Why was it necessary to go bck to work so quickly?"

Jenny shrugged. "I met Kevin MacPartland the summer after I finished college. I'd been a fine arts major at Fordham University in Lincoln Center. Kev had a small part in an off-Broadway show. Nana told me I was making a mistake but naturally I didn't listen."

"Nana?"

"My grandmother. She raised me since I was a year old. Anyhow Nana was right. Kev's a nice enough guy but he's a— lightweight. Two children in two years of

16

marriage wasn't on his schedule. Right after Tina was born he moved out. We're divorced now."

"Does he support the children?"

"The average income for an actor is three thousand dollars a year. Actually Kev is quite good and with a break or two might make it. But at the moment the answer to the question is no."

"Surely you haven't had those children in a day-care center from the time they were born?"

Jenny felt the lump start to form in her throat. In a minute her eyes would be filling with tears. She said hurriedly, "My grandmother took care of them while I worked. She died three months ago. I really don't want to talk about her now."

She felt his hand close over hers. "Jenny, I'm sorry. Forgive me. I'm not usually so dense."

She managed a smile. "My turn. *Do* tell *me* all about *you.*"

She nibbled on the sandwich while he talked. "You probably read the bio on the brochure—I'm an only child. My mother died in an accident on the farm when I was ten . . . on my tenth birthday to be exact. My father died two years ago. The farm manager really runs the place. I spend most of my time in my studio."

"It would be a waste if you didn't," Jenny said. "You've been painting since you were fifteen years old, haven't you? Didn't you realize how good you were?"

Erich twirled the wine in his glass, hesitated, then shrugged. "I could give the usual answer, that I painted strictly as an avocation, but it wouldn't be the whole truth. My mother was an artist. I'm afraid she wasn't very good but her father was reasonably well known. His name was Everett Bonardi."

"Of *course* I know of him," Jenny exclaimed. "But why didn't you include that in your bio?"

"If my work is good, it will speak for itself. I hope I've inherited something of his talent. Mother simply sketched and enjoyed doing it, but my father was terribly jealous of her art. I suppose he'd felt like a bull in a china shop when he met her family in San Francisco. I gather they treated him like a Midwest hunky with hayseed in his shoes. He reciprocated by telling mother to use her skill to do useful things like making quilts. Even so he idolized her. But I always knew he would have hated to find me 'wasting my time painting,' so I kept it from him."

The noonday sun had broken through the overcast sky and a few stray beams, colored by the stained-glass window, danced on their table. Jenny blinked and turned her head.

Erich was studying her. "Jenny," he said suddenly, "you must have wondered about my reaction when we met. Frankly I thought I was seeing a ghost. Your resemblance to Caroline is quite startling. She was about your height. Her hair was darker than yours and her eyes were a brilliant green. Yours are blue with just a suggestion of green. But there are other things about you. Your smile. The way you tilt your head when you listen. You're so slim, just as she was. My father was always fretting over her thinness. He'd keep trying to make her eat more. And I find myself wanting to say, 'Jenny, finish that sandwich. You've barely touched it.'"

"I'm fine," Jenny said. "But would you mind ordering a quick coffee? Mr. Hartley will be having a heart attack as it is that you arrived when he was out. And I have to sneak away from the reception early which won't endear me to him."

Erich's smile vanished. "You have plans for tonight?"

"Big ones. If I'm late picking up the girls at Mrs. Curtis' Progressive Day Care Center, I'm in trouble."

Jenny raised her eyebrows, pursed her lips, imitated Mrs. Curtis. "'My usual time for closing is five P.M. but I make an exception for working mothers, Mrs. MacPartland. But five-thirty is the finish. I don't want to hear anything about missed buses or last-minute phone calls. You be here by five-thirty, or you keep your kids home the next morning. Understan?'"

Erich laughed. "I *understan*. Now tell me about your girls."

"Oh, that's easy," she said. "Obviously they're brilliant and beautiful and lovable and . . ."

"And walked at six months and talked at nine months. You sound like my mother. People tell me that's the way she used to talk about me."

Jenny felt an odd catch at her heart at the wistful expression that suddenly came over his face. "I'm sure it was true," she said.

He laughed. "And I'm sure it wasn't. Jenny, New York staggers me. What was it like growing up here?"

Over coffee they talked. She about city life: "There isn't a building in Manhattan I don't love." He, drily, "I can't imagine that. But then you've never really experienced the other way of life." They talked about her marriage. "How did you feel when it was over?"

"Surprisingly, only the same degree of regret that I imagine I'd have for the typical first love. The difference is I have my children. For that I'll always be grateful to Kev."

When they got back to the gallery, Mr. Hartley was waiting. Nervously Jenny watched the angry red points on his cheekbones, then admired the way Erich placated him. "As I'm sure you'll agree, airline food is not fit to eat. Since Mrs. MacPartland was just leaving for lunch, I prevailed on her to allow me to join her. I merely nibbled and now look forward to lunching with you. And may I compliment you on the placement of my work."

The red points receded. Thinking of the thick sandwich Erich had consumed, Jenny said demurely, "Mr. Hartley, I recommended the chicken Kiev to Mr. Krueger. Please make him order it."

Erich quirked one eyebrow and as he passed her he murmured, "Thanks a lot."

Afterward she regretted her impulsive teasing. She hardly knew the man. Then why this sense of rapport? He was so sympathetic and yet gave an impression of latent strength. Well, if you're used to money all your life and have good looks and talent thrown in, why wouldn't you feel secure?

The gallery was busy all afternoon. Jenny watched for the important collectors. They'd all been invited to the reception but she knew many of them would come in early to have a chance to study the exhibit. The prices were steep, very steep, for a new artist. But Erich Krueger seemed to be quite indifferent whether or not they sold.

Mr. Hartley got back just as the gallery was closed to the public. He told Jenny that Erich had gone to his hotel to change for the reception. "You made quite an impression on him, Jenny," he said, sounding rather puzzled. "He did nothing but ask questions about you."

By five o'clock the reception was in full swing. Efficiently Jenny escorted Erich from critics to collectors, introducing him, making small talk, giving him a chance to chat, then extricating him to meet another visitor. Not infrequently they were asked, "Is this young lady your model for *Memory of Caroline?*"

Erich seemed to enjoy the question. "I'm beginning to think she is."

Mr. Hartley concentrated on greeting guests as they arrived. From his beatific smile, Jenny could surmise that the collection was a major success.

It was obvious that the critics were equally impressed by Erich Krueger, the man. He had changed his sports jacket and slacks for a well-tailored dark blue suit; his white French-cuffed shirt was obviously custom-made; a maroon tie against the crisp white collar brought out his tanned face, blue eyes and the silver tints in his hair. He wore a gold band on the little finger of his left hand. She'd noticed it at lunch. Now Jenny realized why it looked familiar. The woman in the painting had been wearing it. It must be his mother's wedding ring.

She left Erich talking with Alison Spencer, the elegant young critic from *Art News* magazine. Alison was wearing an off-white Adolfo suit that complemented her ash-blond hair. Jenny became suddenly aware of the drooping quality of her own wool skirt, the fact that her boots still looked scuffed even though she'd had them resoled and shined. She knew that her sweater looked just like what it was, a cheap, misshapen, polyester rag.

She tried to rationalize her sudden depression. It had been a long day and she was tired. It was time for her to leave and she almost dreaded picking up the girls. When Nana was still with them, going home had been a pleasure.

"Now sit down, dear," Nana would say, "and get yourself relaxed. I'll fix us a nice little cocktail." She'd enjoyed hearing what was going on at the gallery, and she'd read the children a bedtime story while Jenny got dinner. "From the time you were eight years old, you were a better cook than I am, Jen."

"Well, Nana," Jenny would tease, "maybe if you didn't cook hamburgers so long they wouldn't look like hockey pucks . . ."

Since they'd lost Nana, Jenny picked up the girls at the day-care center, bused them to the apartment and placated them with cookies while she threw a meal together.

As she was reaching for her coat, one of the most important collectors cornered her. Finally at 5:25 she managed to get away. She debated about saying good night to Erich but he was still deep in conversation with Alison Spencer. What possible difference would it make to him that she was going? Shrugging away the renewed sensation of depression, Jenny quietly left the gallery by the service door.

2

Patches of ice on the sidewalk made the going treacherous. Avenue of the Americas, Fifth, Madison, Park, Lexington, Third. Second. Long, long blocks. Whoever said Manhattan was a narrow island had never run across it on slick pavements. But the buses were so slow, she was better off on foot. Still she'd be late.

The day-care center was on Forty-ninth Street near Second Avenue. It was quarter of six before, panting from running, Jenny rang the bell of Mrs. Curtis' apartment. Mrs. Curtis was clearly angry, her arms folded, her lips a narrow slash in her long, unpleasant face. "Mrs. MacPartland!"

"We had a terrible day," the grim lady continued. "Tina wouldn't stop crying. And you told me that Beth was terlet-trained, but let me tell you she isn't."

"She is terlet-, I mean toilet-trained," Jenny protested. "It's probably that the girls aren't used to being here yet."

23

"And they won't get the chance. Your kids are just too much of a handful. You try to understand my position; a three-year-old who isn't trained and a two-year-old who never stops crying are a full-time job by themselves."

"Mommy."

Jenny ignored Mrs. Curtis. Beth and Tina were sitting together on the battered couch in the dark foyer that Mrs. Curtis grandly referred to as the "play area." Jenny wondered how long they'd been bundled in their outside clothes. With a rush of tenderness, she hugged them fiercely. "Hi, Mouse. Hello, Tinker Bell." Tina's cheeks were damp with tears. Lovingly, she smoothed back the soft auburn hair that spilled over their foreheads. They'd both inherited Kev's hazel eyes and thick, sooty lashes as well as his hair.

"Her was scared today," Beth reported, pointing at Tina. "Her cried and cried."

Tina's bottom lip quivered. She reached up her arms to Jenny.

"And you're late again," Mrs. Curtis accused.

"I'm sorry." Jenny's tone was absentminded. Tina's eyes were heavy, her cheeks flushed. Was she starting another siege of croup? It was this place. She never should have settled on it.

She picked up Tina. Fearful of being left behind, Beth slid off the couch. "I'll keep both girls until Friday, which is a favor," Mrs. Curtis said, "but that's *it.*"

Without saying good night, Jenny opened the door and stepped out into the cold.

It was completely dark now and the wind was sharp. Tina burrowed her head in Jenny's neck. Beth tried to shield her face in Jenny's coat. "I only wet once," she confided.

Jenny laughed. "Oh, Mouse, love! Hang on. We'll be in the nice warm bus in a minute."

But three buses went by full. At last she gave up and began walking downtown. Tina was a dead weight. Trying to hurry meant she had to half-drag Beth. At the end of two blocks, she bent down and scooped her up. "I can walk, Mommy," Beth protested. "I'm big."

"I know you are," Jenny assured her, "but we'll make better time if I carry you." Locking her hands together, she managed to balance both small bottoms on her arms. "Hang on," she said, "the marathon is under way."

She had ten more blocks to go downtown, then two more across town. They're not heavy, she told herself. They're your children. Where in the name of God would she find another day care by next Monday? Oh, Nana, Nana, we need you so much! She couldn't dare take more time off from the gallery. Had Erich asked Alison Spencer to have dinner with him? she wondered.

Someone fell in step beside her. Jenny looked up startled as Erich reached down and took Beth from her arms. Beth's mouth formed a half-surprised, half-frightened circle. Seeming to realize she was about to protest, he smiled at her. "We'll get home a lot faster if I carry you and we race Mommy and Tina." His tone was conspiratorial.

"But . . ." Jenny began.

"Now surely you're going to let me help you, Jenny?" he said. "I'd like to carry the little one too but I'm sure she wouldn't come to me."

"She wouldn't," Jenny agreed, "and I'm grateful, of course, Mr. Krueger, but . . ."

"Jenny, will you please stop calling me Mr. Krueger? Why did you leave me stuck with that tiresome woman from *Art News?* I kept expecting you to rescue me. When I realized you were gone, I remembered the day-care center. That awful woman told me you'd left but I got your address from her. I decided to walk down to your apartment and ring your bell. Then right in front of me I see a pretty girl in need of help, and here we are."

She felt his arm tuck firmly under her elbow. Suddenly instead of feeling fatigued and depressed, she was absurdly happy. She glanced at his face.

"Do you go through this every night?" he asked. His tone was both incredulous and concerned.

"We usually manage to get a bus in bad weather," she said. "Tonight they were so full, there was hardly room for the driver."

The block between Lexington and Park was filled with high-stooped brownstones. Jenny pointed to the third house on the uptown side. "That's it." She eyed the street affectionately. To her the rows of brownstones offered a sense of tranquillity: houses nearly one hundred years old, built when Manhattan still had large neighborhoods of single-family homes. Most of them were gone now, reduced to rubble to make way for skyscrapers.

Outside her building, she tried to say good night to Erich but he refused to be dismissed.

"I'll see you in," he told her.

Reluctantly she preceded him into the ground-level studio. She'd made slipcovers in a cheerful yellow-and-orange pattern for the battered secondhand upholstery; a piece of dark brown carpet covered most of the scarred parquet floor; the cribs fit into the small dressing room off the bathroom and were almost concealed by the louver door. Chagall prints hid some of the peeling wall paint and her plants brightened the ledge over the kitchen sink.

Glad to be released Beth and Tina ran into the room. Beth spun around. "I'm very glad to be home, Mommy," she said. She glanced at Tina. "Tina is glad to be home too."

Jenny laughed. "Oh, Mouse, I know what you

mean. You see," she explained to Erich, "it's a little place but we love it."

"I can see why. It's very pleasant."

"Well, don't look too hard," Jenny said. "The management is letting it run down. The building is going co-op so they're not spending any more money on it now."

"Are you going to buy your apartment?"

Jenny began to unzip Tina's snowsuit. "I haven't a prayer. It will cost seventy-five thousand dollars, if you can believe it, for this room. We'll just hang in till they evict us and then find someplace else."

Erich picked up Beth. "Let's get out of those heavy clothes." Quickly he unfastened her jacket, then said, "Now we've got to make up our minds. I've invited myself to dinner, Jenny. So if you have plans for the evening, kick me out. Otherwise point me to a supermarket."

They stood up together and faced each other. "Which is it, Jenny," he asked, "the supermarket or the door?"

She thought she detected a wistful note in the question. Before she could answer, Beth tugged at his leg. "You can read to me if you want," she invited.

"That settles it," Erich said decisively. "I'm staying. You have nothing more to say about it, Mommy."

Jenny thought, He really wants to stay. He honestly wants to be with us. The realization sent unexpected waves of delight through her. "There's no need to go shopping," she told him. "If you like meatloaf we're in great shape."

She poured Chablis, then turned on the evening news for him while she bathed and fed the children. He read a story to them while she prepared dinner. As she set the table and made a salad she stole glances at the couch. Erich was sitting, one little girl under each arm, reading *The Three Bears* with appropriate histrionics. Tina began to doze and quietly he pulled her on his lap. Beth listened rapturously, her eyes never leaving his face. "That was very, very good," she announced when he finished. "You read almost as good as Mommy."

He lifted one eyebrow to Jenny, smiling triumphantly.

After the children were in bed they ate at the dinette table that overlooked the garden. The snow in the yard was still white. The bare-limbed trees glistened in the reflection of the lights from the house. Thick, high evergreens almost hid the fence that separated the property from the adjacent yards.

"You see," Jenny explained, "country within the city. After the girls are settled, I linger over coffee here and imagine I'm gazing at my acreage. Turtle Bay, about ten blocks uptown, is a beautiful area. The brownstones have magnificent gardens. This is sort of mock turtle bay but I'll be very sorry when moving day arrives."

"Where will you go?"

"I'm not sure but I've got six months to worry about it. We'll find something. Now how about coffee?"

The bell rang. Erich looked annoyed. Jenny bit her lip. "It's probably Fran from upstairs. She's between boyfriends now and pops in to visit every couple of nights."

But it was Kevin. He filled the doorway, boyishly handsome in his expensive ski sweater, a long scarf casually knotted over his shoulder, his dark red hair well-barbered, his face evenly tanned.

"Come in, Kevin," she said, trying not to sound exasperated. Timing, she thought. By heaven, he's got it.

He strode into the room, kissing her quickly. She felt suddenly embarrassed, knowing Erich's eyes were on them.

"Kids in bed, Jen?" Kevin asked. "Too bad. I was hoping to see them. Oh, you have company."

His voice changed, became formal, almost English. Ever the actor, Jenny thought. The former husband meeting the ex-wife's new friend in a drawing-room comedy. She introduced the men and they nodded to each other without smiling.

Kevin apparently decided to lighten the atmosphere. "Smells good in here, Jen. What have you been cooking?" He examined the stove top. "My word, what a fancy meatloaf." He sampled it. "Excellent. I can't imagine why I let you get away from me."

"It was a dreadful mistake," Erich said, his voice chipped with ice.

"It surely was," Kevin agreed easily. "Well, look I won't delay. Just thought I'd pop by on my way past. Oh, Jen, could I speak with you outside for a minute?"

She knew exactly why he wanted to speak with her. It was payday. Hoping Erich wouldn't notice she slipped her purse under her arm as she went out to the foyer. "Kev, I really haven't . . ."

"Jen, it's just that going overboard for Christmas for you and the kids left me short. My rent is due and the landlord is getting nasty. Just lend me thirty dollars for a week or so."

"Thirty dollars. Kevin, I can't."

"Jen, I *need* it."

Reluctantly she took out her wallet. "Kevin, we've got to talk. I think I'm going to lose my job."

Quickly he took the bills. Stuffing them in his pocket, he turned toward the outside door. "That old joker would never let you go, Jen. He knows a good thing when he has it. Call his bluff and strike for a raise. He'll never hire anyone for what he's paying you. You'll see."

She went back into the apartment. Erich was clearing the table, running water in the sink. He picked up the pan with the remaining meatloaf and walked over to the garbage can.

"Hey, hold it," Jenny protested. "The kids can have that tomorrow night for dinner."

Deliberately he dumped it out. "Not after that actor-ex of yours touched it they won't!" He looked directly at her. "How much did you give him?"

"Thirty dollars. He'll pay me back."

"You mean to say you allow him to walk in here, kiss you, joke about abandoning you and breeze out with your money to spend at some expensive bar?"

"He's short on his rent."

"Don't kid yourself, Jenny; how often does he pull that? Every payday, I suppose."

Jenny smiled wearily. "No, he missed one last month. Look, Erich, please leave those dishes. I can do them myself."

"You've got far too much work to do as it is."

Silently Jenny picked up a towel. Why had Kevin chosen just this evening to walk in? What a fool she was to hand him money.

The rigid disapproval in Erich's face and stance began to ease. He took the towel from her hands. "That's enough of that," he smiled.

He poured wine into fresh glasses and brought it over to the couch. She sat beside him, keenly aware of a deep but vague intensity about him. She tried to analyze her feelings and could not. In a little while Erich would leave. Tomorrow morning he was going back to Minnesota. Tomorrow night at this time she'd be here by herself again. She thought of the happiness on the children's faces when Erich read to them, the blessed relief she'd felt when he appeared beside her and took Beth from her. Lunch and dinner had been such fun, as though by his very presence he could dispel worry and loneliness.

"Jenny." His voice was tender. "What are you thinking?"

She tried to smile. "I don't think I was thinking. I was . . . just content, I suppose."

"And I don't know when I've been this content. Jenny, you're sure you're not still in love with Kevin MacPartland."

She was astonished enough to laugh. "Good Lord, no."

"Then why are you so willing to give him money?"

"A misguided feeling of responsibility, I suppose. The worry that maybe he does need his rent."

"Jenny, I have an early flight tomorrow morning. But I can get back to New York for the weekend. Are you free on Friday night?"

He was coming back to see her. The same delicious sense of relief and pleasure that had been hers when he suddenly appeared on Second Avenue filled her. "I'm free. I'll find a sitter."

"How about Saturday? Do you think the children would enjoy going to the Central Park Zoo if it isn't too cold? And then we could take them to Rumpelmayer's for lunch."

"They'd love it. But, Erich, really . . ."

"I'm not only sorry I can't just stay in New York for a while. But I've got a meeting in Minneapolis about some investments I'm planning to make. Oh, may I . . . ?"

He had spotted the photo album on the shelf under the cocktail table.

"If you wish. It's not terribly exciting."

They sipped wine as he inspected the book. "That's me being picked up at the children's home," she told him. "I was adopted. Those are my new parents."

"They're a nice-looking young couple."

"I don't remember them at all. They were in an

automobile accident when I was fourteen months old. After that it was just Nana and me."

"Is that a picture of your grandmother?"

"Yes. She was fifty-three when I was born. I remember when I was in the first grade and came home with a long face because the kids were making Father's Day cards and I didn't have a father. She said, 'Listen, Jenny, I'm your mother, I'm your father, I'm your grandmother, I'm your grandfather. I'm all you need. You make *me* a card for Father's Day!'"

She felt Erich's arm around her shoulders. "No wonder you miss her so."

Hurriedly Jenny went on: "Nana worked in a travel agency. We took some terrific trips. See, here we are in England. I was fifteen. This is our trip to Hawaii."

When they came to the pictures of her wedding to Kevin, Erich closed the album. "It's getting late," he said. "You must be tired."

At the door he took both her hands in his and held them to his lips. She had kicked off her boots and was in her stocking feet. "Even this way you are so like Caroline," he said, smiling. "You look tall in heels and quite small without them. Are you a fatalist, Jenny?"

"What is to be will be. I suppose I believe that."

"That will do." The door closed behind him.

3

At exactly eight o'clock the phone rang. "How did you sleep, Jenny?"

"Very well." It was true. She had drifted off to sleep in a kind of euphoric anticipation. Erich was coming back. She would see him again. For the first time since Nana's death she did not wake up around dawn with the sickening feeling of heavyhearted pain.

"I'm glad. So did I. And I might add I enjoyed some very pleasant dreams. Jenny, starting this morning, I've arranged for a limousine to come for you and the girls at eight-fifteen. He'll take them to the day-care center and you to the gallery. And he'll pick you up evenings at ten after five."

"Erich, that's impossible."

"Jenny, *please*. It's such a little thing for me. I simply can't be worrying about you struggling with those babies in this weather."

"But, Erich!"

"Jenny, I have to run. I'll call you later."

At the day-care center Mrs. Curtis was elaborately pleasant. "Such a distinguished boyfriend you have, Mrs. MacPartland. He phoned this morning. And I want you to know that you don't have to transfer the children. I think we just need to get to know each other better and give them a chance to settle in. Isn't that right, girls?"

He called her at the gallery. "I just landed in Minneapolis. Did the car get there?"

"Erich, it was a blessing. Not having to rush the girls out made such a difference. Whatever did you say to Mrs. Curtis? She was oozing sweetness and light."

"I'll bet she was. Jenny, where do you want to eat Friday night?"

"It doesn't matter."

"Choose a restaurant that you've always wanted to try . . . someplace you've never been with anyone else."

"Erich, there are thousands of restaurants in New York. The ones on Second Avenue and Greenwich Village are my speed."

"Have you ever been to Lutèce?"

"Good Lord, no."

"Fine. We'll eat there Friday night."

In a daze Jenny got through the day. It didn't help to have Mr. Hartley repeatedly comment how taken Erich had been with her. "Love at first sight, Jenny. He's got it."

Fran, the flight attendant who lived in apartment 4E of the brownstone, dropped in that evening. She was consumed with curiosity. "I saw that gorgeous guy in the foyer last night. I figured he had to have been here. And you have a date with him Friday. Wow!"

She volunteered to mind the girls for Jenny. "I'd love to meet him. Maybe he has a brother or a cousin or an old college pal."

Jenny laughed. "Fran, he'll probably think this through and call to tell me to forget it."

"No, he won't." Fran shook her tightly curled head. "I've got a hunch."

The week dragged. Wednesday. Thursday. And then miraculously it was Friday.

Erich came for her at seven-thirty. She had decided to wear a long-sleeved dress she'd bought on sale. The gold locket was set off by the oval neckline and its center diamond gleamed brilliantly against the black silk. She had twisted her hair into a French braid.

"You're lovely, Jenny." He looked quietly expensive in a dark blue suit with a faint pinstripe, a dark blue cashmere coat, a white silk scarf.

She phoned Fran to come down, caught the amused gleam in Erich's eye at Fran's open approval.

Tina and Beth were enchanted with the dolls Erich had brought them. Jenny looked at the beautiful painted faces on the dolls, the eyelids that opened and closed, the dimpled hands, the curling hair and compared them with the shabby gifts Kevin had chosen for Christmas.

She caught Erich's frown as she handed him her well-worn thermal coat and for a moment wished that she'd accepted Fran's suggestion that she borrow her fur jacket. But Nana always told her not to borrow.

Erich had hired a limousine for the evening. She leaned back against the upholstery and he reached for her hand. "Jenny, I've missed you. These were the longest four days of my life."

"I've missed you too." It was the simple truth but she wished she hadn't sounded so fervent.

In the restaurant she glanced around at the other tables, spotting celebrity faces.

"Why are you smiling, Jenny?" Erich asked.

"Culture shock. Jet lag from one life-style to another. Do you realize not one person in this room is even aware of Mrs. Curtis' Day Care Center."

"Let's hope not." His eyes had a look of amused tenderness.

The waiter poured champagne. "You were wearing that locket the other day, Jenny. It's quite lovely. Did Kevin give it to you?"

"No. It was Nana's."

He leaned across the table; his slender, sculptured fingers entwined around hers. "I'm glad. Otherwise it would have been bothering me all night. Now I can enjoy seeing it on you."

In excellent French he discussed the menu with the captain. She asked him where he had acquired the language.

"Abroad. I did quite a bit of traveling. Finally I realized I was happiest and least lonely when I was at the farm, painting. But these last few days were pretty bad."

"Why?"

"I was lonely for you."

On Saturday they went to the zoo. Endlessly patient, Erich rotated having the girls on his shoulders and at their entreaties returned to the monkey section three times.

At lunch he cut Beth's food as Jenny prepared Tina's plate. He talked Tina into finishing her milk by promising to finish his Bloody Mary and with mock solemnity shook his head at Jenny's twitching lips.

Over Jenny's protests he insisted the girls each select one of Rumpelmayer's famed stuffed animals and seemed blissfully unaware of the interminable time Beth took to make her decision.

"Are you sure you don't have six kids on your Minnesota farm?" Jenny asked him as they stepped onto the street. "Nobody comes naturally by that kind of patience with children."

"But I was raised by someone who had that kind of patience and it's all I know."

"I wish I'd known your mother."

"I wish I'd known your grandmother."

"Mommy," Beth asked, "why do you look so happy?"

On Sunday Erich arrived with double-runner ice skates for Tina and Beth and took them all to the rink at Rockefeller Center to skate.

That evening he took Jenny to the Park Lane for a quiet dinner. Over coffee they both became silent. Finally he said, "It's been a very happy two days, Jenny."

"Yes."

But he didn't say anything about coming back. She turned her head and looked out at Central Park, now sparkling from the combination of streetlights, headlights and the windows of the apartments that bordered it. "The park is always so pretty, isn't it?"

"Would you miss it very much?"

"Miss it?"

"Minnesota has a different kind of beauty."

What was he saying? She turned to face him. In a spontaneous gesture their hands met, their fingers entwined. "Jenny, it's fast but it's right. If you insist I'll come to New York every weekend for six months —for a year—and court you. But is it necessary?"

"Erich, you hardly know me!"

"I've always known you. You were a solemn baby; you swam when you were five; you won the general excellence medal in the fifth, sixth and seventh grades."

"Seeing an album doesn't mean you know me."

"I think it does. And I know myself. I've always understood what I was looking for, was confident that when it came I would recognize it. You feel it too. Admit it."

"I've already made one mistake. I thought I felt all the right things for Kevin."

"Jenny, you're not fair to yourself. You were very young. You told me he was the first date you ever cared about. And don't forget, wonderful as your grandmother was, you have to have missed having a man in your life, a father, a brother. You were *ready* to fall in love with Kevin."

She considered. "I suppose that's true."

"And the girls. Don't lose their childhood, Jenny. They're so happy when you're with them. I think they could be happy with me. Marry me, Jenny. Soon."

A week ago she hadn't known him. She felt the warmth of his hand, looked into his questioning eyes, felt that her own reflected the same blaze of love.

And she knew without a doubt what her answer would be.

They sat up till dawn in the apartment and talked. "I want to adopt the girls, Jenny. I'll have my lawyers prepare forms for MacPartland to sign."

"I don't think he'll give up the children."

"My guess is that he will. I want them to have my name. When we have a family of our own I don't want Beth and Tina to feel like outsiders. I'll be a good father to them. He's worse than a bad one. He's indifferent to them. By the way, what kind of engagement ring did you get from MacPartland?"

"I didn't."

"Good. I'll have Caroline's ring reset for you."

Wednesday evening on the phone he told her that he'd arranged to meet Kevin on Friday afternoon. "I think it's best if I see him alone, dear."

All week Tina and Beth kept asking when "Mr. Kruer" would come back. When he arrived at the apartment on Friday evening they flew into his arms. Jenny felt happy tears in her eyes at their whoops of joy as he hugged them.

Over dinner at The Four Seasons he told her about his session with Kevin. "He wasn't too friendly. I'm afraid he's something of a spoiler, darling. He doesn't want you or the children, but he doesn't want anyone else to have you. But I persuaded him it was in their best interest. We'll complete the formalities by the end of the month. Then the adoption will take about six months to finalize. Let's get married on February third; that will be almost a month to the day we met.

"Which reminds me." He opened his attaché case. She'd been surprised that he brought that case to the dinner table. "Let's see how this fits."

It was an emerald-cut solitaire. As Erich slipped it on her finger, Jenny stared down into the fiery beauty of the perfect stone.

"I decided not to have it reset," he told her. "It really is perfect just as it is."

"It's beautiful, Erich."

"And, darling—let's get this out of the way too." He pulled out a sheaf of papers. "When my lawyers prepared the adoption papers, they also insisted on taking care of the premarital agreement."

"The premarital agreement?" Jenny asked absently. She was absorbed in admiring her ring. It was not all a dream. It was real. It was happening. She was going to marry Erich. She almost laughed thinking of Fran's reaction. "Jenny, he's too perfect. He's handsome; he's rich; he's talented; he worships you. God, he can't take his eyes off you; he's crazy about the kids. Let me tell you there's got to be something wrong. He's gotta be a gambler or a drinker or a bigamist."

She'd almost told Erich that and then decided

against it. She knew Fran's brash humor didn't go over very well with him. What was he saying?

"It's just that I am a rather—wealthy—man. . . . My lawyers weren't happy about the way things have moved so rapidly. This simply says that if we were to break up before ten years have passed the Krueger interests will remain intact."

She was taken aback. "If we broke up, I wouldn't want anything from you, Erich."

"I would rather die than lose you, Jen. This is just a formality." He laid the papers by her plate. "Of course you may want your lawyers to go over these carefully. In fact I was instructed to tell you that even if you or they are satisfied with all the clauses, you should not mail them back before you've held them two days."

"Erich, I don't have a lawyer." She glanced at the top page, was aghast at the legal jargon and shook her head. Incongruously she remembered Nana's habit of carefully checking the grocery tape, her occasional triumphant, "He charged me *twice* for the lemons." Nana would scrutinize any document like this before she signed it.

"Erich, I don't want to wade through all this. Where shall I sign?"

"I've marked the places for you, darling."

Quickly Jenny scrawled her name. Obviously Erich's lawyers feared that she might be marrying him for his money. She supposed she couldn't blame them but even so it felt uncomfortable.

"And, darling, besides that one provision, this sets up a trust fund for each of the girls which they'll inherit at twenty-one. It goes into effect as soon as the adoption is complete. It also provides that you will inherit everything I have on my death."

"Don't even *talk* about that, Erich."

He put the papers back in his case. "What a terribly

unromantic thing to have to do," he said. "What do you want for our fiftieth anniversary, Jen?"

"Darby and Joan."

"What?"

"They're Royal Doulton figurines. An old man and an old woman sitting contentedly side by side. I've always loved them."

The next morning when Erich came to the house he had a gift box under his arm. The two figurines were in it.

Even more than the ring, they made Jenny sure about the rest of her life.

4

I appreciate this, Jen. Three hundred bucks is a big help. You were always a good sport."

"Well, you and I collected this stuff together. The money is rightfully half yours, Kev."

"God, when I think of how we'd go around late at night to pick up the furniture people were leaving out with their garbage. Remember how we just beat someone to the love seat? You sat on it before the other guy could get to it."

"I remember," Jenny said. "He was so mad I thought he'd pull a knife on me. Look, Kevin, I wish you'd come earlier. Erich will be here in a few minutes and I don't think he'll be pleased to run into you."

They were standing in the dismantled apartment. The furniture had been taken out—Jenny had sold everything for just under six hundred dollars. The walls, now bare of the cheerful prints, looked soiled and cracked. The basic shabbiness of the apartment was cruelly revealed without the furniture and carpet to hide its nakedness. The handsome new suitcases were the only items in the room.

Kevin was wearing an Ultrasuede jacket. No wonder he's always broke, she thought. Dispassionately she studied him, noticing the puffy lines under his eyes. Another hangover, she guessed. With guilt she realized that she felt more nostalgia at leaving this tiny apartment than she did at the prospect of not seeing Kevin again.

"You look beautiful, Jen. That blue is a great color on you."

She was wearing a two-piece blue silk dress. On one of his visits, Erich had insisted on outfitting her and the children at Saks. She'd protested but he'd overridden her objection. "Look at it this way. By the time the bill comes in you'll be my wife."

Now her Vuitton bags were filled with designer suits and blouses and sweaters and slacks and evening skirts, Raphael boots and Magli shoes. After her first uneasiness about having Erich paying for them before they were married, she'd had a marvelous time. And what joy it had been to shop for the girls. "You're so good to us." It became a constant refrain.

"I love you, Jenny. Every penny I spend is pleasure for me. I've never been happier."

He'd helped her select the clothes. Erich had an excellent sense of style. "The artist's eye," she joked.

"Where are the girls?" Kevin asked. "I'd like to say goodbye to them."

"Fran took them for a walk. We'll pick them up after the ceremony. Fran and Mr. Hartley are having lunch with us. Then we'll go right to the airport."

"Jen, I think you've rushed into this too fast. You've only known Krueger a month."

"That's long enough when you're sure, when you're very sure. And we both are."

"Well, *I'm* still not sure about the adoption. I don't want to give up my kids."

Jenny tried not to show irritation. "Kevin, we've been through this. You've signed the papers. You don't bother with the girls. You don't support them. In fact whenever you're interviewed you deny having a family."

"How are they going to feel when they're grown and understand that I gave them up?"

"Grateful for giving them the chance to be with a father who wants them. You seem to forget I'm adopted. And I'll always be grateful to whoever gave me up. Being raised by Nana was mighty special."

"I agree Nana was mighty special. But I don't like Erich Krueger. There's something about him . . ."

"Kevin!"

"All right. I'll go. I'll miss you, Jen. I still love you. You know that." He took her hands. "And I love my kids too."

Act three, curtain, Jenny thought. Not a dry eye in the house. "Please, Kevin. I don't want Erich to find you here."

"Jen, there's a chance I may be coming to Minnesota. I've got a good crack at getting in the repertory company at the Guthrie Theater in Minneapolis. If I do, I'll look you up."

"Kevin, don't look me up!"

Firmly she opened the apartment door. The buzzer rang. "That must be Erich," Jenny said nervously. "Darn it. I didn't want him to see you here. Come on, I'll walk you out."

Erich was waiting behind the locked French-glass foyer doors. He was holding a large gift-wrapped box. Dismayed, she watched his expression change from anticipation to displeasure as he saw her coming down the hall with Kevin.

She opened the outer door to admit him then said

quickly, "Kevin stopped over for just a minute. Good-bye, Kevin."

The two men stared at each other. Neither spoke. Then Kevin smiled and bent over Jenny. Kissing her on the mouth, he said, his tone intimate. "It was wonderful being with you. Thanks again, Jen. See you in Minnesota, darling."

5

We are crossing over Green Bay, Wisconsin. Our altitude is thirty thousand feet. We'll be landing at the Twin Cities Airport at five-fifty-eight P.M. The temperature in Minneapolis is eight degrees Fahrenheit. It's a clear, beautiful afternoon. Hope you're enjoying your flight, folks. Thanks again for flying Northwest."

Erich's hand covered Jenny's. "Enjoying your flight?"

She smiled at him. "Very much." They both looked down at his mother's gold wedding band now on her finger.

Beth and Tina had fallen asleep. The flight attendant had removed the center arm and they were curled up together, auburn ringlets overlapping, their new green velvet jumpers and white turtleneck pullovers somewhat rumpled now.

Jenny turned to study the cushion of clouds that floated outside the plane window. Underneath her happiness she was still furious with Kevin. She'd known he was weak and irresponsible but she'd always thought of him as being casually good-natured. But he was a spoiler. He'd managed to cloud their wedding day.

In the apartment after he left, Erich had said, "Why did he thank you and what did he mean? Did you invite him to our home?"

She'd tried to explain but the explanation felt hollow in her own ears.

"You gave him three hundred dollars?" Erich asked incredulously. "How much does he owe you in support payments and loans?"

"But I don't need that and the furniture was half his."

"Or maybe you wanted to be sure he had fare to come visit you?"

"Erich, how can you believe that?" She'd forced back the tears that threatened to fill her eyes but not before Erich had seen them.

"Jenny, forgive me. I'm sorry. I'm jealous of you. I admit that. I hate the fact that man ever touched you. I don't want him to ever put a finger on you again."

"He won't. I can promise you that. God, if anything I'm so grateful to him for signing the adoption papers. I kept my fingers crossed right to the last minute on that."

"Money talks."

"Erich, you didn't pay him?"

"Not much. Two thousand dollars. A thousand per girl. A very cheap price to get rid of him."

"He sold you his children." Jenny had tried to keep the contempt from showing in her voice.

"I'd have paid fifty times more."

"You should have told me."

"I wouldn't have told you now except I don't want any leftover pity for him. . . . Let's forget him. This is our day. How about opening your wedding present?"

It was a Blackglama mink coat. "Oh, Erich."

"Come on—try it on."

It felt luxurious, soft, lightweight, warm. "It's exactly right with your hair and eyes," Erich said, pleased. "Do you know what I was thinking this morning?"

"No."

He'd put his arms around her. "I slept so badly last night. I hate hotels and all I could think is that tonight Jenny will be with me in my own home. Do you know that poem, 'Jenny Kissed Me'?"

"I'm not sure."

"I could only remember a couple of the lines. 'Say I'm weary, say I'm sad' . . . and then the triumphant last line is 'Jenny kissed me.' I was thinking that as I rang the bell and then a minute later I have to watch Kevin MacPartland kiss you."

"Please, Erich."

"Forgive me. Let's get out of this place. It's depressing."

She hadn't had time to take a final look before he rushed her to the limousine.

Even during the ceremony Kevin had been on her mind, especially her marriage to him at St. Monica's four years ago. They'd chosen that church because Nana had been married there. Nana sat beaming in the first row. She hadn't approved of Kevin but put her doubts behind her when she couldn't dissuade Jen. What would she think of this ceremony before a judge instead of a priest? "I, Jennifer, take you . . ." She hesitated. Dear God, she'd almost said *Kevin*. She felt Erich's questioning eyes and began again. Firmly. "I, Jennifer, take you, Erich . . ."

"What God has joined together, man must not separate."

The judge had spoken the words solemnly.

But they'd said that at her wedding to Kevin.

They arrived in Minneapolis one minute ahead of schedule. A large sign said, WELCOME TO THE TWIN

48

CITIES. Jenny studied the airport with avid interest. "I've been all over Europe but never farther west than Pennsylvania," she laughed. "I had a mental image of landing in the midst of a prairie."

She was holding Beth by the hand. Erich was carrying Tina. Beth looked backward at the ramp that led to the plane. "More plane, Mommy," she begged.

"You may have started something, Erich," Jenny said. "They seem to be developing a taste for first-class travel."

Erich was not listening. "I told Clyde to have Joe waiting for us," he said. "He should have been at the arrival gate."

"Joe?"

"One of the farmhands. He's not too bright but he's excellent with horses and a good driver. I always have him chauffeur me when I don't want to leave the car at the airport. Oh, here he is."

Jenny saw rushing toward them a straw-haired, slenderly built young man of about twenty, with wide innocent eyes and rosy cheeks. He was neatly dressed in a thermal coat, dark knit trousers, heavy boots and gloves. A chauffeur's cap sat incongruously on his thick hair. He pulled it off as he stopped in front of Erich, and she had time to reflect that for such a handsome young man he looked awfully worried.

"Mr. Krueger, I'm sorry I'm late. The roads are pretty icy."

"Where's the car?" Erich asked brusquely. "I'll get my wife and children settled, then you and I can attend to the luggage."

"Yes, Mr. Krueger." The worried look deepened. "I'm really sorry I'm late."

"Oh, for heaven sake," Jenny said. "We're early, one minute early." She held out her hand. "I'm Jenny."

He took it, holding it gingerly as though he feared

hurting it. "I'm Joe, Mrs. Krueger. Everybody's looking forward to seeing you. Everybody's been talking about you."

"I'm sure they have," Erich said shortly. His arm urged Jenny forward. Joe fell back behind them. She realized Erich was annoyed. Maybe she wasn't supposed to have been so friendly. Her life in New York and Hartley gallery and the apartment on Thirty-seventh Street suddenly seemed terribly far away.

6

Erich's maroon Fleetwood was mint-new and the only car in the parking area not spattered with crusted snow. Jenny wondered if Joe had taken precious minutes to have it washed before arriving at the airport. Erich settled her and Tina in the back seat, gave permission to Beth to ride in front, and hurried away to help Joe collect the baggage.

A few minutes later they were pulling onto the highway. "It's nearly a three-hour drive to the farm," Erich told her. "Why don't you lean against me and nap?" He seemed relaxed, even genial now, the spasm of anger forgotten.

He reached for Tina, who willingly settled in his lap. Erich had a way with the little girl. Seeing the contentment on Tina's face snapped Jenny out of her momentary homesickness.

The car sped into the country. The lights along the highway began to disappear. The road darkened and narrowed. Joe switched on the high beams of the headlights and she could discern clumps of graceful maples and irregular, poorly shaped oaks. The land seemed absolutely flat. It was all so different from New York. That was why she'd felt that terrible sense of alienation as they left the airport.

She needed time to think, to get in focus, to adjust. Settling her head on Erich's shoulder, she murmured, "You know something, I am tired." She didn't want to talk any more, not right now. But, oh, how good it was to lean against him, to know that their time together wouldn't ever again be rushed and frantic. He had suggested that they defer an official honeymoon. "You don't have anyone to leave with the girls," he'd said. "Once they're comfortably settled on the farm, we'll find a reliable sitter and take a trip." How many other men would have been that thoughtful? she wondered.

She felt Erich looking down at her.

"Awake, Jenny?" he asked but she didn't answer. His hand smoothed back her hair; his fingers kneaded her temple. Tina was asleep now; her breathing came soft and measured. In the front seat, Beth had stopped chattering to Joe so she too must be napping.

Jenny made her own breath rise and fall evenly. It was time to plan ahead, to turn away from the life she had left and begin to anticipate the one that was waiting for her.

Erich's home had been without a woman's touch for a quarter of a century. It probably needed a massive overhaul. It would be interesting to see how much of Caroline's influence remained in it.

Funny, she mused, I never think of Erich's mother as his mother. I think of her as Caroline.

She wondered if his father hadn't referred to her that way. If instead of saying "your mother" to Erich, when he reminisced he'd say, "Caroline and I used to . . ."

Redecorating would be a joy. How many times had

she studied the apartment and thought, If I could afford it, I'd do this . . . and this . . . and this . . .

What a sense of freedom it would be to wake up in the morning and know she didn't have to rush off to work. Just to be with the children, to spend time with them, real time, not end-of-the-day exhausted time! She'd already lost the best part of their baby years.

And to be a wife. Just as Kevin had never been a real father to the children, he'd never been a real husband to her. Even in their most intimate moments, she'd always felt that Kevin had a mental image of himself playing the romantic lead in an M-G-M film. And she was certain that he'd been unfaithful to her even during the short time they lived together.

Erich was mature. He could have married long before now but he'd waited. He welcomed responsibility. Kevin had shunned it. Erich was so reticent. Fran said she thought he was a bit stodgy and Jenny knew that even Mr. Hartley wasn't comfortable with him. They didn't realize that his seeming aloofness was simply a cover for an innately shy nature. "I find it easier to paint my sentiments than to express them," he'd told her. There was so much love expressed in everything he painted. . . .

She felt Erich's hand stroking her cheek. "Wake up, darling, we're nearly home."

"What? Oh. Did I fall asleep?" She pulled herself up.

"I'm glad you slept, darling. But look out the window now. The moon is so bright you should be able to see quite a bit." His voice was eager. "We're on county road twenty-six. Our farm begins at that fence, on both sides of the road. The right side eventually ends at Gray's Lake. The other side winds and twists. The woods take up nearly two hundred acres alone; they end at the river valley that slopes into the Minnesota River. Now, watch, you'll see some of the outer buildings. Those are the polebarns, where we feed the cattle in the winter. Beyond them are the grainery and stables and the old mill. Now as we come around this bend you can see the west side of the house. It's set on that knoll."

Jenny pressed her face against the car window. From the background glimpses she'd seen in some of Erich's paintings, she knew that at least part of the exterior of the house was pale red brick. She'd imagined a Currier and Ives kind of farmhouse. Nothing Erich had said had prepared her for what she was looking at now.

Even viewed from the side, it was obvious that the house was a mansion. It was somewhere between seventy and eighty feet long and three stories high. Lights streamed from the long graceful windows on the first floor. Overhead the moon blanched the roof and gables into glistening tiaras. The snow-covered fields shone like layers of white ermine, framing the structure, enhancing its flowing lines.

"Erich!"

"Do you like it, Jenny?"

"Like it? Erich, it's magnificent. It's twice, no five times larger than I expected. Why didn't you warn me?"

"I wanted to surprise you. I told Clyde to be sure and have it lighted for your first impression. I see he took me at my word."

Jenny stared, trying to absorb every detail as the car moved slowly along the road. A white wooden porch with slender columns began at the side door and extended to the rear of the house. She recognized it as the setting of *Memory of Caroline*. Even the swing in the painting was still there, the only piece of furniture on the porch. A gust of wind was making it sway gently to and fro.

The car turned left and drove through open gates. A sign, KRUEGER FARM, was lighted by the torchères that topped the gateposts. The car followed the driveway skirting snow-covered fields. To their right the woods began, a thick heavy forest of trees whose branches were bare and skeletal against the moon. The car turned left and completed the arc, stopping in the driveway in front of wide stone steps.

Massive, ornately carved double doors were illuminated by the fan window arching over them. Joe hurried to open Jenny's door. Quickly Erich handed the sleeping Tina to him. "You bring in the girls, Joe," he said.

Taking Jenny's hand, he hurried up the steps, turned the latch and pushed open the doors. Pausing, he looked directly into her eyes. "I wish I could paint you now," he said. "I could call the painting *Coming Home*. Your long, lovely dark hair, your eyes so tender looking at me . . . You do love me, don't you, Jenny?"

"I love you, Erich," she said quietly.

"Promise you'll never leave me. Swear that, Jenny."

"Erich, how can you even think that now?"

"Please promise, Jenny."

"I'll never leave you, Erich." She put her arms around his neck. His need is so great, she thought. All this month she'd been troubled by the one-sided aspect of their relationship, he the giver, she the taker. She was grateful to realize it wasn't that simple.

He picked her up. "Jenny kissed me." Now he was smiling. As he carried her into the house he kissed her lips, at first tentatively, then with gathering emotion. "Oh, Jenny!"

He set her down in the entrance hall. It had gleaming parquet floors, delicately stenciled walls, a crystal and gold chandelier. A staircase with an ornately carved balustrade led to the second floor. The walls were covered with paintings, Erich's bold signature in the right-hand corner. For a moment Jenny was speechless.

Joe was coming up the steps with the girls. "Now don't run," he was cautioning them. But the long nap had revived them and they were eager to explore. Keeping one eye on them, Jenny listened as Erich began to show her through the house. The main parlor was to the left of the entry foyer. She tried to absorb everything he was telling her about the individual pieces. Like a child showing off his toys, he pointed out the walnut étagère, kidney-shaped and marble-based. "It's early eighteenth century," he said. Ornate oil lamps, now wired, stood on either side of a massive high-backed couch. "My grandfather had that made in Austria. The lamps are from Switzerland."

Memory of Caroline was hung above the couch. An overhead light revealed the face in the portrait more intimately than it had appeared in the gallery window. It seemed to Jenny that in this lighting, in this room, her own resemblance to Caroline was accentuated. The woman in the painting seemed to be looking directly at her. "It's almost like an icon," Jenny whispered. "I feel as though her eyes are following me."

"I always feel that way," Erich said. "Do you think they might be?"

An immense rosewood reed organ on the west wall immediately attracted the children. They climbed onto the velvet-cushioned bench and began to press the keys. Jenny saw Erich wince as the buckle of Tina's shoe scratched the leg of the bench. Quickly she lifted the protesting girls down. "Let's see the rest of the house," she suggested.

The dining room was dominated by a banquet table

large enough to accommodate twelve chairs. An elaborate heart motif was carved out of each of the chairbacks.

A quilt was hung like a tapestry on the far wall. Pieced entirely of hexagons with a scalloped border and stitched in flower motifs, it added a bright note to the austerely handsome room. "My mother made it," Erich said. "See her initials."

All the walls of the large library were covered with walnut bookcases. Each shelf held an even row of precisely placed books. Jennie glanced at some of the titles. "Am I going to have a good time!" she exclaimed. "I can't wait to catch up on reading. About how many books have you got?"

"Eleven hundred and twenty-three."

"You know *exactly* how many?"

"Of course."

The kitchen was huge. The left wall contained the appliances. A round oak table and chairs were placed exactly in the center of the room. On the east wall, a giant old iron stove with highly polished nickel chrome and isinglass windows looked capable of heating the whole house. An oak cradle next to the stove held firewood. A couch covered in a colonial print and matching chair were at rigid right angles to each other. In this room, as in the others she had seen, absolutely nothing was out of place.

"It's a little different from your apartment, isn't it, Jenny?" His tone was proud. "You see why I didn't tell you. I wanted to enjoy your reaction."

Jenny felt an urge to defend the apartment. "It's certainly bigger," she agreed. "How many rooms are there?"

"Twenty-two," Erich said proudly. "Let's just have a quick look at our bedrooms. We'll finish the tour tomorrow."

He put his arm around her as they walked up the stairs. The gesture was comforting and helped to relieve some of the strangeness she was feeling. All right, she thought, I do feel as though I'm on a guided tour: Look but don't touch.

The master bedroom was a large corner room in the front of the house. Dark mahogany furniture gleamed with a fine velvet patina. The massive four-poster bed was covered with a spread of cranberry-colored brocade. The brocade was repeated in the canopy and draperies. A leaded crystal bowl on the left side of the dresser was filled with small bars of pine soap. An initialed silver dressing set, each piece an inch apart, was to the right of the bowl. The dressing set had been Erich's great-grandmother's; the bowl was Caroline's and had come from Venice. "Caroline never wore perfume but loved the scent of pine," Erich said. "That soap is imported from England."

The pine soap. That was what she had detected as she came into the room—the faint aroma of pine, so subtle it was almost impossible to distinguish.

"Is this where Tina and I sleep, Mommy?" Beth asked.

Erich laughed. "No, Mouse. You and Tina will be across the hall. But do you want to see my room first? It's right next door."

Jenny followed, expecting to see the room of a bachelor in the family home. She was anxious to experience Erich's personal taste in furnishing. Almost everything she had seen so far seemed to have been left to him.

He threw open the door of the room next to the master bedroom. Here too the overhead light was already on. She saw a single maple bed covered by a colorful quilt. A rolltop desk, half-open, revealed pencils and crayons and sketch pads. A three-shelf bookcase contained the *Book of Knowledge*. A Little League trophy stood on the dresser. A high-backed rocker was in the left corner near the door. A hockey stick was propped against the right wall.

It was the room of a ten-year-old child.

7

I never slept here after Mother died," Erich explained. "When I was little I used to love lying in bed, listening to the sound of her moving around in her room. The night of the accident I couldn't stand to come in here. To calm me down, Dad and I both moved to the two back bedrooms. We never moved back."

"Are you saying that this room and the master bedroom haven't been slept in in nearly twenty-five years?"

"That's right. But we didn't close them off. We just didn't use them. But someday our son will use this room, sweetheart."

Jenny was glad to go back into the foyer. Despite the cheerful quilt and warm maple furniture there was something disquieting about Erich's boyhood room.

Beth tugged at her restlessly. "Mommy, we're hungry," she said positively.

"Oh, Mouse, I'm sorry. Let's go to the kitchen." Beth raced down the long hall, her footsteps noisy for such little feet. Tina ran behind her. "Wait for me, Beth."

"Don't run," Erich called after them.

"Don't break anything," Jenny warned, remembering the delicate porcelain in the parlor.

Erich lifted the mink off her shoulders, dropped it over his arm. "Well, what do you think?"

Something about the way he asked the question was disturbing. It was as though he was too eager for approval, and she reassured him now the same way she answered a similar question from Beth. "It's perfect. I love it."

The refrigerator was well-stocked. She heated milk for cocoa and made ham sandwiches. "I have champagne for us," Erich said. He put his arm over the back of her chair.

"I'll be ready for it in a little while." Jenny smiled at him and tilted her head toward the girls. "As soon as I clear the decks."

They were just about to get up when the doorbell rang. Erich's scowl changed to a look of pleasure when he opened the door. "Mark, for heaven sake! Come on in."

The visitor filled the entry. His windblown sandy hair almost touched the top of the doorway. Rangy shoulders were not hidden by his heavy hooded parka. Piercing blue eyes dominated his strong-featured face. "Jenny," Erich said. "This is Mark Garrett. I've told you about him."

Mark Garrett. *Dr.* Garrett, the veterinarian, who had been Erich's closest friend since boyhood. "Mark's like a brother," Erich had told her. "In fact if anything had happened to me before I married, he would have inherited the farm."

Jenny extended her hand, felt his, cold and strong, cover hers.

61

"I've always said you had good taste, Erich," Mark commented. "Welcome to Minnesota, Jenny."

She liked him immediately. "It's lovely to be here." She introduced the girls to him. They were both unexpectedly shy. "You're very, very big," Beth told him.

He refused coffee. "I hate to barge in," he told Erich, "but I wanted you to hear it from me. Baron pulled a tendon pretty badly this afternoon."

Baron was Erich's horse. Erich had talked about him. "A thoroughbred, flawless breeding, nervous, bad-tempered. A remarkable animal. I could have raced him but prefer having him for myself."

"Were any bones broken?" Erich's voice was absolutely calm.

"Positively not."

"What happened?"

Mark hesitated. "Somehow the stable door was left open and he got out. He stumbled when he tried to jump the barbed-wire fence on the east field."

The stable door was open? Each word was precisely enunciated. "Who *left* it open?"

"No one admits to it. Joe swears he closed it when he left the stable after he fed Baron this morning."

Joe. The driver. No wonder he had looked so frightened, Jenny thought. She looked at the girls. They were sitting quietly at the table. A minute ago they'd been ready to scamper away. Now they seemed to sense the change in the atmosphere, the anger Erich wasn't bothering to hide.

"I told Joe not to discuss it with you until I had a chance to see you. Baron will be fine in a couple of weeks. I think Joe probably didn't pull the door fast when he left. He'd never be deliberately careless. He loves that animal."

"Apparently no one in his family inflicts harm

deliberately," Erich snapped. "But they certainly manage to inflict it. If Baron is left lame . . ."

"He won't be. I've hosed him down and bandaged him. Why don't you walk out and see him now? You'll feel better."

"I might as well." Erich reached into the kitchen closet for his coat. His expression was coldly furious.

Mark followed him out. "Again, welcome, Jenny," he said. "My apologies for being the bearer of bad news." As the door closed behind them, she heard his deep, calm voice: "Now, Erich, don't get upset."

It took a warm bath and bedtime story before the children finally settled down. Jenny tiptoed out of the room exhausted. She'd pushed the beds together with one against the wall. Then she'd shoved the steamer trunk against the exposed side of the other one. The room that an hour before had been in perfect order was a mess. The suitcases were open on the floor. She'd rifled through them hunting for pajamas and Tina's favorite old blanket, but had not bothered to unpack properly. She was too tired now. It could wait till morning. Erich was there just as she came out. She watched his expression change as he surveyed the untidiness inside.

"Let's leave it, darling," she said wearily. "I know it's every which way but I'll put it right tomorrow."

It seemed to her that he made a deliberate attempt to sound casual. "I'm afraid I couldn't go to bed and leave this."

It took him only a few minutes to completely unpack, to stack underwear and socks in furniture drawers, to hang dresses and sweaters in the closet. Jenny gave up trying to help. If they wake up they'll be around for hours, she thought, but was suddenly too tired to protest. Finally Erich pushed the outer bed so that it was lined exactly with its twin, straightened the small shoes and boots, stacked the suitcases on an upper shelf and closed the closet door which Jenny had left ajar.

When he was finished, the room was infinitely neater and the children hadn't awakened. Jenny shrugged. She knew she should be grateful but could not help feeling that the risk of waking the children should have overcome the need for a clean-up session, particularly on a wedding night.

In the hall, Erich put his arms around her. "Sweetheart, I know what a long day this has been. I drew a tub for you. It should be about the right temperature now. Why don't you get changed and I'll fix a tray for us. I've got champagne cooling and a jar of the best caviar I could find in Bloomingdale's. How does that sound?"

Jenny felt a rush of shame at her feeling of irritation. She smiled up at him. "You're too good to be true."

The bath helped. She soaked in it, enjoying the unaccustomed length and depth of the tub, which was still mounted on its original brass claw feet. As the hot water soothed the muscles in her neck and shoulders she determined to relax.

She realized now that Erich had carefully avoided describing the house to her. What had he said? Oh, yes, things like, "Nothing much has been changed since Caroline died. I think the extent of the redecorating was to replace some curtains in the guest bedroom."

Was it just that nothing had worn out in these years or was Erich religiously preserving intact everything that reminded him of his mother's presence here? The scent she loved was still lingering in the master bedroom. Her brushes and combs and nail buffer were on the dresser. She wondered if there might not still be a few strands of Caroline's hair caught in one of the brushes.

His father had been desperately wrong to have allowed Erich's childhood bedroom to be left intact, frozen in time, as though growth in this house had stopped with Caroline's death. The thought made her uneasy and she deliberately pushed it aside. Think of Erich and yourself, she told herself. Forget the past. Remember that you belong to each other now. Her pulse quickened.

She thought of the lovely new nightgown and peignoir inside her new suitcase. She'd bought them in Bergdorf Goodman with her last paycheck, splurging extravagantly, but wanting to truly look like a bride tonight.

Suddenly lighthearted, she got out of the tub, released the stopper and reached for a towel. The mirror above the sink was clouded over. She started to dry herself then paused and began to wipe away the steam. She felt that in the midst of all the newness she needed to see herself, find her own image. As the glass dried, she glanced into it. But it was not her own blue-green eyes that she saw reflected back.

It was Erich's face, Erich's midnight-blue eyes meeting hers in the reflection. He had opened the door so silently she hadn't heard him. Spinning around, she instinctively clutched the towel in front of her, then deliberately let it fall.

"Oh, Erich, you scared me," she said. "I didn't hear you come in."

His eyes never left her face. "I thought you'd want your gown, darling," he said. "Here it is."

He was holding an aquamarine satin nightgown with a deep V cut in the front and back.

"Erich, I have a new gown. Did you just buy this one for me?"

"No," Erich said, "it was Caroline's." He ran his tongue nervously over his lips. He was smiling strangely. His eyes as they rested on her were moist with love. When he spoke again his tone was pleading. "For my sake, Jenny, wear it tonight."

8

For minutes Jenny stood staring at the bathroom door, not knowing what to do. I don't want to wear a dead woman's nightgown, she protested silently. The satin felt soft and clinging under her fingers.

After Erich handed her the gown he'd abruptly left the room. She began to shiver as she looked at the suitcase. Should she simply put on her own gown and peignoir, simply say, "I prefer this, Erich."

She thought of his expression when he handed his mother's gown to her.

Maybe it won't fit, she hoped. That would solve everything. But when she pulled it over her head, it might have been made for her. She was thin enough for the tapered waist, the narrowly cut hips, the straight line to the ankles. The V cut accentuated her firm breasts. She glanced in the mirror. The steam was evaporating now and tiny driblets of water were running down. That must be why she looked different. Or was it that something in the aqua tone of the gown emphasized the green in her eyes?

She could not say the gown did not fit and certainly it was becoming. But I don't want to wear it, she thought uneasily. I don't feel like myself in it.

She was about to pull it over her head when there was a soft tap on the door. She opened it. Erich was wearing gray silk pajamas and a matching dressing gown. He had turned off all the lights except for the one on the night table and his burnished gold hair was a counterpoint to the glow of the lamp.

The brocaded cranberry-colored spread was off the bed. The sheets were turned back. Lace embroidered pillows were propped against the massive headboard.

Erich was holding two glasses of champagne. He handed one of them to her. They walked to the center of the room and he touched his glass to hers. "I looked up the rest of the poem, darling." His voice soft, he spoke the words slowly:

> "Jenny kissed me when we met,
> Jumping from the chair she sat in;
> Time, you thief, who love to get
> Sweets into your list, put that in:
> Say I'm weary, say I'm sad,
> Say that health and wealth have missed me,
> Say I'm growing old, but add,
> Jenny kissed me."

Jenny felt tears in her eyes. This was her wedding night. This man who had offered so much love to her and whom she loved so much was her husband. This beautiful room was theirs. What difference what nightgown she wore! It was such a little thing to do for him. She knew her smile was as happy as his as they toasted each other. When he took the glass from her hand and set it down, she joyfully went into his arms.

Long after Erich slept, his arm pillowing her head, his face buried in her hair, Jenny lay awake. She was so accustomed to the street noises that were part of the night sounds of the New York apartment that she was not yet able to absorb the absolute stillness of this room.

The room was very cool. She liked that and reveled in the clear fresh air. But it was so quiet, so absolutely still, except for the even breathing that rose and fell against her neck.

I am so happy, she thought. I didn't know it was possible to be this happy.

Erich was a shy, tender and considerate lover. She had always suspected that there were far deeper emotions possible than Kevin had ever aroused in her. It was true.

Before Erich fell asleep they had talked. "Was Kevin the only one before me, Jenny?"

"Yes, he was."

"There's never been anyone before for me."

Did he mean he'd never *loved* anyone before or he'd never slept with anyone before? Was that possible?

She drifted off to sleep. Light was just beginning to trickle into the room when she felt Erich stir and slip out of bed.

"Erich."

"Darling, I'm sorry to wake you. I never sleep more than a few hours. In a little while I'll go to the cabin and paint. I'll be back around noon."

She felt his kiss on her forehead and lips as she drifted back to sleep. "I love you," she murmured.

The room was flooded with light when she awoke again. Quickly she ran to the window and pulled up the shade. As she watched she was surprised to see Erich disappearing into the woods.

The scene outside was like one of his paintings. The tree branches were white with frozen snow. Snow covered the gambrel roof of the barn nearest the house. Far back in the fields she could catch glimpses of cattle.

She glanced at the porcelain clock on the night table. Eight o'clock. The girls would be waking up soon. They might be startled to find themselves in a strange room.

Barefoot she hurried out of the bedroom and started down the wide foyer. As she passed Erich's old room, she glanced into it, then stopped. The coverlet was tossed back. The pillows were bunched up. She went into the room and touched the sheet. It was still warm. Erich had left their room and come in here. Why?

He doesn't sleep much, she thought. He probably didn't want to toss and turn and wake me up. He's used to sleeping alone. Maybe he wanted to read.

But he said he'd never slept in this room since he was ten years old.

Footsteps were running down the hall. "Mommy. Mommy."

Quickly she hurried to the foyer, bent down and opened her arms. Beth and Tina, their eyes shining from the long sleep, ran to her.

"Mommy, we were looking for you," Beth said accusingly.

"Me like it here," Tina chirped in.

"And we have a present," Beth said.

"A present? What have you got, love?"

"Me too," Tina cried. "Thank you, Mommy."

"It was on our pillows," Beth explained.

Jenny gasped and stared. Each little girl was holding a small round cake of pine soap.

She dressed the children in new red corduroy overalls and striped tee shirts. "No school," Beth said positively.

"No school," Jenny agreed happily. Quickly she put

on slacks and a sweater and they went downstairs. The cleaning woman had just arrived. She had a scrawny frame with incongruously powerful arms and shoulders. Her small eyes set in a puffy face were guarded. She looked as though she rarely smiled. Her hair, too tightly braided, seemed to be pulling up the skin around her hairline, robbing her of expression.

Jenny held out her hand. "You must be Elsa. I'm . . ." She started to say "Jenny" and remembered Erich's annoyance at her too friendly greeting to Joe. "I'm Mrs. Krueger." She introduced the girls.

Elsa nodded. "I do my best."

"I can see that," Jenny said. "The house looks lovely."

"You tell Mr. Krueger that stain on the dining-room paper was not my fault. Maybe he had paint on his hand."

"I didn't notice a stain last night."

"I show you."

There was a smudge on the dining-room paper near the window. Jenny studied it. "For heaven sake, you almost need a microscope to see it."

Elsa went into the parlor to begin cleaning and Jenny and the girls breakfasted in the kitchen. When they were finished she got out their coloring books and crayons. "Tell you what," she proposed, "let me have a cup of coffee in peace and then we'll go out for a walk."

She wanted to think. Only Erich could have put those cakes of soap on the girls' pillows. Of course it was perfectly natural that he'd look in on them this morning and there was nothing wrong with the fact that he obviously liked the smell of pine. Shrugging, she finished her coffee and dressed the children in snowsuits.

The day was cold but there was no wind. Erich had told her that winter in Minnesota could range from severe to vicious. "We're breaking you in easy this year," he'd said. "It's just middlin bad."

At the doorway she hesitated. Erich might want to show them around the stables and barns and introduce her to the help. "Let's go this way," she suggested.

She led Tina and Beth around the back of the house and toward the open fields on the east side of the property. They walked on the crunching snow until the house was almost out of sight. Then as they strolled toward the country road that marked the east boundary of the farm, Jenny noticed a fenced-off area and realized they had come upon the family cemetery. A half-dozen granite monuments were visible through the white pickets.

"What's that, Mommy?" Beth asked.

She opened the gate and they went inside the enclosure. She walked from one to the other of the tombstones, reading the inscriptions. Erich Fritz Krueger, 1843–1913, and Gretchen Krueger, 1847–1915. They must have been Erich's great-grandparents. Two little girls: Marthea, 1875–1877, and Amanda, 1878–1890. Erich's grandparents, Erich Lars and Olga Krueger, both born in 1880. She died in 1941, he in 1948. A baby boy, Erich Hans, who lived eight months in 1911. So much pain, Jenny thought, so much grief. Two little girls lost in one generation, a baby boy in the next one. How do people bear that kind of hurt? At the next monument, Erich John Krueger, 1915–1979. Erich's father.

There was one grave at the south end of the plot, as separate from the others as it was possible to be. It was the one she realized she had been looking for. The inscription read Caroline Bonardi Krueger, 1924–1956.

Erich's father and mother were not buried together. Why? The other monuments were weathered. This one looked as though it had been recently cleaned. Did Erich's love for his mother extend to taking extraordinary care of her tombstone? Inexplicably Jenny felt a stab of anxiety. She tried to smile. "Come on, you two. I'll race you across the field."

Laughing, they ran after her. She let them catch and then pass her, pretending to try to keep up with them. Finally they all stopped breathless. Clearly Beth and Tina were elated to have her with them. Their cheeks were rosy, their eyes sparkled and glowed. Even Beth had lost her perpetually solemn look. Jenny hugged them fiercely.

"Let's walk as far as that knoll," she suggested, "then we'll turn back."

But when they reached the top of the embankment, Jenny was surprised to see a fair-sized white farmhouse nestled on the other side. She realized it had to be the original family farmhouse now used by the farm manager.

"Who lives there?" Beth asked.

"Some people who work for Daddy."

As they stood looking at the house, the front door opened. A woman came out on the porch and waved to them, clearly indicating she wanted them to come up to the house. "Beth, Tina, come on," Jenny urged. "It looks as though we're about to meet our first neighbor."

It seemed to her that the woman stared at them unrelentingly as they walked across the field. Unmindful of the cold day she stood in the doorway, the door wide open behind her. At first Jenny thought from her slight frame and sagging body that she was elderly. But as she got closer, she realized that the woman was no more than in her late fifties. Her brown hair was streaked with gray and twisted high on her head in a carelessly pinned knot. Her rimless glasses magnified sad gray eyes. She wore a long, shapeless sweater over baggy, double-knit slacks. The sweater accentuated her bony shoulders and acute thinness.

Still there were vestiges of prettiness about the face, and the drooping mouth had well-shaped lips. There was a hint of a dimple in her chin, and somehow Jenny visualized this woman younger, more joyous. The woman stared at her as she introduced herself and the girls.

"Just like Erich told me," the woman said, her voice low and nervous. "'Rooney,' he said, 'wait till you meet Jenny, you'll think you're looking at Caroline.' But he didn't want me talking about it." She made a visible effort to calm herself.

Impulsively Jenny held out both her hands. "And Erich has told me about you, Rooney, how long you've been here. I understand your husband is the farm manager. I haven't met him yet."

The woman ignored that. "You're from New York City?"

"Yes, I am."

"How old are you?"

"Twenty-six."

"Our daughter Arden is twenty-seven. Clyde said she went to New York. Maybe you met her?" The question was asked with fierce eagerness.

"I'm afraid I haven't," Jenny said. "But of course New York is so big. What kind of work does she do? Where does she live?"

"I don't know. Arden ran away ten years ago. She didn't have to run away. Could just as easily have said, 'Ma, I want to go to New York.' I never denied her. Her dad was a bit strict with her. I guess she knew he wouldn't let her go so young. But she was such a good girl, why she was president of the 4-H club. I didn't know she wanted to go so bad. I thought she was really happy with us."

The woman's gaze was fixed on the wall. She

seemed to be in a reverie of her own, as though explaining something she had explained many times before. "She was our only one. We waited a long time for her. She was such a pretty baby, and so *wanting,* you know what I mean. So active, right from the minute she was born. So I said, let's call her Arden, short for ardent. It suited her real nice."

Beth and Tina shrank against Jenny. There was something about this woman, about the staring eyes and slight tremor, that frightened them.

My God, Jenny thought. Her only child and she hasn't heard from her in ten years. I would go mad.

"See her picture here." Rooney indicated a framed picture on the wall. "I took that just two weeks before she left."

Jenny studied the picture of a sturdy, smiling teenager with curly blond hair.

"Maybe she's married and has babies too," Rooney said. "I think about that a lot. That's why when I saw you coming along with the little ones, I thought maybe that's Arden."

"I'm sorry," Jenny said.

"No, it's all right. And please don't tell Erich I've been talking about Arden again. Clyde said Erich is sick of listening to me always going on about Arden and Caroline. Clyde said that's why Erich retired me from my job at the house when his dad died. I took real good care of that house, just like my own. Clyde and I came here when John and Caroline were married. Caroline liked the way I did things and even after she died I kept everything just so for her, as though she'd be walking in any minute. But come on in the kitchen. I made doughnuts and the coffeepot's on."

Jenny could smell the perking coffee. They sat around the white enamel table in the cheerful kitchen. Hungrily Tina and Beth munched at still-warm powdered doughnuts and drank milk.

"I remember when Erich was that age," Rooney said. "I used to make those doughnuts for him all the time. I was the only one Caroline ever left him with if she went out shopping. Felt almost like he was my own. Still do, I guess. I didn't have Arden for ten years after we wuz married but Caroline had Erich that first year. Never saw a little boy loved his mother more. Never wanted her out of his sight. Oh, you do look like her, you do."

She reached for the coffeepot and refilled Jenny's cup. "And Erich's been so good to us. He spent ten thousand dollars on private detectives trying to find where Arden went."

Yes, Jenny thought, Erich would do that. The clock over the kitchen sink began to chime. It was noon. Hastily Jenny got up. Erich would be home. She wanted terribly to be with him. "Mrs. Toomis, we'd better run. I do hope you'll come and visit us."

"Call me Rooney. Everybody does. Clyde don't want me to go to the big house anymore. But I fool him. I go up there a lot to make sure everything's nice. And you come back here again and visit. I like having company."

A smile made a remarkable transformation in her face. For a moment the drooping, sad lines disappeared and Jenny knew she'd been right in guessing that at one time Rooney Toomis had been a very pretty woman.

Rooney insisted they take a plate of doughnuts home. "They're good for an afternoon snack." As she held open the door for them she started to turn up the collar of her sweater. "I think I'll start looking for Arden now," she sighed. Once again her voice had become vague.

The noon sun was brilliant, high in the heavens, shining on the snow-covered fields. As they turned the bend, the house came into view. The pale red of the brick glowed under the sun's rays. Our home, Jenny thought. She held the girls by the hand. Was Rooney going to walk aimlessly around these acres looking for her lost child?

"That was a very nice lady," Beth announced.

"Yes, she was," Jenny agreed. "Come on, now. On the double. Daddy's probably waiting for us."

"Which daddy?" Beth asked matter-of-factly.

"The only one."

Just before she opened the kitchen door, Jenny whispered to the children. "Let's tiptoe in and surprise Daddy."

Eyes sparkling, they nodded.

Noiselessly she turned the handle. The first sound they heard was Erich's voice. It was coming from the dining room, each angry word pitched slightly higher than its predecessor. "How dare you tell me that I might have caused that stain! It's obvious that you let the oil rag touch the wallpaper when you dusted the windowsill. Do you realize the entire room will have to be repapered now? Do you know how difficult it will be to get that pattern again? How many times have I warned you about those oil rags?"

"But, Mr. Krueger . . ." Elsa's protest, nervously loud, was cut off.

"I want you to apologize for blaming that mess on me. Either apologize or get out of this house and don't come back."

There was silence.

"Mommy," Beth whispered, frightened.

"Sshh," Jenny said. Erich couldn't be that upset over that little smudge on the paper, could he? she wondered. Stay out of it, some instinct warned. There's nothing you can do.

As she heard Elsa's sullen, unhappy voice say, "I apologize, Mr. Krueger," she pulled the children outside and closed the door.

9

"Why is Daddy mad?" Tina asked.

"I'm really not sure, love. But we'll pretend that we didn't hear him. All right?"

"But we did hear him," Beth said seriously.

"I know," Jenny agreed, "but it doesn't have anything to do with us. Now, come on. Let's go in again."

This time she called, "Erich, hi," before they were even in the house. Not pausing to allow an answer she called again, "Is there a husband in this place?"

"Sweetheart!" Erich hurried into the kitchen, his smile welcoming, his entire manner relaxed. "I've just been asking Elsa where you were. I'm disappointed you went out. I wanted to show you around myself."

His arms were around her. His cheek, still cold from the outdoors, rubbed against hers. Jenny blessed the instinct that had kept her from visiting the farm buildings.

"I knew you'd want to give us the tour," she said, "so we just walked across the east fields and got some fresh air. You can't imagine how wonderful it is not to stop for a traffic light every few feet."

"I'll have to teach you to be sure to avoid the fields where the bulls are kept," Erich smiled. "Believe me, you'd prefer the traffic lights." He became aware of the plate she was holding. "What's that?"

"Mrs. Toom gave that to Mommy," Beth told him.

"Mrs. Toomis," Jenny corrected.

"Mrs. Toomis," Erich said. His arms dropped to his sides. "Jenny, I hope you're not going to tell me you were in Rooney's house?"

"She waved to us," Jenny explained. "It would have been so rude . . ."

"She waves to anyone who passes," Erich interrupted. "This is why you really ought to have waited for me to take you around, darling. Rooney is a very disturbed woman and if you give her an inch she'll take a stranglehold on you. I finally had to lay it to Clyde that he must keep her away from this house. Even after I retired her, I'd come home and find her puttering in here. God help her, I'm sorry for her, Jenny, but it got pretty rough waking up in the middle of the night and hearing her walking around the hall or even standing in my room." He turned to Beth. "Come on, Mouse. Let's get that snowsuit off." He lifted Beth in the air and to her delight sat her on top of the refrigerator.

"Me too, me too," Tina cried.

"You too, you too," he mimicked. "Now isn't this a good way to get your boots off?" he asked them. "Just the right height isn't it, Mommy?"

Apprehensively Jenny moved nearer to the refrigerator to make sure that one of the girls didn't lean forward too far and topple off it but she realized there was no need to worry. Erich quickly yanked the small overshoes off and lifted the girls down. Before he put them on the ground he said, "Okay, you two, what's my name?"

Tina looked at Jenny. "Daddy?" she said, her voice a question.

"Mommy said you're the only daddy," Beth informed him.

"Mommy said that?" Erich put the girls down and smiled at Jenny. "Thank you, Mommy."

Elsa came into the kitchen. Her face was flushed and set in angry, defensive lines. "Mr. Krueger, I finish upstairs. You want me to do something special now?"

"Upstairs?" Jenny asked quickly. "I meant to tell you. I hope you didn't bother to separate the beds in the children's room. They're on their way up for a nap."

"I told Elsa to straighten the room," Erich said.

"But, Erich, they can't sleep on those high beds the way they are," Jenny protested. "I'm afraid we'll really have to get them youth beds." A thought occurred to her. It was a gamble but it would be a natural request. "Erich, couldn't the girls nap in your old room? That bed is quite low."

She studied his face, waiting for his reaction. Even so she did not miss the sly look Elsa threw at him. She's enjoying this, Jenny thought. She knows he wants to refuse.

Erich's expression became closed. "As a matter of fact, Jenny," he said, his tone suddenly formal, "I intended to speak to you about allowing the children to use that room. I thought I made myself plain about the fact that that room is not to be occupied. Elsa tells me she found the bed unmade this morning."

Jenny gasped. Of course it had never occurred to her that Tina and Beth might have gotten into that bed when they were wandering around before she woke up.

"I'm sorry."

His face softened. "It's all right, darling. Let the girls nap in the beds they used last night. We'll order youth beds for them immediately."

Jenny prepared soup for the children, then took them upstairs. As she pulled down the shades, she said, "Now, look, you two, when you wake up, I don't want you getting into any other beds. Understand?"

"But we always get into your bed at home," Beth said, her tone injured.

"That's different. I mean any other beds in this house." She kissed them gently. "Promise. I don't want Daddy to get upset."

"Daddy yelled loud," Tina murmured, her eyes closing. "Where's my present?"

The cakes of soap were on the night table. Tina slipped hers under her pillow. "Thank you for giving that to me, Mommy. We didn't get into your bed, Mommy."

Erich had begun slicing turkey for sandwiches. Deliberately Jenny closed the door that shut the kitchen off from the rest of the house.

"Hi," she said. Putting her arms around him, she whispered, "Look, we had our wedding dinner with the children. At least let me fix our first by-ourselves meal on Krueger Farm and you pour us some of that champagne we never got around to finishing last night."

His lips were on her hair. "Last night was beautiful for me, Jenny. Was it for you?"

"It was beautiful."

"I didn't get much done this morning. All I could think of is how you look when you're asleep."

He made a fire in the cast-iron stove and they sipped the champagne and ate the sandwiches, curled up together on the couch in front of it. "You know,"

Jenny said, "walking around today made me realize the sense of continuity this farm has. I don't know my roots. I don't know if my people lived in the city or country. I don't know if my birth mother liked to sew or paint or if she could carry a tune. It's so wonderful that you know everything about your people. Just looking at the burial plot made me appreciate that."

"You went to the burial plot?" Erich asked quietly.

"Yes, do you mind?"

"Then you saw Caroline's grave?"

"Yes, I did."

"And you probably wondered why she and my father aren't together the way the others are?"

"I was surprised."

"It isn't any mystery. Caroline had those Norwegian pines planted. At that time she told my father she wanted to be buried at the south end of the graveyard where the pines would shelter her. He never really approved, but he respected her wishes. Before he died he told me he'd always expected to be placed in the grave next to his parents. Somehow I felt that was the right thing to do for both of them. Caroline always wanted more freedom than my father would give her anyway. I think that afterward he regretted the way he ridiculed her art until she threw out her sketch pad. What difference would it have made if she'd painted instead of making quilts? He was wrong. *Wrong!*"

He paused, staring into the fire. Jenny felt that Erich seemed to be unaware of her presence. "But so was she," he whispered.

With a tremor of anxiety Jenny realized that for the first time Erich was hinting that the relationship between his mother and father had been troubled.

Jenny settled into a daily routine that she found immensely satisfying. Each day she realized how much she had missed by being away from the children so much. She learned that Beth, the practical, quiet child, had a definite musical talent and could pick out simple tunes on the spinet in the small parlor after hearing them played only a few times. Tina's whiny streak vanished as she blossomed in the new atmosphere. She who had always cried so easily became positively sunny-dispositioned and showed signs of a natural sense of humor.

Erich usually left for the studio by dawn and never returned until noon. Jenny and the girls had breakfast around eight and at ten o'clock, when the sun was becoming stronger, bundled up in snowsuits and went for a walk.

The walks soon assumed a pattern. First the chicken house, where Joe taught the girls to collect the fresh-laid eggs. Joe had decided that Jenny's presence had saved his job after Baron's accident. "I bet if Mr. Krueger wasn't so happy about your being here, he'd have fired me. My maw says he's not a forgiving man, Mrs. Krueger."

"I really didn't have a thing to do with it," Jenny protested.

"Dr. Garrett says I'm taking real good care of Baron's leg. When the weather gets warmer and he can exercise a little it will be fine. And, Mrs. Krueger, I tell you, now I check that stable door ten times every day."

Jenny knew what he meant. Unconsciously she had begun to check so many little things a second time, things she never would have dreamed of noticing before. Erich was more than tidy, he was a perfectionist. She quickly learned to tell by a certain tenseness in his face and body if something had upset him—a closet door left open, a glass standing in the sink.

The mornings Erich didn't go to the cabin, he worked in the farm office next to the stable with Clyde Toomis, the farm manager. Clyde, a stocky man of about sixty with a leathery, wrinkled face, and thick, yellow-white hair, had a matter-of-fact manner that approached brusqueness.

When he introduced Jenny to him, Erich said, "Clyde really runs the farm. Sometimes I think I'm just window dressing around here."

"Well, you're certainly not window dressing in front of an easel," she laughed, but was surprised that Clyde did not make even a perfunctory effort to contradict Erich.

"Think you'll like it here?" Clyde asked her.

"I do like it here," she smiled.

"It's quite a change for a city person," Clyde said abruptly. "Hope it isn't too much for you."

"It isn't."

"Funny business," Clyde said. "The country girls hanker after the city. The city girls claim they love the country." She thought she heard a note of bitterness in his voice and wondered if he was thinking about his own daughter. She decided he was when he added, "My wife's all excited about having you and the children here. If she starts dropping in on you, just let me know. Rooney don't mean to bother people but sometimes she kind of forgets herself."

It seemed to Jenny there was a defensive tone in his voice when he spoke of Rooney. "I enjoyed visiting with her," she said sincerely.

The brusque manner softened. "That's good to hear. And she's looking up patterns to make jumpers or some such things for your girls. Is that all right?"

"It's fine."

When they left the office Erich said, "Jenny, Jenny, don't encourage Rooney."

"I promise I won't let it get out of hand. Erich, she's just lonely."

Every afternoon after lunch while the children napped, she and Erich put on cross-country skis and explored the farm. Elsa was willing to mind the children as they slept. In fact it was she who suggested the arrangement. It occurred to Jenny that Elsa was trying to make up for accusing Erich of damaging the dining-room wall.

And yet she wondered if it weren't possible that he *had* caused the stain. Often when he came in for lunch his hands would still have paint or charcoal smudges. If he noticed anything out of order, a curtain not centered on the rod, bric-a-brac not exactly in place, he would automatically adjust it. Several times Jenny stopped him before he touched something with paint-spattered fingers.

The paper in the dining room was replaced. When the paperhanger and his assistant came in, they were incredulous. "You mean to say that he bought eight double rolls at these prices and he's replacing exactly what he has?"

"My husband knows what he wants."

When they were finished, the room looked exactly the same except that the smudge was gone.

During the evenings she and Erich liked to settle in the library reading, listening to music, talking. He asked her about the faint scar at her hairline. "An automobile accident when I was sixteen. Someone jumped the divider and plowed into us."

"You must have been frightened, darling."

"I don't remember a thing about it," Jenny laughed. "I'd just leaned my head back and fallen asleep. The next thing I was aware of was being in the hospital three days later. I had a pretty bad concussion— enough to give me amnesia for those days. Nana was frantic. She was sure I'd be brain-damaged or something. I did have headaches for a while and even did some sleepwalking around final exam time. Stress brought it on according to the doctor. But gradually it stopped."

At first hesitantly, then the words tumbling out, Erich talked about his mother's accident. "Caroline and I had just gone into the dairy barn to see the new calf. It was being weaned and Caroline held the nursing bottle to its lips. The stock tank—that's that thing that looks like a bathtub in the calving pen—was full of water. It was muddy underfoot and Caroline slipped. She tried to grab something to keep from falling. The something was the lamp cord. She fell into the tank, pulling the lamp with her. That fool of a workman, Joe's uncle incidentally, was rewiring the barn and he'd left the lamp slung over a nail on the wall. In a minute it was all over."

"I hadn't realized you were with her."

"I don't like to talk about it. Luke Garrett, Mark's father, was here. He tried to revive her but it was hopeless. And I stood there holding the hockey stick she'd just given me for my birthday. . . ."

Jenny was sitting on the hassock at the foot of Erich's leather easy chair. She raised his hands to her lips. Leaning down he lifted her up and held her tightly against him. "For a long time I hated the sight of that hockey stick. Then I started to think of it as her last present to me." He kissed her eyelids. "Don't look so sad, Jenny. Having you makes up for everything. Please, Jenny, promise me."

She knew what he wanted to hear. With a wrench of tenderness, she whispered, "I'll never leave you."

10

One morning when she was walking with Tina and Beth, Jenny spotted Rooney leaning over the picket fence at the southern end of the graveyard. She seemed to be looking down at Caroline's grave.

"I was just thinking of all the nice times I had when Caroline and I were young and Erich was little and then when Arden was born. Caroline drew a picture of Arden once. It was so pretty. I don't know what happened to it. It disappeared right out of my room. Clyde says I was probably carrying it around like I used to do sometimes. Why don't you come visit me again?"

Jenny had braced herself for the question. "It's just we've been so busy settling. Beth, Tina, aren't you going to say hello to Mrs. Toomis?"

Beth said hello, shyly. Tina ran forward and raised her face for a kiss. Rooney bent down and smoothed Tina's hair from her forehead. "She reminds me of Arden, this one. Always jumping from one place to the next. Erich probably told you to keep away from me.

Well, I can't say I blame him. I guess I am an awful nuisance sometimes. But I found the pattern I was looking for. Can I make the jumpers for the girls?"

"I'd like that," Jenny said, deciding that Erich would have to get used to the idea that she would become friendly with Rooney. There was something infinitely appealing about the woman.

Rooney turned so that once again she was gazing into the graveyard. "Do you get lonesome here yet?" she asked.

"No," Jenny said honestly. "It's different, of course. I was used to a busy job and talking to people all day, and the phones ringing and friends popping into my apartment. Some of that I miss, I suppose. But mostly I'm just so glad to be here."

"So was Caroline," Rooney said. "So happy for a while. And then it changed." She stared down at the simple headstone on the other side of the fence. There were snow clouds in the air and the pines threw restless shadows across the pale pink granite. "Oh, indeed it changed for Caroline," she whispered, "and after she was gone, it started right then to change for us all."

"You're trying to get rid of me," Erich protested. "I don't want to go."

"Sure I'm trying to get rid of you," Jenny agreed. "Oh, Erich, this is perfectly beautiful." She held up a three-by-four-foot oil to examine it more closely. "You've caught the haze that comes around the trees just before they start to bud. And that dark spot circling the ice in the river. That shows the ice is about to break up, that there's moving water below, doesn't it?"

"You've got a good eye, darling. That's right."

"Well, don't forget I was a fine arts major. *Changing Seasons* is a lovely title. The change is so subtle here."

Erich draped an arm across her shoulders and studied the painting with her. "Remember, anything you want us to keep, I won't exhibit."

"No, that's foolish. This is the time to keep building your reputation. I won't mind at all eventually being known as the wife of the most prestigious artist in America. They'll point me out and say, 'See, isn't she lucky? And he's gorgeous too!'"

Erich pulled her hair. "Is that what they'll say?"

"Uh-huh, and they'll be right."

"I could just as easily send word that I can't make the show."

"Erich, don't do it. They've already planned a reception for you. I just wish I could go but I can't leave the kids yet and dragging them with us won't work. Next time."

He began to stack the canvases. "Promise you'll miss me, Jenny."

"I'll miss you lots. It's going to be a lonesome four days." Unconsciously Jenny sighed. In nearly three weeks, she'd spoken only to a handful of people: Clyde, Joe, Elsa, Rooney and Mark.

Elsa was taciturn almost to the point of absolute silence. Rooney, Clyde and Joe were hardly companions. She'd only chatted with Mark briefly once since that first evening, even though she knew from Joe that he'd checked on Baron at least half a dozen times.

She'd been on the farm a week before she realized that the telephone never rang. "Haven't they heard about the 'reach out and touch someone' campaign around here?" she joked.

"The calls all go through the office," Erich explained. "I only have them come directly to the house if I'm expecting a particular one. Otherwise whoever is in the office will buzz me."

"But suppose no one's in the office?"

"Then the Phone-Mate will take messages."

"But Erich, *why?*"

"Darling, if I have one quirk, it's that I despise the intrusion of a telephone ringing constantly. Of course whenever I'm away, Clyde will set the line to ring through to the house at night so I can call you."

Jenny wanted to protest, then decided against it. Later on when she had friends in the community it would be time enough to coax Erich into normal phone service.

He finished separating the canvases. "Jenny, I was thinking. It's about time I showed you off a bit. Would you like to go to church next Sunday?"

"I swear you can read my mind," she laughed. "I was just thinking that I'd like to meet some of your friends."

"I'm better at donating money than attending services, Jen. How about you?"

"I never missed Sunday Mass growing up. Then after Kev and I were married, I got careless. But as Nana always said the apple doesn't fall far from the tree. I'll probably be back at Mass regularly one of these days."

They attended Zion Lutheran the following Sunday. The church was old and not very large, actually almost chapel-sized. The delicate stained-glass windows diffused the winter light so that it shone blue and green and gold and red on the sanctuary. She could read the names on some of the windows: DONATED BY ERICH AND GRETCHEN KRUEGER, 1906 . . . DONATED BY ERICH AND OLGA KRUEGER, 1930.

The window over the alter, an Adoration of the Magi scene, was particularly beautiful. She gasped at the inscription: IN LOVING MEMORY OF CAROLINE BONARDI KRUEGER, DONATED BY ERICH KRUEGER.

She tugged at his arm. "When did you give that window?"

"Last year when the sanctuary was renovated."

Tina and Beth sat between them, sedately conscious of their new blue coats and bonnets. People looked over at the children throughout the service. She knew Erich was aware of the glances too. He had a contented smile on his face and during the sermon slipped his hand into hers.

Midway through the sermon he whispered, "You're beautiful, Jenny. Everybody is looking at you and the girls."

After the service he introduced her to Pastor Barstrom, a slight man in his late sixties with a gentle face. "We're happy to have you with us, Jenny," he said warmly. He looked down at the girls. "Now who's Beth and who's Tina?"

"You know their names," Jenny commented, pleased.

"Indeed I do. Erich told me all about you when he stopped by the parsonage. I hope you realize what a very generous husband you have. Thanks to him our new senior citizen center will be very comfortable and well-equipped. I've known Erich since he was a boy and we're all very happy for him now."

"I'm mighty happy too," Jenny smiled.

"There's a meeting of the women in the parish Thursday night. Perhaps you'd like to join them? We want to get to know you."

"I'd love to," Jenny agreed.

"Darling, we'd better start," Erich said. "There are others who want to visit with the pastor."

"Of course." As she extended her hand, the pastor said, "It certainly must have been very difficult for you to be widowed so young with such little babies, Jenny. Both you and Erich are surely deserving of much good fortune and many blessings now."

Erich propelled her forward before she could do more than gasp. In the car she exclaimed, "Erich, surely you didn't tell Pastor Barstrom that I was widowed, did you?"

Erich steered the car from the curb. "Jenny, Granite Place isn't New York. It's a small town in the Midwest. People around here were shocked to hear I was getting married a month after I met you. At least a young widow is a sympathetic image; a New York divorcée says something quite different in this community. And I never exactly said you were a widow. I told Pastor Barstrom you had lost your husband. He surmised the rest."

"So you didn't lie but in effect I've lied for you by not correcting him," Jenny said. "Erich, don't you understand the kind of position that places me in?"

"No, I don't, dear. And I won't have people around here wondering if I had my head turned by a sophisticated New Yorker taking advantage of a hayseed."

Erich had a mortal fear of looking ridiculous, so much so that he would lie to his clergyman to avoid the possibility.

"Erich, I will have to tell Pastor Barstrom the truth when I go to the meeting Thursday night."

"I'll be gone Thursday."

"I know. That's why I think it would be pleasant to be there. I'd like to meet the people around here."

"Are you planning to leave the children alone?"

"Of course not. Surely there are baby-sitters?"

"Surely you don't intend to leave the children with just anyone?"

"Pastor Barstrom could recommend . . ."

"Jenny, please wait. Don't start getting involved in activities. And don't tell Pastor Barstrom you're a divorcée. Knowing him, he'll never bring up the subject again unless you introduce it."

"But why do you object to my going?"

Erich took his eyes from the road and looked at her. "Because I love you so much I'm not ready to share you with other people, Jenny. I *won't* share you with anyone, Jenny."

11

Erich was leaving for Atlanta on February 23. On the twenty-first, he told Jenny he had an errand to do and would be late for lunch. It was nearly one-thirty when he returned. "Come over to the stable," he invited. "I've got a surprise for you." Grabbing a jacket, she ran out with him.

Mark Garrett was waiting there, smiling broadly. "Meet the new tenants," he said.

Two Shetland ponies stood side by side in the stalls nearest the door. Their manes and tails were full and lustrous, their copper bodies gleaming. "My present to my new daughters," Erich said proudly. "I thought we'd call them Mouse and Tinker Bell. Then the Krueger girls will never forget their pet names."

He hurried her to the next stall.

"And this is your gift."

Speechless, Jenny stared at a bay Morgan mare who returned her gaze amiably.

"She's a treasure," Erich exulted. "Four years old,

impeccable breeding, gentle. She's already won half a dozen ribbons. Do you like her?"

Jenny reached a hand to pat the mare's head and was thrilled that the animal did not draw back. "What's her name?"

"The breeder called her Fire Maid. Claims she has fire and heart as well as heritage. Of course you can call her anything you want."

"Fire and heart," Jenny whispered. "That's a lovely combination. Erich, I'm so delighted."

He looked pleased. "I don't want you riding yet. The fields are still too icy. But if you and the girls start making friends with the horses and visiting them every day, by next month you can get started on lessons. Now if you don't mind, how about lunch?"

Impulsively Jenny turned to Mark. "You can't have had lunch either. Won't you join us? It's just cold meat and a salad."

She caught Erich's frown but was relieved to see it disappear as fast as it came. "Please do, Mark," he urged.

Over lunch Jenny realized that she was constantly thinking about Fire Maid. Finally Erich said, "Darling, you have the most happy-child smile on your face. Is it me or the bay mare?"

"Erich, I have to say I'm so darn delighted about that horse I haven't even begun to think about thanking you."

"Have you ever had a pet, Jenny?" Mark asked.

There was something sturdy and easygoing about Mark that made her feel instantly at home in his presence. "I *almost* had a pet," she laughed. "One of our neighbors in New York had a miniature poodle. When puppies were born I used to stop every afternoon on my way home from school to help take care of them. I was about eleven or twelve. But we weren't allowed to have pets in our apartment."

"So you always felt cheated," Mark guessed.

"I certainly felt as though I missed something growing up."

They finished coffee and Mark pushed back his chair. "Jenny, thank you. This has been very pleasant."

"I wish you'd come to dinner when Erich gets back from Atlanta. Bring a date."

"That's a good idea," Erich agreed, and she thought he sounded as though he meant it. "How about Emily, Mark? She's always had an eye for you."

"She always had an eye for *you*," Mark corrected. "But yes, I will ask her."

Before Erich left, he held her tightly. "I'll miss you so, Jenny. Be sure to lock the doors at night."

"I will. We'll be fine."

"The roads are icy. If you want something from the store let Joe drive you."

"Erich, I'm a big girl," she protested. "Don't worry about me."

"I can't help it. I'll call you tonight, darling."

That night Jenny felt a guilty sense of freedom as she lay propped up in bed reading. The house was still except for the occasional hum of the furnace as it went off and on. From across the hallway she could hear Tina occasionally talking in her sleep. She smiled, realizing that Tina never woke up crying anymore.

Erich should have gotten to Atlanta by now. He'd be calling soon. She glanced around the room. The closet door was half open and she'd left her robe tossed over the slipper chair. Erich would have objected, of course, but tonight she didn't have to worry.

She returned to her book. An hour later the telephone rang. She reached for the receiver eagerly. "Hello, darling," she said.

"What a nice way to be greeted, Jen."

It was Kevin.

"Kevin." Jenny pulled herself up from the pillows so suddenly that her book slid from the bed onto the floor. "Where are you?"

"In Minneapolis. The Guthrie Theater. I'm auditioning."

Jenny felt acute uneasiness. "Kevin, that's wonderful." She tried to sound convincing.

"We'll see what happens. How's it going with you, Jen?"

"Very, very well."

"And the kids?"

"They're simply fine."

"I'm coming down to see them. You gonna be home tomorrow?" His words were slurred, his tone aggressive.

"Kevin, no."

"I want to see my kids, Jen. Where's Krueger?"

Something warned Jenny not to admit that Erich would be gone for four days.

"He's out at the moment. I thought he was calling now."

"Give me directions for getting to your place. I'll borrow a car."

"Kevin, you can't do that. Erich would be furious. You have no right here."

"I have every right to see my children. That adoption isn't final yet. I can stop it by snapping my fingers. I want to be sure Tina and Beth are happy. I want to be sure you're happy, Jen. Maybe we both made a mistake. Maybe we should talk about it. Now how do I get to your place?"

"You're not coming!"

"Jen, Granite Place is on the map. And I guess everybody there knows where Mr. High and Mighty lives."

Jenny felt her palms become sticky as she gripped

the phone. She could imagine the gossip in town if Kevin showed up asking directions to Krueger Farm. It would be just like him to say he'd been married to her. She remembered the look in Erich's face when he'd seen Kevin in the foyer of the apartment on their wedding day.

"Kev," she pleaded, "don't come here. You'll spoil everything for us. The girls and I are very happy. I've always been pretty decent to you. Have I ever once turned you down when you asked me for money even when I hardly had my own rent? That should count for something."

"I know you did, Jen." Now his voice took on the intimate, coaxing tone she knew so well. "As a matter of fact I'm a little short right now and you're loaded. How about giving me the rest of the furniture money?"

Jenny felt relief flood her. He was just looking for money. That would make it a lot easier. "Where do you want me to send it?"

"I'll come down for it."

He was obviously determined to see her. There was no way she could allow him to come to this house, even to this town. She shuddered, thinking how painstakingly Erich had been teaching the girls to say Beth Krueger, Tina Krueger.

There was a small restaurant in the shopping center twenty miles away. It was the only place she could think of to suggest. Quickly she gave Kevin directions and agreed to meet him at one o'clock the next day.

After he hung up she leaned back on the pillows. The relaxed pleasure of the evening was gone. Now she dreaded Erich's call. Should she tell him that she was going to see Kevin?

When Erich's call came she still was not sure what to do. Erich sounded tense. "I miss you. I'm sorry I came, darling. Did the girls ask for me tonight?"

She still hesitated to tell him about Kevin. "Of course they did. And Beth is starting to call her dolls 'critters.'"

Erich laughed. "They'll end up talking like Joe yet. I should let you go to sleep."

She had to tell him. "Erich . . ."

"Yes, darling."

She paused, suddenly remembering Erich's astonishment when she admitted giving Kevin half the furniture money, his suggestion that maybe she wanted him to have plane fare to Minnesota. She *couldn't* tell him about meeting Kevin. "I . . . I love you so much, Erich. I wish you were here right now."

"Oh, darling, so do I. Good night."

She could not sleep. The moonlight filtered into the room, reflecting against the crystal bowl. Jenny thought that the bowl seemed almost urn-shaped as it stood silhouetted on the dresser. Could ashes be pine-scented? she wondered. What a crazy, horrible thought, she chided herself restlessly. Caroline was buried in the family cemetery. Even so, Jenny suddenly felt uneasy enough to want to go in and check the girls. They were deeply asleep. Beth had her cheek pillowed on her hand. Tina was fetal-positioned, the satin binding of the blanket hugged against her face.

Jenny kissed them softly. They looked so content. She thought about how happy they were to have her home with them all day, about their ecstasy when Erich had shown them the ponies. Silently she vowed that Kevin was not going to spoil this new life for them.

12

The keys to the Cadillac were in the farm office, but Erich kept spare keys to all the buildings and machines in the library. It would make sense that the extra Cadillac keys were there as well.

Her guess was right. Slipping them in the pocket of her slacks, she fed the girls an early lunch and settled them for a nap. "Elsa, I have an errand to do. I'll be back by two o'clock."

Elsa nodded. Was Elsa naturally this taciturn? She didn't think so. Sometimes when she'd come in after skiing with Erich, Tina and Beth would be already awake and she'd hear Elsa chatting with them, her Swedish accent more pronounced when she spoke quickly. But when Jenny or Erich was around, she was silent.

The country roads had a few patches of ice but the highway was completely clear. Jenny realized how good it felt to drive again. She smiled to herself, remembering the weekend jaunts she and Nana took in her secondhand Beetle. But after she and Kev were married she'd had to sell it; the upkeep had become too expensive. Now she would ask Erich to pick up a small car for her.

It was twenty of one when she got to the restaurant. Surprisingly Kevin was already there, a nearly empty carafe of wine in front of him. She slid into the booth and looked across the table. "Hello, Kev." Incredible that in less than a month he could seem older, less buoyant. His eyes were puffy. Was Kevin drinking too much? she wondered.

He reached for her hand. "Jenny, I've missed you. I've missed the kids."

She disengaged her fingers. "Tell me about the Guthrie."

"I'm pretty sure I've got the job. I'd better have it. Broadway is tight as a drum. And I'll be that much nearer you and the kids out here. Jen, let's try again."

"Kev, you're crazy."

"No, I'm not. You're beautiful, Jenny. I like that outfit. That jacket must have cost a fortune."

"I guess it was expensive."

"You're classy, Jen. I always knew it but didn't think about it. I always believed you'd be there for me."

Again he covered her hand with his. "Are you happy, Jen?"

"Yes, I am. Look, Erich would be terribly upset about my seeing you. I have to tell you you didn't make much of an impression on him the last time you met."

"And he didn't make much of an impression on me when he stuck a piece of paper in front of me and told me you'd sue me for nonsupport and attach every nickle I ever made if I didn't sign."

"Erich said that!"

"Erich said that. Come on, Jen. That was a lousy trick. I was up for a part in the new Hal Prince

musical. That would have really queered me. Too bad I didn't know I'd already been eliminated. Believe me, there wouldn't have been any adoption papers signed."

"It isn't that simple," Jenny said. "I know Erich gave you two thousand dollars."

"That was just a loan."

She was torn between pity for Kevin and the nagging certainty that he would always use the girls as a wedge for staying in her life. She opened her pocketbook. "Kev, I must get back. Here's the three hundred dollars. But after today, please don't contact me; don't try to see the children. If you do, you'll make trouble for them, for you, for me."

He took the money, flipped his fingers idly through the bills, then put them in his wallet. "Jen, you want to know something. I have a bad feeling about you and the kids. It's something I can't explain. But I do."

Jenny got up. In an instant Kevin was beside her, his arms were pulling her to him. "I still love you, Jenny." His kiss was harsh and demanding.

She could not pull away without creating a scene. It was fully half a minute before she felt his arms loosen and she could step back. "Leave us alone," she whispered. "I beg you, I *warn* you, Kevin, leave us alone."

She almost bumped into the waitress who was standing behind her, order pad in hand. The two women at the window table were staring at them.

As Jenny fled from the restaurant she realized why one of the women seemed familiar. She had sat across the aisle from them at church on Sunday morning.

13

After that first evening, Erich did not call again. Jenny tried to rationalize her uneasiness. Erich had a thing about telephones. But he had planned to call every night. Should she try to reach him at the hotel? A half-dozen times she put her hand on the phone and then removed it.

Did Kevin get hired by the Guthrie? If he did, he'd be trying the same thing here that he'd done at the apartment, dropping in when he was broke or feeling sentimental. Erich would never stand for it and it was no good for the children.

Why didn't Erich phone?

He was due home on the twenty-eighth. Joe was picking him up at the airport. Should she ride up to Minneapolis with Joe? No, she'd wait at the farm and have a good dinner ready. She missed him. She hadn't realized how totally she and the girls had embraced their new life in these past weeks.

* * *

If it weren't for the miserable feeling of guilt over meeting Kevin, Jenny knew she wouldn't be troubled that Erich hadn't phoned. Kevin was the spoiler. Suppose when the three hundred dollars was gone, he came back? It would be twice as bad if Erich learned she'd met him and said nothing.

She flew into Erich's arms when he opened the door. He held her against him. In the short distance from the car to the porch the chill of the evening had caught in his coat and his lips were cool. They warmed quickly as he kissed her. With a half-sob she thought, *It will be all right.*

"I've missed you so." They said it together.

He hugged the girls, asked them if they'd been good, and at their enthusiastic response presented them with brightly wrapped packages. He smiled indulgently at their squeals of delight over their new dolls.

"Thank you very, very much," Beth said solemnly.

"Thank you, Daddy," he corrected.

"That's what I mean," Beth said, her tone puzzled.

"What did you bring Mommy?" Tina asked.

He smiled at Jenny. "Has Mommy been a good girl?"

They agreed that she had.

"You're sure, Mommy?"

Why was it that the most ordinary teasing seemed double-edged when you have something to hide? Jen thought of Nana shaking her head about an acquaintance. "That one's bad news; she'd lie even when the truth would serve her better."

Was that what she'd done? "I've been a good girl." She tried to make her voice sound amused, casual.

"Jenny, you're blushing." Erich shook his head.

She knew her smile was forced. "Where's my present?"

He reached into his suitcase. "Since you like Royal

Doulton figurines, I thought I'd try to find another one for you in Atlanta. This one leaped out at me. It's called *The Cup of Tea.*"

She opened the box. The figurine was of an old woman sitting in a rocking chair, a cup of tea in her hand, a look of contentment on her face.

"It even looks like Nana," she sighed.

His eyes were tender as he watched her examine the figurine. Her eyes bright with tears, she smiled at him. And Kevin would spoil this for me, she thought.

She had made a fire in the stove; a carafe of wine and wedge of cheese were on the table. Linking her fingers in his, she brought him over to the couch. Smiling, she poured wine into his glass and handed it to him. "Welcome home." She sat beside him, turning so that her knee touched his. She was wearing a green, ruffle-necked Yves St. Laurent silk blouse and tweed slacks in a brown-and-green weave. She knew it was one of Erich's favorite outfits. Her hair was growing longer and fell loosely on her shoulders. Except when it was bitterly cold she liked to go bareheaded and the winter sun had bleached gold highlights in her dark hair.

Erich studied her, his face inscrutable. "You're a beautiful woman, Jen. Aren't you quite dressed up?"

"It isn't every night my husband comes home after being away four days."

"If I hadn't come home tonight, it would have been a waste getting all dolled up, I hope."

"If you hadn't come home tonight, I'd have worn this for you tomorrow." Jenny decided to change the subject. "How did it go in Atlanta?"

"It was miserable. The gallery people spent most of their time trying to persuade me to sell *Memory of Caroline*. They had a couple of big offers for it and could smell the commission."

"You ran into the same thing in New York. Maybe you'll have to stop showing that painting."

"And maybe I choose to show it because it's still my best work," Erich said quietly. Was there an implied criticism of her suggestion in his voice?

"Why don't I finish putting dinner together?" As she got up, Jenny leaned over and kissed him. "Hey, ' she whispered, "I love you."

While she was tossing the salad and stirring hollandaise sauce, he called Beth and Tina over. A few minutes later he had both girls on his lap and was animatedly telling them the story of the Peachtree Hotel in Atlanta where the elevators were glass and went up outside the building just like a magic carpet. Someday he'd take them there.

"Mommy too?" Tina asked.

Jenny turned, smiling, but the smile ended when Erich said, "If Mommy wants to come with us."

She'd cooked a rib roast. He ate well but his fingers drummed restlessly on the table and no matter what she said he answered in monosyllables. Finally Jenny gave up and started talking only to the children. "Did you tell Daddy that you sat on the ponies' backs?"

Beth put down her fork and looked at Erich. "It was fun. I said giddyap but Mouse didn't go."

"I said giddyap too," Tina chimed in.

"Where were the ponies?" Erich asked.

"Right in the stalls," Jenny said hastily, "and Joe lifted them up for just a minute."

"Joe takes too much on himself," Erich interrupted. "I want to be there when the girls are put on the ponies. I want to be sure he's watching them carefully. How do I know he's not as careless as that fool of an uncle was?"

"Erich, that was so long ago."

"It doesn't seem long ago when I bump into that

drunken sot. And Joe tells me he's back in town again."

Was that the reason Erich was so upset? "Beth, Tina, if you're finished you can excuse yourselves and play with your new dolls." When the children were out of earshot she said, "Is Joe's uncle the problem, Erich, or is it something else?"

He reached across the table in that familiar gesture of entwining their fingers. "It's that. It's the fact that I think Joe has been tootling around in the car again. It has at least forty extra miles on it. Of course he denies driving it but he used it once in the fall without permission. He didn't drive you anywhere, did he?"

She clenched her fist. "No."

She had to say something about Kevin. She wouldn't have Erich believe that Joe had deceived him.

"Erich . . . I . . ."

He interrupted her. "And it's the damn art galleries. For four days I had to keep telling that fool in Atlanta that *Memory of Caroline* was not for sale. I think it's still my best work and I want to exhibit it but . . ." His voice stopped. When he spoke again, it was calmer. "I'll be doing more painting, Jen. You don't mind, do you? It means I'll have to hole up in the cabin for three or four days at a stretch. But it's necessary."

Dismayed, Jenny thought how these last days had dragged. She tried to make her voice sound casual. "If it's necessary, of course."

When she came back to the library from putting the girls to bed, Erich's eyes were filled with tears.

"Erich, what is it?"

Hastily he brushed his eyes with the back of his hand. "Forgive me, Jenny. It's just I was so depressed. I missed you so much. And Mother's anniversary is next week. You can't know how hard a time that always is for me. Every year it's still as though it's just happened. When Joe told me his uncle is around, it was like a punch in the stomach. I felt so lousy. Then the car turned in from the road and the house was lighted. I was so afraid it would be dark and empty; and I opened the door and you were there, so beautiful, so glad to see me. I was so afraid that maybe while I was away somehow I'd lost you."

Jenny slipped to her knees. She smoothed the hair back from his forehead.

"Glad to see you. You can't guess!"

His lips silenced her.

When they went up to bed, Jenny reached for one of her new nightgowns then stopped. Reluctantly she opened the dresser drawer that held the aqua gown. The bosom of the gown felt too small. Well, maybe that's one solution, she thought. I'll outgrow the damn thing.

Later just before she fell asleep she realized what it was that had been teasing her subconscious. The only times Erich made love to her was when she was wearing this gown.

14

She heard Erich walking around the bedroom before dawn. "Are you going to the cabin?" she murmured, trying to pull herself from sleep.

"Yes, darling." His whisper was barely audible.

"Will you be back for lunch?" As she started to wake up she remembered that he had talked about staying at the cabin.

"I'm not sure." The door closed behind him.

She and the girls took their usual walk after breakfast. The ponies had replaced the chickens as first attraction for Beth and Tina. They ran ahead of her now. "Hold it, you two," she called. "Make sure Baron is locked up."

Joe was already in the stable. "Good morning, Mrs. Krueger." His round face broke into a smile. The soft, sandy hair spilled out from under his cap. "Hello, girls."

The ponies were immaculate. Their thick manes and tails were brushed and shining. "Just groomed them for you," Joe said. "Did you bring some sugar with you?"

He held the girls up to feed the sugar. "Now how about sitting on their backs for a couple of minutes?"

"Joe, I'm afraid not," Jenny said. "Mr. Krueger didn't approve of putting the girls on the ponies."

"I want to sit on Tinker Bell's back," Tina said.

"Daddy will let us," Beth said positively. "Mommy, you're mean."

"Beth!"

"Mean Mommy," Tina said. Her lip trembled.

"Don't cry, Tina," Beth said. She looked up at Jenny. "Mommy, *please."*

Joe was looking at her too.

"Well . . ." Jenny wavered, then thought of Erich's face when he said that Joe took too much on himself. She could not have Erich accuse her of deliberately ignoring his wishes.

"Tomorrow," she said positively. "I'll talk to Daddy. Now let's go see the chickens."

"I want to ride my pony," Tina cried. Her small hand slapped Jenny's leg. "You're a bad mommy."

Jenny reached down. In a reflex action she swatted Tina's bottom. "And you're a very fresh little girl."

Tina ran from the barn, crying. Beth was right behind her.

Jenny hurried after the girls. They were holding hands, walking toward the barn. As she caught up with them she heard Beth say soothingly, "Don't be sad, Tina. We'll tell Daddy on Mommy."

Joe was at her side. "Mrs. Krueger."

"Yes, Joe." Jenny turned her face from him. She did not want him to see the tears that were swimming in her eyes. In her bones she knew that when they asked him, Erich would give permission to the girls to sit on the ponies in the stable.

"Mrs. Krueger, I was wondering. We have a new puppy at our place. We're just down the road about half a mile. Maybe the girls would like to see Randy. It might take their minds off the ponies."

"Joe, that would be nice." Jenny caught up with the children. She crouched in front of Tina. "I'm sorry I spanked you, Tinker Bell. I want to ride Fire Maid just as much as you want to ride your pony, but we have to wait till Daddy says okay. Now Joe wants to take us to see his puppy. Want to go?"

They walked together, Joe pointing out the first signs of the approaching spring. "See how the snow is going. In a couple of weeks the ground will be real muddy. That's because all the frost will be coming out of it. Then the grass starts to grow. Your dad wants me to build a ring for you to ride in."

Joe's mother was home; his father had died five years ago. She was a heavyset woman in her late fifties with a practical, no-nonsense approach. She invited them in. The small house was comfortably shabby. Souvenir knickknacks covered the tables. The walls were strewn with family pictures indiscriminately hung.

"Nice to meet you, Mrs. Krueger. My Joe talks about you all the time. No wonder he says you're pretty. You sure are. And oh, my land, how you look like Caroline! I'm Maude Ekers. You call me Maude."

"Where's Joe's dog?" Tina asked.

"Come on in the kitchen," Maude told them.

They followed her eagerly. The puppy looked to be a combination of German shepherd and retriever. Awkwardly it struggled up on ungainly legs. "We found it on the road," Joe explained. "Somebody must have pushed it out of a car. If I hadn't come along it probably would have frozen to death."

Maude shook her head. "He's always bringing home stray animals. My Joe has the kindest heart I ever come across. Never was one for schoolwork, but let me tell you, he's magic with animals. You shoulda seen his last dog. He was a beauty. Smart as a whip too."

"What happened to him?" Jenny asked.

"We don't know. We tried to keep him fenced in but sometimes he'd get away. He used to want to trail after Joe to your farm. Mr. Krueger didn't like it."

"I don't blame Mr. Krueger," Joe said hastily. "He had a purebred bitch and he didn't want Tarpy to get near her. But one day Tarpy did follow me and was on Juna. Mr. Krueger was real mad."

"Where's Juna now?" Jenny asked.

"Mr. Krueger got rid of her. Said she wouldn't be any use if she carried a litter from a mongrel."

"What happened to Tarpy?"

"We don't know," Maude said. "He got out again one day and never came back. I've got my suspicions," she hinted darkly.

"Maw," Joe said hastily.

"Erich Krueger threatened to shoot that dog," she continued simply. "If Tarpy ruined his expensive bitch I don't much blame him for getting sore. But least he coulda told you. Joe hunted high and low for that dog," she told Jenny. "I thought he'd get sick."

Tina and Beth squatted on the floor beside Randy. Tina's face was rapturous. "Mommy, can we have a dog, please?"

"We'll ask Daddy," she promised.

The children played with the puppy while she had coffee with Maude. The woman immediately began interrogating her. How did she like the Krueger home? Pretty fancy, wasn't it? Must be tough to come out from New York City to a farm. Jenny replied that she was sure she'd be happy.

"Caroline said that too," Maude hinted darkly. "But the Krueger men aren't very sociable. Kind of makes it hard on their wives. Everybody around here thought the world of Caroline. And they respected John Krueger. Same as they do Erich. But the Kruegers aren't warm even with their own. And they're not forgiving people. When they get angry, they stay angry."

Jenny knew Maude was referring to her brother's role in Caroline's accident. Quickly she finished her coffee. "We'd better get back."

The kitchen door was pushed open just as she stood up. "Well, who's this?" The voice was raspy, as though the vocal cords had been strained. The man was in his mid-fifties. His eyes were bloodshot and faded with the bleary expression of the heavy drinker. He was painfully thin, so that the waist of his pants settled somewhere around his hips.

He stared at Jenny, then his eyes narrowed thoughtfully. "You gotta be the new Mrs. Krueger I've been hearing about."

"Yes, I am."

"I'm Josh Brothers, Joe's uncle."

The electrician who had been responsible for the accident. Jenny sensed immediately that Erich would be furious if he heard about this meeting.

"I can see why Erich picked you," Josh said heavily. He turned to his sister. "Swear it was Caroline, wouldn't you, Maude?" Without waiting for an answer he asked Jenny, "Heard all about the accident, I suppose?"

"Yes, I did."

"The Krueger version. Not mine." Clearly Josh Brothers was about to tell an often-repeated story. Jenny got the smell of whiskey from his breath. His voice took on a reciting quality. "In spite of the fact they were divorcing, John was crazy about Caroline. . . ."

"Divorcing!" Jenny interrupted. "Erich's father and mother *divorcing!*"

The bleary eyes became crafty. "Oh, Erich didn't tell you that? He likes to pretend it didn't happen. Lots of gossip here, let me tell you, when Caroline didn't even *try* to get custody of her only child. Anyhow the day of the accident I was working in the dairy barn and Caroline and Erich came in. She was leaving for good that afternoon. It was his birthday and he was holding his new hockey stick and crying his eyes out. She waved me away; that's why I hung the lamp over the nail. I heard Caroline say, 'Just like this little calf has to be weaned away from its mother . . .' Then I pulled the door closed behind me so they could say good-bye to each other and a minute later Erich began screaming. Luke Garrett pounded on her chest and did that mouth-to-mouth breathing, but we all knew it was no good. When she slipped and fell into the stock tank, she grabbed the cord and pulled the lamp in with her. That voltage went right through her. . . . She never had no chance."

"Josh, keep quiet," Maude said sharply.

Jenny stared at Josh. Why had Erich never told her that his parents were divorcing, that Caroline was leaving him and his father? And to have witnessed that ghastly accident! No wonder Erich was so terribly insecure now, so afraid of losing her.

Deep in thought, she collected the girls and murmured goodbyes.

As they walked back home, Joe spoke timidly to Jenny. "Mr. Krueger wouldn't be pleased to hear my mom talked so much and that you met my uncle."

"I'm not going to discuss it, Joe, I promise," she reassured him.

The country road back to Krueger Farm was peaceful in the late morning. Beth and Tina ran ahead of them, happily scooping up loose snow. Jenny felt depressed and frightened. She thought of the countless times Erich had talked about Caroline. Never once had he even hinted about the fact that she had been planning to leave him.

If only I had a friend here, Jenny thought, someone I could talk to. She remembered how she and Nana had been able to talk through any problem that came up in their lives, how she and Fran would have coffee after the girls were in bed and exchange confidences.

"Mrs. Krueger," Joe said softly, "you look as though you feel real bad. I hope my uncle didn't upset you. I know Mom talks kind of mean about the Kruegers but please don't take offense."

"I won't," Jenny promised. "But, Joe, will you please do one thing for me?"

"Anything."

"For God sake when Mr. Krueger isn't around, call me Jenny. I'm beginning to forget my own name around here."

"I call you Jenny whenever I think about you."

"Terrific," Jenny laughed, feeling better, then glanced at Joe. The open worship on his face was unmistakable.

Oh, dear God, she thought, if he ever looks at me like that in front of Erich there'll be hell to pay.

15

As they neared the big house Jenny thought she saw someone watching them from the window of the farm office. Erich often stopped there on his way back from the cabin.

She hurried the girls into the house and began preparing grilled cheese sandwiches and hot cocoa. Tina and Beth perched at the table, expectantly watching the toaster oven as the bubbling smell of melting cheese filled the kitchen.

What could have made Caroline so desperately unhappy that she would leave Erich? How much resentment was mixed in with Erich's love for her? Jenny tried to visualize any circumstance under which she'd leave Beth and Tina. There was none.

The children were tired from the long walk and fell asleep as soon as she put them in for their nap. She watched as their eyes drooped and closed. She was reluctant to leave the room. She sat on the window seat for a moment, realizing she felt lightheaded. Why?

Finally she went downstairs, pulled on a jacket and walked over to the office. Clyde was working at the big desk. Trying to sound casual, she remarked, "Erich hasn't come in yet for lunch. I thought he might have been delayed over here."

Clyde looked puzzled. "He just stopped in for a couple of minutes on his way back from getting supplies. He told me you knew he's planning to stay up at the cabin and paint."

Wordlessly Jenny turned to leave. Then her eye spotted the incoming mail basket. "Oh, Clyde, if I get any mail while Erich is at the cabin, will you be sure that someone brings it over to me?"

"Sure will. Usually I just give anything for you to Erich."

Anything for you . . . In the month she'd been here, even though she'd written to Fran and Mr. Hartley, she hadn't received a single piece of mail. "I'm afraid he forgot about it." She could hear the strain in her voice. "How much has come in?"

"A letter last week, a couple of postcards. I don't know."

"I see." Jenny looked at the telephone. "How about phone calls?"

"Someone from church phoned last week about a meeting. And the week before you got a call from New York. You mean Erich didn't give you those messages?"

"He was so concerned with getting ready for the trip," Jenny murmured. "Thanks, Clyde."

Slowly she started back to the house. The sky was overcast now. Snow was beginning to fall in stinging, slapping gusts. The ground that had begun to thaw had hardened again. The temperature was dropping swiftly.

I won't share you, . . . Jenny. Erich had meant that literally. Who had phoned from New York? Kevin to say he was coming to Minnesota? If so, why didn't Erich warn her?

Who had written? Mr. Hartley? Fran?

I can't let this happen, Jenny thought. I've got to do something.

"Jenny!" Mark Garrett was hurrying from the barn. With his long strides he covered the distance between them in seconds. His sandy hair was rumpled. He was smiling but his eyes were serious. "Haven't had a chance to say hello for a while. How's everything?"

How much did he suspect? Could she discuss Erich with him? No, that wouldn't be fair to Erich. But there was one thing she could do.

She tried to make her smile seem natural. "I'm fine," she replied. "And you're just the person I wanted to see. Remember we talked about having you and your friend—is it Emily?—for dinner?"

"Yes."

"Let's make it March eighth. That's Erich's birthday. I want to have a little party for him."

Mark frowned. "Jenny, I have to warn you. Erich still finds his birthday a pretty rough day."

"I know," Jenny said. She looked up at Mark, aware of his tallness. "Mark, that was twenty-five years ago. Isn't it about time that Erich got over losing his mother?"

Mark seemed to be choosing his words. "Go easy, Jenny," he suggested. "It takes time to wean someone like Erich off imprinted reactions." He smiled. "But I must say it shouldn't take him very long to start to appreciate what he has now."

"Then you will come?"

"Definitely. And Emily's been dying to meet you."

Jenny laughed wistfully. "I've been dying to meet some people too."

She said good-bye and went into the house. Elsa was

just ready to leave. "The girls are still asleep. Tomorrow I can shop on my way in. I have the list."

"List?"

"Yes, when you were out with the girls this morning, Mr. Krueger came in. He said I should do the shopping from now on."

"That's nonsense," Jenny protested. "I can go or Joe can take me."

"Mr. Krueger said he was taking the keys to the car."

"I see. Thank you, Elsa." Jenny would not let the woman see the dismay she felt.

But when the door closed behind Elsa, she realized she was trembling. Had Erich taken the keys to make sure Joe didn't use the car? Or was it possible he guessed that *she* had used it? Nervously she glanced around the kitchen. In the apartment whenever she'd been upset she'd calmed herself by tackling some big cleaning job that needed to be done. But this house was immaculate.

She stared at the canisters on the counter space. They took up so much room and were so seldom used. Every room here was formal, cold, overcrowded. It was her home. Surely Erich would be pleased if she put her own stamp on this place?

She made room for the canisters on a pantry shelf. The round oak table and chairs were exactly centered in the middle of the room. Placed under the window on the south wall, they'd be infinitely more convenient to the buffet bar, and at meals it would be pleasant to look out at the far fields. Not caring if the table legs scuffed the floor, Jenny dragged it over.

The hook rug that had been in the girls' bedroom had been taken up to the attic. She decided that placing it near the cast-iron stove and grouping the couch, its matching chair and a slipper chair from the library on it would create a pleasant den area in the kitchen.

Fired now with nervous energy, she went into the parlor, swept some of the bric-a-brac into her arms and carried it to a cupboard. Tugging and straining, she managed to pull down the lace curtains that blocked sunlight and view from the parlor and the dining room. The couch in the parlor was almost too heavy to push. Somehow she managed to reverse it with the mahogany trestle table. When she was finished the room seemed airier, more inviting.

She went through the rest of the downstairs rooms, making mental notes. A little at a time, she promised herself. She folded the curtains neatly and carried them up to the attic. The braided rug was there. If she couldn't manage to bring that down by herself she'd call Joe.

She yanked at the rug she wanted, realized there was no way she could manage it alone and with idle curiosity glanced at the other pieces in the room.

A small blue leather vanity case with the initials C.B.K. caught her eye. She pulled it out to examine it. Was it unlocked? Hesitating for only an instant, she deflected one then the other of the catches. The lid swung up.

Toilet articles were set in a traylike holder. Creams and makeup and pine-scented soap. A leather-bound daily reminder notebook was under the tray. The date on the cover was twenty-five years old. Jenny opened the book and flipped through the pages. January 2, 10 A.M., teacher conference, Erich. January 8: dinner, Luke Garrett, the Meiers, the Behrends. January 10: return library books. She skimmed through the entries. February 2: judges chambers, 9 A.M. Would that have been the divorce hearing? Feb. 22: order hockey stick for E. The last entry, March 8: Erich b-day. That had been written in light blue ink. Then with a different pen, 7 P.M., Northwest flight 241, Minneapolis to San Francisco. A ticket unused, one-way, clipped to that page, a note under it.

The name printed across the top of the note: EVERETT BONARDI. Caroline's father, Jenny thought. Quickly she read the uneven handwriting: "Caroline, dear. Your mother and I are not surprised to learn you are leaving John. We are deeply concerned about Erich but after reading your letter agree it is best if he stays with his father. We had no idea of the true circumstances. Neither of us has been well but are looking forward to having you with us. Our love to you."

Jenny folded the letter, slipped it back in the notebook and closed the lid of the vanity case. What had Everett Bonardi meant when he wrote "We had no idea of the true circumstances"?

Slowly she went down the attic stairs. The girls were still asleep. Lovingly she looked down at them, then her mouth went dry. The girls' dark red hair was tumbled out on their pillows. On the top of each pillow, positioned so it almost seemed to be a hair ornament, was a small round cake of pine soap. The faint scent of pine permeated the air.

"Aren't they the little beauties?" a voice sighed in her ear. Too startled to scream, Jenny spun around. A thin, bony arm encircled her waist. "Oh, Caroline," Rooney Toomis sighed, her eyes vacant and moist, "don't we just love our babies?"

Somehow Jenny got Rooney out of the room without waking the girls. Rooney went willingly although she kept her arm wrapped around Jenny's waist. Awkwardly they descended the stairs.

"Let's have a cup of tea," Jenny suggested, trying to keep her voice normal. How had Rooney gotten in? She must still have a house key.

Rooney sipped the tea silently, never taking her

gaze from the window. "Arden used to love those woods," she said. "Course she knew she wasn't to go any farther than the edge. But she was always climbing trees. She'd perch up there in that one"—Rooney pointed vaguely to a large oak—"and watch the birds. Did I tell you she was president of the 4-H club one year?"

Her voice was calming. Her eyes were clearer when she turned to look at Jenny. "You're not Caroline," she said, puzzled.

"No, I'm not. I'm Jenny."

Rooney sighed. "I'm sorry. I guess I forgot. Something came over me, one of my spells. I was thinking I was late getting to work. Thought I'd overslept. Course Caroline would never care but Mr. John Krueger was so exacting."

"And you had a key?" Jenny asked.

"I forgot my key. The door was unlocked. But I don't have a key anymore, do I?"

Jenny was positive the lock had been on the kitchen door. On the other hand . . . She decided not to try to pin Rooney down.

"And I went upstairs to make the beds," Rooney said. "But they were all finished. And then I saw Caroline. No, I mean I saw you."

"And you put the pine soap on the children's pillows?" Jenny asked.

"Oh, no. Caroline must have done that. She was the one who loved that scent."

It was useless. Rooney's mind was too confused to attempt to separate imagination from reality. "Rooney, do you ever go out to church or to any meetings? Do you ever have friends in?"

Rooney shook her head. "I used to go to all the activities with Arden, the 4-H, the school plays, her band concerts. But no more."

Her eyes were clear now. "I shouldn't be here. Erich won't like it." She looked fearful. "You won't tell him or Clyde, will you? Promise you won't tell."

"Of course I won't."

"You're like Caroline, pretty and gentle and sweet. I hope nothing happens to you. That would be such a shame. Toward the end Caroline was so anxious to get away. She used to say, 'I just have a feeling, Rooney, that something terrible is going to happen. And I'm so helpless.'" Rooney got up to go.

"Didn't you wear a coat?" Jenny asked.

"I guess I didn't notice."

"Wait a minute." Jenny dug her thermal coat out of the foyer closet. "Put this on. Look, it fits you perfectly. Button it up around the neck. It's cold out."

Hadn't Erich said practically the same thing to her at that first lunch in the Russian Tea Room? Was that really less than two months ago?

Rooney glanced around uncertainly. "If you want I'll help you move the table back before Erich comes."

"I don't intend to move the table back. It's staying right where it is."

"Caroline had it at the window once but John said she was just trying to show herself off to the men on the farm."

"What did Caroline say?"

"Nothing. She just put on her green cape and went outside and sat on the porch swing. Just like in the picture. Once she told me she used to like to sit out there and face west because that's where her folks were. She got awful homesick for them."

"Didn't they ever come here to visit?"

"Never. But Caroline still loved the farm. She was raised in the city but she'd always say, 'This country is so beautiful, Rooney, so special in what it does for me.'"

"And then she left?"

"Something happened and she decided she had to go."

"What was that?"

"I don't know." Rooney glanced down. "This coat is nice. I like it."

"Please keep it," Jenny told her. "I've hardly worn it since I came here."

"If I do, can I make the girls jumpers like you promised?"

"Of course you can. And, Rooney, I'd like to be your friend."

Jenny stood at the kitchen door, watching the slight figure, now warmly wrapped, bend forward against the wind.

16

It was the waiting that was so hard. Was Erich angry? Had he simply become so involved in painting that he hadn't wanted to break his concentration? Did she dare go into the woods, try to find the cabin and confront him?

No, she must not do that.

The days seemed endlessly long. Even the children became restless. Where's Daddy? was a constant inquiry. In this short time, Erich had become terribly important to them.

Let Kevin stay away, Jenny prayed. Make him leave us alone.

She spent her time concentrating on the house. Room by room she rearranged furniture, sometimes switching only a chair or table, sometimes making radical adjustments. Unwillingly Elsa helped her take down the rest of the heavy lace curtains. "Look, Elsa," Jenny finally said firmly, "these curtains are coming down and I don't want any more talk about checking with Mr. Krueger first. Either help me or don't."

Outside, the farm seemed gray and depressing. When the snow was on the ground, it had had a Currier and Ives beauty. When spring came, she was sure the lush green of the fields and trees would be magnificent. But now the frozen mud, the brown fields, the dark tree trunks and overcast skies chilled and depressed her.

Would Erich come back to the house for his birthday? He'd told her that he was always on the farm that day. Should she cancel his birthday dinner?

The evenings alone were interminable. In New York when the children were settled for the night, she'd often gone to bed with a book and a cup of tea. The library on the farm was excellent. But the books in this library didn't invite leisurely reading. They were placed in exact rows, seemingly by size and color rather than author or subject. To her, they had the same effect as furniture with plastic covers; she hated to touch them. Her problem was solved when on one of her trips to the attic she noticed a box marked BOOKS—CBK. Happily she helped herself to a couple of the comfortably shabby, well-read volumes.

But even though she read far into the night, she was finding it harder and harder to sleep. All her life she'd only had to close her eyes and instantly she'd be in a sound sleep for hours. Now she began to wake up frequently, to dream vague, frightening dreams in which shadowy figures slithered through her subconscious.

On March 7, following a particularly restless night, she made up her mind. She needed more exercise. After lunch she went out to hunt for Joe and found him in the farm office. His unaffected pleasure at the visit was reassuring. Quickly she explained: "Joe, I want to start riding lessons today."

126

Twenty minutes later she was sitting astride the mare, trying to keep Joe's instructions straight in her head.

She realized she was enjoying herself thoroughly. She forgot the chill, the sharp wind, the fact that her thighs were getting sore, that her hands were tingling against the reins. Softly she spoke to Fire Maid. "Now you at least give me a chance, old girl," she suggested "I'll probably make mistakes but I'm new at this business."

By the end of an hour she was getting the feel of moving her body in cadence with the horse. She spotted Mark watching her and waved to him. He came over.

"You look pretty good. This your first time on a horse?"

"The very first." Jenny started to dismount. Quickly Mark took the horse's bridle. "The other side," he said.

"What, oh, sorry." She slid down easily.

"You did real good, Jenny," Joe told her.

"Thank you, Joe. Monday okay with you?"

"Anytime, Jenny."

Mark walked with her to the house. "You've got a fan in Joe."

Was there some kind of warning in his voice?

She tried to sound matter-of-fact. "He's a good teacher and I think Erich will be pleased that I'm learning to ride. It will be a surprise for him that I've started taking lessons."

"I hardly think so," Mark commented. "He was watching you for quite a while."

"Watching me?"

"Yes, for nearly half an hour from the woods. I thought he didn't want to make you nervous."

"Where is he now?"

"He went up to the house for a minute and then started back to the cabin."

"Erich was in the house?" I sound stupid, Jenny thought, hearing the astonishment in her voice.

Mark stopped, took her arm and turned her to him. "What's the matter, Jenny?" he asked. Somehow she could imagine him examining an animal, searching for the source of pain.

They were almost at the porch. She said tiffly, "Erich has been staying at the cabin since he came back from Atlanta. It's just that it's rather lonely for me now. I'm used to being terribly busy and around people and now . . . I guess I feel out of touch all around."

"See if it doesn't get much better after tomorrow," Mark advised. "By the way, are you sure you want us for dinner?"

"No. I mean, I'm not even sure Erich will be home. Could we make it the thirteenth instead? That will separate his birthday party from the anniversary. If he still hasn't come back by then, I'll give you a call and you two can decide if you want to come just to visit me or go out and enjoy yourselves."

She was afraid she sounded resentful. What's the matter with me? she thought, dismayed.

Mark took both her hands in his. "We'll come, Jenny, whether Erich is home or not. For what it's worth I've had Erich turn on me when he gets in one of his moods. The rest of the picture is that when he comes out of them, he's all the good things— intelligent, generous, talented, kind. Give him a chance to get through tomorrow and see if he isn't the real Erich again."

With a quick smile, he squeezed her hands, released them and left her. Sighing, Jenny entered the house. Elsa was ready to go. Tina and Beth were cross-legged on the floor, crayons in hand. "Daddy brought us new coloring books," Beth announced. "Aren't they good?"

"Mr. Krueger left note for you." Elsa pointed to a sealed envelope on the table.

Jenny felt the curiosity in the woman's eyes. She slipped the note into her pocket. "Thank you."

As the door closed behind the cleaning woman, Jenny pulled the envelope from her pocket and ripped it open. The sheet of paper, covered by oversized letters in Erich's bold handwriting, held one sentence: *You should have waited for me to ride with you.*

"Mommy, Mommy." Beth was tugging at her jacket. "You look sick, Mommy." Trying to smile, Jenny looked down at the woebegone face. Tina was next to Beth now, her face puckered, ready to cry.

Jenny crumbled the note and shoved it in her pocket. "No, love, I'm fine. I just didn't feel so well for a minute."

She was not reassuring Beth. A wave of nausea had come over her as she read the note. Dear God, she thought, he can't mean this. He won't let me go to the church meetings. He won't let me use the car. Now he won't let me even learn to ride when he's painting.

Erich, don't spoil it for us, she protested silently. You can't have it both ways. You can't hole up and paint and expect me to sit with my hands folded waiting for you. You can't be so jealous that I'm afraid to be honest with you.

She glanced around wildly. Should she take a stand, pack and go back to New York? If there was any chance to keep their relationship from being destroyed, he'd have to get counseling, get some help to overcome this possessiveness. If she left, he'd know she meant it.

Where could she go? And with what?

She didn't have a dollar in her pocketbook. She had no money for fare, no place to go, no job. And she didn't want to leave him.

She was afraid she was going to be sick. "I'll be right back," she whispered and hurried upstairs. In the bathroom she wrung out a cold cloth and washed her face. Her reflection had a sickly, unnatural pallor.

"Mommy, Mommy." Beth and Tina were in the hallway. They had followed her upstairs.

She knelt down, swooped them to her, hugging them fiercely.

"Mommy, you're hurting me," Tina protested.

"I'm sorry, Moppet." The warm, wiggling bodies close to hers restored her balance. "You two certainly got yourselves one brilliant mother," she said.

The afternoon dragged slowly. To pass the time, she sat with the girls at the spinet and began to teach them to pick out notes. Without the curtains it was possible to look out the parlor windows and see the sunset. The clouds had been blown away and the sky was coldly beautiful in shades of mauve and orange, gold and pink.

Leaving the children banging on the keyboard, she walked to the kitchen door that opened onto the west porch. The wind was making the porch swing move gently. Ignoring the cold, Jenny stood on the porch and admired the last of the sunset. When the final lights were ebbing into grayness, she turned to go back into the house.

A movement in the woods caught her attention. She stared. Someone was watching her, a shadowy figure, nearly concealed by the double trunk of the oak tree that Arden used to climb.

"Who's there?" Jenny called sharply.

The shadow receded into the woods as though trying to step back into the protection of the underbrush.

"Who's there?" Jenny called again sharply. Aware only of her anger at the intrusion on her privacy, she started down the porch steps toward the woods.

Erich stepped out from the shelter of the oak and with outstretched arms started running toward her.

"But, darling, I was only joking. How could you have thought for a minute that I wasn't joking?" He took the crumbled note from her. "Here, let's throw that out." He shoved it in the stove. "There, it's gone."

Bewildered, Jenny looked at Erich. There wasn't a trace of nervousness about him. He was smiling easily, shaking his head at her in amusement. "It's hard to believe you took that seriously, Jenny," he said, then he laughed. "I thought you'd be flattered that I pretended to be jealous."

"Erich!"

He locked his arms around her waist, rubbed his cheek against hers. "Umm, you feel good."

Nothing about the fact that they hadn't seen each other for a week. And that note *wasn't* a joke. He was kissing her cheek. "I love you, Jen."

For a moment she held herself rigid. She had vowed that she would have it out with him, the absences, the jealousy, her mail. But she didn't want to start an argument. She'd missed him. Suddenly the whole house seemed cheerful again.

The girls heard his voice and came running back into the room. "Daddy, Daddy." He picked them up.

"Hey, you two sounded great on the piano. Guess we'll have to start lessons for you pretty soon. Would you like that?"

Jenny thought, Mark's right. I've got to have patience, give him time. Her smile was genuine when he looked at her over the children's heads.

Dinner had a festive air. She prepared carbonara

and an endive salad. Erich brought a bottle of Chablis from the wine rack. "It gets harder and harder to work in the cabin, Jen," he said. "Especially when I know I'm missing dinners like this." He tickled Tina. "And it's no fun being away from my family."

"And your home," she said. It seemed a good moment to bring up the changes she'd made. "You haven't mentioned how you like the way I've moved things around."

"I'm slow to react," he said lightly. "Let me think about it."

It was better than she'd hoped for. She got up, walked around the table and put her arms around his neck. "I was so afraid you might be upset."

He reached up and smoothed her hair. As always the feel of his nearness thrilled her, pushed away the doubts and uncertainties.

Beth had just left the table. Now she came running back. "Mommy, do you love Daddy better than our other daddy?"

Why in the name of God had she thought to ask that question now? Jenny wondered despairingly. Desperately she tried to frame an answer. She could only find the truth. "I loved your first daddy mostly because of you and Tina. Why do you want to know that?" To Erich she said, "They haven't mentioned Kevin for weeks."

Beth pointed at Erich. "Because *this daddy* asked me if I love him better than our first daddy."

"Erich, I wouldn't discuss that with the girls."

"I shouldn't," he said contritely. "I guess I was just anxious to see if their memory of him was beginning to fade." He put his arms around her. "How about your memory, darling?"

She took a long time with the children's baths. Somehow it was calming to watch their uncomplicated pleasure splashing in the tub. She wrapped them in thick towels, rejoicing in the sturdy little bodies and brushing back the freshly shampooed ringlets. Her hands trembled as she buttoned their pajamas. I'm getting so nervous, she fumed at herself. It's just I feel so dishonest that the smallest thing Erich says I take the wrong way. *Damn* Kevin.

She heard the girls' prayers. "God bless Mommy and Daddy," Tina intoned. She paused then looked up. "Should we say God bless both daddies?"

Jenny bit her lip. Erich had started this. She wasn't going to tell the children not to pray for Kevin. Still . . . "Why not tonight say God bless everyone?" she suggested.

"And Fire Maid and Mouse and Tinker Bell and Joe . . ." Beth added.

"And Randy," Tina reminded her. "Can we have a puppy too?"

Jenny tucked them into bed, realizing how every night she was becoming more and more reluctant to go downstairs again. When she was alone, the house seemed too big, too silent. On windy nights there was a mournful wail from the trees that penetrated the quiet.

And now when Erich was here she didn't know what to expect. Would he stay overnight or go back to the cabin?

She went downstairs. He had made the coffee. "They must have been pretty dirty for you to be so long with them, sweetheart."

She had planned to ask him for the keys to the car but he didn't give her the chance. He picked up the tray with the coffee service. "Let's sit in the front parlor and let me absorb your changes."

As she followed him she realized how well the white cableknit sweater he was wearing set off his dark, gold hair. My handsome, successful, talented husband, she thought, and with a tinge of irony remembered Fran saying, "He's too perfect."

In the parlor she pointed out to him how moving some furniture and putting away the excessive bric-a-brac made it possible to appreciate the lovely pieces in the room.

"Where did you put everything?"

"The curtains are in the attic. The small pieces are in the cupboard in the pantry. Don't you think having the trestle table under *Memory of Caroline* is better? I always felt the pattern in the couch was distracting so near the painting."

"Perhaps."

She couldn't be sure of his reaction. Nervously she tried to fill the silence with conversation. "And don't you think with the light that way, we see more of the little boy—of you? Before this your face was rather shadowed."

"That's a bit fanciful. The child's face was never meant to be defined. As a fine arts major who worked in a prominent gallery, you should realize that, Jenny."

He laughed.

Was he intending to joke? Was it just that no matter what he said tonight, there seemed to be a sting in it? Jenny picked up her coffee cup and realized her hand was shaking. The cup slipped from her hand and the coffee splattered on the couch and Oriental rug.

"Jenny, darling. Why are you so nervous?" Erich's face creased into worried lines. With his napkin he began to swab the stain.

"Don't rub it in," Jenny cautioned. Rushing into the kitchen, she grabbed a bottle of club soda from the refrigerator.

With a sponge she dabbed furiously at the spots. "Thank God I hadn't put cream in yet," she murmured.

Erich said nothing. Would he consider the couch and carpet destroyed as he had the dining-room wallpaper?

But the club soda did the trick. "I think I've got it all." She got up slowly. "I'm sorry, Erich."

"Sweetheart, don't worry about it. But can't you tell me why you're so upset? You *are* upset, Jen. That note for example. A few weeks ago you would have known I was teasing you. Darling, your sense of humor is one of the most delightful parts of your personality. Please don't lose it."

She knew he was right. "I'm sorry," she said miserably. She was going to tell Erich about meeting Kevin. No matter what, she had to clear the air. "The reason I'm so . . ."

The phone rang.

"Answer it, please, Jenny."

"It won't be for me."

It rang again.

"Don't be so sure. Clyde tells me in the last week there have been a dozen disconnects where someone didn't want to leave a taped message. That's why I told him to let it ring through tonight."

With a sense of fatality she preceded him into the kitchen. The phone rang a third time. She knew even before she picked it up that it was Kevin.

"Jenny, I can't believe I finally got through to you. That damn answering machine! How are you?" Kevin's voice was buoyant.

"I'm all right, Kev." She felt Erich's eyes on her face; he bent over the phone so he could hear the conversation. "What do you want?" *Would Kevin talk about their meeting?* If only she'd told Erich first.

"To share the good news. I'm officially in the repertory company at the Guthrie, Jen."

"I'm glad for you," she said stiffly. "But, Kevin, I don't want you calling me. I forbid you to call me.

Erich is right here and he's very upset that you're contacting me."

"Listen, Jen, I'll call all I want. You tell Krueger for me that he can tear up those adoption papers. I'm going to court to stop the adoption. You can have custody, Jen, and I'll pay support, but those kids are MacPartlands and that's the way it's going to be. Who knows? Someday Tina and I might be doing a Tatum and Ryan O'Neal number. She's a real little actress. Oh, Jen. Gotta run. They're calling for me. I'll get back to you. Bye."

Slowly Jenny hung up the phone. "Can he stop the adoption?" she asked.

"He can try. He won't succeed." Erich's eyes were cold, his tone icy.

"A Tatum and Ryan O'Neal number, my God," Jenny said disbelievingly. "I'd almost admire him if I thought he wanted the children, really wanted them. But this!"

"Jenny, I predicted you were making a mistake letting him sponge off you," Erich said. "If you'd been yanking him into court for support payments, you'd have been finished with him two years ago."

As usual, Erich was right. Suddenly she felt infinitely weary and the faint nausea she'd experienced earlier was coming back. "I'm going to bed," she said abruptly. "Are you staying here tonight, Erich?"

"I'm not sure."

"I see." She started down the foyer from the kitchen to the staircase. She had gone only a few feet when he caught up with her.

"Jenny."

She turned. "What is it, Erich?"

His eyes were warm now, his face concerned and gentle. "I know it isn't your fault that MacPartland is bothering you. I promise I know that. I shouldn't get upset with you."

"It makes it so much harder for me when you do."

"We'll work this out. Let me get through these next few days. I'll feel better then. Try to understand. Maybe it's because Mother promised me just before she died that she'd always be here on my birthday. Maybe that's why I'm so depressed around this time. I feel her presence—and her loss—so much. Try to understand me; try to forgive me when I hurt you. I don't *mean* it, Jenny. I love you."

They were wrapped in each other's arms. "Erich, *please,*" Jenny begged, "let this be the last year you react like this. Twenty-five years. *Twenty-five years.* Caroline would be fifty-seven years old. You still see her as a young woman whose death was a tragedy. It was, but it's over. Let's get on with life. It could be good for us. Let me share your life, really share it. Bring your friends in. Take me to see your studio. Get me a small car so I can go shopping or to an art gallery or take the kids to a movie when you're painting."

"You want to be able to meet Kevin, don't you?"

"Oh, my God." Jenny pulled away. "Let me go to bed, Erich. I really don't feel well."

He did not follow her up the stairs. She looked in on the girls. They were fast asleep. Tina stirred when she kissed her.

She went into the master bedroom. The faint scent of pine that always lingered in the room seemed heavier tonight. Was it because she felt queasy? Her eyes fell on the crystal bowl. Tomorrow she'd move that bowl to a guest bedroom. Oh, Erich, stay tonight, she pleaded silently. Don't go away feeling like this. Suppose Kevin started pestering them with calls? Suppose he stopped the adoption? Suppose he had regular visitation rights? It would be unbearable for Erich. It would destroy their marriage.

She got into bed and determinedly opened her book. But it was impossible to concentrate. Her eyes were heavy and her body ached in unaccustomed places. Joe had warned her the riding would cause that. "You'll hear from muscles you didn't know you had," he'd grinned.

Finally she turned off the light. A little later she heard footsteps in the hall. Erich? She pulled herself up on one elbow but the footsteps continued up the stairs to the attic. What was he doing there? A few minutes later she heard him coming down. He must be dragging something. There was a thudding sound every few steps. What was he doing?

She was about to get up and investigate when she heard sounds from downstairs, the sounds of furniture being moved.

Of course, she thought.

Erich had gone upstairs for the carton of curtains. Now he was rearranging the furniture, putting it back in its original places.

In the morning when Jenny went downstairs, the curtains were rehung; every table and chair and piece of bric-a-brac was in place and her plants were missing. Later she found them in the trash container behind the barn.

17

Slowly Jenny walked through the downstairs rooms a second time. Erich had not failed to return a single vase or lamp or footstool to its original exact spot. He'd even found the ornately ugly owl sculpture that she'd poked away in an unused cabinet over the stove.

She had known what to expect but even so the absolute rejection of her wishes and taste shocked her. Finally she made coffee and went back to bed. Shivering, she pulled the covers around her and leaned back on the pillows propped against the massive headboard. It would be another cold and gloomy day. The sky was gray and misty; a sharp wind rattled the windowpanes.

The eighth of March, Erich's thirty-fifth birthday, Caroline's twenty-fifth anniversary. That last morning of her life had Caroline awakened in this bed, heartsick that she was leaving her only child? Or had she awakened counting the hours until she could leave this house?

Jenny rubbed her forehead. It ached dully. Once again her sleep had been restless. She'd been dreaming of Erich. Always he had that same expression on his face, an expression she could never quite understand. Once this anniversary was over and he came back to the house she'd talk to him quietly. She would ask him to go with her for counseling. If he refused she'd have to consider taking the children to New York.

Where?

Maybe her job would be available again. Maybe Kevin would lend her a few hundred dollars for airfare. *Lend.* He owed her hundreds. Fran would let her and the girls bunk in her place for a short time. It was a terrible inconvenience to ask of anyone but Fran was a good scout.

I don't have a cent, Jenny thought, but it isn't that. I don't want to leave Erich. I love him. I want to spend the rest of my life with him.

She was still so chilled. A hot shower might help. And she'd wear that warm argyll sweater. It was in the closet.

Jenny glanced at the closet and understood what had been subconsciously bothering her.

When she got up she'd taken her robe from the closet. But last night she had left the robe thrown over the vanity bench. The bench had been pulled back from the dressing table. Now it was precision-straight.

No wonder she dreamed of Erich's face. She must have subconsciously realized he was in the room. Why hadn't he stayed? She shivered. Her skin felt prickly. But it wasn't the cold. She was afraid. Afraid of Erich, of her own husband? Of course not, she told herself. I am afraid of his rejection. He came to me and then left me. Had Erich gone back to the cabin during the night or had he slept in the house?

Quietly she put on her robe and slippers and went into the hall. The door of Erich's boyhood room was closed. She listened at the door. There was no sound. Slowly she turned the handle and opened the door.

Erich was curled up in bed, the gaily patterned patchwork quilt wrapped around him. Only his ear and hairline showed. His face was buried in folds of soft material. Silently Jenny entered the room and became aware of a familiar faint scent. She bent over Erich. In his sleep he was nuzzling the aqua nightgown to his face.

She and the children had almost finished breakfast when Erich came downstairs. He refused even coffee. He was already wearing one of his heavy parkas and was carrying what was obviously an expensive hunting rifle, even to Jenny's inexperienced eye. Jenny eyed it nervously.

"I don't know if I'll be back tonight," he told her. "I don't know what I'll do. I'll just be around the farm today."

"All right."

"Don't go changing any of the furniture again, Jenny. I didn't like it your way."

"I gathered that," Jenny said evenly.

"It's my birthday, Jen." His tone sounded high-pitched, *young,* like the voice of a boy. "Aren't you going to wish me a happy birthday?"

"I'd rather wait until Friday night. Mark and Emily are coming to dinner. We'll celebrate it with them. Wouldn't you prefer that?"

"Maybe." He came over to her. The cold steel of the rifle brushed her arm. "Do you love me, Jenny?"

"Yes."

"And you'll never leave me?"

"I'd never want to leave you."

"That's what Caroline said, those very words." His eyes became reflective.

The children had been silent. "Daddy, can I go with you?" Beth begged.

"Not now. Tell me your name."

"Beth Crew-grr."

"Tina, what's your name?"

"Tina Crew-grr."

"Very good. I'll get both of you presents." He kissed them and came back to Jenny. Propping the rifle against the stove, he took her hands and ran them through his hair. "Do it like that," he whispered. "Please, Jen."

His eyes were on her intently now. They looked as they had in her dream. With a wrench of tenderness she obeyed. He looked so vulnerable, and last night he had not been able to come to her for comfort.

"That's good," he smiled. "That feels so good. Thank you."

He picked up the rifle and walked to the door. "Good-bye, girls."

He smiled at Jenny, then hesitated. "Sweetheart, I have an idea. Let's go out together for dinner tonight, just the two of us. I'll ask Rooney and Clyde to stay with the children for a few hours."

"Oh, Erich, I'd love that!" If he began to share this date with her . . . it's a breakthrough, she thought, a good omen.

"I'll phone and make reservations for eight o'clock at the Groveland Inn. I've been promising to take you there, darling. It's the best food around."

The Groveland Inn where she had met Kevin. Jenny felt her face pale.

When she and the girls got to the stable, Joe was waiting for them. His usually sunny smile was missing; his young face was set in unfamiliar lines of worry.

"Uncle Josh came over this morning. He was pretty drunk and Maw told him to get lost. He left the door open and Randy got out. I just hope nothing happens to him. He's not used to cars."

"Go look for him," Jenny said.

"Mr. Krueger won't like . . ."

"It will be all right, Joe. I'll see it is. The girls would be heartsick if anything happened to Randy."

She watched him hurry down the dirt road, then said, "Come on, girls. Let's take our walk now. You can visit the ponies later."

They ran ahead of her across the fields. Their rubber boots made soft squishing sounds. The ground was thawing. Maybe it would be an early spring after all. She tried to imagine these fields fleshed out with alfalfa and grass, those sparse empty trees weighted with leaves.

Even the wind had lost something of its biting edge. In the south pastures she could see that the cattle had their heads down and were sniffing at the ground as though anticipating the shoots of grass that would soon be coming.

I'd like to start a garden, Jenny thought. I don't know a thing about it but I could learn. Maybe it was because she needed exercise that she was feeling physically rotten. It wasn't just nerves; once again the clammy, queasy feeling was back. She stopped abruptly. Was it possible? Dear God, was it possible?

Of course it was.

She'd felt this way when she was carrying Beth.

She was pregnant.

That explained why the nightgown felt too tight in the bodice; it explained the light-headedness, the queasiness; it even explained the periods of depression.

What a marvelous gift to tell Erich tonight that she believed she was expecting a child! He wanted a son to inherit this farm. Surely the night staff at the restaurant was different from the lunchtime help? It would be all right. *Erich's son.*

"Randy," Tina called. "Look, Mommy, there's Randy."

"Oh, good," Jenny said. "Joe was so worried." She called to him. "Randy come here."

The puppy must have cut through the orchard. He stopped, turned and looked at her. Squealing, Beth and Tina began running toward him. With a bark of delight he turned tail and began to run toward the south fields. "Randy, stop," Jenny shouted. Now barking noisily, the puppy loped ahead. Don't let Erich hear him, she prayed. Don't let him run toward the cow pastures. Erich would be furious if he upset the cows. Nearly a dozen of them were coming to term with calves.

But he wasn't heading toward the pastures. Instead he veered and started running along the east line of the property.

The cemetery. He was heading straight for it. Jenny remembered how Joe joked about Randy digging around their house. "Swear he's trying to get to China, Jenny. You should just see him. Every spot that shows a bit of thawing, he's into."

If the dog ever started digging in the graves . . .

Jenny passed the girls, running as fast as she could on the mushy ground. "Randy," she called again. "Randy, *come here.*"

Suppose Erich heard her? Puffing heavily she ran around the line of Norwegian pines that screened the graveyard and into the clearing. The gate was open and the puppy was leaping among the tombstones. In its isolated corner Caroline's grave was covered with a blanket of fresh roses. Randy romped over it, crushing the flowers.

Jenny saw the glint of metal coming from the

woods. Instantly she realized what it was. "No, no," she screamed, "don't shoot! Erich, don't shoot him!"

Erich stepped from the shelter of the trees. With slow-motion precision he raised it to his shoulder. "Don't, please!" she screamed.

The sharp crack of the rifle sent sparrows squawking from the trees. With a howl of pain the puppy crumbled to the ground, his small body sinking into the roses. As Jenny watched in disbelieving horror, Erich worked the bolt with a well-oiled click, and shot the whimpering animal again. As the echo of the blast died away, the whimpering ceased.

18

Later Jenny remembered the hours after the shooting as a nightmare, blurred and difficult to piece together. She remembered her own frantic rush to head off the girls before they saw what had happened to Randy, yanking their hands. "We have to go home now."

"But we want to play with Randy."

She thrust them in the house. "Wait here. Don't come out again."

A shirt-sleeved, grave Erich was carrying Randy's still form; the parka he had wrapped the animal in was soaked with blood. Joe tried to blink back tears.

"Joe, I thought it was one of those damn strays. You know half of them are rabid. If I'd only realized . . ."

"You shouldn't have put him on your good coat, Mr. Krueger."

"Erich, how can you be so cruel? You shot him twice. You shot him after I called to you."

"I had to, darling," he insisted. "The first bullet shattered his spine. Do you think I could have left him

146

like that? Jenny, I was frantic when I thought the girls were chasing a stray. A child nearly died last year after being bitten by one of them."

Clyde, looking uncomfortable, shifted from one foot to the other. "You just can't go around petting animals on a farm, Miz Krueger."

"I'm sorry to give you so much trouble, Mr. Krueger," Joe said apologetically.

Her own anger dissipated into confusion. Erich smoothed her hair. "Joe, I'll replace him with a good hunter."

"You don't need to do that, Mr. Krueger." But there was hope in his voice.

Joe took Randy to bury him on his own property. Taking her back to the house, Erich insisted she lie on the couch, bringing her a steaming cup of tea. "I forget my darling is still a city girl." And then he left her.

Finally she got up and got the girls' lunch. While they napped she rested, forcing herself to read, willing her mind to stop squirming about in hopeless worry.

"It will be a fast dinner for you two tonight," she told Beth and Tina. "Daddy and I are going out."

"Me too," Tina volunteered.

"No, not you too," Jenny said, hugging her. "For once Daddy and I have a date." But no wonder the girls expected to be included. The few places she and Erich had gone to in this last month, he'd always insisted on bringing them along. How many stepfathers would be so considerate?

She took elaborate care with her own preparations. Soaking in a steaming tub took some of the soreness from her body. Hesitating only a minute, she filled the tub with the pine-scented bath crystals that she'd so far ignored in the bathroom cabinet.

She washed her hair and pulled it back in a Psyche

knot. When she'd been in the restaurant with Kevin her hair had been loose on her shoulders.

She studied the contents of her closet, choosing a long-sleeved, hunter-green wraparound silk that accentuated her narrow waist and the green in her eyes.

Erich came into the room just as she was fastening her locket. "Jenny, you dressed especially for me. I love you in green."

She cupped his face in her hands. "I always dress for you. I always will."

He was carrying a canvas. "Miraculous as it might seem, I managed to finish it this afternoon."

It was a spring scene, a new calf half-hidden in a hollow, the mother watchfully beside it, eyeing the other cattle, seeming to warn them to stay away. The sunlight filtered through pine trees; the sun was a five-pointed star. The painting had the aura of a Nativity scene.

Jenny studied it and felt all her senses quickening to its profound beauty. "It's magnificent," she said quietly. "There's so much tenderness there."

"Today you told me I was cruel."

"Today I was terribly stupid and terribly wrong. Will this be for the next exhibit?"

"No, darling, this is my gift to you."

She pulled the collar of her coat around her face as they went into the restaurant. The other time she'd been so anxious to escape quickly that she'd hardly noticed the details of the place. Now she realized that with its bright red carpeting, pine furniture, mellow lighting, colonial curtains and blazing fire, the inn was immensely appealing. Her eyes slid to the booth where she'd sat with Kevin.

"Right this way." The hostess led them in that direction. Jenny held her breath but mercifully the hostess sailed past it and led them to a window table.

There was a bottle of champagne already in the cooler beside the table.

When their glasses had been filled Jenny held hers up to Erich. "Happy birthday, darling."

"Thank you."

Quietly they sipped.

Erich was wearing a dark gray tweed jacket, a narrow black tie, charcoal gray trousers. His thick charcoal eyebrows and lashes intensified the blue of his eyes. His bronze-gold hair was highlighted by the flickering candle on the table. He reached for her hand.

"I enjoy taking you to places for the first time, darling."

Her mouth went dry. "I enjoy being everywhere . . . anywhere with you."

"I think that's why I left that note. You're right, sweetheart. I wasn't only teasing. I *was* jealous watching Joe teach you to ride. All I could think was that I wanted to share the first minute you were on Fire Maid. I suppose it's as though I'd bought you a piece of jewelry and you'd worn it for someone else."

"Erich," Jenny protested. "I just thought it would be nice for you not to be bothered with the ABCs of the learning process."

"It's not unlike the house, is it, Jenny? You came in, and in four weeks you try to transform a historical treasure into a New York studio complete with bare windows and spider plants. Darling, may I suggest a birthday present for me? Take a little time to find out who I am . . . who we are. You accused me of cruelty when I shot an animal I thought might attack our children. May I suggest that you in a different way shoot from the hip utterly without justification? And, Jenny, I have to say this, you have the distinction of being the first Krueger woman in four generations to create a scene in front of a hired hand. Caroline would have fainted dead away before she would publicly criticize my father."

"I'm not Caroline," Jenny said quietly.

"Darling, just understand that I'm not cruel to animals. I'm not unreasonably rigid. That first night in your apartment I could see you didn't understand why I was astonished that you gave MacPartland money; the same thing on our wedding day. But it's come back to haunt us, hasn't it?"

If you only knew, Jenny thought.

The maître d' was heading toward them with menus, a professional smile plastered on his face. "And now, my sweet," Erich said, "let's consider that we've cleared the air a bit. Let's have a wonderful dinner together and please know that I'd rather be here with you in this place at this moment than anywhere else with anyone else in the world."

When they arrived home she deliberately put on the aqua gown. She had not told Erich at dinner about her possible pregnancy. She'd been too shaken by the truth of his observations. When they were in bed, his arms around her, she would tell him.

But he did not stay with her. "I need to be completely alone. I'll be back by Thursday but not before then."

She did not dare to protest. "Now don't get into a creative haze and forget that Mark and Emily are coming to dinner on Friday."

He looked down at her as she lay in bed. "I won't forget." Without kissing her, he left. Once again she was alone in the cavernous bedroom to fall into the uneasy, dream-filled sleep that was becoming a way of life.

19

In spite of everything, planning the dinner party was a pleasant diversion. She wanted to shop herself but would not make driving the car an issue. Instead she compiled a long list for Elsa. "Coquilles St. Jacques," she told Erich when he came to the house on Friday morning. "Mine is really good. And you say Mark likes a rib roast?" She chatted on, determined to bridge the perceptible estrangement. He'll get over it, she thought, especially when he knows about the baby.

Kevin had not called again. Maybe he had met a girl in the cast and had become involved. If so, they wouldn't hear from him for a while. If necessary, as soon as the adoption became final they could take legal steps to make him stay away. Or if he did try to block the adoption, Erich might as a last resort buy him off. Silently, she prayed: Please let the children have a home, a real family. Let it be good again between Erich and me.

The night of the dinner she set out the Limoges

china, delicately beautiful with its gold-and-blue border. Mark and Emily were due at eight. Jenny found herself eagerly looking forward to meeting Emily. All her life she'd had girlfriends. She'd lost touch with most of them because of lack of time to keep up contacts after Beth and Tina came along. Maybe Emily and she would hit it off.

She said as much to Erich. "I doubt it," he told her. "There was a time when the Hanovers looked very fondly at the prospect of having me as a son-in-law. Roger Hanover is the president of the bank in Granite Place and has a good idea of my net worth."

"Did you ever go out with Emily?"

"A little. But I wasn't interested and didn't want to get into a situation that would prove uncomfortable. I was waiting for the perfect woman, you see."

She tried to make her voice teasing. "Well, you found her, dear."

He kissed her. "I certainly hope so."

She flinched. He's joking, she told herself fiercely.

After she got Beth and Tina into bed, Jenny changed into a white silk blouse with lace cuffs and a multicolored, ankle-length skirt. She studied her reflection in the mirror and realized she was deathly pale. Adding a touch of rouge helped.

Erich had set up the tea table in the parlor as a bar. When she came into the room he studied her carefully. "I like that costume, Jen."

"That's good," she smiled. "You certainly paid enough for it."

"I thought you didn't like it. You've never worn it before."

"It seemed kind of dressed up for just sitting around."

He came over to her. "Is that a spot on your sleeve?"

"That? Oh, it's just a speck of dust. It must have happened in the store."

"Then you haven't worn this outfit before?"

Why did he ask that? Was he simply too sensitive not to know she was hiding something from him?

"First time, girl scout's honor."

The door chimes were a welcome interruption. Her mouth had begun to go dry. It's getting so that no matter what Erich says, I'm afraid of giving myself away, she thought.

Mark was wearing a pepper-and-salt jacket that suited him well. It brought out the gray in his hair, accentuated his broad shoulders, the lean strength of his tall frame. The woman with him was about thirty, small-boned, with wide inquisitive eyes and dark blond hair that skimmed the collar of her well-cut brown velvet suit. Jenny decided that Emily had the air of someone who never had experienced an instant of self-doubt. She made no secret of looking Jenny over from head to toe. "You do realize I have to report to everyone in town what you're like; the curiosity is overwhelming. My mother gave me a list of twenty questions I'm to discreetly toss in. You haven't exactly made yourself available to the community."

Before Jenny could answer, she felt Erich's arm slip around her waist. "If we'd taken a two-month honeymoon cruise nobody would have thought a thing of it. But as Jenny says, because we chose to honeymoon in our own home, Granite Place is outraged not to be camped in our living room."

I never said that! Jenny thought helplessly as she watched Emily's eyes narrow.

Over cocktails, Mark waited until Erich and Emily were deep in conversation before he commented, "You look pale, Jenny. Are you all right?"

"Fine!" She tried to sound as though she meant it.

"Joe told me about his dog. I understand you were pretty upset."

"I guess I have to learn to understand that things are different here. In New York we cliff dwellers weep collectively over the picture of a stray about to be destroyed. Then somebody shows up to adopt him and we all cheer."

Emily was looking around the room. "You haven't changed anything, have you?" she asked. "I don't know whether Erich has mentioned it but I am an interior designer and if I were you, I'd get rid of those curtains. Sure they're beautiful but the windows are so overdressed and you lose that glorious view."

Jenny waited for Erich to defend her. "Apparently, Jen doesn't agree with you," he said smoothly. His tone and smile were indulgent.

Erich, that's unfair, Jenny thought furiously. Should she contradict him? *The first Krueger woman in four generations to create a scene in front of a hired hand.* How about a scene in front of friends? What was Emily saying?

". . . and I happen to be never at peace if I'm not switching things around but maybe that isn't your interest. I understand you're an artist too."

The moment had passed. It was too late to correct the impression Erich had left. "I'm not an artist," Jenny said. "My degree is in fine arts. I worked in a gallery in New York. That's where I met Erich."

"So I've heard. Your whirlwind romance has created quite a stir in these parts. How does our rustic life compare with the Big Apple?"

Jenny chose her words carefully. She had to undo the impression that she felt Erich had given that she was scornful of the local people. "I miss my friends, of course. I miss bumping into people who know me and comment on how big the children are getting. I like people and I make friends easily. But once," she glanced at Erich, "once our honeymoon is officially over, I hope to be active in the community."

"Report that to your mother, Emily," Mark suggested.

Jenny thought, Bless you for underscoring. Mark knew what she was trying to do.

Emily laughed, a brittle, mirthless sound. "From what I hear you've got at least one friend to keep you amused."

She had to be referring to the meeting with Kevin. The woman from church had been gossiping. She felt Erich's questioning look and did not meet his eyes.

Jenny murmured something about seeing to the dinner and went into the kitchen. Her hands were shaking so she could hardly lift the roasting pan from the oven. Suppose Emily followed through on her insinuations? Emily believed she was a widow; now her telling the truth would in effect be branding Erich as a liar. What about Mark? The question had not come up but undoubtedly he too thought she had been a widow.

Somehow she managed to get the food onto serving dishes, to light the candles and call them to the table. At least I'm a good cook, she reflected. Emily can tell her mother that.

Erich carved and served the rib roast. "One of our own steers," he said proudly. "Are you sure that doesn't repel you, Jenny?"

He was teasing her. She mustn't overreact. The others didn't seem to notice. "Think, Jenny," he continued in the same bantering tone, "the yearling you pointed out to me in the field last month, the one you said looked so wistful. You're eating him now."

Her throat closed. She was afraid she would gag. Please, God, please don't let me get sick.

Emily laughed. "Erich, you are so mean. Remember you used to bait Arden like that and have her in tears?"

"Arden?" Jenny asked. She reached for her water glass. The knot in her throat started to dissolve.

"Yes. What a nice kid she was. Talk about the all-American girl. Crazy about animals. At sixteen she wouldn't touch meat or poultry. Said it was barbaric and that she was going to be a vet when she grew up. But I guess she changed her mind. I was in college when she ran away."

"Rooney's never given up hope that she'll come back," Mark commented. "It's incredible, the mother instinct. You see it from the first moment of birth. The dumbest animal knows its own calf and will protect it to the death."

"You're not eating your meat, darling," Erich commented.

A flash of anger made it possible for her to square her shoulders and look across the table directly into his eyes. "And you're not eating your vegetables, darling," she told him.

He winked at her. He *was* just teasing. "Touché," he smiled.

The peal of the door chimes startled all of them. Erich frowned. "Now, who could that . . ." His voice trailed off as he stared at Jenny. She knew what he was thinking. Don't let it be Kevin, she prayed, and realized as she pushed back her chair that all evening she'd been sending frantic prayers for divine intervention.

A heavily built man of about sixty, with massive shoulders, a bulging leather jacket and narrow, heavy-lidded eyes, was there. His car was parked directly in front of the house, an official car with a red dome top.

"Mrs. Krueger?"

"Yes." Relief made her weak. No matter what this man wanted, at least Kevin hadn't come.

"I'm Wendell Gunderson, sheriff of Granite County. May I come in?"

"Of course. I'll get my husband."

Erich was hurrying down the hall, into the foyer. Jenny noticed the instant respect that came into the sheriff's face. "Sorry to bother you, Erich. Just have to ask your wife a few questions."

"Ask me a few questions?" But even as she spoke, Jenny knew that this visit had to do with Kevin.

"Yes, ma'am." From the dining room they could hear the sound of Mark's voice. "Could we speak quietly for a few minutes?"

"Why don't you come and join us for coffee?" Erich suggested.

"Perhaps your wife would rather answer my questions privately, Erich."

Jenny felt clammy perspiration on her forehead. She realized her palms were damp. The queasiness was so strong, she had to clamp her lips together. "There's certainly no reason we can't talk at the table," she murmured helplessly.

She led the way into the dining room, listened as Emily greeted the sheriff with quickly concealed surprise, watched as Mark leaned back in his chair, an attitude she had begun to realize meant he was diagnosing a situation. As Erich offered the sheriff a drink which was refused "because of being on official business," she set out the coffee cups.

"Mrs. Krueger, do you know a Kevin MacPartland?"

"Yes." She knew her voice was trembling. "Has Kevin been in an accident?"

"When and where did you last see him?"

She put her hands in her pockets, clenched them

into fists. Of course it had had to come out. But why this way? Oh, Erich, I'm so sorry, she thought. She could not look at Erich. "On February twenty-fourth at the shopping center in Raleigh."

"Kevin MacPartland is the father of your children?"

"He is my former husband and the father of my children." She heard Emily gasp.

"When did you last speak with him?"

"He phoned on the evening of March seventh about nine o'clock. Please tell me. Has anything happened to him?"

The sheriff's eyes narrowed into slits. "On Monday afternoon, March ninth, Kevin MacPartland received a telephone call during a rehearsal at the Guthrie Theater. He said his former wife had to see him about the children. He borrowed a car from one of the other actors and left half an hour later, about four-thirty P.M., promising to return in the morning. That was four days ago and he hasn't been heard from since. The car he borrowed was only six weeks old and the actor who lent it had just met MacPartland so you can understand that he's pretty concerned. Are you saying that you did not ask him to meet you?"

"No, I did not."

"May I ask why you've been in touch with your former husband? We understood around here that you were a widow."

"Kevin wanted to see the girls," Jenny said. "He was talking about stopping the adoption." It surprised her how lifeless her voice sounded. She could see Kevin as though he were in the room: the expensive ski sweater, the long scarf draped over his left shoulder, the dark red hair so carefully barbered, the poses and posturing. Had he deliberately staged a disappearance to embarrass her? She had warned him that

Erich was upset. Did Kevin hope to destroy their marriage before it had a chance?

"And what did you tell him?"

"When I saw him, and when he called, I told him to leave us alone." Her voice was getting higher.

"Erich, were you aware of this meeting, of the phone call on March seventh?"

"I was aware of the phone call on March seventh. I was here when it came. I was not aware of the meeting. But I can understand it. Jenny knew my feelings about Kevin MacPartland."

"You were home with your wife on the evening of March ninth?"

"No, as a matter of fact, I stayed in the cabin that night. I was just completing a new canvas."

"Did your wife know you were planning to be away?"

There was a long silence. Jenny broke it. "Of course I knew."

"What did you do that evening, Mrs. Krueger?"

"I was very tired and went to bed shortly after I had settled my little girls in their room."

"Did you speak to anyone on the phone?"

"No one. I went to sleep almost immediately."

"I see. And you are very sure you did not invite your former husband to visit you during Erich's absence?"

"No, I did not . . . I would never ask him to come here." It was as though she could read their minds. Of course they didn't believe her.

Her untouched plate was on the serving buffet. Congealed fat was forming a narrow rim around the beef. The beef had a crimson center. She thought of Randy's body turning crimson with blood as he collapsed among the roses; she thought of Kevin's dark red hair.

Now the plate was going around and around. She had to get fresh air. She was spinning too. Pushing back her chair, she tried to struggle to her feet. Her last conscious recollection was Erich's expression—was it concern or annoyance?—as her chair slammed against the buffet behind her.

When she woke up she was lying on the couch in the parlor. Someone was holding a cold cloth on her head. It felt so good. Her head hurt so much. There was something she didn't want to think about.

Kevin.

She opened her eyes. "I'm all right. I'm so sorry."

Mark was bending over her. There was so much concern in his face. It was oddly comforting. "Take it easy," he said.

"Can I get something for you, Jenny?" There was an undercurrent of excitement in Emily's voice. She's enjoying this, Jenny thought. She's the kind of person who wants to be in on everything.

"Darling!" Erich's tone was solicitous. He came over and took both her hands.

"Not too close," Mark warned. "Give her air."

Her head started to clear. Slowly she sat up, the taffeta skirt rustling as she moved. She felt Mark slip pillows behind her head and back.

"Sheriff, I can answer any questions you have. I'm sorry. I don't know what came over me. I've not felt quite well these past few days."

His eyes seemed wider and shinier now, as though they'd locked into an intense focus on her. "Mrs. Krueger, I'll make this brief. You did not phone your former husband on the ninth of March to request a meeting, nor did he arrive here that night?"

"That's correct."

"Why would he have told his colleagues that you

had called him? What purpose would he have in lying?"

"The only thought I have is that sometimes Kevin used to say he was visiting me and the children when he wanted to get out of other plans. If he was in the process of dropping one girlfriend for another, he'd often use us as an excuse."

"Then may I ask why you're so upset at his disappearance if you think he might be off with some woman?"

Her lips were so stiff it was hard to form words. She spoke slowly, like a teacher enunciating for a first-year language class. "You must understand there is something terribly wrong. Kevin *had* been accepted by the Guthrie Theater for the repertory company. That is true, isn't it?"

"Yes, it is."

"You must look for him," she said. "He would never jeopardize that opportunity. Kevin's acting is the most important thing in his life."

They all left a few minutes later. She insisted on walking with them to the front door. Jenny could imagine the conversation that would take place when Emily reported back to her mother: *"She's* not a widow . . . that was her ex-husband she was kissing in the restaurant . . . and now he's missing . . . the sheriff obviously thinks she's lying . . . poor Erich . . ."

"I'll treat this as a missing person. . . . Get out some flyers. . . . We'll be back to you, Mrs. Krueger."

"Thank you, Sheriff."

He was gone. Mark pulled on his coat. "Jenny, you ought to go right to bed. You still look mighty rocky."

"Thanks for coming you two," Erich said. "Sorry our evening ended so badly." His arm was around Jenny. He kissed her cheek. "Shows what happens when you marry a woman with a past, doesn't it?"

His tone was amused. Emily laughed. Mark's face showed no emotion. When the door closed behind him, Jenny wordlessly started up the staircase. All she wanted to do was to go to bed.

Erich's astonished voice stopped her. "Jenny, surely you're not planning to leave the house in this condition overnight?"

20

Rooney let herself in as Jenny was sipping a second cup of tea after breakfast. Jenny spun around at the faint click of the door. "Oh!"

"Did I scare you?" Rooney sounded pleased. Her eyes were vague; her thin hair, scattered by the wind, blew around her birdlike face.

"Rooney, that door was locked. I thought you said you're not supposed to have a key."

"I must have found one."

"Where? Mine is missing."

"Did I find yours?"

Of course, Jenny thought. The coat I gave her. It was in the pocket. Thank God I didn't admit to Erich that I lost it. "May I have my key, please?" She held out her hand.

Rooney looked puzzled. "I didn't know there was a key in your coat. We gave you back your coat."

"I don't think so."

"Yes. Clyde made me. He put it back himself. I saw you wear it."

163

"It's not in the closet," Jenny said. What difference? she thought. She tried a new approach. "Let me see your key, Rooney, please."

Rooney pulled a heavy key ring out of her pocket. The large bunch of keys were all individually tagged: house, barn, office, grainery . . .

"Rooney, aren't these Clyde's keys?"

"I guess so."

"You must put them back. Clyde will be angry if you take his keys."

"He says I shouldn't take them."

So that was how Rooney got into the house. I'll have to tell Clyde to hide his keys, Jenny thought. Erich would have a fit if he knew she could get at them.

Jenny looked at Rooney with pity. In the three weeks since the sheriff had come, she hadn't visited Rooney and in fact had tried to avoid running into her. "Sit down and let me pour you a cup of tea," she urged. For the first time she noticed that Rooney had a package tucked under her arm. "What have you got there?"

"You said I could make the girls jumpers. You promised."

"Yes, I did. Let me see."

Hesitantly Rooney opened the brown paper and shook two violet-blue corduroy jumpers from tissue wrapping. The stitching was fine; the strawberry-shaped pockets were embroidered in red and green. Jenny could see that the sizes would be perfect.

"Rooney, these are lovely," she said sincerely. "You sew beautifully."

"I'm glad you like them. I made Arden a skirt with this material and had some left over. I was going to make her a jacket too but then she ran away. Don't you think this is a pretty shade of blue?"

"Yes, I do. It will be wonderful with their hair."

"I wanted you to see the material before I started,

but when I came that night you were on your way out and I didn't want to interfere."

On the way out at night? Not likely, Jenny thought, but let it go. She found herself glad for Rooney's company. These weeks had dragged so. Ceaselessly she thought about Kevin. What had happened to him? He was a fast driver. He'd been driving a strange car. The roads were icy that day. Could he have been in an accident, maybe not hurt himself but have wrecked the borrowed car? Would that have panicked him into leaving Minnesota? Always she got back to one irrefutable fact. Kevin would never walk away from the Guthrie Theater.

She felt so rotten. She should tell Erich she was pregnant. She should see a doctor.

But not yet. Not until something was resolved about Kevin. The news of the baby should be joyful. It shouldn't be told in this tense, hostile atmosphere.

The night of the dinner party Erich had insisted that every piece of china and crystal be handwashed, every pot scrubbed before they went upstairs.

As they got into bed, he'd commented, "I must say you look pretty upset, Jenny. I didn't realize that MacPartland meant that much to you. No, I'll correct myself. Maybe I've sensed it; maybe that's why I'm not even surprised that you had a clandestine meeting with him."

She'd tried to explain but to her own ears the justification seemed feeble and halting. Finally she'd been too tired, too upset, to discuss it any further. As she'd drifted off to sleep, he'd put his arm around her. "I'm your husband, Jenny," he said. "No matter what, I'll stand by you as long as you tell me the truth."

". . . Like I said, I didn't want to interfere with your visit," Rooney was saying.

"What . . . Oh, I'm sorry." Jenny realized she had not been listening to Rooney. She looked across the table. Rooney's eyes were clearer. How much of her problem was her absolute obsession with Arden? How much was the loneliness of no outside contacts? "Rooney, I've always wanted to learn to sew. Do you think you could teach me?"

Rooney brightened. "Oh, I'd love that. I can teach you to sew and knit and crochet if you want."

She left a few minutes later. "I'll get everything together and come back tomorrow afternoon," she promised. "It will be like old times. Caroline didn't know how to do none of those things neither. I was the one who taught her. Maybe you can make a nice quilt before something happens to you."

"Hal-lo, Jenny," Joe called cheerfully.

Oh, God, Jenny thought. Erich was just a few steps behind her with the girls but had not turned the corner into the stable.

"How are you, Joe?" she asked nervously. Something in her voice made him look up quickly. He saw Erich and reddened. "Oh, good morning, Mr. Krueger. Didn't expect you, I guess."

"I'm sure you didn't." Erich's icy tone made Joe blush several shades deeper. "I want to see how my girls are doing with their lessons."

"Yes, sir. I'll tack up the ponies right away." He scurried into the tack room.

"Is he in the habit of addressing you as Jenny?" Erich asked quietly.

"It's my fault," Jenny said, then wondered how many times in the last weeks she'd used those words.

Joe came back with the tack. As the girls squealed impatiently, he put the saddles on. "We'll each lead one of the ponies," Erich told him.

"How about you, Mrs. Krueger?" Joe asked. "You up to riding today?"

"Not yet, Joe."

"Haven't you been riding?" Erich asked.

"No. My back has been hurting quite a bit."

"You didn't tell me that."

"It will be fine."

She still couldn't tell him about the baby. Nearly four weeks had passed since Sheriff Gunderson had come and there hadn't been a single word more.

Spring was about to break. The trees all had a red haze around them. Joe told her that that happened just before the budding started. There were shoots of green coming through the mud in the fields. The chickens were wandering out of the chicken house and exploring the territory around them. The boastful crowing of the roosters could be heard from behind the grainery and polebarn and stable. One of the hens had selected a corner of the stable for her own nest and was brooding her unhatched eggs.

"Since when have you had a backache, Jenny? Do you want to see a doctor?" Erich's tone was loving and concerned.

"No. Let's see if it doesn't just go away. I've had them before." She had had mild backaches during her other pregnancies.

Someone fell into step with them. It was Mark. She hadn't run into Mark since the night of the dinner.

"Hello, you two," Mark said. His manner was easy. There was nothing to indicate he was thinking of what had happened at the dinner party.

"Stay a minute and watch the way my girls sit their ponies," Erich invited.

In the past weeks Tina and Beth had made rapid progress on the ponies. Jenny smiled unconsciously at their delighted faces as they sat straight up, holding the reins with rapt concentration.

"They look good," Mark commented. "They'll grow to be fine riders."

"They love those animals."

Erich left them to lead one of the ponies.

"I've never seen Erich happier. He was showing their pictures to everyone at the Hanovers' the other night. Emily was sorry you couldn't make it."

"Couldn't make it?" Jenny repeated. "Couldn't make what?"

"The Hanovers' party. Erich said you weren't feeling up to par. Have you seen a doctor yet? I just overheard you mentioning your back. And that fainting spell that night, Jenny. Was that unusual? Do you have any history of weak spells?"

"No. I never faint. And I will see a doctor soon."

She felt rather than saw Mark studying her. Somehow she didn't mind. Whatever conclusion he had reached about Kevin's possible visit and her supposed widow status, he had not condemned her.

Should she tell him that she had no idea about Emily's party? What good would it do? Erich left us together here because he knew Mark would probably bring up the party, she thought. Erich wanted me to know about it. Why? Was it simply another way of trying to hurt her, to punish her, for the gossip around the Krueger name? How much did people in this community know? She was sure Emily had told her family and friends about the sheriff's visit.

If Erich believed people thought he had made a mistake and were pitying him, he'd be furious. She remembered his anger when Elsa suggested he had made the smudge on the wall.

Erich was a perfectionist.

As Mark turned to leave, Erich called, "See you tonight." Tonight? Jenny wondered. Another party? Business of some kind? Whatever it was, she wouldn't hear about it.

The girls ran to her when they dismounted. "Daddy is going to ride Baron with us soon," Beth said. "Don't you like to ride with us, Mommy?"

Joe led the ponies into the barn. "See you, Mrs. Krueger," he said. She was very sure he would not call her Jenny again.

"Come along, dear." Erich took her arm. "Didn't my little princesses do beautifully?"

My princesses. *My* girls. *My* daughters. Not *our*, only *my*. When had that begun? Jenny realized that the emotion she was experiencing was stark jealousy. Good Lord, she thought. Don't let me start getting upset about that. The one good thing in my life right now is that the children are so happy.

They were almost to the house when a car pulled into the driveway, a car with a dome light on the roof. Sheriff Gunderson.

Did he have news about Kevin? She forced herself not to hurry, not to let her face show anxiety. As the sheriff got out of the car, Erich linked his arm in hers. He was holding Tina by the other hand. Beth was running in front of them. The devoted husband standing by his wife in time of trouble, Jenny thought. That had to be the impression the sheriff was getting.

Wendell Gunderson's face was grim. There was a trifle more formality in his manner even when he greeted Erich. He wanted to speak with Jenny alone.

They went into the library. Jenny thought how in the first weeks this had been her favorite room. The meeting with Kevin had changed everything. The sheriff ignored the couch and chose the one straight chair.

"Mrs. Krueger, there has been absolutely no sign of your ex-husband. The Minneapolis police are treating his disappearance as possible foul play. There is no evidence he planned to stay away. There was two hundred dollars in cash in a desk drawer; he took only a small overnight bag with him when he left. Everyone he worked with at the Guthrie agreed that he wouldn't walk away from that opportunity. I realize that last time it would have been much easier if I insisted on speaking with you alone. Please tell the truth, because once this investigation is in full swing, I promise you the truth will come out. Did you phone Kevin MacPartland on the afternoon of Monday, March ninth?"

"I did not."

"Did you see him on the night of Monday, March ninth?"

"I did not."

"He left Minneapolis about five-thirty. Driving straight through, that would get him here about nine. We'll assume he might have stopped along the way to get something to eat. Where were you between nine-thirty and ten that Monday night?"

"I was in bed. I turned out the light before nine o'clock. I was very tired."

"You insist you did not see him?"

"I did not."

"The Guthrie operator confirmed that he received a call from a woman. Is there any woman who might have called him in your name? Any close friend?"

"I don't have any close friends here," Jenny said, "man or woman." She stood up. "Sheriff, no one wants more than I do to find Kevin MacPartland. He is the father of my children. There's never been even a hint of animosity between us. So will you please explain to me what you're driving at? Are you suggesting that I invited or enticed Kevin here knowing that my husband planned to be away? And if you believe that, are you insinuating I had something to do with his disappearance?"

"I'm not suggesting anything, Mrs. Krueger. I'm only asking you to tell us everything you know. If MacPartland was definitely on his way here and didn't show up, it gives us a starting point. If he was here and we knew what time he left, it gives us something else.

Can you see what I'm getting at? I can understand why that might be embarrassing for you but . . ."

"I don't think we have anything more to discuss," Jenny said. Turning abruptly, she left the library. Erich was in the kitchen with the girls. He'd made ham and cheese sandwiches. The three of them were eating companionably. Jenny saw there was no place set for her.

"Erich, I think the sheriff is ready to leave," she said. "You might want to see him out."

"Mommy." Beth looked anxious.

Oh, Mouse, Jenny thought, that antenna of yours. She tried to smile. "Say, you two looked terrific on the ponies today." Going to the refrigerator, she poured a glass of milk.

"Don't you know better, Mommy?" Beth asked.

"Know what better?" Jenny picked up Tina, sat at the table with the little girl on her lap.

"Daddy told Joe when we were on our ponies that even if you don't know better than to have Joe call you Mrs. Krueger, Joe should know better."

"Daddy said that?"

"Yes." Beth was positive. "You know what else he said?"

Jenny sipped her milk. "No, what?"

"He said that when Joe got home for lunch today, he'd find a brand-new puppy Daddy bought for him because Randy runned away. Can we see the puppy, Mommy?"

"Sure. Let's walk over there after your nap."

So Randy "runned away," she thought. That's the official version of what happened to that poor little puppy.

21

The new puppy was a golden retriever. Even to Jenny's unpracticed eye, the long nose, thin face and slender body indicated good breeding.

The thick old quilt on the kitchen floor was the same one Randy had curled up on. The bowl with water still had his name in the jaunty red letters Joe had painted on it.

Even Joe's mother seemed mollified by the gift. "Erich Krueger is a fair man," she conceded to Jenny. "Feel as though I was wrong accusing him of maybe doing away with Joe's dog last year. Seems as though if he got rid of that dog he'd a come out and said so."

Except that this time I saw him, Jenny thought, and then felt unfair to Erich.

Beth patted the sleek head. "You must be very careful because he's so little," she instructed Tina. "You must not hurt him."

"They sure are pretty little girls," Maude Ekers said. "They favor you except for the hair."

To Jenny there was something different about the

woman's attitude today. Her welcome had been restrained. She had hesitated before inviting them in. Jenny would not have accepted a cup of coffee from the ever-present percolator but was surprised when it wasn't offered.

"What's the puppy's name?" Beth asked.

"Randy," Maude said. "Joe's decided he's another Randy."

"Naturally," Jenny commented. "Somehow I knew Joe wouldn't just forget that other little dog so quickly. He's much too good-hearted."

They were sitting at the kitchen table. She smiled at the other woman.

But to her astonishment Maude's face showed worried hostility. *You leave my boy alone*, Mrs. Krueger," she burst out. "He's a simple farm boy and I already got enough worries with the way that brother of mine is bringing Joey to the bars with him at night. Joe moons about you too much as it is. Maybe it's not for me to say but you're married to the most important man in this community and you should realize your position."

Jenny pushed the chair back and stood up. "What do you mean?"

"I think you know what I mean. With a woman like you there's bound to be trouble. My brother's life was spoiled because of that accident in the dairy barn. You got to have heard that John Krueger felt my brother was careless with the work light 'cause he got so flustered around Caroline. Joe's all I got. He means the world to me. I don't want accidents or problems."

Now that she had started, the words tumbled from her mouth. Beth and Tina stopped playing with the puppy. Uncertainly they clasped hands. "And something else, it may not be my place but you're awful foolish to have your ex-husband sneaking around here when everyone knows Erich is in his cabin painting."

"What are you talking about?"

"I'm no gossip and this ain't passed my lips but one night last month that actor ex-husband of yours came here looking for directions. He's a talky one. Introduced himself. Boasted you invited him down. Said he'd just been hired by the Guthrie. I pointed the road to your place myself but let me tell you I wasn't happy about doing it."

"You must immediately phone Sheriff Gunderson and tell him what you know," Jenny said, keeping her voice as steady as she could. "Kevin never arrived at our house that night. The sheriff is inquiring for him. He's officially listed as a missing person."

"He never got to your house?" Maude's normally strong voice became louder.

"No, he did not. Please call Sheriff Gunderson immediately. And thank you for letting us visit the puppy."

Kevin had been in Maude's house!

He had specifically told Maude that she, Jenny, had called him.

Maude had pointed the way to the Krueger farmhouse, a three-minute drive away.

And Kevin had not arrived.

If Sheriff Gunderson had been insolent with his insinuations today, what would he be like now?"

"Mommy, you're hurting my hand," Beth protested.

"Oh, sorry, love. I didn't mean to squeeze it."

She had to get out of here. No, that was impossible. She couldn't leave until she knew what had happened to Kevin.

And beyond that. She was carrying in her womb the microcosm of a human being who was a fifth-generation Krueger, who belonged to this place, whose birthright was this land.

* * *

Afterward Jenny thought of that evening of April 7 as the final calm hours. Erich was not in the house when she and the girls got home.

I'm glad, she thought. At least she would not have to keep up some sort of pretense. The next time she saw him she would tell him what Maude had told her.

Maude had probably called the sheriff already. Would he come back here tonight? Somehow she didn't think so, but why would Kevin tell people she'd called him? What had happened to him?

"What do you want for dinner, ladies," she asked.

"Frankfurters," Beth said positively.

"Ice cream," was Tina's hopeful contribution.

"Sounds terrific," Jenny said. Somehow she'd felt the girls slipping away from her. That wouldn't happen tonight.

Recklessly she let the girls bring their plates to the couch. *The Wizard of Oz* was on. Companionably nibbling frankfurters and sipping Cokes they huddled together as they watched it.

By the time it was over Tina was asleep in Jenny's lap and Beth's head was drooping on her shoulder. She carried them both upstairs.

Just over three months had passed since that wintry evening when she'd been carrying them home from the day-care center and Erich had caught up with them. There was no use thinking about that. He probably would stay in the cabin again. Even so she didn't want to sleep in the master bedroom.

She undressed the children, buttoned them into pajamas, patted their faces and hands with a warm washcloth and tucked them into bed. Her back hurt. She should not carry them anymore. Too much weight, too much of a strain. It didn't take long to stack the dishwasher. Carefully she examined the couch for signs of crumbs.

She remembered the nights in the apartment when

if she was very tired she left the dishes stacked and rinsed in the sink and got into bed with a cup of tea and a good book. I didn't know when I was well off, she thought. And then she remembered the leaky ceiling, rushing the girls to the day-care center, the constant worry about money, the relentless loneliness.

When she was finished straightening up it was not quite nine o'clock. She went through the downstairs rooms, checking that no lights had been left on. In the dining room she stopped under Caroline's quilt. Caroline had wanted to paint and had been shamed and ridiculed away from her art. She'd "done something useful."

It had taken Caroline eleven years before she'd been driven away. Had she too experienced the sensation of being the outsider who did not belong?

Slowly climbing the stairs, Jenny realized how close she felt to the woman who had lived in this house. She wondered if Caroline had entered the master bedroom with the same sense of hopeless entrapment that she now felt.

It was midmorning before Sheriff Gunderson came back to the house. Again Jenny had had fitful dreams, dreams of walking in the forest and smelling the pine trees. Was she looking for the cabin?

When she woke up she became ill. How much of the early-morning nausea had to do with the physical aspect of pregnancy and how much was the result of the anxiety over Kevin's disappearance?

Elsa came in as usual at nine o'clock: dour, silent, vanishing upstairs with vacuum and window cleaners and polishing rags.

She was still reading to the girls when Wendell Gunderson came. She had not yet dressed but was wearing a warm wool robe over her nightgown. Would

Erich object to her talking to the sheriff in her robe? No, how could he? The robe zipped up to her neck.

She knew she was pale. She'd tied her hair at the nape of her neck. The sheriff came to the front door.

"Mrs. Krueger." She detected a pitch of excitement. "Mrs. Krueger," he repeated, his voice deepening. "Last night I received a call from Maude Ekers."

"I asked her to phone you," Jenny said.

"So she claims. I didn't talk to you right away because I decided to figure out where Kevin MacPartland might have driven if he didn't come here."

Was it possible the sheriff did believe her? His face, his voice, were so serious. No. He looked like a poker player about to play his winning card.

"I realized it could happen that a stranger might miss your gate if he turned off on the bend that leads to the riverbank."

The riverbank. Oh, dear God, Jenny thought. Could Kevin have made that turn and kept driving, maybe driving quickly, and then gone over the bank. That road was so dark.

"We investigated and I'm sorry to say that's what happened," the sheriff said. "We found a late-model white Buick in the water near the shoreline. It's crusted by ice and that thick brush keeps anyone walking on the bank from seeing it. We pulled it out."

"Kevin?" She knew what he would tell her. Kevin's face flashed before her mind.

"A man's body is in the car, Mrs. Krueger. It's badly decomposed but generally answers the description of the missing Kevin MacPartland, including the clothing he was wearing when last seen. The driver's license in his pocket is MacPartland's."

Oh, Kevin, Jenny mourned silently, oh, Kevin. She tried to speak, but could not.

"We will need you to give us positive identification as soon as possible."

No, she wanted to shriek, no. Kevin was so vain. He worried about a blemish. Badly decomposed! Oh, God.

"Mrs. Krueger, you may want to engage a lawyer."

"Why?"

"Because there'll be an inquest into MacPartland's death and some tough questions will be asked. You don't have to say anything more."

"I'll answer any questions you have now."

"All right. I'm going to ask you again. Did Kevin MacPartland come to this house that Monday night, March ninth?"

"No, I told you *no.*"

"Mrs. MacPartland, do you own a full-length maroon thermal winter coat?"

"Yes, I do. No, I mean I did. I gave it away. Why?"

"Do you remember where you purchased it?"

"Yes, in Macy's in New York."

"I'm afraid you have a lot of explaining to do, Mrs. Krueger. A woman's coat was found on the seat next to the body. A maroon thermal coat with the label of Macy's department store. We'll need you to look at it and see if it's the one you claim you gave away."

22

The inquest was held a week later. For Jenny the week was a blur of unfocused pain.

In the morgue, she stared down at the stretcher. Kevin's face was mutilated but still recognizable, with the long straight nose, the curve of the forehead, the thick, dark red hair. Memories of their wedding day in St. Monica's kept flashing back to her. "I, Jennifer, take thee Kevin . . . Till death do us part." Never had her life been more entwined with his than now. Oh, Kevin, why did you follow me here?

"Mrs. Krueger?" Sheriff Gunderson's voice urging the identification.

Her throat closed. She hadn't even been able to swallow tea this morning.

"Yes," she whispered, "that's my husband."

A low, harsh laugh behind her. "Erich, oh, Erich, I didn't mean . . ."

But he was gone, his footsteps decisively slapping the tiled floor. When she got to the car he was there, stony-faced, and did not speak to her on the way home.

During the inquest the same questions were asked a dozen different ways. "Mrs. Krueger, Kevin Mac-Partland told a number of people you had invited him to come to your home in your husband's absence."

"I did not."

"Mrs. Krueger what is the phone number of your home?"

She gave it.

"Do you know the telephone number of the Guthrie Theater?"

"I do not."

"Let me tell you or perhaps refresh your memory. It is 555-2824. Is it familiar to you?"

"No."

"Mrs. Krueger, I am holding a copy of the March telephone bill from Krueger Farm. A call to the Guthrie Theater appears on this bill dated March *ninth*. Do you still deny making that call?"

"Yes, I do."

"Is this your coat, Mrs. Krueger?"

"Yes, I gave it away."

"Do you have a key to the Krueger residence?"

"Yes, but I've mislaid it." The coat, she thought. Of course it was in the pocket of the coat. She told the prosecutor that.

He held up something, a key; the ring had her initials, J.K. The key Erich had given her.

"Is this your key?"

"It looks like it."

"Did you give it to anyone, Mrs. Krueger? Please tell us the truth."

"No, I did not."

"This key was found in Kevin MacPartland's hand."

"That's impossible."

On the stand Maude unhappily, doggedly, repeated the story she had told Jenny. "He said his ex-wife wanted to see him and I pointed the road. I'm very sure of the date. He came the night after my son's dog was killed."

Clyde Toomis on the stand was embarrassed, tongue-tied, but patiently honest. "I told my wife she had her own good everyday winter coat. I scolded her for accepting it. I put that maroon coat back in the closet in the hall off the kitchen of Krueger farmhouse myself, put it there the very day my wife wore it home."

"Did Mrs. Krueger know that?"

"Don't know how she coulda missed it. The closet ain't that big and I hung it right next to that ski jacket she wears all the time."

I didn't notice, Jenny thought, but knew it was possible she simply hadn't paid attention.

Erich testified. The questions were brief, respectful. "Mr. Krueger, were you at home the night of Monday, March ninth?"

"Did you make known your plans to paint in your cabin that night?"

"Were you aware your wife had been in contact with her former husband?"

Erich might have been talking about a stranger. He answered with detachment, weighing his words, unemotional.

Jenny sat in the first row watching him. Not for a second did his glance meet hers. Erich, who hated even talking on the phone, Erich, who was one of the most private people she had ever known, who had become estranged from her because he was upset about Kevin's phone call and her meeting with him.

The inquest was over. When he summed up, the coroner said that a severe bruise on the right temple of the deceased might have been incurred during the impact of the crash or might have been inflicted previous to it.

The official verdict was death by drowning.

But as Jenny left the courthouse she knew the verdict that the community had passed. At the least she was a woman who had been seeing her former husband clandestinely.

At the worst she had murdered him.

In the three weeks that followed the inquest, the dinners Erich ate with her fell into a pattern. He never spoke directly to her, only to the girls. He would say, "Ask Mommy to pass the rolls, Tinker Bell." His tone was always warm and affectionate. It would have taken sensitive ears to pick up the tension between them.

When she put the girls to bed, she never knew whether she would find him still in the house when she came downstairs. She wondered where he went. To the cabin? To the home of friends? She dared not ask. If he did sleep in the house, it was in the rear bedroom that his father had used for so many years.

There was no one she could talk to. Something told her that he would get over it. There were times she caught him looking at her with such tenderness in his face that she had to restrain herself from putting her arms around him, begging him to believe in her.

Quietly she mourned the waste of Kevin's life. He could have accomplished so much; he had been so talented. If only he had disciplined himself, stayed away from involvements with women, drunk less.

But how did her coat get in the car?

One night she came downstairs to find Erich sipping coffee at the kitchen table.

"Jenny," he said, "we have to talk."

Not sure whether the emotion she felt was relief or

anxiety, she sat down. After the girls were settled, she'd showered and put on her nightgown and the robe Nana had given her. She watched as Erich studied her.

"That red is perfect against your hair. Dark cloud on scarlet. Symbolic, isn't it? Like dark secrets in a scarlet woman. Is that why you wear it?"

So this was to be the "talk." "I put it on because I was cold," Jenny said.

"It's very becoming. Maybe you're expecting someone?"

Odd, she thought, in the midst of all this I can still feel sorry for him. What had been worse for him, she wondered suddenly, Caroline's death or the fact that Caroline had been planning to leave him?

"I'm not expecting anyone, Erich. If you think I am, why not stay with me every night and reassure yourself?" She knew she should be outraged and furious but there was no emotion left in her except pity for him. He looked so troubled, so vulnerable. Always when he was upset he seemed younger, almost boyish.

"Erich, I'm so sorry about all this. I know people are gossiping and how distressing this must be for you. I don't have any logical explanation for what happened."

"Your coat."

"I don't know how it got in that car."

"You expect me to believe that."

"I would believe you."

"Jenny, I want to believe you and I can't. But I do believe this. If you agreed to let MacPartland come here, maybe you did want to warn him to stay away from us. I can accept that. But I can't live with the lie. Admit you invited him down here and I'll put this behind us. I can see how it happened. You didn't want to bring him in the house so you had him drive to the dead end at the riverbank. You warned him and you had your key in your hand. Maybe he made a pass at you. Did you struggle? You slid out of your coat and got out of the car. Maybe when he went to reverse he went forward. *Jenny, it's understandable.* But say so. Just don't look at me with those wide, innocent eyes. Don't look thin and wan like some kind of wounded victim. Admit you're a liar and I promise I'll never mention this again. We love each other so much. It's still there, all that love."

At least he was being totally honest. She felt as though she were sitting on a mountain looking down into a valley, observing what was going on, a disinterested spectator.

"It would almost be easier to do what you wanted," she observed. "But it's funny; we're all the sum total of our lives. Nana despised liars. She was contemptuous of even the social life. 'Jenny,' she used to say, 'don't evade. If you don't want to go on a date with someone just say no thank you, not that you have a headache or have to do math homework. Truth serves everyone best.'"

"We're not talking about math homework," Erich said.

"I'm going to bed, Erich," she said. "Good night." There was no point in continuing like this.

Such a short time ago they'd gone upstairs arms around each other. To think she'd objected to wearing the aqua nightgown. It was so unimportant in retrospect.

Erich did not answer her even though she went up the stairs slowly, giving him the chance to respond.

She dropped off to sleep quickly, the exhaustion weighing her down, forcing her into weary dreams. She slept restlessly, always just under the conscious level, aware of herself moving around the bed. She was dreaming again; this time she was in the car, struggling with Kevin; he wanted the key. . . .

Then she was in the woods, walking in them, searching. She flung up her arm to push away the nearness of the trees and touched flesh.

Her fingers felt the outline of a forehead, the soft membrane of an eyelid. Long hair brushed her cheek.

Biting her lips over the scream that tried to escape her throat, she bolted up and fumbled for the night-table light. She snapped it on and looked around wildly. There was no one there. She was alone in bed, in the room.

She sank back on the pillows, her body trembling helplessly. Even her facial muscles were twitching.

I'm going crazy, she thought. I'm losing my mind. For the rest of the night, she did not turn off the light and the first rays of dawn were filtering through the drawn shades before she finally fell asleep.

23

Jenny awoke to bright sunlight and instantly remembered what had happened. A bad dream, she thought, a nightmare. Embarrassed, she snapped off the table lamp and got out of bed.

The weather was finally breaking. She stood at the window looking out at the woods. The trees were a mass of opening buds. From the chicken house she heard the strident crowing of the largest roosters. Opening the windows, she listened to the sounds of the farm, smiled as she heard the new calves bawling for their mothers.

Of course it had been a nightmare. Even so the vivid memory made her perspire, a cold, clammy sweat. It had seemed so real, the feeling of touching a face. Could she be hallucinating?

And the dream about being in the car with Kevin, struggling with him. Could she have phoned Kevin? She'd been so upset that day thinking about what Erich said at the birthday dinner, realizing that Kevin could destroy her marriage. Could she have forgotten that she called Kevin and asked to see him?

The concussion from the accident. The doctor had warned her to take any future headaches seriously.

She'd been having headaches.

She showered, tied her hair in a knot at the top of her head, pulled on jeans and a heavy wool sweater. The girls weren't awake yet. Maybe if she was very calm, she'd be able to eat some breakfast. She must have lost ten pounds in these three months. It was bound to be bad for the baby.

Just as she put the kettle on, she saw Rooney's head bob past the window. This time Rooney knocked.

Rooney's eyes were clear, her face composed. "I had to see you."

"Sit down, Rooney. Coffee or tea?"

"Jenny!" Today Rooney had none of the vagueness. "I've hurt you but I'll try to make amends."

"How could you hurt me?"

Rooney's eyes filled with tears. "I've been feeling so much better with you here. A young, pretty girl to talk to, teaching you to sew. It's made me so happy. And I didn't blame you a bit for meeting him. Krueger men aren't easy to live with. Caroline found that out. So I understand. And I never was going to talk about it, not ever."

"Talk about what? Rooney, there can't be anything to be so upset about."

"There is, oh, Jenny, there is. Last night I got one of my spells. You know I just keep talking but this time I told Clyde how I came to show you the blue corduroy that Monday night after Caroline's anniversary to see if you liked the color. It was late. Near ten o'clock. But being it was so near the anniversary I was restless. And I thought I'd just look and see if your light was on in the kitchen. And you were just getting in the white car.

I saw you get in. I saw you drive away with him down the road to the riverbank but I swear, Jenny, I never planned to tell. I couldn't hurt you."

Jenny put her arms around the trembling woman. "I know you wouldn't hurt me." I did go with Kevin, she thought. I did go. No, I don't believe that. I can't believe that.

"And Clyde said it was his duty to tell Erich and the sheriff," Rooney sobbed. "This morning I told Clyde I made it up, that I got all mixed up, but Clyde said he remembers he woke up that night and I'd just come in with the material under my arm and he was mad I'd gone out. He's going to talk to Erich and the sheriff. Jenny, I'm going to lie for you. I don't care. But I'm causing trouble for you."

"Rooney," Jenny said carefully, "try to understand. I think you are mistaken. I was in bed that night. I never asked Kevin to come here. You wouldn't be lying if you tell them you got confused. I promise you that."

Rooney sighed. "I'd like that coffee now. I love you, Jenny. Sometimes when you're here I can start to believe that Arden may never come back and that I'll get over it someday."

It was later in the morning that they came into the house together, the sheriff, Erich and Mark. Why Mark?

"You know why we're here, Mrs. Krueger."

She listened attentively. They were talking about someone else, someone she didn't know who had been seen getting into a car, driving away.

Erich didn't look angry anymore, only sorrowful. "Apparently Rooney is trying to retract her statement but we couldn't keep this information from Sheriff Gunderson." He came over to her now, put his hands on her face, smoothed her hair.

Jenny wondered why she felt as though she were being stripped in public. "My darling," Erich said, "these are your friends. Tell the truth."

She reached up, grasped his hands, pulling them from her face. Otherwise she would suffocate.

"I have told the truth as I know it," she said.

"You ever had spells of any kind, Mrs. Krueger?" The sheriff's voice was not unkind.

"I did have a concussion once." Briefly she told them about the accident. All the time she was aware of Mark Garrett's eyes studying her. He probably thinks I'm making this up, she thought.

"Mrs. Krueger, were you still in love with Kevin MacPartland?"

What a terrible question to ask in front of Erich, Jenny thought. How humiliating this is for him. If only she could go away. Take the girls. Leave him to his own life.

But she was carrying his child. Erich would love his son. It would be a boy. She was certain of that.

"Not in the way I presume you mean," she said.

"Isn't it true that you showed public affection for him to the point where the waitress and two patrons of the Groveland Inn were shocked."

For a moment Jenny thought she would laugh. "They shock easily. Kevin kissed me when I left. I didn't kiss him."

"Perhaps I should ask it this way, Mrs. Krueger. Weren't you pretty upset about your ex-husband showing up? Wasn't he a threat to your marriage?"

"What do you mean?"

"Initially you gave out to Mr. Krueger that you were a widow. Mr. Krueger's a wealthy man. He's adopting your kids. MacPartland coulda ruined your pretty setup."

Jenny looked at Erich. She was about to say that the adoption papers would show that Kevin had signed them, that Erich knew about Kevin before their marriage. But what point? This was hard enough on Erich without having his friends and neighbors know that he had deliberately lied to them. She evaded the direct question.

"My husband and I were in complete agreement. We did not want Kevin to come to the house and upset the children."

"But the waitress heard him tell you that he wasn't giving up, that he wasn't letting the adoption go through. She heard you say, 'I warn you, Kevin.' So he was a threat to your marriage, wasn't he, Mrs. Krueger?"

Why didn't Erich help her? She looked at him and watched his face darken with anger. "Sheriff, I think this has gone far enough," he said firmly. "Nothing could ever upset our marriage, certainly not Kevin MacPartland, alive or dead. We all know Rooney is mentally ill. My wife denies being in that car. Are you prepared to press charges? If not I demand that you stop harassing her."

The sheriff nodded. "Okay, Erich. But I have to warn you. There's a possibility the inquest will be reopened."

"If it is, we'll face it."

To a degree he had defended her. Jenny realized she was surprised at his matter-of-fact attitude. Was he becoming resigned to notoriety?

"I'm not saying it *will* be. Whether or not Rooney's testimony would change anything, I'm not sure. Until Mrs. Krueger starts remembering exactly what happened, we're not much further along than we were up till now. I don't think there was much doubt in any juror's mind that she was in that car at some point."

Erich walked the sheriff to his car. They stood for a few minutes deep in conversation.

Mark lingered behind them. "Jenny, I'd like to make an appointment for you with a doctor."

There was deep concern in his face. Was it for her or for Erich? "A shrink, I suppose?"

"No, a good old-fashioned family doctor. I know one in Waverly. You don't look well. This certainly has been a strain for you."

"I'll hold off a bit, I think, but thanks."

She had to get out of the house. The girls were playing in their room. She went upstairs and got them. "Let's go for a walk."

It was springlike outside. "Can we ride?" Tina asked.

"Not now," Beth said positively. "Daddy said he'll take us."

"I want to give Tinker Bell sugar."

"Sure, let's go to the stable," Jenny agreed. For a moment she allowed herself to daydream. Wouldn't it be wonderful if Erich were saddling Baron and she were on Fire Maid and they could go riding together on a beautiful day like this? They'd planned that, looked forward to it.

A somber-faced Joe was in the stable. Since she'd become aware that Erich was angry and jealous about her friendship with Joe, she'd made it a point to avoid him as much as possible. "How's Randy the second?" she asked.

"He's fine. He and I live in town now with my uncle. We've got a place over the post office. You'll have to come and see him there."

"You left your mother?"

"You bet I did."

"Joe, tell me. Why did you move out of your mother's place?"

"Because she's a troublemaker. I'm just sick, Mrs. Krueger, *Jenny*, about the things she said to you. I told

191

her if you say you didn't see that fellow Kevin that night, it's because it was necessary for you to say it. I told her you been so good to me, I'd a lost my job when Baron got away 'cept for you. If Maw'd minded her business, you wouldn't a had all that awful talk round here. That ain't the first time a car went off that road down the riverbank. People woulda said 'That's a shame' and somebody woulda said we need a better sign. Instead everybody in this county is snickering about you and Mr. Krueger and saying shows what happens when you get your head turned by a gold digger from New York."

"Joe, please." Jenny put her hand on his arm. "I've caused enough trouble here. Your mother must be upset. Joe, please move back home."

"No way. And, Mrs. Krueger, if you want a ride anywhere or if the girls want to see Randy, I'll be happy to bring you on my own time. You just say the word."

"Sshh, Joe, that kind of talk doesn't help." She gestured toward the open doors. "Please, someone might hear you."

"I don't care who hears me." The anger died from his face. "Jenny, I'd do anything to help you."

"Mommy, let's go now." Beth pulled at her. But what was it Joe had said that was nagging at her?

She remembered. "Joe, whatever you said to your mother about it being necessary for me to say I wasn't in the car? Joe, why did you put it that way?"

His face flamed red. Awkwardly he thrust his hands in his pocket, half-turned from her. When he spoke, his voice was a near-whisper. "Jenny, you don't have to pretend with me. I was there. I was worried that maybe I hadn't locked Baron's stall door tight. I was just cutting across the orchard when I saw Rooney. She was almost at the big house. I stopped 'cause I didn't want to get stuck talking to her. Then the car pulled up, that white Buick, and the front door opened and you ran out of the house. I saw you get in the car, Jenny, but I swear to God I'll never tell anyone. I . . . I love you, Jenny." Tentatively he took his hand from his pocket and closed it over her arm.

24

Erich came in just as the sun began to send slanting rays across the fields. Jenny had decided that no matter what, it was time to tell him about the baby.

He made it unexpectedly easy. He had brought canvases from the cabin, the ones he was planning to exhibit in San Francisco.

"What do you think of them?" he asked her. There was nothing in his voice or manner to suggest that the exchange with Sheriff Gunderson had taken place this morning.

"They're wonderful, Erich." *Shall I tell him what Joe said? Should I wait? When I go to a doctor, maybe I can find out if amnesia spells can happen to pregnant women.*

Erich was looking at her curiously.

"Do you want to come to San Francisco with me, Jenny?"

"Let's talk about it later."

He put his arms around her. "Don't be afraid,

darling. I'll take care of you. Today when Gunderson was badgering you I realized that no matter what happened that night, you're my whole life. I need you."

"Erich, I'm so confused."

"Why is that, darling?"

"Erich, I don't remember going out with Kevin but Rooney wouldn't lie."

"Don't worry. She's not a reliable witness. It's a good thing. Gunderson told me that he'd reopen the inquest in a shot if she were."

"You mean if someone else came forward and claimed to have seen me get in that car, they'd reopen the inquest and maybe charge me with a crime?"

"There's no need to talk about it. There's no other witness."

Oh, yes, there is, Jenny thought. Could anyone have overheard Joe today? His voice was loud. Joe's mother was starting to worry that Joe, like his uncle, had a tendency to drink. Suppose sometime in a bar he confided that he'd seen her get in the car with Kevin?

"Could I have forgotten that I went out?" she asked Erich.

He put his arms around her. His hands stroked her hair. "It would have been a shocking experience. Your coat was off. He had the key in his hand when he was found. Maybe, as I suggested to you, Kevin made a pass at you, grabbed the key. Maybe you resisted him. The car started to roll. You got out before it went over the bank."

"I don't know," Jenny said. "I can't believe it."

Later when it was time to go upstairs, Erich said, "Wear the aqua gown, darling."

"I can't."

"Can't? Why not?"

"It's too small for me. I'm going to have a baby."

Kevin had responded with dismay the first time she told him she thought she was pregnant. "Hell, Jen, we can't afford it. Get rid of it."

Now Erich shouted with joy. "My darling! Oh, Jen, that's the reason you've been looking so ill. Oh, my sweet. Will it be a boy?"

"I'm sure it is." Jenny laughed, savoring the momentary release from anxiety. He's already given me a harder time in three months than both girls did in nine."

"We'll have to get you right to a good doctor. My *son*. Do you mind if we call him Erich? It's the family tradition."

"I want it that way."

With her wrapped in his arms on the couch, all the mistrust between them was forgotten. "Jen, we've had a rotten break. We'll put all this misery behind us. We'll have a big party when I come back from San Francisco. You shouldn't travel now, should you, not if you haven't been feeling well? We'll face this community down. We'll be a real family. The adoption will be complete by the summer. I'm sorry for MacPartland, but at least he's not a threat anymore. Oh, Jen. . . ."

Not a threat, Jenny thought. Should she tell Erich about Joe? No, this was the baby's night.

Finally they went upstairs. Erich was already in bed when she came out of the bathroom. "I've missed sleeping with you, Jen," he said. "I've been so lonely."

"I've been so lonely too." The intense physical relationship between them, heightened and fired by separation, helped her forget the weeks of suffering. "I love you, Jenny. I love you so."

"Erich, I thought I'd go crazy, feeling so estranged from you. . . ."

"I know."

"Jen?"

"Yes, darling."

"I'm anxious to see whom the baby looks like."

"Mmm, I hope like you. . . . Just like you."

"How much I hope that too." His breathing became even.

She began to drift off to sleep, then felt that she'd been slapped with ice water. Oh, God, Erich couldn't doubt that he was the baby's father, could he? Of course not. It was just that her nerves were so shot. Everything upset her. But it was the way he'd put it . . .

In the morning, he said, "I heard you crying in your sleep last night, darling."

"I wasn't aware of it."

"I love you, Jenny."

"Love is trust, Erich. Please, darling, remember love and trust go hand in hand."

Three days later he took her to an obstetrician in Granite Place. When she met Dr. Elmendorf she liked him instantly. He was anywhere between fifty and sixty-five, small and bald with knowing eyes.

"You've been spotting, Mrs. Krueger?"

"Yes, but that happened both times before and I was fine."

"Did you lose so much weight at the beginning of your first two pregnancies?"

"No."

"Were you always anemic?"

"No."

"Were there any complications about your own birth?"

"I don't know. I was adopted. My grandmother never mentioned anything. I was born in New York City. That's about all I know of my background."

"I see. We've got to build you up. I'm aware you've been under a great strain."

What a delicate way of putting it, Jenny thought.

"I'll want to start you on vitamins. Also no lifting, no pushing or hauling. Get a great deal of rest."

Erich was sitting beside her. He reached for her hand and stroked it. "I'll take good care of her, Doctor."

The eyes rested on Erich speculatively. "I think it would be well if you abstain from marital relations for the next month at least and possibly through the pregnancy if the spotting continues. Will that be too much of a problem?"

"Nothing is too much of a problem if it means that Jenny will have a healthy child."

The doctor nodded approvingly.

But it is a problem, Jenny thought, dismayed. You see, Doctor, our marital relations give us the one area where we are simply two people who love and want each other and we manage to close the door on jealousy and suspicion and outside pressures.

25

The late spring was warm with afternoon showers and the rich abundant land became thick and green. The tough, heady alfalfa plants, now decorated with blue blossoms, were ready for the first cutting of the season.

Cattle strayed far away from the polebarns, happy with the grazing in the sloping fields that led to the riverbank. Tree branches rustled against each other, dressed in the leaves that made a solid green wall of the edge of the woods. Deer sometimes ran through that wall, paused, listened, then escaped back into the protective arms of the trees.

Even the house brightened with the fair weather. Rigid as they were, the heavy curtains could not withstand the delicate breezes that brought the scent of irises and violets and sunflowers and roses indoors.

For Jenny the change was welcome. The warmth of the spring sun seemed to penetrate the constant chill of her body. The scent of flowers in the house almost overcame the pervasive hint of pine. In the mornings she would get out of bed, open the windows and lie back against the pillows, enjoying the fresh, delicate breeze.

The pills for morning sickness weren't helping. Every morning she was racked by nausea. Erich insisted she stay in bed. He brought her tea and saltines, and after a while the feeling would subside.

He stayed in the house every night now. "I don't want you to be alone, darling, and I'm all ready for the San Francisco exhibit." He was leaving on the twenty-third of May. "By then Dr. Elmendorf said you'll probably be feeling a lot better."

"I hope so. Are you sure you're not interrupting your painting?"

"Very sure. It's good to spend more time with the girls. And face it, Jen. Between Clyde on the farm and the manager at the limeworks and Emily's father at the bank, I can manage my time my way."

Now it was Erich who took the girls to the stable during the mornings and led them on their ponies. Rooney came over regularly. The sweater Jenny was knitting was going well and she was already starting Jenny on a patchwork quilt.

Jenny was still helpless to explain how her coat got in Kevin's car. Suppose Kevin did come down, and tried that door on the west porch? It could have been unlocked. Suppose he came in? The closet door was right there. He might have panicked. After all, he didn't know whether or not a housekeeper slept in. Perhaps he took her coat, planning to insinuate that he'd seen her, started driving away, took the wrong turn, put his hand in the pocket in the hope of finding money, pulled out the key and with that the car went off the bank.

It still didn't explain the phone call.

After their nap the girls loved to roam in the fields. Jenny sat on the west porch watching them as her fingers knitted the rows of wool or made patchwork squares. Rooney had dug up material from the attic, leftover goods that had been used for dresses long ago, a bag of scraps, a bolt of dark blue cotton. "John bought that blue material for me to make curtains for the back bedroom when he took it over. I warned him they'd be too dark. He hated to admit it but he had me take them down after a couple of months. Then I made the ones that are there now."

Somehow Jenny could not bring herself to sit in Caroline's swing. Instead she chose a wicker chair, high-backed with comfortable cushions. Nevertheless Caroline had sat on this porch, sewing, watching her child play in these fields.

She no longer felt the lack of company. Now she always refused Erich's suggestions of dinner at one of the local restaurants. "Not yet, Erich. I don't even like the smell of food."

He began taking the children with him when he went out on errands. They came back chatting about the people they'd met, the places where they'd stopped to visit and stayed for cookies and milk.

Now Erich always slept in the back bedroom. "Jen, it's easier this way. I can stay away from you if I'm not too near you but I can't lie beside you night after night and not have my hands on you. Besides you're a restless sleeper. You'll probably sleep better alone."

She should be grateful but she wasn't. The nightmares happened regularly; over and over again she'd had that sensation of touching flesh, a face in the dark, of feeling long hair against her cheek. She didn't dare tell him that. He'd surely think she was mad.

The day before he was to leave for San Francisco, he suggested she go to the stable with him. The morning nausea hadn't occurred for two days.

"I'd rather you be there when the girls ride. I'm getting pretty unhappy with Joe."

A quick thrill of worry. "Why?"

"I've heard rumors he's boozing it up every night with his uncle. Josh Brothers is exactly the wrong influence on Joe at this stage. Anyhow if you think he seems hung over, I don't want the girls out with him. I may have to get rid of him."

Mark was in the stable. His normally calm voice was raised and icy. "Don't you know how dangerous it is to leave rat poison five feet from the oat supply? Suppose some of it got mixed in with the feed? Those horses would go crazy. What the hell is the matter with you lately, Joe? Let me tell you, if this happens again, I'll recommend that Erich fire you. Those children ride the ponies every day. Erich's horse is hard enough to handle even for an experienced rider like him. Give Baron a taste of the strychnine in that stuff and he'd trample anyone who came near him."

Erich dropped Jenny's arm. "What's all this about?"

A red-faced Joe who seemed on the verge of tears admitted, "I was going to put the poison in the traps. I pulled the box in here when it started to rain and I forgot it."

"You're fired," Erich said evenly.

Joe looked at Jenny. Was there something significant in his expression or simple pleading? She wasn't sure.

She stepped forward, took Erich's hand. *"Please,* Erich. Joe's been wonderful with the children. He's so patient teaching them to ride. They'd miss him terribly."

Erich studied her face. "If it means that much to you," he said shortly, then turned back to Joe. "Any mistake, Joe, *any* mistake, a stall door open, a dog running around my property, this sort of thing . . ." He glanced contemptuously at the box of rat poison. "That's *it.* Got it?"

"Yes, sir," Joe whispered. "Thank you, sir. Thank you, Mrs. Krueger."

"And make sure it's *Mrs. Krueger,*" Erich snapped. "Jenny, I don't want the girls riding till I come back. Is that clear?"

"Yes." She agreed with him. Joe looked ill. There was a bruise on his forehead.

Mark left the stable with them. "You've got a new calf in the dairy barn, Erich. That's why I'm here. Keep an eye on Joe. He was in another fight last night."

"What the hell is he fighting about?" Erich asked irritably.

Mark's face closed. "Give people not used to liquor a couple of boilermakers and you don't need much excuse."

"Come back to lunch with us," Erich suggested. "We haven't seen much of you."

"Please come," Jenny murmured.

They walked up to the house together.

"You two go on in," Erich suggested. "Mark, pour us a sherry, will you? I want to pick up the mail at the office."

"Sure thing."

He waited until Erich was out of earshot then said quickly, "Two things, Jenny. I heard the good news about the baby. Congratulations. How do you feel?"

"Much better now."

"Jenny, I have to warn you. It was very good of you to save Joe's job for him but it's a mistaken kindness. The reason he's getting into fights is that he's too open about his feelings for you. He worships you and the guys who hang around the bars at night are teasing him about it. Joe would be better off far away from this farm."

"And from me?"

"Bluntly, yes."

26

When Erich was leaving for San Francisco he decided to drive the Cadillac to the airport and leave it there. "Unless you particularly want to use it, darling?"

Was there an edge to the question? The last time he'd been away she'd used the car to meet Kevin. "I don't want it," she said quietly. "Elsa can pick up anything I need."

"You have your vitamins."

"Plenty of them."

"If you don't feel well, Clyde will drive you to the doctor." They were at the door. "Girls," Erich called, "come give Daddy a kiss."

They ran to him. "Bring me a present," Beth begged.

"Me too," Tina chimed in.

"Oh, Erich, before you go, tell the girls that you don't want them on the ponies until you get back."

"Daddy!" There were two wails of protest.

"Oh, I don't know. Joe came to apologize to me.

Says he knows he's been off-base. He's even going to move back in with his mother. I think it's all right to let him take the girls out. You just be sure to be with them every minute, Jen."

"I'd rather not," she said evenly.

"Any reason?" His eyebrows quirked.

She thought of what Mark had told her. But there was no way she could discuss that with Erich. "If you're sure it's safe."

His arms were around her. "I'll miss you."

"I'll miss you too."

She walked with him to the car. Clyde had driven it out of the garage. Joe was polishing it with a soft cloth. Rooney was standing by it, ready to come in and sew with Jenny. Mark had come over to say good-bye.

"I'll call you as soon as I get to the hotel," Erich told Jenny. "That will be ten your time."

That night she lay in bed waiting for the phone to ring. This house is too large, she thought. Anyone could come in the front door, the west door, the back door, come up the back staircase and I'd never hear him or her. The keys were hanging in the office. They were locked up at night but often during the day the office was empty. Suppose someone took a house key, made a copy and returned the first key to the office? No one would ever know.

Why am I worrying about that now? she wondered.

It was just that dream, that recurring dream of touching flesh, of her fingers grazing a cheek, an ear, hair. It was happening almost nightly now. And always the same. The heavy scent of pine, the feeling of a presence, the touching, and then a faint sighing sound. And always when she turned on the light the room was empty.

If only she could talk to someone about it. But who? Dr. Elmendorf would suggest she see a psychiatrist. She was sure of that. That's all Granite Place would need, she thought. Now that Krueger woman is going to have her head examined.

It was not quite ten o'clock. The phone rang. Quickly she picked it up. "Hello."

The line was dead. No, she could hear something. Not breathing but something.

"Hello." She felt herself start to tremble.

"Jenny." The voice was a whisper.

"Who is this?"

"Jenny, are you alone?"

"Who is this?"

"Have you got another boyfriend from New York with you yet, Jenny? Does he like to swim?"

"What are you talking about?"

Now the voice burst forth, a shriek, a scream, half-laugh, half-sob, unrecognizable. "Whore. Murderer. Get out of Caroline's bed. Get out of it *now.*"

She slammed the phone down. Oh, God, help me. She held her hands against her cheek feeling a tic under her eye. Oh, God.

The phone rang. I won't pick it up. I won't.

Four times, five times, six times. It stopped. It began to ring again. Erich, she thought. It was after ten o'clock. She grabbed the receiver.

"Jenny," Erich's voice was concerned, "what's the matter? I called a few minutes ago and the line was busy. Then no answer. Are you all right? Who was on the phone?"

"I don't know. It was just a voice." Her own voice was near hysteria.

"You sound upset. What did whoever called you say?"

"I . . : I couldn't make out the words." She couldn't tell him.

"I see." A long pause, then in a resigned tone, Erich said, "We won't discuss it now."

"What do you mean we won't discuss it?" Shocked,

Jenny heard the shriek in her own voice. She sounded exactly like the caller. "I want to discuss it. Listen, listen to what they said." Sobbing, she told him. "Who would accuse me like that? Who could hate me so much?"

"Darling, calm yourself, please."

"But, Erich, *who?*"

"Darling, *think.* It was Rooney, of course."

"But *why?* Rooney likes me."

"She may *like* you but she *loved* Caroline. She wants Caroline back and when she gets upset she sees you as an intruder. Darling, I warned you about her. Jenny, please don't cry. It's going to be all right. I'll take care of you. I'll always take care of you."

Sometime during the long, sleepless night the cramps began. First they were shooting pains in her abdomen. Then they settled into a steady off-on pattern. At eight she phoned Dr. Elmendorf. "You'd better come in," he told her.

Clyde had left early for a cattle auction and had taken Rooney with him. She didn't dare ask Joe to drive her. There were a half-dozen other men on the farm, the daily help who came in the morning and went to their own homes at night. She knew their names and faces but Erich had always cautioned her "not to get familiar."

She didn't want to ask one of them. She called Mark and explained. "By any chance . . .?"

His answer was prompt. "No problem. If you don't mind waiting until after office hours for me to drive you back. Or better still my dad can do it. He just got up from Florida. He'll stay most of the summer with me."

Mark's father, Luke Garrett. Jenny was anxious to meet him.

Mark came for her at nine-fifteen. The morning was

warm and hazy. It would be a hot day. Jenny had gone to her closet for something to wear and realized that all the new clothes Erich bought her when they were married were for cool weather. She'd had to rummage to find a summer cotton from last year in New York. Putting it on she'd felt peculiarly herself again. The two-piece pink-checked dress was an Albert Capraro, one she'd bought at an end-of-the-season sale. The soft, wide skirt was only a little tight at the waist; the blouson top concealed her thinness.

Mark's car was a four-year-old Chrysler station wagon. His bag was tossed in the back. A stack of books was scattered next to it on the seat. The car had an air of comfortable untidiness.

It was the first time she'd ever really been alone with Mark. I'll bet even the animals know instinctively he'll make things better when he's around, she thought. She told him that.

He glanced over at her. "I'd like to think so. And I hope Elmendorf is having the same effect on you. He's a good doctor, Jenny. You can trust him."

"I do."

They drove down the dirt road that led past the farm into Granite Place. Acre on acre of Krueger land, she thought. All those animals grazing on the fields. Krueger prize cattle. And I really had visualized a pleasant farmhouse and some cornfields. I never understood.

Mark said, "I don't know whether you heard that Joe is moving back in with his mother."

"Erich told me."

"The best possible situation. Maude is a smart woman. Drink runs in that family. She'll keep a tight rein on Joe."

"I thought her brother started drinking because of the accident?"

"I wonder. I heard my father and John Krueger talk about it afterward. John always said that Josh Brothers had been drinking that day. Maybe the accident was his excuse for coming out in the open with his boozing."

"Will Erich ever forgive me for all this gossip? It's destroying our marriage." She hadn't expected to ask the question. She heard it come from her flat and lifeless. Did she dare tell Mark about the phone call, about Erich's response to it?

"Jenny." There was a long silence then Mark began to speak. She'd already noticed that his voice had a tendency to deepen when he was particularly intent on what he was saying. "Jenny, I can't tell you what a different person Erich is since the first day he came back here after meeting you. He's always been a loner. He's always spent a lot of time in that cabin. Now of course we understand why. But even so . . . picture it. I doubt whether John Krueger ever so much as kissed Erich when he was a child. Caroline was the kind who'd scoop you up, hug you when you came in, run her fingers through your hair when she talked to you. People around here aren't like that. We're not outwardly expressive. Caroline was half-Italian, as you know. I remember my father teasing her about that Latin warmth in her. Can you imagine what it must have been like for Erich to know she was planning to leave him? No wonder he was so upset about your former husband. Just give him time. The gossip will die down. By next month people will have something else to chew on."

"You make it sound so easy."

"Not easy, but maybe not as bad as you think."

He dropped her at the doctor's office. "I'll just sit out here and catch up on some reading. You shouldn't be too long."

The obstetrician did not mince words. "You've had false labor and I certainly don't like it at this stage. You haven't been exerting yourself?"

"No."

"You've lost more weight."

"I just can't eat."

"For the sake of the baby, you've got to try. Malted milks, ice cream, just get something down. And stay off your feet as much as possible. Are you worried about anything?"

Yes, Doctor, she wanted to say. I'm worried because I don't know who calls me when my husband is away. Is Rooney sicker than I realize? How about Maude? She resents the Kruegers, particularly resents me. Who else knows so much about when Erich is away?

"Are you worried about anything, Mrs. Krueger?" he repeated.

"Not really."

She told Mark what the doctor had said. His arm was slung around the back of the seat. He's so big, she thought, so overpoweringly, comfortably male. She could not imagine him exploding in fury. He had been reading. Now he tossed the book in the backseat, and started the car. "Jenny," he suggested, "don't you have a friend or a cousin or someone who could come out and spend a couple of months with you? You seem so alone here. I think that might help to take your mind off things."

Fran, Jenny thought. With absolute longing she wanted Fran to come and visit. She thought of the amusing evenings they had spent together while Fran expounded on her latest boyfriend. But Erich disliked Fran intensely. He'd told her to make sure that Fran didn't visit. Jenny thought of some of her other friends. None of them could spend nearly four hundred dollars to fly out for a weekend visit. They had jobs and families. "No," she said, "I don't have anyone who can come."

The Garrett farm was on the north end of Granite Place. "We're small potatoes next to Erich," Mark said. "We have a section, six hundred and forty acres. I have my clinic right on the property."

The farmhouse was like the one she'd pictured Erich would have. Large and white, black-shuttered, with a wide front porch.

The parlor was lined with bookshelves. Mark's father was reading in an easy chair there. He looked up when they came in. Jenny watched as a startled expression came over his face.

He was a big man too, with rangy shoulders. The thick hair was pure white but the part broke at the same place as his son's. His reading glasses enhanced his blue-gray eyes, and his lashes were gray-white. Mark's were dark. But Luke's eyes had that same quizzical expression.

"You have to be Jenny Krueger."

"Yes, I am." Jenny liked him at once.

"No wonder Erich . . ." He stopped. "I've been anxious to meet you. I'd hoped to get the chance when I was here in late February."

"You were here in February?" Jenny turned to Mark. "Why didn't you bring your father over?"

Mark shrugged. "Erich pretty well sent out signals you two were doing an at-home honeymoon. Jenny, I've got ten minutes before the clinic opens. What would you like? Tea? Coffee?"

Mark disappeared into the kitchen and she was alone with Luke Garrett. She felt as though she were being looked over by the school counselor, as though any minute he'd ask, "And how do you like your courses? Are you comfortable with your teachers?"

She told him that.

He smiled. "Maybe I am analyzing. How is it going?"

"How much have you heard?"

"The accident? The inquest?"

"You've heard." She raised her hands as though pushing away a weight that was closing in on her. "I can't blame people for thinking the worst. My coat was in the car. A woman did call the Guthrie Theater from our telephone that afternoon.

"I keep thinking there's a reasonable explanation and once I find it out, everything will be all right again."

She hesitated, then decided against discussing Rooney with him. If Rooney had made that call last night in one of her spells, she'd probably have forgotten it by now. And Jenny did not want to repeat what the caller had said to her.

Mark came in followed by a short, stocky woman carrying a tray. The warm, enticing scent of coffee cake reminded Jenny of Nana's one great baking success, a Bisquick coffee cake. A wave of nostalgia made her blink back tears.

"You're not very happy here, are you, Jenny?" Luke asked.

"I expected to be. I could be," she replied honestly.

"That's exactly what Caroline said," Luke commented softly. "Remember, Mark, when I was putting her bags in the car that last afternoon?"

A few minutes later Mark left for the clinic and Luke drove her home. He seemed quiet and distracted and after a few efforts at conversation, Jenny became quiet too.

Luke steered the station wagon through the main gate. They circled around to the west entrance. She saw Luke's eyes rest on the porch swing. "The problem," he said suddenly, "is that this place doesn't change. If you took a picture of this house and compared it to one that was thirty years old, it would be the same. Nothing is added, nothing is renovated, nothing is moved. Maybe that's why everyone here has that same feeling of her presence, as though the door might fling open and she'd come running out, always glad to see you, always urging you to stay for dinner. After Mark's mother and I were divorced she had Mark here so much. Caroline was a second mother to him."

"And to you?" Jenny asked. "What was she to you?"

Luke looked at her through eyes that were suddenly anguished. "Everything I ever wanted in a woman." He cleared his throat abruptly as though fearing he had revealed too much of himself. As she got out of the car Jenny said, "When Erich comes back, promise you'll come for dinner with Mark."

"I'd enjoy that, Jenny. Sure you have everything?"

"Yes." She started to walk toward the house.

"Jenny," he called.

She turned. Luke's face was filled with pain. "Forgive me. It's just that you resemble Caroline so strongly. It's rather frightening. Jenny, be careful. Be careful of accidents."

27

Erich was due home on June third. He called the night of the second. "Jen, I've been miserable. Darling, I'd give anything not to have you so upset."

She felt the hard knot of tension ease. It was as Mark said, eventually the gossip would blow over. If only she could hang on to that thought. "It's all right. We're going to get through all this."

"How do you feel, Jen?"

"Pretty good."

"Eating better?"

"Trying to. How did the exhibit go?"

"Very, very well. The Gramercy Trust bought three oils. Stiff prices too. The reviews were fine."

"I'm so glad. What time does your plane get in?"

"Around eleven. I should be home between two and three. I love you so much, Jen."

That night the room seemed less threatening. Maybe it will be all right, she promised herself. For the first time in weeks she slept without dreaming.

She was sitting at the breakfast table with Tina and

Beth when the screaming started, a hideous cacophony of wild neighing and frantic sounds of human pain.

"Mommy!" Beth jumped off her chair and ran for the door.

"Stay there," Jenny ordered. She ran toward the sounds. They were coming from the stable. Clyde was rushing from the office, a rifle in his hand. "Stay back, Miz Krueger, stay back."

She could not. Joe. It was Joe who was screaming.

He was in the stall, crouched against the back wall, trying frantically to dodge the flying hooves. Baron was rearing on his hind legs, his eyes rolling in his head, the sharp metal-shod hoofs flailing the air. Joe was bleeding from the head; one arm hung limply at his side. As she watched he slumped onto the floor and Baron's front legs trampled his chest.

"Oh, God, oh, God, oh, God!" She heard her own voice weeping, praying, entreating. She was shoved aside. "Get out of his way, Joe. I'm gonna shoot." Clyde took aim as the hooves reared up again. There was a sharp crack of the rifle, followed by a screeching, protesting neighing; Baron stood poised statuelike in midair, then crumbled into the straw in the stall.

Somehow Joe managed to press against the wall, to avoid the crushing weight of the falling animal. Joe lay still, his breath coming in sharp gasps, his eyes glazed with shock, his arm twisted grotesquely. Clyde threw down the rifle and ran over to him.

"Don't move him!" Jenny shouted. "Call for an ambulance. Hurry."

Trying to avoid Baron's body, she kneeled beside Joe, her hand smoothing his forehead, wiping the blood from his eyes, pressing against the gaping tear near his hairline. Men came running from the fields. She could hear the sounds of a woman sobbing. Maude Ekers. "Joey, Joey."

"Maw . . ."

"Joey."

The ambulance arrived. Efficient white-clad attendants ordered everyone back. Then Joe was on the stretcher, his eyes closed, his face ashen. An attendant's low voice whispered, "I think he's going."

There was a shriek from Maude Ekers.

Joe's eyes opened, fastening on Jenny. His voice was bewildered, amazingly clear. "I'd never a told anyone I saw you get in the car that night, honest I wouldn't," he said.

Maude turned on Jenny, as she climbed in the ambulance after her son. "If my boy dies, it's your fault, Jenny Krueger," she screamed. "I *curse* the day you came here! God *damn* you Krueger women for what you've done to my family! God damn the baby you're carrying, whoever it belongs to!"

The ambulance sped away, the wail of its siren shattering the peace of the summer morning.

Erich arrived home a few hours later. He chartered a plane to fly a chest surgeon down from the Mayo Clinic, and phoned for private nurses. Then he walked into the stable and crouched beside Baron, his hand patting the sleek, beautiful head of the dead animal.

Mark had already analyzed the bucket of oats. The report: strychnine mixed with oats.

Later Sheriff Gunderson showed up at the front door with his now familiar car. "Mrs. Krueger, a half-dozen people heard Joe say he wouldn't have told that he saw you get in the car that night. What did he mean by that?"

"I don't understand what he meant."

"Mrs. Krueger, you were present a short time ago when Dr. Garrett admonished Joe for leaving the rat poison near the oats. You knew what effect it would have on Baron. You heard Dr. Garrett warn Joe that strychnine would drive Baron wild."

"Did Dr. Garrett tell you that?"

"He told me that Joe had been careless with the rat poison and that you and Erich were present when he dressed Joe down."

"What are you trying to say?"

"Nothing I can say, Mrs. Krueger. Joe claims he got the boxes mixed up. I don't believe him. No one does."

"Will Joe live?"

"Too soon to tell. Even if he does, he'll be a mighty sick boy for a long time. If he makes it through the next three days, they're moving him up to Mayo." The sheriff turned to go. "Like his maw said, at least he'll be safe up there."

28

Caught up in the rhythm of her pregnancy, Jenny began counting days and weeks until the baby was due. In twelve weeks, in eleven weeks, in ten weeks, Erich would have a son. He would move back into their room. She would be well again. The talk in town would die out for lack of fresh fuel. The baby would look exactly like Erich.

The operation on Joe's chest had been successful, though he would not leave Mayo Clinic until the end of August. Maude was staying in a furnished apartment near the hospital. Jenny knew that Erich was paying all the bills.

Now Erich rode Fire Maid when he took the girls riding. He never mentioned Baron to her. She did hear from Mark that Joe had persisted in his story that he must have mixed the poison in with the oats himself and that he had no idea what he'd meant when he talked about seeing Jenny that night.

She didn't need Mark to tell her that no one believed him.

Erich was working less at the cabin and more on the farm with Clyde and the men. When she asked him about that he said, "I can't quite get in the mood for painting."

He was kind to her but remote. Always she felt that he was watching her. In the evenings they'd sit in the parlor and read. He rarely spoke to her, but when she glanced up, she'd see his eyes drop as though he didn't want to be caught studying her.

About once a week Sheriff Gunderson would drop by, seemingly just to chat. "Let's go over the night Kevin MacPartland came here, Mrs. Krueger." Or he would speculate: "Joe has a real big crush on you, don't he? Enough to make him pretty protective. Anything you feel like talking about, Mrs. Krueger?"

The sensation of someone being in the room with her at night was constant. Always the pattern was the same. She would start dreaming of being in the woods; something would come toward her, hover over her; she'd push out her hand and feel long hair, a woman's hair. The sighing sound came next. She would fumble for the light and when she turned it on she'd be alone in the room.

Finally she told Dr. Elmendorf about the dream.

"How do you explain it?" he asked.

"I don't know." She hesitated. "No, that's not quite true. I always think it has something to do with Caroline." She told him about Caroline, told him that everyone close to her seemed to have a sense of her presence.

"I'd guess that your imagination is playing tricks on you. Would you like me to arrange counseling?"

"No. I'm sure you're right."

She started to sleep with the light on in the room, then determinedly snapped it off. The bed was to the right of the door. The massive headboard was against the north wall. One side of the bed was close to the east wall of the room. She wondered if Erich would move the bed for her so that it was between the windows on the south wall. There would be more moonlight there. She'd be able to look out when she wasn't sleeping. The corner where the bed was placed was terribly dark.

She knew better than to make the request.

One morning Beth asked, "Mommy, why didn't you talk to me when you came into my room last night?"

"I didn't come to you, Mouse."

"Yes, you did!"

Was she sleepwalking?

The tiny flutters of life inside her seemed unlike the sturdy kicks she'd known from Beth and Tina. Let the baby be healthy, she pleaded in silent prayer. Let me give Erich his son.

The hot August afternoons dissolved into cool evenings. The woods held the first touches of gold. "It will be an early fall," Rooney commented. "And by the time the leaves are all turned, your quilt will be finished. You can hang it in the dining room too."

Jenny avoided Mark as much as possible, staying in the house whenever she glimpsed his station wagon parked near the office. Did he too believe she might have deliberately put poison in Baron's feed? She felt she could not stand it if she sensed accusation from him too.

In early September, Erich invited Mark and Luke Garrett for dinner. He told her about it casually. "Luke's going back to Florida until the holidays. I haven't seen enough of him. Emily's coming too. I can have Elsa stay and cook."

"No, that's the one thing I get to do around here."

The first dinner party since the night Sheriff Gunderson had come to tell her Kevin was missing. She found herself looking forward to seeing Luke again. She knew Erich went over to the Garrett farm regularly. He'd taken Tina and Beth with him. He never cleared the outings with her anymore. He'd simply announce, "I'll keep the girls out of your hair for the afternoon. Get a good rest, Jen."

It wasn't that she wanted to go. She didn't want to run the risk of seeing any of the townspeople. How would they treat her? Smile to her face and gossip about her as she passed?

When Erich was away with the girls, she would take long walks on the farm. She would wander along the river and try not to think that Kevin's car plunged over the bank just around that bend. She walked past the cemetery. Caroline's grave was planted with summer flowers.

She found herself longing to slip into the woods, to find Erich's cabin. Once she went fifty yards into them. The thick branches blotted out the sun. A fox passed her, brushing her legs, in pursuit of a rabbit. Startled, she'd turned back. Birds nesting in the trees sent up a flutter of protest as she passed.

She'd ordered some maternity clothes from a Dayton's catalog. Nearly seven months pregnant, she thought, and my own clothes aren't that much too tight. But the new blouses and slacks and skirts buoyed her spirits. She remembered how carefully she'd shopped when she was pregnant with Beth. She'd worn those same clothes for Tina. For this baby Erich had said, "Order as much as you want."

The night of the dinner she wore an emerald-green two-piece silk dress with a white lace collar. It was simple and well-cut. She knew Erich liked her to wear green. It did something to her eyes. Like the aqua gown.

The Garretts and Emily came together. Jenny decided there seemed to be a new intimacy between Mark and Emily. They sat side by side on the couch. At one point Emily's hand rested on Mark's arm.

Maybe they are engaged, she thought. The possibility brought a queer stab of pain. Why?

Emily was making a distinct effort to be pleasant. But it was hard to find common ground. She talked about the county fair. "Corny as they are, I always enjoy them. And everyone was talking about how darling your girls are."

"Our girls," Erich smiled. "Oh, by the way, you'll all be glad to know the adoption is complete. The girls are legally and bindingly Kruegers."

Jenny'd expected that, of course. But how long had Erich known? A few weeks ago he'd stopped asking her if she minded if he took the girls out. Was that the reason: they were "legally and bindingly Kruegers"?

Luke Garrett was very quiet. He had chosen to sit in the wing chair. After a while Jenny understood why. It gave the clearest view of Caroline's portrait. His eyes seldom strayed from it. What had he meant by that warning about accidents?

The dinner turned out well. She'd made tomato bisque from a recipe she found in an old cookbook in the kitchen. Luke raised his eyebrows. "Erich, if I'm not mistaken that must be the recipe your grandmother used when I was a boy. Excellent, Jenny."

As though to make up for his earlier silence, Luke began reminiscing about his youth. "Your dad," he said to Erich, "was as close to me growing up as you and Mark ever were."

At ten o'clock they went home. Erich helped her to clear the table. He seemed pleased at the way the evening had gone. "Looks as though Mark and Emily are pretty close to an engagement," he said. "Luke would be glad. He's been after Mark to settle down."

"I thought so too," Jenny agreed. She tried to sound pleased but knew the effort was a failure.

* * *

In October it became sharply colder. Biting winds stripped the trees of their autumn finery; frost dulled the grass to brown; rain became icy. The furnace hummed constantly now. Every morning Erich started a fire in the kitchen stove. Beth and Tina came to breakfast wrapped in warm robes, eagerly anticipating the first snowfall.

Jenny seldom left the house. The long walks were too tiring and Dr. Elmendorf advised against them. Her legs cramped frequently and she was afraid of falling. Rooney came to visit every afternoon. Between them they'd made a layette for the baby. "I'll never sew properly," Jenny sighed, but even so it was gratifying to make simple kimonos from the flowered cloth that Rooney ordered from town.

It was Rooney who showed Jenny the corner of the attic where the Krueger bassinette was covered with sheets. "I'll make a new skirt for it," Rooney said. The activity seemed to brighten her and for days at a time she was never confused.

"I'll put the bassinette in Erich's old room," she told Rooney. "I don't want to move the girls and the other rooms are too far away. I'd be afraid I wouldn't hear the baby at night."

"That's what Caroline said," Rooney volunteered. "You know Erich's room used to be part of the master bedroom, kind of an alcove of it. Caroline put the bassinette and baby dresser there. John didn't like having the baby in his room. Said he didn't have a big house so he'd have to tiptoe around an infant. That's when they put the partition in."

"The partition?"

"Didn't Erich ever tell you that? Your bed used to be on the south wall. Behind the headboard where it is now is the sliding wall."

"Show me, Rooney."

They went upstairs to Erich's old room. "Course you can't open it from your side with the headboard there," Rooney said, "But look-see." She pushed the high-back rocker aside and pointed to a recessed handle in the wallpaper. "Just watch how easy it works."

Noiselessly the panel slid open. "Caroline had it made like that so when Erich was bigger you could just close off the two rooms. My Clyde made the partition and Josh Brothers helped him. Didn't they do a good job? Would you ever guess it was there?"

Jenny stood in the opening. She was behind the headboard of her bed. She leaned over. That was why she had felt a presence, reached out, touched a face. She remembered the constant sensation of long hair. Rooney's hair removed from that tight bun was surely quite long. "Rooney," she tried to sound casual, "do you ever come into this room and open the partition at night? Maybe look in at me?"

"I don't think I do. But, Jenny . . ." Rooney put her lips to Jenny's ear. "I wouldn't tell Clyde because he'd think I'm crazy. Sometimes he scares me. He talks about putting me away for my own good. But, Jenny, I've seen Caroline walking around the farm at night these last few months. Once I followed her here to the house and she came up the back stairs. That's why I keep thinking if Caroline is able to come back, maybe my Arden will be here soon too."

29

This time it wasn't false labor. Quietly Jenny lay in bed timing the contractions. From ten minutes apart for two hours, they suddenly accelerated to five-minute intervals. Jenny patted the small mound in her abdomen. We've made it, young Mr. Krueger, she thought. For a while I wasn't sure we would.

Dr. Elmendorf had been cautiously pleased on her last visit. "The baby is about five pounds," he said. "I'd wish it bigger but that's a comfortable weight. Frankly I was sure you were going to deliver prematurely." He'd done a scan. "You're right, Mrs. Krueger. You're going to have a boy."

She went down the hall to call Erich. The door of his bedroom was closed. She never went there. Hesitating she knocked. "Erich," she called softly.

There was no answer. Could he have gone to the cabin during the night? He'd started painting again but always came home for dinner. Even if he went back to the cabin for the evening he returned to the house at some point.

She'd asked him about the panel that separated his old room from the master bedroom. "My God, Jen, I'd forgotten all about it. Why do you get the idea someone has been opening it? I'll bet Rooney is in and out of this place more than we realize. I warned you against getting so cozy with her."

She hadn't dared tell him that Rooney talked about seeing Caroline.

Now she pushed open the door to the room he'd been using and reached for the light. The bed was made. Erich wasn't here.

She'd have to get to the hospital. It was only four o'clock. There wouldn't be anyone up until seven. Unless . . .

Padding softly on bare feet down the wide foyer, Jenny passed the closed doors of the other bedrooms. Erich would never use any of those except . . .

Cautiously she opened the door of his old room. The Little League trophy on the dresser glistened in the moonlight. The bassinette, now frothy with a yellow silk skirt overlaid with white net, was next to the bed.

The bedcovers were rumpled. Erich was asleep, his body hunched in his favorite fetal position. His hand was thrown over the bassinette as though he'd fallen asleep holding it. Something Rooney had said came back to her. "I can see Caroline rocking that bassinette by the hour with Erich fussing in it. I used to tell him he was lucky to have had such a patient mother."

"Erich," Jenny whispered, touching his shoulder.

His eyes flew open. He jumped up. "Jenny, what's the matter?"

"I think I'd better get to the hospital." He got out of bed quickly, put his arms around her. "Something told me to come in here tonight, to be near you. I fell asleep thinking how wonderful it will be when our little boy is in that bassinette."

It had been weeks since he had touched her. She had not realized how starved she had been for the feeling of arms around her. She reached up her hands to his face.

In the dark her fingers felt the curve of his face, the softness of his eyelids.

She shivered.

"What is it, dear? Are you all right?"

She sighed. "I don't know why but just for a minute I was so frightened. You'd think this was my first baby, wouldn't you?"

The overhead light in the delivery room was very bright. It hurt her eyes. She was slipping in and out of consciousness. Erich, masked and coated like the doctors and nurses, was watching her. Why did Erich watch her all the time?

A last rush of pain. Now, she thought, now. Dr. Elmendorf held up a small, limp body. All of them bending over it. "Oxygen."

The baby had to be all right. "Give him to me." But her lips didn't form the words. She couldn't move her lips.

"Let me see him," Erich said. He sounded anxious, nervous. Then she heard his dismayed whisper. "He has hair like the girls, *dark red hair!*"

When she opened her eyes again the room was dark. A nurse was sitting by the bed.

"The baby?"

"He'll be fine," the nurse said soothingly. "He just gave us a little scare. Try to sleep."

"My husband?"

"He's gone home."

What was it Erich had said in the delivery room? She couldn't remember.

She drifted in and out of sleep. In the morning a pediatrician came in. "I'm Dr. Bovitch. The baby's lungs aren't fully developed. He's in trouble but we'll pull him through, Mother. I promise you that. However, since you gave your religion as Roman Catholic we thought it best to have him baptized last night."

"Is he that sick? I want to see him."

"You can walk down to the nursery in a little while. We can't take him out of the oxygen yet. Kevin's a beautiful little baby, Mrs. Krueger."

"Kevin!"

"Yes. Before the priest baptized him he asked your husband what you planned to call him. That is right, isn't it? Kevin MacPartland Krueger?"

Erich came in with an armful of long-stemmed red roses. "Jenny, Jenny, they say he'll make it. The baby will make it. When I went home I spent the night crying. I thought it was hopeless."

"Why did you tell them his name was Kevin MacPartland?"

"Darling, they said they didn't think he'd survive more than a few hours. I thought we'd save the name Erich for a son who would live. It was the only other name that came to my mind. I thought you'd be pleased."

"Change it."

"Of course, darling. He'll be Erich Krueger the fifth on his birth certificate."

The week she was in the hospital Jenny forced herself to eat, husbanded her strength, pushed back the depression that sapped her energy. After the fourth day they took the baby out of oxygen and let her hold him. He was so frail. Her being ached with tenderness as his mouth reached for her breast. She had not nursed Beth or Tina. It had been too important to get back to work. But to this child she could give all her time, all her energy.

She was discharged from the hospital when the baby was five days old. For the next three weeks she went back there every four hours during the day to nurse him. Sometimes Erich drove her. Other times he gave her the car. "Anything for the baby, darling."

The girls got used to her leaving them. At first they fussed, then became resigned. "It's all right," Beth told Tina. "Daddy will mind us and we have fun with him."

Erich heard. "Who do you like best, Mommy or me?" He tossed them in the air.

"You, Daddy," Tina giggled. Jenny realized she'd learned the answers Erich wanted to hear.

Beth hesitated, glanced at Jenny. "I like you both the same."

Finally, the day after Thanksgiving, she was allowed to bring the baby home. Tenderly, she dressed the small body, glad to hand back the coarse hospital shirt and replace it with a new one, washed once to soften the cotton fibers. A long flowered nightgown, the blue woolen sacque and bonnet, a receiving blanket, the brushed wool bunting lined in satin.

It was bitterly cold out. November had brought snow, ice-tipped, constant. Wind whispered through the trees, stirring the naked branches into restless movement. Smoke wisped constantly from the chimneys in the house, from the office, blew over the ridge from Clyde and Rooney's home near the cemetery.

The girls were ecstatic over their little brother, each pleading to hold him. Sitting beside them on the couch, Jenny let them have a turn. "Gently, gently. He's so tiny."

Mark and Emily dropped by to see him. "He's

beautiful," Emily declared. "Erich is showing his picture to everyone."

"Thank you for your flowers," Jenny murmured, "and your father and mother sent a beautiful arrangement. I phoned to thank your mother but apparently she wasn't home."

The "apparently" was a deliberate choice of words. She was certain that Mrs. Hanover was home when she called.

"They're so happy for you . . . and for Erich, of course," Emily said hastily. "I'm just hoping I'm giving someone over here ideas." She laughed in Mark's direction.

He smiled back at her.

You don't make remarks like that until you're pretty sure of yourself, Jenny thought.

She tried to make conversation. "Well, Dr. Garrett, how do you judge my son? Would he win a prize at the county fair?"

"A thoroughbred, for sure," Mark replied. What was there in his voice? A worried tone? Pity? Did he see something as fragile in the baby as she did?

She was sure of it.

Rooney was a born nurse. She loved to give the baby the supplemental bottle after Jenny breast-fed him. Or she would read to the girls when the baby was sleeping.

Jenny was grateful for the help. The baby worried her. He slept too much; he was so pale. His eyes began to focus. They would be wide with the hint of almond shaping that Erich's had. They were china blue now. "But I swear I see some green lights in them. I bet they're like your mother's eyes, Erich. You'd like that?"

"I'd like that."

He moved the four-poster to the south wall of the

230

master bedroom. She left the partition open between that room and the small one. The bassinette was kept there. She could hear every sound the baby made.

Erich still hadn't moved back into their room. "You need your rest a little longer, Jenny."

"You can come in with me. I'd like that."

"Not yet."

Then she realized she was relieved. The baby consumed her every thought. At the end of the first month he had lost six ounces. The pediatrician looked grave. "We'll increase the formula in the supplemental bottle. I'm afraid your milk isn't rich enough for him. Are you eating properly? Is anything upsetting you? Remember a relaxed mother has a happier baby."

She forced herself to eat, to nibble, to drink milk shakes. The baby would start to nurse eagerly then tire and fall asleep. She told the doctor that.

"We'd better do some tests."

The baby was in the hospital three days. She slept in a room near the nursery. "Don't worry about my girls, Jenny. I'll take care of them."

"I know you will, Erich."

She lived for the moments she could hold the baby.

One of the valves in the baby's heart was defective. "He'll need an operation later on, but we can't risk it yet."

She thought of Maude Ekers' curse: "God damn the baby you're carrying." Her arms tightened around the sleeping infant.

"Is the operation dangerous?"

"Any operation has potential risk. But most babies come through nicely."

Again she brought the baby home. The tiny birth fuzz started to fall out. Fine golden shades of down began to replace it. "He'll have your hair, Erich."

"I think he'll stay red like the girls."

December came. Beth and Tina made up long lists

for Santa Claus. Erich set up a huge tree in the corner near the stove. The girls helped him. Jenny held the baby as she watched. She hated to put him down. "He sleeps better this way," she told Erich. "He always feels so cold. His circulation is poor."

"Sometimes I don't think you care about anyone except him," Erich observed. "I have to tell you, Tina and Beth and I are feeling pretty left out, aren't we?"

He took the girls to see Santa Claus in a nearby shopping mall. "What a list," he commented indulgently. "I had to write everything down that they were ordering. The big things they seem to want are bassinettes and baby dolls."

Luke had come back to Minnesota for the holidays. He, Mark and Emily stopped in on Christmas afternoon. Emily looked subdued. She showed an exquisite leather pocketbook. "Mark's present. Isn't it lovely?"

Jenny wondered if she had been expecting an engagement ring.

Luke asked to hold the baby. "He's a little beauty."

"And he's put on eight ounces," Jenny announced joyfully. "Didn't you, Pumpkin?"

"Do you always call him Pumpkin?" Emily asked.

"I suppose it sounds silly. It's just that Erich sounds like too much name for such a tiny little scrap. He'll have to grow into it."

She looked up smiling. Erich looked impassive. Mark, Luke and Emily were exchanging startled glances. Of course. They'd probably seen the birth notice in the paper the day after the baby was born, the notice that listed his name as Kevin. But hadn't Erich explained?

Emily rushed to fill the awkward silence. Bending over the baby again, she said, "I think he'll have the same coloring as the girls."

"Oh, I'm sure he's going to be blond like Erich."

Jenny smiled again. "Just give him six months. We'll have a Krueger towhead." She took him from Luke. "You'll look just like your daddy, won't you, Pumpkin?"

"That's what I've been saying right along," Erich commented.

Jenny felt the smile freeze on her face. Did he mean what she thought he meant? She looked searchingly from one face to the other. Emily looked acutely embarrassed. Luke stared straight ahead. Mark was stony-faced. She felt the anger in him. Erich was smiling warmly at the baby.

She knew with absolute certainty that Erich had not changed the name on the birth certificate.

The baby began to whimper. "My poor little darling," he said. She stood up. "If you'll excuse me, I have to . . ." She paused, then finished quietly, "I have to take care of Kevin."

Long after the baby fell asleep she sat by the bassinette. She heard Erich bring the girls upstairs, his voice soft. "Don't wake up the baby. I'll kiss Mommy good night for you. Didn't we have a wonderful Christmas?"

Jenny thought: I can't live like this.

At last she went downstairs. Erich had closed the gift boxes and stacked them neatly around the tree. He was wearing the new velvet jacket she'd ordered from Dayton's for him. The deep blue suited him. All strong colors suit him, she thought objectively.

"Jen, I'm really happy with my present. I hope you're as pleased with yours." He'd bought her a white mink jacket.

Without waiting for a reply, he continued to straighten the gifts, then said, "The girls really went for those bassinettes, didn't they? You'd never guess they got anything else. And the baby. Well, he's a little too young to appreciate them but before long he'll have fun with those stuffed animals."

"Erich, where is the baby's birth certificate?"

"It's on file in the office, dear. Why?"

"What name is on it?"

"The baby's name. Kevin."

"You told me you'd changed that."

"I realized it would have been a terrible mistake to change it."

"Why?"

"Jenny, hasn't there been enough talk about us? What do you think the people around here would say if we corrected the baby's name? My God, that would give them fuel for the next ten years. Don't forget we weren't married quite nine months when he was born."

"But *Kevin*. You called him *Kevin*."

"I explained the reason for that. Jenny, already the talk is dying down. When people talk about the accident, they don't mention Kevin's name. They talk about Jenny Krueger's first husband, the guy who followed her to Minnesota and somehow went over the riverbank. But I can tell you this. If we changed the baby's name now, they'd be trying to figure out why for the next fifty years. And by God, then they'd remember Kevin MacPartland."

"Erich," she asked fearfully, "is there a better reason you didn't change the birth certificate? Is the baby sicker than I realize? Is it because you're saving your name for a child who will live? Tell me, Erich, please. Are you and the doctor hiding anything from me?"

"No, no, no." He came over to her, his eyes tender. "Jenny, don't you see? Everything will be fine. I want you to stop worrying. The baby is getting stronger."

There was another question she had to ask him.

"Erich, there was something you said in the delivery room, that the baby had dark red hair like the girls. Kevin had dark red hair. Erich, tell me, promise me, that you're not suggesting that Kevin was the baby's father. You can't believe that?"

"Jenny, why would I believe that?"

"Because of what you said about his hair." She felt her voice quivering. "The baby's going to be the image of you. Wait and see. All his new hair is blond. But when the others were here . . . The way you picked me up when I said he'll look just like his daddy. The way you said, "That's what I've been saying right along.' Erich, surely you can't think Kevin is the baby's father?"

She stared at him. The blue velvet gave an almost burnished look to his blond hair. She'd never really appreciated how dark his lashes and brows were. She was reminded of the paintings in the palace in Venice where generations of lean-faced, smoldering-eyed doges looked disdainfully down on the tourists. There was something of that contempt in Erich's eyes now.

His facial muscles tightened. "Jenny, is there any end to the ways you misunderstand me? I've been good to you. I brought you and the children out of that miserable apartment to this beautiful home. I gave you jewelry and clothes and furs. You could have had anything you wanted and still you allowed Kevin MacPartland to contact you and cause a scandal. I'm sure there isn't a house in this community that doesn't discuss us over the dinner table every night. I forgive you but you have no right to be angry with me, to question every word out of my mouth. Now let's go upstairs. I think it's time I moved back in with you."

His hands tightened on her arms. His entire body was so rigid. There was something frightening about him. Confused, she looked away.

"Erich," she said carefully, "we're both very tired.

We've been under a strain for a long time. I think what you should do is start painting again. Do you realize how few times you've gone to the cabin since the baby was born? Go to your own room tonight and get an early start in the morning. But bundle up; it's probably very cold there now."

"How do you know it's cold? When did you go there?" His voice was quick and suspicious.

"Erich, you know I've never been there."

"Then how did you know . . .?"

"Sshh, listen." From upstairs they heard a wailing.

"It's the baby." Jenny turned and ran up the stairs, Erich behind her. The baby's arms and legs were flailing. His face was damp. As they watched he began to suck his clenched fist.

"Oh, Erich, look, he's crying real tears." Tenderly she bent over and picked him up. "There, there, Pumpkin. I know you're hungry, my precious lamb. Erich, he is getting stronger."

From behind her, she heard the door close. Erich had left the room.

30

She dreamed of a pigeon. Somehow it seemed terribly ominous. It was flying through the house and she had to catch it. It mustn't be allowed in the house. It sailed into the girls' room and she followed it. It flew frantically round and round the room. It escaped her hands and fluttered past her into the baby's room. It settled on the bassinette. She began to cry, no, no, no.

She woke up with tears drenching her face and rushed in to the baby. He was sleeping contentedly.

Erich had left a note on the kitchen table. "Taking your advice. Will be at cabin painting for a few days."

At breakfast, Tina paused over her cereal and said, "Mommy, why didn't you talk to me when you came into my room last night?"

That afternoon Rooney stopped in to visit and it was she who first realized that the baby had a fever.

She and Clyde had had Christmas dinner with Maude and Joe. "Joe's doing fine," Rooney informed

Jenny. "Going down to Florida right from the hospital did wonders for him and for Maude too. Both of them that tanned and healthy. Joe gets rid of the brace next month."

"I'm so glad."

"Course Maude says she's happy to be home now. She told me Erich was real generous to them. But I guess you know that. He paid every cent of the medical bills and gave them a check for five thousand dollars beside. He wrote Maude that he felt responsible."

Jenny was stitching the last of her quilt together. She looked up. *"Responsible?"*

"I don't know what he means. But Maude told me she feels real bad that the baby hasn't been well. Says she remembers saying awful things to you."

Jenny remembered the awful things Maude had said.

"Guess Joe admitted that he'd had a pretty good hangover that morning; insists it was likely he'd mixed up the poison and oats."

"Joe said that?"

"He did. Anyhow I think Maude wanted me to give you her apologies. I know when they got back last week Joe went down and spoke to the sheriff himself. Joe's real upset about all the rumors flying around his accident. You know, because of the wild thing he said about seeing you. He said he don't know why he ever said anything like that."

Poor Joe, Jenny thought. Trying to undo irreparable harm and then making it worse by stirring it up again.

"My, Jenny, do you realize that your quilt is just about finished? Real lovely too. That took patience."

"I was glad to have it to do," she said.

"Will you hang it in the dining room near Caroline's?"

"I haven't thought about it."

She hadn't thought about very much today except the possibility that she was sleepwalking. In her dream she'd been trying to chase a pigeon out of the girls' room. But had she actually been in the room?

There were too many episodes like this now over the past few months. The next time she went in to see Dr. Elmendorf, she'd talk to him about them. Maybe she did need some counseling.

I am so afraid, she thought.

She had begun to doubt whether Erich would ever forgive her for the notoriety that she had caused. No matter how hard they both tried, it would never be right again. And no matter what Erich said, she believed that subconsciously he was not sure that the baby was his son. She couldn't live her life out with that between them.

But the baby was a Krueger and deserved the best medical attention Erich's wealth could obtain for him. After the baby had the operation and was well, if things hadn't gotten much better, she'd leave. She tried to visualize living in New York, working in the gallery, the day-care center, picking up the children, hurrying home to start dinner. It wouldn't be easy. But nothing was easy and many women managed it. And anything would be better than this terrible feeling of isolation, this sense of losing touch with reality.

Nightmares. Sleepwalking. Amnesia. Was even amnesia possible? She'd never had any trouble in the apartment in New York. She'd be bone-tired at the end of the day but always slept. She might not have had nearly enough time for the girls but now it seemed she had no time. She was so worried about the baby and Erich kept whisking Tina and Beth off on outings that she couldn't or wouldn't attend.

I want to go home, she thought. Home wasn't a

place, maybe not even a house or apartment. Home was where you could close your door and be at peace.

This land. Even now. The snow falling, the wind blowing. She liked the savageness of the winter. She imagined the house as she had started to arrange it. The heavy curtains down, this table at the window, the friends she'd expected to make, the parties she would have given over the holidays.

"Jenny, you look so sad," Rooney said suddenly.

She tried to smile. "It's just . . ." Her voice trailed off.

"This is the best Christmas I've had since Arden went. Just watching the children so happy and being able to help you with the baby . . ."

Jenny realized that Rooney never called the baby by name.

She held up the quilt. "Here it is, Rooney, complete."

Beth and Tina were playing with their new picture puzzles. Beth looked up. "That is very pretty, Mommy. You're a very good sewer."

Tina volunteered, "I like it better than the one on the wall. Daddy said that yours won't be as nice as the one on the wall and I thought that was mean."

She bent her head over her book. Every line of her body suggested injury.

Jenny could not help smiling. "Oh, Tinker, you're such an actress." She went over, knelt down and hugged her.

Tina returned the hug fiercely. "Oh, Mommy."

I've given them so little time since the baby came, Jenny thought. "Tell you what," she said, "we're going to bring Pumpkin down in a few minutes. If you two wash your hands you can have a chance to hold him."

Rooney interrupted their squeals of delight. "Jenny, may I get him?"

"Of course. I'll fix his cereal."

Rooney was back downstairs in a few minutes, carefully holding the blanketed baby. She looked concerned. "I think he has a fever."

At five o'clock Dr. Bovitch came. "We'd better take him to the hospital."

"No, please." Jenny tried not to have her voice quiver.

The pediatrician hesitated. "We could give it till morning," he said. "Trouble is—with infants the fever can go high pretty fast. On the other hand, I'm not crazy about taking him out in the cold. All right. Let's see how he is in the morning."

Rooney stayed and prepared supper for them. Jenny gave the baby aspirin. She was chilled herself. Was she catching cold or was she simply numb with anxiety? "Rooney, hand me my shawl, please."

She wrapped it around her shoulders, sheltered the baby in it as she held him.

"Oh, dear." Rooney's face was ashen.

"What is it, Rooney?"

"It's just that the shawl, I didn't realize when I made it that the color . . . with your dark hair . . . for just a minute it was like watching that painting of Caroline. Made me feel kind of queer."

Clyde was coming at seven-thirty to walk Rooney home. "He won't have me out of the house alone at night," Rooney confided. "Says he doesn't like my wild talk after I've been out alone."

"What kind of wild talk?" Jenny asked absently. The baby was sleeping. His breathing sounded heavy.

"You know," Rooney said, her tone lowered to a whisper. "Once in one of my spells, when I just spill out words, I told Clyde I've been seeing Caroline around an awful lot. Clyde got real mad."

Jenny shivered. Rooney had seemed so well. She hadn't talked about seeing Caroline since before the baby was born.

There was a sharp knock at the door and Clyde stepped into the kitchen foyer. "Come on, Rooney," he said, "let's get started. I want my dinner."

Rooney brought her lips up to Jenny's ear. "Oh, Jenny, you have to believe me, she's here. Caroline's come back. I can understand, can't you? She just wants to see her grandchild."

For the next four nights Jenny kept the bassinette by the side of her bed. A vaporizer circulated warm, moist air, a dim nightlight made it possible for her, between snatches of sleep, to see that the baby was covered, that he was breathing easily.

The doctor came every morning. "Just have to watch for any signs of pneumonia," he said. "In an infant a cold can go into the lungs in a few hours."

Erich did not come back from the cabin. During the day, Jenny brought the baby down and put him in the cradle near the stove. That way she could watch him all the time and still be with Beth and Tina.

The possibility that she was sleepwalking haunted Jenny. Dear God, could she be wandering outside at night? From a distance she would look like Caroline, especially if she had the shawl wrapped around her.

If she were sleepwalking, it would explain Rooney's claims of seeing Caroline, Tina's, "Why didn't you talk to me when you came into my room," Joe's absolute certainty that he had watched her get in Kevin's car.

On New Year's Eve, the doctor's smile was genuine. "I think he's just about over it. You're a good nurse, Jenny. Now you've got to get some rest yourself. Put him back in his own room. If he doesn't look for a feeding during the night, don't wake him up."

After she nursed the baby at ten o'clock, Jenny rolled the bassinette back. "I'm going to miss you as my bunky, Pumpkin," she said. "But it's awfully nice to have you over that cold."

The baby's eyes, deep midnight blue, looked solemnly up at her from under long sooty lashes. The incoming blond fuzz sent silky gold lights through his dark strands of birth hair. "Do you know you're eight weeks old?" she asked. "What a great big boy."

She tied the drawstring on the long nightgown. "Now kick all you want," she smiled. "You're going to be covered in spite of yourself."

For a long minute she held him against her, sniffing the faint scent of talcum. "You smell so good," she whispered. "Good night, Pumpkin."

She left the sliding panel open only a crack and got into bed. The new year would begin in a few hours. A year ago tonight, Fran and some of the other people in the brownstone had stopped in. They'd known that she was bound to be feeling low; the first New Year that Nana hadn't been with her.

Fran had joked about Nana. "She's probably up in heaven, leaning out the window rattling a noise-maker."

They'd laughed together. "It's going to be a good year for you, Jen," Fran had said. "I feel it in my bones."

Good year! When she finally got back to New York she'd tell Fran to get her bones checked. They were sending out the wrong vibes.

But the baby! He made everything else that had happened this year unimportant. I take it back, she thought quickly. It *was* a good year.

When she awakened, the sun was streaming in, a clear, cold light that warned of a frigid day outside. The small porcelain clock on the night table said five minutes of eight.

The baby had slept through the night, slept through his six o'clock feeding. She bolted out of bed, shoved the panel aside and rushed to the bassinette.

The long lashes cast tranquil shadows on the pale cheeks. A blue vein on the side of the tiny nose was dark against the translucent skin. The baby's arms were flung over his head; his tiny hands were open, the fingers spread so they resembled stars.

The baby was not breathing.

Afterward she remembered screaming, remembered running with the baby in her arms; running out in her nightgown, barefoot, across the snow to the office. Erich, Clyde, Luke and Mark were there. Mark grabbed the baby from her, putting his mouth down to the tiny lips.

"Crib death, Mrs. Krueger," Dr. Bovitch said. "He was a very sick infant. I don't know how he could have survived the operation. This is so much easier for him."

Rooney intoned over and over again, "Oh, no, oh, no!"

"Our little boy," Erich wailed. *My* little boy, she thought fiercely. You denied him your name.

"Why did God take our baby to heaven?" Tina and Beth asked.

Why indeed.

"I'd like to bury him with your mother, Erich," Jenny said. "Somehow it would be less lonesome leaving him there." Her arms ached and felt empty.

"I'm sorry, Jenny," Erich said firmly. "I can't disturb Caroline's grave."

After a Mass of the Angels, Kevin MacPartland Krueger was placed next to the three babies who had been lost in other generations. Dry-eyed, Jenny watched as the small casket was lowered. That first morning on this farm she'd looked at those tombstones and wondered how anyone could bear the grief of losing a child.

Now that grief was hers.

She began to weep. Erich put his arm around her. She shook it off.

They filed back to the house, Mark, Luke, Clyde, Emily, Rooney, Erich, herself. It was so cold. Elsa was inside. She had made sandwiches. Her eyes were red and swollen. So Elsa has feelings, Jenny thought bitterly, and then was ashamed.

Erich led them into the front parlor. Mark was beside her. "Jenny, drink this. It will warm you up." The brandy burned her throat. She hadn't touched liquor from the moment she knew she was pregnant. Now it didn't matter.

Numbly she sat down, sipped the brandy. It was so hard to swallow.

"You're trembling," Mark said.

Rooney heard him. "I'll get your shawl."

Not the green one, Jenny thought, not the one I wrapped the baby in. But Rooney was laying it over her shoulders, tucking it around her.

Luke's eyes were riveted on her. She knew why. She tried to shrug off the shawl.

Erich had allowed Tina and Beth to bring their bassinettes into the parlor so they could be with everyone. They looked frightened.

Beth said, "Look, Mommy, this is the way God will cover our baby in heaven." Lovingly she tucked the blanket under her doll's chin.

There was absolute silence in the room.

Then Tina's voice, sweet and clear: "And this is the way that lady"—she pointed to the painting—"covered the baby the night God took him to heaven."

Slowly, deliberately, she opened her palms and pressed them over her doll's face.

Jenny heard a harsh, drawn-out gasp. Had it come from her own lips? Everyone was staring at the painting now, and then in a single gesture, every head turned and eyes that burned and questioned stared at her.

31

Oh, no, no." Rooney's voice was singsong. "Caroline would never hurt the baby, love." She rushed over to Tina. "You see Caroline always used to cup her hands on Erich's face when he was little. Like this." Gently she placed her palms on the doll's cheeks. "And she would laugh and say, *'Caro, caro.'* That means dear one."

Rooney straightened up and looked around. Now her pupils were enormous. "Jenny, it's just like I told you. She came back. Maybe she knew the baby was sick and wanted to help."

Erich's voice was low. "Get her out of here, Clyde."

Clyde grasped Rooney's arm. "Come on. And be quiet."

Rooney pulled away. "Jenny, tell them how I've been seeing Caroline. Tell them I told you that. Tell them I'm not crazy."

Jenny tried to get up from the chair. Clyde was hurting Rooney. His fingers were digging into the thin arm. But her legs wouldn't hold her up. She tried to speak but no words came. Tina's small hands over the doll's mouth and nostrils. . . .

It was Luke who pried Clyde's fingers loose. "Leave her alone, man. For God sake, can't you see this has been too much for her?" His tone was soothing. "Rooney, why don't you go home and lie down? It's been a terrible day for you too."

Rooney did not seem to hear. "I've been seeing her and seeing her. Sometimes at night I sneak out after Clyde's asleep because I want to talk to her. I bet she knows where Arden went. And I see her coming into the house. Once I saw her at the window of the baby's room. The moonlight was shining on her, just as clear as day. I wish she'd talk to me sometimes. Maybe she thinks I'm afraid of her. But why would I be? If Caroline is here that means that even if Arden is dead she might be able to come back. Isn't that right?"

She pulled away from Clyde and ran over to Jenny. Sinking on her knees she put her arms around her. "That means maybe the baby will come back too. Won't that be nice? Jenny, will you let me hold him when he comes back?"

It was nearly two o'clock. Her breasts were heavy with milk. Dr. Elmendorf had bound them to stop the lactation but at the hours she'd fed the baby they still filled. They hurt, but she was glad to have the physical pain. It balanced the agony of grief. Rooney's frail body was shaking. Jenny reached out, put her arms around the thin shoulders. "He isn't coming back, Rooney," she said. "Neither is Caroline or Arden. Tina was dreaming."

"Of course she was," Mark said brusquely.

Luke and Clyde lifted Rooney up. "She needs a sedative," Luke said, "I'll drive with you to the hospital." Luke looked ill himself.

Emily and Mark stayed a little longer. Emily made

halfhearted attempts to talk to Erich about his painting.

"I have an exhibit in Houston in February," Erich told her. "I'll take Jenny and the girls with me. The change will do us all good."

Mark sat next to her. There was something so quietly comforting about him. She could feel his compassion and it helped.

After he and Emily left, Jenny managed to prepare dinner for the girls and Erich. Somehow she found the strength to get the children ready for bed. Tina splashed in the tub. Jenny thought about holding the baby in the crook of her arm while she bathed him. She brushed Beth's long, thick curls. The baby was losing that dark hair. His would have been golden. She heard their prayers. "God bless Nana and our baby in heaven." She closed her eyes as waves of pain washed over her.

Downstairs Erich had brandy waiting. "Drink this, Jenny. It will help you relax." He pulled her down beside him. She did not resist. His hands ran through her hair. Once that gesture had thrilled her. "Jen, you heard the doctor. The baby wouldn't have made it through the surgery. He really was much sicker than you knew."

She listened, waiting for the numbness to wear off. Don't try to make it easier, Erich, she thought. Nothing you can say matters.

"Jenny, I'm worried. I'll take care of you. But Emily is a gossip. By now what Tina said is going to be all over town." He put his arms around her. "Thank God, Rooney is an unreliable witness and Tina is so small. Otherwise . . ."

She tried to pull away from him. His hands held her fast. His voice so soft, so hypnotically gentle. "Jenny, I'm terribly afraid for you. Everyone has remarked how much you resemble Caroline. They're going to hear what Tina said. Oh, my darling, don't you see what they're going to say?"

Soon she would wake up and be back in the apartment. Nana would be there. "Now, Jen, you're talking in your sleep again. You must have had a nightmare. You've got too much on your mind, dear."

But she was not in the apartment. She was in this cold, overfurnished parlor listening to the incredible suggestion that people might think she had killed her own baby.

"The trouble is, Jen, you *have* been sleepwalking. How many times have the girls asked why you don't speak to them when you go into their room at night? It's entirely possible you were in the baby's room, maybe patting the baby's face. Tina didn't understand what she saw. You yourself told Dr. Elmendorf you've been hallucinating. He called me about that."

"He called *you?*"

"Yes. He's quite concerned. He says you've refused to see a psychiatrist."

Jenny stared past him at the curtains. The lace seemed web-like. Once she had taken those curtains down, blindly trying to change the stifling atmosphere of this house. Erich had put them back up.

Now the curtains seemed to be closing in on her, enmeshing her, smothering her.

Smothering. She closed her eyes against the memory of Tina's small hands covering her doll's face, pressing down.

Hallucinating. Had she imagined the face, the feeling of hair hanging over the bed? All those nights, had she been imagining that?

"Erich, I'm so confused. I don't know what reality is anymore. Even before this. But now. I've got to get away. I'll take the girls."

"Impossible, Jenny. You're much too upset. For your sake, for their sake, you can't be alone. And don't forget. The girls are legally Kruegers. They're just as much my children as yours."

"I'm their mother, their natural mother and guardian."

"Jenny, please remember this. In the eyes of the law I have every bit as much right to them as you. And believe me if you ever tried to leave me, I'd get custody. Do you think any court would award them to you with your reputation in this community?"

"But they're *mine!* The baby was yours and you wouldn't give him your name. The girls are mine and you want them. Why?"

"Because I want you. No matter what you've done, no matter how sick you are, I want you. Caroline was willing to leave me but I know you, Jenny. You'd never leave your children. That's why we'll be together always. We're going to start over as of right now. I'm moving back in with you tonight."

"No."

"You have no choice. We'll put the past behind. I'll never mention the baby again. I'll be there to help if you start to sleepwalk. I'll take care of you. If they investigate the baby's death, I'll hire a lawyer."

He was pulling her to her feet. Helplessly she allowed him to propel her up the stairs. "Tomorrow we'll put the room back the old way," he told her. "Just pretend the baby never was born."

She had to humor him until she could plan. They were in the bedroom; he opened the bottom drawer of the large dresser. She knew what he was reaching for. The aqua gown. "Wear it for me, Jen. It's been so long."

"I can't." She was so afraid. His eyes were so strange. She didn't know this man who could tell her that people believed she was a murderer, tell her to forget the baby she'd buried a few hours ago.

"Yes, you can. You're very thin now. You're lovely."

She took it from him and went into the bathroom. She changed and the nightgown did fit her again. She stared into the mirror over the sink. And understood why people thought she looked like Caroline.

Her eyes had the same sad, haunted look as those of the woman in the painting.

In the morning Erich slid out of bed quietly and began to tiptoe around the room. "I'm awake," she told him. It was six o'clock. It should have been time to feed the baby.

"Try to go back to sleep, darling." He pulled on a heavy ski sweater. "I'm going to the cabin. I've got to finish the paintings for the Houston exhibition. We'll go together, darling, the two of us and the girls. We'll have a wonderful time." He sat down on the edge of the bed. "Oh, Jen, I love you so."

She stared up at him.

"Tell me you love me, Jen."

Dutifully she said, "I love you, Erich."

It was a bleak morning. Even by the time the girls had had breakfast, the sun was still hidden by patches of wintry clouds. The air had a chilly, dark feeling as before a storm.

She dressed Tina and Beth for a walk. Elsa was going to take down the Christmas tree and Jenny broke small branches from it.

"What are you going to do with those, Mommy?" Beth asked.

"I thought we'd put them on the baby's grave."

The fresh dirt had frozen during the night. The luminous pine needles softened the starkness of the little mound.

"Mommy, don't look so sad," Beth begged.

"I'll try not to, Mouse." They turned away. If I could only feel something, she thought. I am so empty, so terribly empty.

On the way back to the house, she saw Clyde drive into the farm road. She waited for him to find out about Rooney.

"They won't let her come home for a while," he said. "They're doing all kinds of tests and they say maybe I should put her in a special hospital for a while. I said no way. She's been a lot better since you came here, Miz Krueger. I guess I never knew how lonesome Rooney was. She's always afraid to leave the farm for long. Just in case Arden suddenly called or came back. But then lately she's been worse again. You saw."

He swallowed, fiercely blinking back tears.

"And, Miz Krueger, what Tina said, got out. The sheriff . . . he's been talking to Rooney. He had a doll out with him. Told her to show him the way Caroline used to pat the baby's face, and how Tina said the lady in the painting touched the baby. I don't know what he's up to."

I do, Jenny thought. Erich's right. Emily couldn't wait to spill that story to the people in town.

Sheriff Gunderson came out three days later. "Mrs. Krueger, I have to warn you there's been talk. I have an order to exhume your baby's body. The medical examiner wants to do an autopsy."

She stood and watched as sharp spades opened the newly frozen earth, as the small casket was loaded onto the funeral car.

She felt someone standing beside her. It was Mark. "Why torture yourself, Jenny? You shouldn't be here."

"What are they looking for?"

"They want to make sure there are no bruises or signs of pressure on the baby's face."

She thought of long lashes throwing shadows on the pale cheeks, the tiny mouth, the blue vein on the side of his nose. The blue vein. She'd never noticed it before that morning when she'd found him.

"Did you notice any bruises on him?" she asked. Mark would have known the difference between a bruise and a vein.

"When I tried the mouth-to-mouth resuscitation I held his face pretty hard. There could be some."

"You told them that."

"Yes."

She turned to him. The wind wasn't strong but every stir of air sent fresh shivers through her. "You told them that to protect me. It wasn't necessary."

"I told them the truth," he said.

The hearse drove onto the dirt road. "Come back to the house," Mark urged.

She tried to analyze her feelings as she trudged by his side through the fresh fallen snow. He was so tall. She'd never realized how used she'd become to Erich's relatively small stature. Kevin had been tall, over six feet. Mark. What would he be? Six four or five?

She had a headache. Her breasts were burning. Why didn't the milk stop flowing? It wasn't needed. She could feel her blouse getting damp. If Erich was in the house he'd be mortified. He hated untidiness. He was so neat. And so private. If he hadn't married her, the Krueger name wouldn't have been dragged through the mud.

Erich believed she had scandalized his name and still he claimed he loved her. He liked her to look like his mother. That's why he always asked her to wear the aqua gown. Maybe when she was sleepwalking she tried to look like his mother to please him.

"I guess I'm trying," she said. Her voice startled her. She didn't know she'd spoken aloud.

"What did you say, Jenny? *Jenny!*"

She was falling; she could not stop herself from

254

falling. But something stopped her just as her hair brushed the snow.

"Jenny!" Mark was holding her, was carrying her. She hoped she wasn't too heavy.

"Jenny, you're burning up."

Maybe that was why she couldn't keep her thoughts straight. It wasn't just the house. Oh, God, how she hated the house.

She was riding in a car. Erich was holding her. She remembered this car. It was Mark's station wagon. He had books in it.

"Shock, milk fever," Dr. Elmendorf said. "We'll keep her here."

It was so nice to float away, so nice to wear one of those rough hospital gowns. She hated the aqua gown.

Erich was in and out of her room. "Beth and Tina are fine. They send their love."

Finally Mark brought the message she needed to have. "The baby is back in the cemetery. They won't disturb him again."

"Thank you."

His fingers closing over her hands. "Oh, Jenny."

That night she had two cups of tea, a piece of toast.

"Good to see you feeling better, Mrs. Krueger." The nurse was genuinely kind. Why was it that kindness made her want to weep? She used to take for granted that people liked her.

The fever was low-grade persistent. "I won't allow you to go home until we've licked it," Dr. Elmendorf insisted.

She cried a lot. Often when she'd dozed off, she'd wake up to find her cheeks wet with tears.

Dr. Elmendorf said, "While you're here, I'd like Dr. Philstrom to have a few talks with you."

Dr. Philstrom was a psychiatrist.

He sat by her bed, a tidy little man who looked like a

bank clerk. "I understand you had a series of pretty bad nightmares."

They all wanted to prove that she was crazy. "I don't have them anymore."

And it was true. In the hospital she was starting to sleep through the night. Each day she began to feel stronger, more like herself. She realized she was joking with the nurse in the morning.

The afternoon was the hardest. She didn't want to see Erich. The sound of his footsteps in the hall made her hands clammy.

He brought the girls to see her. They weren't allowed inside the hospital but she stood at the window and waved to them. Somehow they seemed so forlorn, waving back up at her.

That night she ate a full dinner. She had to get her strength back. There was nothing to hold her on Krueger Farm any longer. There was no way she and Erich could recapture what they once had. She could plan to get away. And she knew how she could manage it. On the trip to Houston. Somehow on that trip, she and Beth and Tina would leave Erich and get on a plane for New York. Erich might be able to get custody of the children in Minnesota but New York would never give it to him.

She could sell Nana's locket to get some money. A jeweler had offered Nana eleven hundred dollars for it a few years ago. If she got anything like that, it would be enough to buy airline tickets and tide her over until she got a job.

Away from Caroline's house, Caroline's portrait, Caroline's bed, Caroline's nightgown, Caroline's *son*, she'd be herself again—able to think calmly, to try to capture all the awful thoughts that kept rising almost to the surface of her mind and then slipping away. There were so many of them—so many impressions that seemed to be eluding her.

Jenny fell asleep, the hint of a smile on her lips, her cheeks pillowed in her hands.

The next day she phoned Fran. Oh, blessed, blessed freedom, knowing no one would pick up the extension in the office.

"Jenny, you haven't answered my letters. I thought you'd jettisoned me into outer space."

She didn't bother to explain that she'd never received them. "Fran, I need you." As quickly as possible she explained: "I have to get out of here."

Fran's usual matter-of-fact laughter disappeared. "It's been bad, Jenny. I can hear it in your voice."

Later she could tell Fran everything. Now she simply agreed, "It's been bad."

"Trust me. I'll get back to you."

"Call after eight o'clock. That's when visiting hours end."

Fran called at ten after seven the next night. The minute the phone rang, Jenny knew what had happened. Fran had not allowed for the time difference. It was ten after eight in New York. Erich was sitting by her bed. His eyebrows raised as he handed her the receiver. Fran's voice was vibrant, carrying. "I've got great plans!"

"Fran, how good to hear from you." Turning to him: "Erich, it's Fran, say hello."

Fran caught on. "Erich, how are you? So sorry to hear Jenny hasn't been well."

After they hung up, Erich's question: "What plans, Jenny?"

32

She went home on the last day in January. Beth and Tina seemed like strangers, curiously quiet, curiously petulant. "You're always gone, Mommy."

She'd spent more time with them in the evenings and weekends in New York than she had here this past year.

How much did Erich suspect about Fran's calls? She'd been evasive. "I just realized I hadn't spoken to Fran in ages and picked up the phone. Wasn't it dear of her to call me back?"

She'd called Fran after Erich left the hospital that night. Fran had exulted: "I have a friend who runs a nursery school near Red Bank, New Jersey. It's marvelous and goes right through kindergarten. I told her you can teach music and art and she has a job for you if you want it. She's looking for an apartment for you."

Jenny bided her time.

Erich was preparing for the Houston exhibition. He began bringing in paintings from the cabin.

"I call this one *The Provider,*" he said, holding up an oil on canvas in tones of blue and green. High on the branches of an elm, a nest could be seen. The mother bird was flying toward the tree, a worm in its beak. The leaves sheltered the nest so it was impossible to see the baby birds. But somehow the viewer sensed their presence.

"The idea for that painting came to me that first night on Second Avenue, when I came on you carrying the girls," Erich said. "You had a purposeful look on your face and you could just tell you were anxious to get the kids home and fed."

His tone was affectionate. He put his arm around her. "How do you like it?"

"It's beautiful."

The one time she was not nervous with Erich was when she studied his work. This was the man with whom she had fallen in love, the artist whose wondrous talent at once could capture the simplicity of daily life and the complicated emotions that attended that simplicity.

The trees in the background. She recognized the line of Norwegian pines that grew near the graveyard. "Erich, you just finished this painting?"

"Yes, darling."

She pointed. "But that tree is gone. You had most of the elms near the cemetery taken down because of the Dutch elm disease last spring."

"I started a painting using that tree in the background but couldn't make it express what I wanted to say. Then one day I saw a bird flying with food for its young and thought of you. You inspire everything I do, Jenny."

In the beginning, a statement like that would have melted her heart. Now it only caused her fear. Invariably it was followed by a remark that would reduce her to trembling nerves for the rest of the day.

The remark wasn't long in coming. Erich covered the painting. "I'm sending thirty canvases. The shippers will pick them up in the morning. Will you be here to make sure they take them all?"

"Of course I'll be here. Where else would I be?"

"Don't be edgy, Jenny. I thought Mark might try to see you before he goes."

"What do you mean?"

"Luke had a heart attack just after he got back to Florida. But that doesn't give him the right to try to break up our marriage."

"Erich, what are you talking about?"

"Luke called me last Thursday. He's out of the hospital. He suggested that you and the girls visit him in Florida. Mark is leaving today to spend a week with him. Luke had the nerve to think I'd let you travel down there with Mark."

"How kind of him." Jenny knew the offer had been refused.

"It wasn't kind of him. Luke just wanted to get you down there away from me. I told him so."

"Erich!"

"Don't be surprised, Jenny. Why do you think Mark and Emily have stopped seeing each other?"

"Have they stopped?"

"Jenny, why are you always so blind? Mark told Emily he realized he wasn't interested in getting married and that it wasn't fair to take her time."

"I didn't know that."

"A man doesn't do that unless he has some other woman in mind."

"Not necessarily."

"Mark's crazy about you, Jenny. If it weren't for him the sheriff would have ordered an inquest into the baby's death. You know that, don't you?"

"No, I don't." All the hard-won calm of the hospital

was deserting her. Her mouth was dry; her hands were sweaty. She felt herself trembling. "Erich, what are you saying?"

"I'm saying that there was a bruise near the baby's right nostril. The coroner said that it probably preceded death. Mark insisted that he was rough when he was trying to resuscitate the baby."

The memory of Mark holding the tiny form flashed through her mind.

Erich was standing next to her now, his lips against her ear. "Mark knows. You know. I know. The baby was bruised, Jenny."

"What are you telling me?"

"Nothing, darling. I'm just warning you. We both know how delicate the baby's skin was. That last night the way he was flailing his fists. He probably bruised himself. But Mark lied. He's just like his father. Everyone knew the way Luke felt about Caroline. Even now whenever he's here he sits in the wing chair so he can see her portrait. He was driving Caroline to the airport that last day. All she had to do was snap her fingers and he was there.

"And now Mark thinks he can pull the same thing. Well he can't. I called Lars Ivanson, the veterinarian from Hennepin Grove. He'll start caring for my animals. Mark Garrett will never set foot on this farm again."

"Erich, you can't mean that."

"Oh, but I can. I know you didn't mean it but you encouraged him, Jenny. I saw it. How many times did he come to the hospital?"

"He came twice. Once to tell me that the baby was back in his grave. Once to bring fruit Luke had ordered for me from Florida. Erich, don't you see? You read so much into the simplest, most innocent situation. Where does it end?"

She did not wait for a reply. She walked out of the room and opened the door onto the west porch. The last of the sun was slipping behind the woods. The evening wind was making Caroline's swing rock. No wonder Caroline had sat out here. She had been driven from the house too.

That night Erich came into the bedroom shortly after her. She held herself rigid, not wanting to be close to him. But he simply turned on his side and went to sleep. She felt her body go limp with relief.

She would not see Mark again. By the time he returned from Florida she would be in New Jersey. Was Erich right? Had she been sending out some kind of signal to Mark? Or was it simply that he and Emily had decided they weren't right for each other and Erich, always suspicious, was reading more into it?

For once, she thought, Erich may be right.

The next morning she prepared a list of odds and ends she needed for the trip. She expected Erich to argue about her requesting the car but he was unexpectedly indifferent. "But leave the girls with Elsa," he told her.

After he left for the cabin she circled a jewelry store listed in the classified ad section that advertised HIGHEST PRICES PAID FOR YOUR GOLD. It was in a shopping center two towns away. She called and described Nana's locket. Yes, they'd be interested in buying it. Immediately she phoned Fran. Fran wasn't home but her recorder was on. She left a message. "We'll be in New York on the seventh or eighth. Don't phone here."

While the children napped she rushed to the jewelry store.

She was offered eight hundred dollars for the locket. It wasn't enough but she had no choice.

She bought makeup and underwear and panty hose with the credit card Erich had given her. She made a point of showing the things to him.

Their first wedding anniversary was February third. "Why don't we celebrate in Houston, darling?" Erich asked. "I'll give you your present there."

"That will be fine." She wasn't a good enough actress to keep up the farce of celebrating this marriage. But, oh, God, soon, soon it would be over. The anticipation put a sparkle in her eye that had not been there in months. Tina and Beth responded to it. They had become so quiet. Now they brightened as she chatted with them. "Do you remember when we were on the plane and had that lovely ride? We're going on a plane again to a big city."

Erich came in. "What are you talking about?"

"I'm telling them about our trip to Houston, what fun it will be."

"You're smiling, Jenny. Do you know how long it's been since you looked happy?"

"Too long."

"Tina, Beth, come on with Daddy to the store. I'll buy you ice cream."

Beth put her hand on Jenny's arm. "I want to stay with Mommy."

"I do too," Tina said positively.

"Then I won't go," Erich said.

He seemed unwilling to leave her alone with the children.

On the night of the fifth she packed. She only took what would appear reasonable for three days. "What fur should I take, my coat or jacket?" she asked Erich. "What's the weather like in Houston?"

"The jacket would be enough, I think. Why are you so nervous, Jenny?"

"I'm not nervous. It's just that I'm out of the habit of traveling. Will I need a long dress?"

"Maybe one. That taffeta skirt and blouse would do. Wear your locket with it."

Was there an edge in his voice; was he toying with her? She tried to sound natural. "That's a good idea."

They had a two o'clock flight from Minneapolis. "I've asked Joe to drive us to the airport," Erich said.

"Joe!"

"Yes, he's able to start working again. I'm going to rehire him."

"But, Erich, after all that happened."

"Jenny, we've put all that behind us."

"Erich, after all the gossip you propose to rehire him!" She bit her lip. What difference who was here?

Rooney would be coming back from the hospital around the fourteenth. They had persuaded Clyde to let her stay a full six weeks. Jenny wished she could say good-bye to her. Maybe she could write and have Fran mail the letter for her from some city on one of her flights. There was nothing else she could do.

At last it was time to go. The girls were dressed in their velvet coats and matching hats. Jenny's heart surged. I'm going to take them to the Village for linguine the night we get to New York, she decided.

From the bedroom window she could barely see a corner of the cemetery. After breakfast she'd slipped over to the baby's grave to say good-bye.

Erich had packed the car. "I'll get Joe," he told her. "Come with me, girls. Give Mommy a chance to finish dressing."

"I am finished," she said. "Hold a minute. I'll go with you."

He seemed not to have heard. "Hurry up, Mommy," Beth called as she and Tina clattered down the stairs behind Erich. Jenny shrugged. Just as well to have five minutes to be sure she had everything. The locket money was in the inside jacket pocket of the suit she had packed.

On her way downstairs she glanced into the girls' room. Elsa had made the beds and straightened the room. Now it seemed inordinately neat, with a quality of emptiness as though it sensed that the girls would not be returning.

Had Erich sensed the same thing?

Suddenly troubled, Jenny ran down the stairs, pulling on her jacket. Erich should be back any minute.

Ten minutes later, she went out on the porch. She was getting so warm. Surely he'd be along any second now? He always left so much time to get to the airport. She stared at the road, straining to see the first sign of the car coming.

At the end of half an hour, she phoned the Ekers'. Her fingers fumbled with the dial. Twice she had to break the connection and start again.

Maude answered. "What do you mean have they left yet? I saw Erich drive past here over forty minutes ago with the girls in the car . . . Joe? Joe wasn't driving them to the airport. Where did you get that idea?"

Erich had gone without her. Taken the girls and gone without her. The money was in the luggage he'd taken. Somehow he had guessed her plans.

She called the hotel in Houston. "I want to leave a message for Erich Krueger. Tell him to call his wife as soon as he arrives."

The reservation clerk's hearty Texan voice: "There must be a misunderstanding. Those reservations were canceled nearly two weeks ago."

At two o'clock Elsa came in to her. "Good-bye, Mrs. Krueger."

Jenny was sitting in the parlor, studying Caroline's painting. She did not turn her head. "Good-bye, Elsa."

Elsa did not go at once. Her long frame hovered in the doorway. "I'm sorry to leave you."

"Leave me?" Yanked from lethargy, Jenny jumped up. "What do you mean?"

"Mr. Krueger said that he and the girls would be going away. He said he'd let me know when to come back."

"When did he tell you that, Elsa?"

"This morning, when he was getting in the car. Are you staying here alone?"

There was a curious mixture of emotion in the stolid face. Ever since the baby's death Jenny had felt a compassion in Elsa she would not have expected. "I guess I am," she said quietly.

For hours after Elsa left, she sat in the parlor waiting. Waiting for what? A phone call. Erich would phone. She was certain of that.

How would she handle the call? Admit she'd been planning to leave him? He already knew that. She was sure of it. Promise to stay with him? He wouldn't trust the promise.

Where had he taken the girls?

The room grew dark. She should turn on some lamps. But somehow the effort was too great. The moon came up. It shone in through the lace of the curtains, throwing a weblike beam on the painting.

Finally Jenny went into the kitchen, made coffee, sat by the telephone. At nine o'clock it began to ring. Her hand trembled so she could barely pick up the receiver. "Hello." Her voice was so low she wondered if it could be heard.

"Mommy!" Beth sounded so far away. "Why didn't you want to come with us today? You promised."

"Bethie, where are you?"

The sound of the phone being moved.

Beth's voice changing to a protest. "I want to talk to Mommy."

Tina interrupted. "Mommy, we didn't go for a plane ride and you said we would."

"Tina, where are you?"

"Hello, darling." Erich's voice was warmly solicitous. Tina and Beth were wailing in the background.

"Erich, where are you? Why did you do this?"

"Why did I do what, darling? Prevent you from taking my children from me? Keep them from danger?"

"Danger? What are you talking about?"

"Jenny, I told you I'd take care of you. I mean it. But I'll never let you leave me and take my girls away."

"I won't, Erich. Bring them home."

"That's not good enough. Jenny, go over to the desk. Get writing paper and a pen. I'll hold on."

The girls were still crying. But she could hear something else. Road sounds. A truck in gear. He must be calling from a phone booth on a highway. *"Erich, where are you?"*

"I said get paper and pen. I'll dictate. You write. Hurry up, Jenny."

The Edwardian desk was held closed by a large gold key. As she tried to turn it, she pulled it out and dropped it. Awkwardly she bent down, scooped it up. The sudden rush of blood to her head made her dizzy. Tripping in her rush to return to the phone, she had to steady herself against the wall.

"I'm ready, Erich."

"It's a letter to me. *Dear Erich . . .*"

Wedging the receiver between her shoulder and ear, she scrawled the two words.

He spoke slowly:

"I realize I am very ill. I know I sleepwalk constantly. I think I do terrible things that I can't remember. I lied when I said I didn't get in the car with Kevin. I asked him to come down here so I could persuade him to leave us alone. I didn't mean to hit him so hard."

Mechanically she was writing, anxious not to make him angry. The meaning of the words filtered through.

"Erich, I won't write that. That's not true."

"Let me finish. Just listen." He spoke rapidly now.

"Joe was threatening to tell that he saw me get in the car. I couldn't let him talk. I dreamed I mixed the poison with the oats. But I know it wasn't a dream. I thought you would accept the baby but you knew it wasn't yours. I thought it would be better for our marriage if the baby didn't live. He was taking all my attention. Tina saw me go in to the baby. She saw me press my hands on his face. Erich, promise you will never trust me alone with the children. I am not responsible for what I do."

The pen dropped from her fingers. *"No!"*

"When you write and sign that statement, Jenny, I'll come back. I'll put it in the safe. No one will ever know about it."

"Erich, please. You can't mean this?"

"Jenny, I can be gone months at a time, years if necessary. You know that. I'll call you in a week or two. Think it over."

"I won't."

"Jenny, I know what you've done." His voice became warm. "We love each other, Jenny. We both know it. But I can't risk losing you and I can't risk the girls with you."

The phone clicked. She stared into it, stared at the crumbled paper in her hand.

"Oh, God," she said, "please help me. I don't know what to do."

She called Fran. "We're not coming."

"Jenny, why not? What's wrong?" The connection was poor. Even Fran's normally strong voice sounded so remote.

"Erich's taken the girls on a trip. I'm not sure when they'll be back."

"Jenny, do you want me to come out? I've got four days off."

Erich would be furious if Fran came. It was the phone call from Fran in the hospital that had alerted him to her plans.

"No, Fran, don't come. Don't even call. Just pray for me. Please."

She could not sleep in the master bedroom. She could not sleep anywhere upstairs: the long dark hallway, the closed doors, the girls' room across from the master bedroom, the room where the baby had slept those few short weeks.

Instead she lay down on the couch by the iron stove and covered herself with the shawl Rooney had made. The heat automatically went off at ten. She decided to make a fire in the stove. The wood was in the cradle. The cradle moved as she touched it. Oh, Pumpkin, she mourned, remembering the solemn eyes that had gazed steadily back at her, the small fist that had curled around her finger.

She could not write that letter. The next time Erich had an outburst of jealousy he might give it to the sheriff. How long would he stay away?

She heard the clock strike one . . . two . . . three

. . . Sometime after that she dozed off. A sound awakened her. The house creaking and groaning as it settled. No, she was hearing footsteps. Someone was walking upstairs.

She had to know. Slowly, step by step, she made herself go up the stairs. She clutched the shawl around her against the chill. The hallway was empty. She made herself go into the master bedroom, switch on a lamp. There was no one there.

Erich's old room. The door was open a crack. Hadn't it been closed? She went into it, flipped on the overhead light. No one.

And yet, there was something, a feeling of presence. What was it? The pine scent. Was it stronger again? She couldn't be sure.

She walked over to the window. She needed to open it, to breathe fresh air. Her hands on the sill, she looked down.

A figure was standing outside in the yard, the figure of a man gazing up at the house. The moonlight flickered on his face. It was Clyde. What was he doing there? She waved to him.

He turned and ran.

33

For the rest of the night she lay on the couch, listening.

Sometimes she fancied she heard sounds, footsteps, a door closing. Imagination. All of it.

At six o'clock she got up and realized she hadn't undressed. The printed silk suit she'd planned to wear on the trip was hopelessly wrinkled. No wonder I couldn't sleep, she thought.

A long, hot shower cleared some of the numbing fatigue. With the heavy bath towel wrapped around her she went into the bedroom and opened the drawer. A faded pair of jeans were there, a pair she used to wear in New York. She put them on and rummaged until she found one of her old sweaters. Erich had wanted her to give everything away. But she'd hung onto a few things. It was important to wear something of her own now, something she'd bought herself. She remembered how badly dressed she'd felt that day she met Erich. She'd been wearing that cheap sweater Kevin gave her and Nana's gold locket.

She'd come here with that one piece of jewelery of her own and the girls. Now she didn't have Nana's locket and Erich had the girls.

Jenny stared at the dark oak floor. Something was shining on it, just outside the closet. She bent down and picked it up. It was a scrap of mink. She yanked open the closet door. The mink coat was half off the hanger. One sleeve drooped raggedly round the hem. What was the matter? Jenny went to adjust it, then pulled back. Her fingers had slid through to the skin beneath the fur at the collar line. Bits of fur clung to her fingers.

The coat had been slashed to ribbons.

At ten o'clock she went over to the office. Clyde was sitting at the large desk, the one Erich always used. "I always base here when Erich is going to be gone for a spell. Makes it easier." Clyde looked older. The heavy wrinkles around his eyes were more pronounced. She waited for him to explain why he'd been looking up at the house in the middle of the night. But he said nothing.

"How long is Erich planning to be gone?" she asked.

"He didn't say for sure, Miz Krueger."

"Clyde, why were you outside the house last night?"

"You saw me?"

"Yes, of course."

"Then you saw her too?"

"Her?"

Clyde burst out: "Miz Krueger, maybe Rooney ain't so crazy after all. You know she keeps saying she sees Caroline? Last night I couldn't sleep. Knowing they still don't want to let Rooney home more'n a few days at a time, wondering if I'm doing the right thing by her, anyhow I got up. And you know, Miz Krueger, how you can see a piece of the cemetery from our window? Well, I saw something moving there. And I went out."

Clyde's face became unnaturally pale. "Miz Krueger, I *saw Caroline.* Just like Rooney's been saying. She was walking from the cemetery to the house. I followed her. That hair, that cape she always wore. She went in the back door. I tried it after her but it was locked. I wasn't carrying my keys.

"I walked around and just waited. In a little while I saw the light go on in the master bedroom, then the light in Erich's old room. Then she came to the window and looked out and waved at me."

"Clyde, *I* was at the window. *I* waved at you."

"Oh, Jesus," Clyde whispered. "Rooney's been saying she sees Caroline. Tina talks about the lady in the painting. I think I'm following Caroline. Oh, Jesus"—he stared at her, horror in his face—"and all the time, just like Erich said, it's you we've been seeing."

"It wasn't me, Clyde," she protested. "I went upstairs because I heard someone walking around." She stopped, repelled by the disbelief in his face. She fled back to the house. Was Clyde right? Had she been walking near the graveyard? She'd been dreaming about the baby. And this morning she'd been thinking how much she hated the clothes Erich had bought her. Had she dreamed that too and then slashed the coat? Maybe she hadn't heard anyone after all. Maybe she'd just been sleepwalking and woke up when she was upstairs.

She was the lady Tina saw, the lady in the painting.

She made coffee, drank it scalding hot. She had not eaten since yesterday morning. She toasted an English muffin, forced herself to nibble on it.

Clyde would tell the doctors that he'd seen the woman he thought was Caroline. He'd say that he followed her to the house and I admitted I waved to him.

Erich would come back and take care of her. She'd sign that statement and Erich would take care of her. For hours she sat at the kitchen table, then went to the desk and got the box of writing paper. Carefully she wrote, trying to remember Erich's exact words. She'd tell about last night too. She wrote:

And last night I must have been sleepwalking again. Clyde saw me. I walked in from the cemetery. I guess I went to the baby's grave. I woke up in the bedroom and saw Clyde from the window. I waved to him.

Clyde had been standing out there, standing in the ice-crusted snow.

The snow.

She'd been in her stocking feet. If she'd been outside her feet would have been wet. The boots she'd been planning to wear on the trip were by the couch, still freshly polished. They hadn't been worn outside.

She might have imagined the draft of cold air, imagined the footsteps, forgotten about sleepwalking. But if she'd been out by the cemetery, her feet would have gotten wet, her stockings would have been stained.

Slowly she tore up the letter, tore it till it scattered in tiny pieces. Dispassionately she watched the pieces scatter around the kitchen. For the first time since Erich had gone, the sense of hopelessness began to lift.

She hadn't been outside. But Rooney had seen Caroline. Tina had seen her. Clyde had seen her. She, Jenny, had heard her upstairs last night. Caroline had slashed the mink coat. Maybe she was angry with Jenny for causing Erich so much trouble. Maybe she was still upstairs. *She had come back.*

Jenny got up. "Caroline," she called. "Caroline."

She could hear her voice getting higher. Maybe Caroline couldn't hear her. Step by step she ascended the stairs. The master bedroom was empty. She detected the faint scent of pine that was always there. Maybe if she left some pine soap out, Caroline would feel more at home. She reached into the crystal bowl, brought out three small cakes, left them on the pillow.

The attic. Perhaps she was in the attic. That's where she might have gone last night. "Caroline," Jenny called, trying to sound coaxing, "don't be afraid of me. Please come. You have to help me get the girls."

The attic was nearly dark. She walked up and down it. Caroline's vanity case with her ticket and appointment book. Where was the rest of her luggage? Why did Caroline keep coming back to this house? She had been so anxious to get away.

"Caroline," Jenny called softly, "please talk to me."

The bassinette was in the corner, covered now with a sheet. Jenny walked over to it, touched it tenderly, began to rock it. "My little love," she whispered. "Oh, little love."

Something was sliding across the sheet, something slipping toward her hand. A delicate gold chain, a heart-shaped pendant, the filigree workmanship like spun-gold thread, the center diamond that flashed in the dusk.

Jenny closed her hand over Nana's locket.

"Nana." Saying the name aloud was like a drenching of cold water. What would Nana think of her, standing here, trying to talk to a dead woman?

The attic seemed intolerably confining. Clasping her hand over the locket she ran downstairs to the second floor, down to the main floor, into the kitchen. I am going mad, she thought. Aghast, she remembered calling Caroline's name.

Think about what Nana would tell her to do.

Everything looks better over a cup of tea, Jenny. Mechanically she put on the kettle.

What did you eat today, Jen? It's not good this business of skipping meals.

She went to the refrigerator, pulled out sandwich makings. A BLT down, she thought, and managed a smile.

As she ate, she tried to picture telling Nana about last night. "Clyde said he saw me but my feet weren't wet. Could it have been Caroline?"

She could just hear Nana's reaction. *There are no such things as ghosts, Jen. When you're dead, you're dead.*

Then how did the locket get upstairs?

Find out.

The telephone book was in the drawer under the wall phone. Holding the sandwich, Jenny went over and got it. She flipped the classified section to JEWELRY, BOUGHT AND SOLD. The jeweler to whom she'd sold the locket. She'd circled his ad with Magic Marker.

She dialed the number, asked to speak to the manager. Quickly she explained: "I'm Mrs. Krueger. I sold a locket to you last week. I think I'd like to buy it back."

"Mrs. Krueger, I wish you'd stop wasting my time. Your husband came in and told me you had no right to sell a family piece. I let him buy it for just what I paid you."

"My husband!"

"Yes, he came not twenty minutes after you sold it to me." The line went dead.

Jenny stared into the phone. Erich had suspected her. He had followed her that afternoon, probably in one of the farm vehicles. But how had the locket gotten to the attic?

She went to the desk, got out a pad of lined paper. One hour ago she'd planned to write the statement Erich had demanded. Now there was something else she needed to see in black and white.

She settled at the kitchen table. On the first line she wrote, *There are no ghosts.* On the second: *I could not have been outside last night.* One more, she thought. The next line she printed in caps: *I AM NOT A VIOLENT PERSON.*

Begin at the beginning, she thought. Write everything down. All the trouble began with that first phone call from Kevin. . . .

Clyde did not come near the house. The third day she went into the office. It was the tenth of February. Clyde was on the phone talking to a dealer. She sat watching him. When Erich was around, Clyde tended to fade into the background. With Erich gone, his voice took on a new note of authority. She listened as he arranged the sale of a two-year-old bull for over one hundred thousand dollars.

When he hung up, he looked at her warily. Obviously he was remembering their last conversation.

"Clyde, don't you have to consult with Erich when you sell a bull for that kind of money?"

"Miz Krueger, when Erich is here, he gets into the business as much as he wants. But the fact is he's never been much interested in running this farm or the limeworks."

"I see. Clyde, I've been doing a lot of thinking. Tell me. Where was Rooney Wednesday night when you thought you saw Caroline?"

"What do you mean, where was Rooney?"

"Just that. I called the hospital and spoke to Dr. Philstrom. He's the psychiatrist who came in to see me."

"I know who he is. He's Rooney's doctor."

"That's right. You didn't tell me Rooney had an overnight pass on Wednesday night."

"Wednesday night Rooney was in the hospital."

"No, she wasn't. She was staying with Maude Ekers. It was Maude's birthday. You were supposed to go to a cattle auction and you'd given permission for Maude to pick up Rooney. Rooney thought you were in St. Cloud."

"I was. I got back home round midnight. I'd forgotten Rooney was going to Maude's."

"Clyde, isn't it possible Rooney slipped out of Maude's house and was walking around on the farm?"

"No, it ain't."

"Clyde, she often walks around at night. You know that. Isn't it possible you saw her with a blanket wrapped around her, a blanket that might seem like a cape from a distance? Think of Rooney with her hair down."

"Rooney ain't worn her hair out of a bun for twenty years, 'cept of course . . ." He hesitated.

"Except when?"

"'cept at night."

"Clyde, don't you see what I'm trying to tell you? Just one more question. Did Erich put a gold locket in the safe or give it to you to put there?"

"He put it in himself. He said you kept mislaying it and didn't want it lost."

"Did you tell Rooney that?"

"I might a mentioned it, just to talk, just to pass the time of day."

"Clyde, Rooney knows the combination of this safe, doesn't she?"

He frowned, a worried frown. "She might."

"And she's home on passes more than you've admitted?"

"She's been home some."

"And it's possible she was wandering around here Wednesday night. Clyde, open the safe. Show me my locket."

Silently he obeyed. His fingers fumbled as he worked the combination. The door swung open. He reached in, pulled out a small strongbox and opened it expectantly. Then he held it up as though hoping that a stronger light would reveal what he was seeking. Finally he said, his voice unnaturally soft, "The locket ain't here."

Two nights later, Erich phoned. "Jenny!" There was a sing-song, teasing quality in his voice.

"Erich! Erich!"

"Where are you, Jen?"

"I'm downstairs, on the couch." She looked at the clock. It was after eleven. She had dozed off.

"Why?"

"It's lonesome upstairs, Erich." She wanted to tell him what she suspected about Rooney.

"Jenny." The anger in his voice bolted her awake. "I want you where you belong in our room, in our bed. I want you to wear the special nightgown. Do you hear me?"

"Erich, please. Tina. Beth. How are they?"

"They're fine. Read the letter to me."

"Erich, I found out something. Maybe you've been *wrong.*" Too late she tried to call back the words. "I mean, Erich, maybe we've both just not understood . . ."

"You haven't written the letter. . . ."

"I started to. But Erich what you think isn't true. I'm sure of that now."

The connection broke.

* * *

279

Jenny rang the bell at Maude Ekers' kitchen door. How many months had it been since she'd been here? Since Maude told her to leave Joe alone?

Maude had been right to worry about Joe.

She was about to ring the bell again when the door opened. Joe was there, a much thinner Joe, the boyish face matured by tired lines around his eyes.

"Joe!"

He held his hands out. Impulsively she grasped them; with a rush of affection she kissed his cheek. "Joe."

"Jenny, I mean, Mrs. Krueger . . ." Awkwardly he stood aside to let her pass.

"Is your mother here?"

"She's working. I'm by myself."

"I'm just as glad. I have to talk to you. I've wanted to talk to you so much but you know . . ."

"I know, Jenny. I've caused you so much trouble. I'd like to go down on my knees for what I said the morning of the accident. I guess everyone thought I was saying that you . . . well, you'd hurt me. Like I told the sheriff I didn't mean that at all. I just meant, I thought I was dying and I was worried about telling you I'd seen you that night."

She took the seat across the kitchen table from him.

"Joe, do you mean you don't think you saw me that night?"

"Just like I tried to explain to the sheriff and like I told Mr. Krueger last week . . . there was something always bothering me about that night."

"Bothering you?"

"It's the way you move. You're so graceful, Jenny. You have such a quick, light step, like a deer. Whoever came down the porch that night walked *different*. It's hard to explain. And she was sort of leaning forward, so her hair was almost covering her face. You always stand so straight. . . ."

"Joe, do you think you might have seen Rooney wearing my coat that night?"

Joe looked puzzled. "How could that be? The reason I was standing there is because I saw Rooney on the path leading to the house and I didn't want to bump into her. Rooney was there all right but somebody else got in that car."

Jenny rubbed her hand over her forehead. These last few days she'd come to believe that Rooney was the key to everything that had happened. Rooney could let herself in and out of the house so silently. Rooney could even have overheard Erich and her talking about Kevin. Rooney could have made the phone call. Rooney knew about the panel between the bedrooms. Everything fit into place if Rooney, wearing her coat, had met Kevin that night.

Then who was wearing that coat? Who had arranged the meeting?

She didn't know.

But at least Joe had verified that he believed she, Jenny, was not that person.

She got up to go. There was no point in being here when Maude came home. Maude would be horrified. She tried to make herself smile. "Joe, I'm so glad to have seen you. We've missed you. It's good news that you'll be working for us again."

"I sure was glad when Mr. Krueger offered me the job. And like I say, I told him what I just told you."

"What did Erich say?"

"He told me I should keep my mouth shut, that I'd only start trouble raking up that story. And I swore I wouldn't mention it again to a soul. But of course he never meant I couldn't tell you."

She made a business of pulling on her gloves. She mustn't let him see how shattered she was. *Erich had demanded that she sign that statement, saying she got*

in the car with Kevin, even after Joe told him he was
sure someone else was wearing her coat.

She had to think it through.

"Jenny, I guess I had an awful crush on you. I think I made it hard for you with Mr. Krueger."

"Joe, it's all right."

"But I have to tell you. Like I told Maw, it's just that you're the kind of person I want to find when I get serious about a girl. I explained that to Maw. She was so worried because she always said my uncle would have had such a different life if it wasn't for Caroline. But even that's working out. My uncle hasn't had a drop since my accident and they're getting together again."

"Who's getting together again?"

"My uncle was keeping company at the time of the accident. When John Krueger told everybody Uncle Josh had been so careless 'cause he was mooning around Caroline, his girl got so upset she broke the engagement. And then my uncle began drinking. But now after all these years, they're starting to see each other."

"Joe, who is your uncle seeing?"

"The girl he used to go around with. Woman, now, of course. You know, Jenny. Your housekeeper, Elsa."

34

Elsa had been engaged to Josh Brothers. She had never married. How much bitterness might have built up over the years against the Kruegers? Why had she taken the job at the farmhouse? The way Erich treated her was so belittling. Elsa could have taken the coat from the closet. Elsa could have overheard her and Erich talking. Elsa might have pumped the girls about Kevin.

But why?

She had to talk to someone; she had to trust someone.

Jenny stopped. The wind slapped at her forehead. There was one person she could trust, someone whose face now filled her vision.

She could trust Mark and he should be back from Florida by now.

As soon as she reached the house, she looked up the number of Mark's clinic and phoned. Dr. Garrett was expected any minute; who was calling?

She did not want to leave her name. "What time would be good to reach him?"

"His clinic hours are between five and seven P.M." She'd call him at home after that.

She walked over to the office. Clyde was just locking the desk. There was a wariness, a constraint between them now. "Clyde, how's Rooney?" she asked.

"I'm bringing her home for good tomorrow. But, Miz Krueger, one thing. I'd appreciate it if you stay away from Rooney. I mean don't ask her to your house; don't visit her." He looked unhappy. "Dr. Philstrom says Rooney getting into a stress situation could set her back."

"And I'm that stress situation?"

"All I know, Miz Krueger, is that Rooney ain't seen Caroline walking around the hospital."

"Clyde, before you lock up that desk, I wish you'd give me some money. Erich left so suddenly that I only have a few dollars and I need to get some odds and ends. Oh, yes, may I borrow your car to go into town?"

Clyde turned the key and dropped it in his pocket. "Erich was real plain about that, Miz Krueger. He don't want you borrowing cars and he told me anything you need till he gets back, you should just tell me and I'll see you get it. But he said real emphatic that he don't want no money given to you. He said it'll cost me my job if I give you a dime from the farm funds or lend my own money to you."

Something in her face made him adapt a friendlier tone. "Miz Krueger, you're not to want for anything. Just tell me what you need."

"I need . . ." Jenny bit her lip, turned and slammed out of the office. She ran along the path, tears of rage and humiliation blinding her.

The late-afternoon shadows were spreading like curtains on the pale brick of the farmhouse. At the edge of the woods the tall Norwegian pines were vividly lush against the stark nakedness of the maples and birches. The sun, hidden behind heavy charcoal clouds, was sending diffused rays over the horizon, streaking the sky with coldly beautiful shades of mauve and pink and cranberry.

A winter sky. A winter place. It had become her prison.

At eight minutes after seven, Jenny reached for the phone to call Mark. Her hand was touching the receiver when the phone rang. She grabbed it off the cradle. "Hello."

"Jenny, you must be sitting on top of the phone. Are you waiting for a call?" There was an edge to the teasing quality in Erich's tone.

Jenny felt her palms go damp. Instinctively she tightened her grasp on the receiver. "I've been hoping to hear from you." Did she sound natural? Did her nervousness show? "Erich, how are the girls?"

"They're fine, of course. What have you been doing today, Jenny?"

"Not much. Now that Elsa doesn't come in, I'm a bit busier in the house. I rather like that." Closing her eyes, trying to choose her words, she added lightly, "Oh, I saw Joe." She hurried on, not wanting to lie, not wanting to admit that she'd gone to the Ekers home. "He's so pleased that you rehired him, Erich."

"I suppose he told you the rest of the conversation I had with him?"

"What do you mean?"

"I mean that garbled story about seeing you get in the car and then deciding he hadn't seen you. You never admitted to me that Joe actually told you he'd seen you in the car that night. I always thought it was only Rooney who saw you."

"But Joe said . . . he told me that he told you . . . he's positive it was someone else wearing my coat."

"Jen, have you signed that statement?"

"Erich, don't you see we have a witness who swears . . ."

"What you mean is we have a witness who knows he saw you and who, to ingratiate himself with me, to get back his job, is now willing to change his story. Jenny, stop trying to avoid the truth. Either have that statement ready to read to me next time I call or forget about seeing the girls until they're adults."

Jenny's control snapped. "You can't do this. I'll swear out a warrant. They're my children. You can't run away with them."

"Jenny, they're just as much mine as yours. I've only taken them on a vacation. I've warned you there's no judge who would award them to you. I have a townful of witnesses who'll swear I'm a wonderful father. Jenny, I love you enough to give you a chance to live with them, to be cared for yourself. Don't push me too hard. Good-bye, Jenny. I'll call you soon."

Jenny stared at the dead receiver. All the tenuous confidence she had started to build vanished. Give up, something said to her. Write the confession. Read it to him. Be finished with it.

No. Biting her lips into a thin, firm line she dialed Mark's number.

He answered on the first ring. "Dr. Garrett."

"Mark." Why did that deep, warm voice bring quick tears to her eyes?

"Jenny. What's the matter? Where are you?"

"Mark, I . . . Could you . . . I *have* to talk to you." She paused, then went on: "But I wouldn't want anyone to see you here. If I cut through the west field, would you pick me up? Unless . . . I mean . . . If you have plans, don't bother. . . ."

"Wait near the millhouse. I'll be there in fifteen minutes."

Jenny went up to the master bedroom and turned on the reading light by the bed. She left a light on in the kitchen, a smaller one in the parlor. Clyde might investigate if the house was completely dark.

She'd have to take the chance that Erich wouldn't phone again in the next few hours.

She left the house and walked in the shadow of the stable and polebarns. Behind the electric fences she could see the outlines of the cattle as they hunched near the barns. There was no grazing on the snow-covered ground and they tended to stay near the buildings where they were fed.

Less than ten minutes after she reached the mill, she heard the faint sound of a car approaching. Mark was driving with his parking lights on. She stood out in the clearing and waved. He stopped, leaned over and opened the door for her.

He seemed to understand that she wanted to get away quickly. It wasn't until they reached the county road that he spoke. "I understood you were in Houston with Erich, Jenny."

"We didn't go."

"Does Erich know you called me?"

"Erich's away. He took the children."

He whistled. "That's what Dad . . ." Then he stopped. She felt his glance, was acutely aware of his wind-tanned skin, his thick, sandy hair, the long capable fingers that gripped the steering wheel. Erich always made her uneasy; his very presence charged the atmosphere. Mark's presence had exactly the opposite effect.

It had been months since the one time she'd been in his home. At night it had the same welcoming atmosphere that she remembered. The wing chair, its velvet upholstery somewhat worn, was drawn up to the fireplace. An outsized oak coffee table in front of a Lawson couch held newspapers and magazines. The shelves on either side of the fireplace were crammed with books of every shape and size.

Mark took her coat. "Farm life certainly hasn't fattened you up," he observed. "Have you had dinner yet?"

"No."

"I thought not." He poured sherry for them. "My housekeeper was off today. I was just about to cook a hamburger when you phoned. I'll be right back."

Jenny sat on the couch, then instinctively reached down, pulled off her boots and curled up. She and Nana had had a Lawson sofa when she was growing up. She could remember wedging herself into a corner of it on rainy afternoons and happily reading the hours away.

In a few minutes Mark returned with a tray. "Minnesota plush," he smiled. "Hamburgers, French fries, lettuce and tomato."

The food smelled delicious. Jenny took a bite from hers and realized she'd been famished. She knew Mark was taking his cue from her, waiting for her to explain to him why she had called him. How much should she tell? Would Mark be horrified to know what Erich believed about her?

He was sitting in the wing chair, his long legs stretched toward her, his eyes concerned, his forehead creased in thought. She realized she didn't mind being studied by him. Oddly it was comforting, as though he would analyze what was wrong and make it right. His father had much that same look. Luke! She hadn't asked about him. "How is your father?"

"Coming along, but he gave me a real scare. He wasn't feeling well even before he went back to Florida. Then he had the attack. But he's in his own place now and looks good. He really wanted you to come visit him, Jenny. He still does."

"I'm glad he's better."

Mark leaned forward. "Tell me about it, Jenny."

She told him everything, looking straight at him, watching his eyes darken, watching as tight lines formed around his eyes and mouth, watching as his expression softened when she talked about the baby and her voice broke.

"You see. I can understand why Erich believed I've done these terrible things. But now I don't believe I did them. So that means some woman is impersonating me. I was so sure it was Rooney but it can't be her. Now I wonder . . . Do you think Elsa? It seems so farfetched that she'd hold a grudge for twenty-five years. . . . Erich was only a child. . . ."

Mark did not reply. His face was troubled now, grave. "You don't think I could do those things?" Jenny burst out. "My God, are you like Erich? Do you think . . ."

The nerve under her left eye began to jump. She put her hand up to her face to stop it, then felt her knees start to tremble. Throwing her head down on her lap, she hugged her legs. Her whole body was shaking now, out of control.

"Jenny. Jenny." Mark's arms were around her, holding her. Her head was against his throat. His lips were on her hair.

"I couldn't hurt anyone. I can't sign and say that I could . . ."

His arms tightened. "Erich is in . . . insecure. . . . Oh, Jenny."

Long minutes passed before the trembling stopped. She made herself pull away. She felt his arms release her. Wordlessly they looked at each other, then Jenny turned away. There was an afghan draped over the back of the couch. He tucked it around her. "I think we could both use coffee."

While he was in the kitchen, she looked into the fireplace, watched as the log split and broke and caved into glowing embers. Suddenly she felt exhausted. But it was a different kind of fatigue, not tense and numbing but relaxing, the kind that came after a race had been run.

Unburdening herself to Mark, she felt as though she had rolled a stone off her shoulders. Listening to the clink of the cups and saucers in the kitchen, smelling the perking coffee, hearing his footsteps as he walked between stove and cabinet, remembering the feel of those arms . . .

When Mark brought in the coffee, she was able to make practical statements that helped dispel the emotionally charged atmosphere. "Erich knows I won't stay with him. The minute he brings the girls back I'll leave."

"You're sure you're going to leave him, Jenny?"

"As fast as I can. But first I want to force him to bring the girls back. They're my children."

"He's right that as their adoptive father, legally they're just as much his as yours. And, Jenny, Erich is capable of staying away indefinitely. Let me talk to a few people. I have a lawyer friend who's an expert in family law. But until then, when Erich phones, whatever you do, don't antagonize him; don't tell him you've been talking to me. Promise me that?"

"Of course."

He drove her home, stopping the car at the millhouse. But he insisted on walking with her through the quiet fields to the house. "I want to be sure you're in," he said. "Go right upstairs and if everything is all right, pull down the shades in your room."

"What do you mean, if everything is all right?"

"I mean that if by any chance Erich decided to come back tonight and realized that you were out, there might be trouble. I'll call you tomorrow after I speak to a few people."

"No, don't. Let me phone you. Clyde knows every call I get."

When they got to the dairy barn, he said, "I'll watch you from here. Try not to worry."

"I'll try. The one thing I don't worry about is that Erich does adore Tina and Beth. He'll be very good to them. That at least is a consolation."

Mark squeezed her hand but did not answer. Quickly she slipped along the side of the path through the west door into the kitchen and looked around. The cup and saucer she had left draining on the sink were still there. She smiled bitterly. She could be sure Erich hadn't come. That cup and saucer would have been put away.

Hurrying upstairs, she went into the master bedroom and began to pull down the shades. From one of the windows she watched as Mark's tall form disappeared into the darkness.

Fifteen minutes later she was in bed. This was the hardest time of all, when she couldn't walk across the hall and tuck Tina and Beth in. She tried to think of all the ways Erich would find to amuse them. They had loved going to the county fair with him last summer. Several times he'd spent a whole day with them in the amusement park. He was endlessly patient with the children.

But both girls had sounded so fretful when he let them speak to her that first night he'd taken them away.

Of course by now they'd be used to her absence, just the way they'd gotten used to her being in the hospital.

As she had told Mark, there was the one consolation that she wasn't worried about the girls.

Jenny remembered the way Mark had squeezed her hand when she said that.

Why?

All night she lay awake. If not Rooney . . . if not Elsa . . . then who?

At dawn she got up. She could not wait for Erich to come to her. She tried to close off the terrible nagging fears, the awful possibilities that had occurred to her during the night.

The cabin. She had to find it. Every instinct told her the place to begin was in the cabin.

35

She began looking for the cabin at dawn. At four
A.M. she'd turned on the radio and heard the weather
report. The temperature was dropping sharply. It was
now twelve degrees Fahrenheit. A strong cold wind
from Canada was driving it down. A major snowstorm was predicted. It should hit the Granite Place
area by tomorrow evening.

She made a thermos of coffee to take with her, put
an extra sweater under her ski suit. Her breasts were
so sore. Thinking of the baby so much during the
night had been enough to start them throbbing. She
could not let herself think about Tina and Beth now.
She could only pray, numb, pleading words. . . . Take
care of them, please. Let no harm come . . .

She knew the cabin must be about twenty minutes'
walk from the edge of the woods. She'd start at the
spot where Erich always disappeared into the trees
and crisscross back and forth from that spot. It didn't
matter how long it took.

At eleven she returned to the house, heated soup, changed her socks and mittens, found another scarf to tie around her face and set out again.

At five, just as the shadows were lengthening to near darkness, just as she was despairing that she would have to give up the search, she skied over a hilly mound and came on the small, bark-roofed cabin that had been the first Krueger home in Minnesota.

It had a closed-up, unused look, but what had she expected? That the chimney would be capped with smoke, lamps would be glowing, that . . . Yes. She dared to hope that Beth and Tina might be in here with Erich.

She kicked off her skis and with the hammer broke a window, then stepped over the low sill into the cabin. It was frigidly cold, with the deep chill of an unheated, sunless place. Blinking to adjust her eyes to the gloom, Jenny went to the other windows, pulled up the shades and looked around.

She saw a twenty-foot-square room, a Franklin stove, a faded Oriental rug, a couch . . . And paintings.

It seemed that every square inch of the walls was covered with Erich's art. Even the dim light could not hide the exquisite power and beauty of his work. As always the awareness of his genius calmed her. The fears she had harbored during the night suddenly seemed ludicrous.

The tranquillity of the subjects he had chosen: the polebarn in a winter storm, the doe, head poised about to flee into the woods, the calf reaching up to its mother. How could the person who could paint like this with so much sensitivity, so much authority, also be so hostile, so suspicious?

She was standing in front of a rack filled with canvases. Something about the top one caught her eye. Not understanding, she began to flip rapidly through the paintings in the rack. The signature in the right-hand corner. Not bold and scrawling like Erich's but delicately lettered with fine brushstrokes, a signature more in keeping with the peaceful themes in the paintings: *Caroline Bonardi*. Every one of them.

She began to study the paintings on the wall. Those that were framed were signed *Erich Krueger*. The unframed ones, *Caroline Bonardi*.

But Erich had said that Caroline had very little talent. . . .

Her eyes raced back and forth between a framed painting with Erich's signature, an unframed one signed by Caroline. The same use of diffused light, the same signature pine tree in the background, the same blending of color. Erich was copying Caroline's work.

No.

The framed canvases. Those were the ones he'd planned to exhibit next. Those were the ones he'd signed. He hadn't painted them. The same artist had done all of these. Erich was forging his name to Caroline's art. That was why he'd been so flustered when she pointed out that the elm in one of his supposedly new paintings had been cut down months before.

A charcoal sketch caught her eye. It was called *Self-Portrait*. It was a miniature of *Memory of Caroline*, probably the preliminary sketch Caroline had done before she started the painting that was her masterpiece.

Oh, God. Everything. Every emotion that she had attributed to Erich through his work was a lie.

Then why was he here so much? What did he do here? She saw the staircase, rushed up it. The loft sloped with the pitch of the roof and she had to bend forward at the top stair before she stepped into the room.

As she straightened up, a nightmarish blaze of color

from the back wall assaulted her vision. Shocked, she stared at her own image. A mirror?

No. The painted face did not move as she approached it. The dusky light from the slitlike window played on the canvas, shading it in streaks, like a ghostly finger pointing.

A collage of scenes: violent scenes painted in violent colors. The center figure, herself, her mouth twisted in grief, staring down at puppetlike bodies. Beth and Tina slumped together on the floor, their blue jumpers tangled, their eyes bulging, their tongues protruding, blue corduroy belts wound around their throats. Far up on the wall behind her image, a window with a dark blue curtain. Peering through the opening in the curtain Erich's face, triumphant, sadistic. And all through the canvas in shades of green and black, a slithery figure, half-woman, half-snake, a woman with Caroline's face, the cape wrapped around her like the scaly skin of the snake. Caroline's figure bending over a surrealistic bassinette, a bassinette suspended from a hole in the sky, the woman's hands, grotesque, outsized like whale flippers covering the baby's face, the baby's hands thrust over his head, the fingers starlike, spread on the pillow.

The Caroline figure in the maroon coat, reflected in the windshield of a car; another face beside hers. Kevin's face, exaggerated, staring, grotesque, frightened, his bruised temple swelling into the windshield. The Caroline figure, her cape flung around her, holding the hooves of a wild horse, guiding them to descend on the sandy-haired figure on the ground. Joe. Joe cringing away from the hooves.

Jenny heard the sound from her throat, the keening wail, the screams of protest. It wasn't Caroline who was half-woman, half-snake. It was Erich's face peering out from the tangled dark hair, Erich's eyes wildly staring at her from the canvas.

No. No. No. These twisted, tortured revelations, this art—evil incarnate, brilliance beside which the pastel elegance of Caroline's talent faded into insignificance.

Erich had not painted the canvases he claimed as his own. But those he *had* painted were the genius of a twisted mind. They were shocking, awesome in their power, evil—and insane!

Jenny stared at her own image, at the faces of her children, their pleading eyes as the cord tightened around the small white throats.

At last she forced herself to wrench the canvas from the wall, her unwilling fingers grasping it as though they were closing around the fires of hell.

Somehow she managed to snap on her skis, start back through the woods. Night was descending, darkness spreading. The canvas caught the wind like a sail, whipped her from her own vague path, bruised her against trees. The wind mocked the constant screams for help that she heard screeching from her throat. Help me. Help me. Help me.

She lost the path, turned around in the darkness, saw again the outline of the cabin. No. No.

She would freeze out here, freeze and die out here, before she could find anyone to stop Erich if it weren't already too late. She lost track of time, not knowing how long she stumbled and fell and picked herself up and began again; how long she clutched the damning canvas to her, how long she screamed. She only knew that her voice was breaking into hoarse sobs when somehow she saw a glint through a clump of trees and realized she was at the edge of the woods.

The glint she had seen was the reflection of the moon on the granite stone of Caroline's grave.

With a last terrible effort she skied across the open fields. The house was totally dark; only the faint light of the crescent moon revealed its outlines. But the windows of the office were bright. She headed there, the canvas flapping more wildly without the trees to break the sharp wind.

She could no longer scream; there were no sounds left except the guttural moans she heard in her throat; her lips still formed the words help me, help me.

At the door of the office she tried to turn the handle with her frozen hands, tried to kick off her skis, but could not force the binders to release. Finally she banged at the door with her ski pole until it was flung open, and she fell forward into Mark's arms.

"Jenny!" His voice broke. "Jenny!"

"Steady, Mrs. Krueger." Someone was pulling the skis off her feet. She knew that burly body, that thick, blunt profile. It was Sheriff Gunderson.

Mark was trying to pry her fingers loose from the canvas. "Jenny, let me see that." And then his awed voice. "Oh, my God."

Her own voice was a witch's croak: "Erich. Erich painted it. He killed my baby. He dresses like Caroline. Beth. Tina. . . . Maybe he's killed them too."

"Erich painted this?" This sheriff's voice, incredulous.

She whirled on him. "Have you found my girls? Why are you here? Are my girls dead?"

"Jenny." Mark was holding her tightly, his hand stopping the flow of words from her mouth. "Jenny, I called the sheriff because I couldn't reach you. Jenny, where did you find this?"

"In the cabin. . . . So many paintings. But not his. Caroline painted them."

"Mrs. Krueger . . ."

On him she could vent her pain. She mimicked his

heavy voice. "Anything you want to tell me, Mrs. Krueger? Anything you suddenly remembered?" She began to sob.

"Jenny," Mark implored, "it's not the sheriff's fault. I should have realized. Dad had begun to suspect . . ."

The sheriff was studying the canvas, his face suddenly deflated, the skin folding into limp creases. His eyes were riveted on the upper-right-hand corner of the painting, with the bassinette suspended from a hole in the sky and the grotesque Caroline-like figure bending over it. "Mrs. Krueger, Erich came to me. He said he understood that there'd been talk about the baby's death. He urged me to request an autopsy."

The door swung open. Erich, Jenny thought. Oh, my God, Erich. But it was Clyde who rushed in, his expression frightened and disapproving. "What in hell is going on around here?" He looked at the canvas. Jenny watched as his leathery face drained to the color of white suede.

"Clyde, who's in there?" Rooney called. Her footsteps approached, crackling on the icy snow.

"Hide that thing," Clyde begged. "Don't let her see it. Here . . ." He thrust it into the supply closet.

Rooney appeared on the threshold of the office, her face filled out a little, her eyes wide and calm. Jenny felt the thin arms embracing her. "Jenny, I've missed you."

Through stiff lips she managed to say, "I've missed you too." She had begun to blame Rooney for everything that had happened. She had dismissed everything Rooney told her as the imagination of a sick mind.

"Jenny, where are the girls? Can I say hello to them?"

The question was a slap across the face. "Erich's

away with the girls." She knew her voice was trembling, unnatural.

"Come on, Rooney. You can visit tomorrow. You better get home. The doctor wanted you to go straight to bed," Clyde urged.

He took her arm, propelled her forward, looked over his shoulder. "Be right back."

While they waited, she managed to tell them about her search for the cabin. "It was you, Mark. Last night. I said the children would be fine with Erich and you didn't say anything. Later on . . . in bed . . . I knew . . . you were worried about them. And I began to think—if not Rooney, if not Elsa, if not me . . . And my mind kept saying, Mark is afraid for the children. Then I thought. Erich. It has to be Erich.

"That first night . . . He made me wear Caroline's nightgown. . . . He wanted me to *be* Caroline. . . . He even went to sleep in his old bed. And the pine soap he put on the girls' pillows. I knew he'd done that. And Kevin. He must have written—or phoned—to say he was coming to Minnesota. . . . Erich was always toying with me. Erich must have known I met Kevin. He talked about the extra mileage in the car. He must have heard the gossip from the woman in church."

"Jenny."

"No, let me *tell* you. He took me back to that restaurant. When Kevin threatened to stop the adoption he told Kevin to come down. That's why the call was on our phone. Erich and I are the same height when I wear heels. With my coat . . . and the black wig—he could look enough like me until he got in the car. He must have hit Kevin. And Joe. He was jealous of Joe. He could have come home earlier that day; he knew about the rat poison. But my baby. He hated my baby. Maybe because of his red hair. Right from the beginning when he gave him Kevin's name, he must have been planning to kill him."

Were those dry, harsh sobs coming from her? She could not stop talking. She had to let it out.

"Those times I thought I felt someone leaning over me. He was opening the panel. He must have been wearing the wig. The night I went to have the baby. Woke him up. I touched Erich's eyelid. That's what scared me. That was what I'd feel when I reached up in the dark. . . . The soft eyelid and the thick lashes."

Mark was rocking her in his arms.

"He has my children. He has my children."

"Mrs. Krueger, can you find your way back to the cabin?" Sheriff Gunderson's tone was urgent.

A chance to do something. "Yes. If we start at the cemetery . . ."

"Jenny, you can't," Mark protested. "We'll follow your tracks."

But she would not let them go without her. Somehow she led them back, Mark and the sheriff and Clyde. They turned on the oil lamps, bathing the cabin in a mellow Victorian glow that only accentuated the gnawing cold. They stared at the delicate signature, *Caroline Bonardi*, then began to search the cupboards. But there were no personal papers; the cupboards were empty except for dishes and cutlery.

"He's got to keep his painting supplies somewhere," Mark snapped.

"But the loft is empty," Jenny said hopelessly. "There was nothing in it except the canvas and the place is so small."

"It can't be that small," Clyde objected. "It's the size of the house. It might be partitioned off."

There was a storage area that was half again the size of the loft room, accessible by a door in the right-hand corner, a door that Jenny hadn't noticed in the shadowy room. This area had stacks of file baskets; dozens more of Caroline's paintings in them; an easel, a cabinet with painting supplies; two suitcases. Jenny realized they matched the vanity case she'd found in the attic. A long green cape and dark wig were folded over one of the suitcases.

"Caroline's cape," Mark said quietly.

Jenny began rifling through the file cabinets. But they only held painting supplies: charcoals and umbras and turpentine and brushes and empty canvases. Nothing, nothing that might indicate where Erich had gone.

Clyde began searching through a bin of canvases near the door. "Look." His cry was horror-filled. He had pulled out a canvas. This one in the murky green tones of stagnant water. A surrealistic collage of Erich as a child and Caroline. Scenes crowding, overlapping. Erich with a hockey stick in his hand. Caroline bending over a calf; Erich pushing her; her body, sprawled in a tub, no that was the stock tank; her eyes staring up at him. The tip of the hockey stick flipping the overhead lamp into the tank. Erich's child-face demonic now, laughing into the agonized figure in the water.

"He killed Caroline," Clyde moaned. "When he was ten years old, he killed his own mother."

"What did you say?" They all spun around. Rooney was in the doorway of the loft, Rooney with wide eyes no longer calm. "Did you think I couldn't tell something was wrong?" she asked. She was staring not at the canvas Clyde was holding, but beyond to the painting now revealed in the bin. Even with the distortions Jenny recognized Arden's face. Arden peering in the window of the cabin. A caped figure with dark hair and Erich's face behind her. Hands around Arden's throat, the fingers not attached to the hands. Arden lying in a grave on top of a casket, dirt being shoveled over her bright blue skirt, the name on the tombstone behind her head: CAROLINE BONARDI

KRUEGER. And in the corner the slashing signature, *Erich Krueger*.

"Erich killed my little girl," Rooney moaned.

Somehow they made their way back to the house. Mark's hand held hers tightly, a silent Mark, not attempting to offer useless words of comfort.

In the house, Sheriff Gunderson got on the phone. "There's the chance that everything we believe he's done is the fantasy of a sick mind. There's one way we can be sure and we can't waste a minute finding out."

The cemetery was once again violated. Floodlights bathed the tombstones in unnatural night brilliance. Drills bore into the frozen ground of Caroline's grave. Rooney watched, surprisingly calm now.

As they looked down, they saw bits of blue wool mixed with the earth.

A man's voice spoke from the grave: "She's here. For God's sake, get the mother away."

Clyde hugged Rooney, forcing her to retreat. "At least we know," he said.

Back at the house, the daylight was filtering in. Mark made coffee. When had Mark begun to suspect that the children were in danger with Erich? She asked him.

"Jenny, after I left you home last night, I called Dad. I knew he'd been terribly upset about what Tina said about how the lady in the painting had covered the baby. He admitted to me that he'd *known* Erich was psychotic as a child. Caroline had confided in him about Erich's obsession with her. She'd caught him watching her while she slept, keeping her nightgown under his pillow, wrapping himself in her cape. She took him to a doctor but John Krueger flatly refused to allow him to be treated. John said that no Krueger had emotional problems; it was just Caroline spoiling him; spending so much time with him, that was the problem.

"Caroline was on the verge of a breakdown by then. She did the only thing she could. She relinquished custody, with the understanding that John would send Erich to boarding school. She hoped a different atmosphere would help him. But after she died, John broke his promise. Erich never did get help.

"When Dad heard what Tina said about the lady in the painting, heard what Rooney said about seeing Caroline, he began to suspect what was happening. I think the realization brought on his heart attack. I only wish he'd confided in me. Of course he had absolutely no proof. But that was why he told me to urge Erich to allow you and the girls to visit him."

"Mrs. Krueger." Sheriff Gunderson's voice was hesitant. Was he afraid she would keep blaming him? "Dr. Philstrom from the hospital is here. We had him look at what's in the cabin. He has to talk to you."

"Jenny, can you tell me exactly what Erich said the last time he phoned you?" Dr. Philstrom asked.

"He was angry because I tried to tell him that maybe he was wrong about me."

"Did he mention the girls?"

"He said they were fine."

"How long since he put them on to talk to you?"

"Nine days."

"I see. Jenny, I'll be honest. It doesn't look good but it would seem that Erich must have painted that last canvas before he disappeared with the girls. There's quite a lot of detail in it. Even if he's been in the cabin—and we know he has—there's a scissor there with bits of fur on it. Even so, it would seem that he painted that picture before he left with the children."

A whisper of hope. "You mean they may not be dead?"

"I don't want to encourage you unfairly. But think about it. Erich still fantasizes living with you, having you under his total power once he has that confession signed. He knows that without the children he can't hold you. So until he perceives a reunion with you as being hopeless, there's a chance, just a chance. . . ."

Jenny stood up. Tina. Beth. If you were dead I would know it. Just the way I knew Nana wouldn't live through that last night. Just the way I knew something was going to happen to the baby.

But Rooney hadn't known. For ten years now Rooney had waited for Arden to come home. And all the time Arden's body was buried within sight of Rooney's windows.

How often had she seen Rooney standing over Caroline's grave. Was it because something had compelled her to go there? Something deep in her subconscious that had told her she was visiting Arden's grave too?

She asked Dr. Philstrom about that, asked him gravely, heard her voice almost childlike. "Is that *possible,* doctor?"

"I don't know, Jenny. I think Rooney instinctively suspected that Arden wouldn't deliberately run away. She knew her child."

"I want my children," Jenny said. "I want them now. How could Erich hate me so much, that he would hurt them?"

"You're talking about a totally irrational man," Dr. Philstrom said. "A man who wanted you because you bear a startling resemblance to his mother, yet hated you for replacing her; who could not trust your love for him because he perceives himself as unlovable and who lived in mortal fear of losing you."

"We're going to make up flyers, Mrs. Krueger," the sheriff said. "We'll have their pictures in every hamlet in Minnesota and all the bordering states. We'll get television coverage. Somebody's got to have seen them. Clyde is going through all Erich's records of property holdings. We'll search out any property he owns. Don't forget. We know he was here at least once, and that was only five hours after he phoned you. We're concentrating on a radius of five hours' drive from here."

The ringing of the telephone made them all jump. Sheriff Gunderson reached to pick it up. Some instinct made Jenny push his hand away.

"Hello." Her voice so unsteady. Would it be Erich? Oh, God, would it be Erich?

"Hello, Mommy."

It was Beth.

36

B eth!" She closed her eyes, jammed her knuckles against her mouth. Beth was still alive. Whatever he planned to do to them hadn't happened yet. The memory of the painting, Beth and Tina, stiff little puppets, the corduroy belts around their necks. She could not blot it out.

She felt Mark's hands, those strong hands on her shoulders, steadying her. She held out the receiver so he could try to listen too.

"Beth, hello, darling." She tried to sound carefree and pleased. It was so hard not to scream, *Beth, where are you?* "Are you having a good time with Daddy?"

"Mommy, you're mean. You came into our room last night and you wouldn't talk to us. And you covered Tina too tight."

Beth's plaintive voice was high-pitched enough for Mark to hear. She saw the agony in his eyes, knew it was reflected in her own. *Covered Tina too tight.* No. No. Please, God. No. The baby. Now Tina.

"Tina cried so hard."

"Tina cried." Jenny tried to fight the waves of dizziness. She mustn't faint. "Let me talk to her, Bethie. I love you, Mouse."

Now Beth began to cry. "I love you too, Mommy. Please come soon."

"Mommy." Tina's helpless sobbing. "You hurt me. The blanket was in my face."

"Tina, I'm sorry, I'm sorry." Jenny tried not to let her voice break. "I'm sorry, Tina."

There was a clunk as the phone was moved, then Tina's wail.

"Jenny, why are you so upset? The girls were dreaming. It's just that they miss you as I do, darling."

"Erich." Jenny knew she was shouting. "Where are you Erich? Please, I promise you. I'll sign that confession. I'll sign anything. But please, I need my children."

She felt Mark's grip on her shoulder, cautioning her. "I mean I need my family, Erich." She forced her voice to calm, bit her lips over the urge to plead with him not to hurt them. "Erich, we can be so happy. I don't know why I do such strange things when I'm asleep but you promised to take care of me. I'm sure I'll get better."

"You were going to leave me, Jenny. You just pretended to love me."

"Erich, come home and we'll talk. Or let me send the letter to you. Tell me where you are."

"Have you talked to anyone about us?"

Jenny looked at Mark. He shook his head warningly. "Why would I tell anyone about us?"

"I tried to phone you three times yesterday afternoon. You were out."

"Erich, I hadn't heard from you for so long. I needed to get some fresh air. I skied for a while. I want

308

to be able to ski with you again. We had such fun, remember?"

"I tried to phone Mark last evening. He wasn't home. Were you with him?"

"Erich, I was here. I'm always here waiting for you." Tina was screaming now. From the background she could hear road sounds again, like heavy trucks shifting gears on a grade. Could Erich have been at the farm last night? If so had he gone to the cabin? No, if he had been in the cabin and seen the broken window, realized that people had been there, he wouldn't be calling now.

"Jenny, I'll think about coming back. You just stay in the house. Don't go out. Don't go skiing. I want you right there. And someday I'll open the door and be there and we'll be a family again. Will you do that, Jenny?"

"Yes, Erich, yes. Yes. I promise."

"Mommy, I want to talk to Mommy." Beth's pleading. "Please, please. . . ."

There was a sharp, clicking sound and the dial tone began to hum in her ear.

Jenny listened while Mark repeated the conversation. She only interjected when the sheriff asked, "But why would the kids have thought it was you?"

"Because he has my suitcases with him now," Jenny said. "He probably put one of my robes on. . . . Maybe even that red one I've been missing. He must have a dark wig with him. When the children are very sleepy they see what they think they're seeing. Dr. Philstrom, what will he do now?"

"Jenny, anything is possible. I can't deny that. But I suspect that as long as he still holds the hope that you'll stay with him, the girls are fairly safe."

"But Tina—last night. . . ."

"You have that answer. He tried to phone you in the

afternoon and you were gone. He tried to phone Mark in the evening and couldn't reach him. It's uncanny how some psychotics develop almost a sixth sense. Some instinct told him you were together. In his frustration he came very near to harming Tina."

Jenny tried to swallow over the quiver in her voice. "He sounds so strange, almost rambling. Suppose he does come soon? He could conceivably decide to come back tonight. He knows every inch of this property. He could ski in. He could drive a car we wouldn't recognize. He could walk in from the river-bank. If he sees anyone around here who doesn't belong here, that will be the end. You've all got to go away. Suppose, oh, God, suppose he sees Caroline's grave has been disturbed? He'll know that Arden's body was found. Don't you see? You can't have any publicity. You can't send out flyers. You can't have strangers here. The cabin. If he goes to the cabin and sees the broken window . . . those bits of cloth tacked on the trees . . ."

Sheriff Gunderson looked from Mark to Dr. Philstrom. "Obviously you both agree. All right. Mark, will you ask Rooney and Clyde to come in here? I'll get the people from the coroner's office. They're still sifting the dirt in the cemetery."

Rooney was surprisingly composed. Jenny knew that Dr. Philstrom was studying her closely. But Rooney's concern seemed to be only for Jenny. She hugged her, laid her cheek on Jenny's. "I know. Oh, my dear, I know."

Clyde had aged ten years in the past hours. "I'm listing all the property Erich owns," he said. "I'll have that for you soon."

"The painting," Jenny said. "We've got to put that painting back. It was on the long wall in the loft."

"I left it in the supply closet in the office," Dr. Philstrom said. "But I think it might be better if Mrs.

Toomis would agree to come back and stay in the hospital until this is over."

"I want to be with Clyde," Rooney said. "I want to be with Jenny. I'm all right. Don't you see. I *know*."

"Rooney stays with me," Clyde said flatly.

Sheriff Gunderson walked over to the window. "This place is a mess of footprints and tire tracks," he said. "What we need is a good snowstorm to cover them. Keep your fingers crossed. There's one due tonight."

The storm began in the early evening. Snowflakes fine and rapid bit at the house and barns and fields. The wind blew and scattered the flying flakes, eventually banking them in rapidly growing piles against the trees and buildings.

The next morning, in prayerful gratitude, Jenny observed the glaring whiteness outside. The violated grave would be quilted with snow, the tracks to the cabin obliterated. If Erich came he would not be suspicious; even Erich who could instantly sense a book out of place, a vase moved a quarter of an inch, would have nothing to trigger his awareness of their presence in the cabin.

During the night, pushing their way through the treacherous roads, Sheriff Gunderson and two deputies had come back. One had wired the phones to monitor incoming calls, had given Jenny a walkie-talkie and taught her how to use it. The other had made copies of the papers Clyde pulled from the files, the pages and pages of income tax forms showing the Krueger holdings: deeds, rental contracts, office buildings, warehouses. The originals were back in the files, the copies taken to be pored over by investigators who would then begin to search possible hiding places.

Jenny adamantly refused to allow a policeman to stay in the house. "Erich could open the door and walk in. Suppose he realizes that someone else is here. And he *would*. You can count on it. I won't risk it."

She began keeping track of days with the awareness of seconds turning into minutes, minutes crawling to the quarter hour, the half hour. She had found the cabin on the fifteenth. On the morning of the sixteenth, the grave had been opened and Erich had phoned. The snowstorm ended on the eighteenth. All through Minnesota the cleanup began. The phone lines were down all of the seventeenth and most of the eighteenth. Suppose Erich tried to call? Would he realize that it wasn't her fault he couldn't get through. The entire area of Granite Place where the farm was located was harder hit than the rest of the county.

Don't let him get angry, she prayed. Don't let him take it out on the girls.

On the morning of the nineteenth she saw Clyde coming to the house. The upright set of his head and chest was gone. He bent forward as he walked the freshly plowed path, his face puckered not so much against the wind as under an invisible burden he seemed to be carrying.

He stepped into the kitchen foyer, stamping his feet to break the cold. "He just called."

"Erich! Clyde, why didn't you ring through? Why didn't you let me talk to him."

"He didn't want to talk to you. He just wanted to know if the lines were down around here last night. He asked me whether or not you've been out. Miz Krueger, Jenny, he's uncanny. He told me I sounded funny. I said I didn't know about that; it's been pretty busy trying to feed all the cattle in this storm. That seemed to satisfy him. Then he said the other day . . . Remember when he called right after we found Arden?"

"Yes."

"He said he'd been thinking about it. He said that I

should have been in the office at that time, that the call should have been picked up there first. Jenny, it's like he's right here watching us. He seems to know every move we make."

"What did you tell him?"

"I said that I'd gotten Rooney out of the hospital that morning and hadn't been to the office yet so that it was still on the night setting where it rings in the house. Then he asked me if Mark has been poking around here; that was the way he put it, 'poking around.'"

"What did you say?"

"I told him Dr. Ivanson had been checking the animals and should I have called Mark instead? He said no."

"Clyde, did he mention the children?"

"No, ma'am. Just said to tell you he'd be phoning and he wanted you in the house waiting for the call. Jenny, I tried to keep him on so they could maybe trace where he is but he talked so fast and got off so quick."

Mark phoned every day. "Jenny, I want to see you."

"Mark, Clyde's right. He is uncanny. He particularly asked about you. Please, stay away."

On the afternoon of the twenty-fifth Joe came to the house. "Mrs. Krueger, is Mr. Krueger all right?"

"What do you mean, Joe?"

"He phoned to see how I was feeling. Wanted to know if I've been seeing you. I said just the one time I bumped into you. I didn't say you'd come to our place. You know what I mean. He said he wanted me to come back to work when I'm ready but if I ever came near you or if he ever heard me call you Jenny, he'd shoot me with the same rifle he used to kill my dogs. He said my *dogs*. That means he did kill the

313

other one too. He sounds crazy. I think it won't do no good for either you or me if I'm around here. You tell me what to do."

He sounds crazy. He was openly threatening Joe now. Despair anesthetized Jenny's terror. "Joe, did you tell anyone about this; did you tell your mother?"

"No, ma'am. I don't want to get her started."

"Joe, I beg you, don't tell anyone about that call. And if Erich phones back, just be very calm and easy with him. Tell him the doctor wants you to wait a few weeks more but don't tell him you refuse to work. And Joe, for God sake, don't tell him you've seen me again."

"Jenny, there's real bad trouble, isn't there?"

"Yes." It was useless to deny it.

"Where is he with your girls?"

"I don't know."

"I see. Jenny, I swear to God you can trust me."

"I know I can. And if he phones you again, let me know right away, please."

"I will."

"And, Joe . . . If—I mean he might come back here. If you happen to see him or the car. I need to know at once."

"You will. Elsa was over at our place for dinner with Uncle Josh. She was talking about you, saying what a lovely person you were."

"She never acted as though she liked me."

"She was scared of Mr. Krueger. He told her to know her place, to keep her mouth shut, to make sure nothing was ever out of place or changed in the house."

"I never could understand why she worked for us, the way Erich treated her."

"The kind of money he paid. Elsa said that she'd work for the devil for that big a salary." Joe put his

314

hand on the doorknob. "Sounds like she *was* working for the devil, don't it, Jenny?"

February is not the shortest month of the year, Jenny thought. It seemed an eternity. Day after day. Minute after minute. The nighttime madness of lying in bed, watching the outline of the crystal bowl against the darkness. She wore Caroline's nightgown every night, kept a cake of pine soap under the pillow so the bed always held the faint scent of pine.

If Erich came in some night, quietly, stealthily, if he came into this room, this nightgown, this scent, might lull him into security.

When she did sleep she dreamt incessantly of the children. In sleep they were waiting for her. They would call *"Mommy, Mommy,"* and tumble into the bed, pressing small, wiggly bodies against her, and then as she tried to put her arms around them she awoke.

She never dreamt of the baby. It was as though the same total involvement she had given to preserving the small flicker of life in that tiny body now belonged to Tina and Beth.

She had the confession memorized; over and over it ran through her head: "I am not responsible . . ."

During the day she was never far from the phone. To pass the time she spent most mornings cleaning the house. She dusted and waxed and mopped, swept, polished silver. But she would not use the vacuum for fear of missing the first peal of the telephone.

Most afternoons Rooney came over, a quiet, different Rooney for whom the waiting was over. "I was thinking we might start quilts for the girls' beds," she suggested. "As long as Erich still thinks he can come here and find you and be a family with you and the girls, he won't hurt them. But in the meantime you

315

gotta be busy at least with your hands. Otherwise you'll go crazy. So let's start quilts."

Rooney went up to the attic to get the bag with the leftover scraps of material. They began to sew. Jenny thought of the legend of the three sisters who spun, measured and cut the threads of time. But we're only two of the three, she thought. Erich is the third. It is he who can cut the strand of life.

Rooney sorted the pieces of material into neat piles on the kitchen table. "We'll want them bright and cheerful," she said, "so we won't use dark colors." She began whisking back into the bag the ones she was rejecting. "This was from a tablecloth old Mrs. Krueger had. That's John's mother. Caroline and I used to laugh that anyone would want such a dismal-looking thing. And that sailcloth was from a bolt she bought to make a cover for the picnic table. That was the summer Erich was five. And, oh, I don't know why I don't just throw out the rest of this blue stuff. Remember I told you I made curtains for the big back room? When they were up you'd think you were in a cave. The whole room was so dark. Oh, well. . . ." She pushed it into the sack. "You never know when you might want to put your hand on it."

They began to sew. It seemed to Jenny that the end of hope had robbed Rooney of intensity. Everything she said was expressed in the same middle key. "Once Erich is found we're going to have a real funeral for Arden. The hardest for me now is to think back and remember how Erich encouraged me to think that Arden was still alive. Clyde said all along that she'd never run away. I shoulda known that. I guess I did know that. But every time I started to say that I guess my Arden is with God, why, then Erich would say, 'I don't believe that, Rooney.' He was so cruel getting up my hopes like that; kind of like never letting the wound heal. I tell you, Jenny, he don't deserve to live."

"Rooney, please, don't talk like that."

"I'm sorry, Jenny."

Sheriff Gunderson phoned her every night. "We've checked out the real estate. We've given pictures to all the police in those areas with the understanding there be no publicity and if they see him or the car they don't apprehend him. He's not at any of the places listed in his tax returns."

He tried to offer cautious comfort. "They say no news is good news, Mrs. Krueger. Right now the kids may be playing on a beach in Florida, getting a nice suntan."

Pray God they were. She didn't believe it.

Mark phoned every night. They stayed on only a minute or two. "Nothing, Jen."

"Nothing."

"All right, I won't tie up the line. Hang in there, Jenny."

Hang in there. She tried to establish some sort of pattern to her days. The nights, either sleepless or wracked with torturing dreams, drove her from bed at dawn. For days she hadn't been outside the house. An early-morning television program featured a yoga exercise. Faithfully she sat in front of the set at six-thirty, mechanically following the prescribed routine of the day.

At seven o'clock *Good Morning America* came on. She forced herself to listen to the news, listen politely to the interviews. One day as she watched, pictures were flashed on the screen of children who had disappeared. Some of them had been missing for years. Amy . . . Roger . . . Tommy . . . Linda . . . José . . . one after the other. Each representing heartbreak. Someday would they add Elizabeth and

Christine . . . "nicknamed Beth and Tina" to the list. "Their adoptive father left with them on February sixth, three years ago. If anyone has knowledge . . ."

The evenings had a ritual too. She sat in the family-room section of the kitchen and read or tried to watch television. Usually she would spin the dial and leave the set at where it stopped. Unseeingly she endured situation comedies, hockey games, old movies. She tried to read, but pages later she'd realize her mind hadn't taken in a thing.

The last night in February she was particularly restless.

It seemed as though there was a stillness in the house that was particularly jarring. The canned laughter during a program depicting a couple throwing bric-a-brac at each other made her snap off the set. She sat staring ahead, seeing nothing. The phone rang. By now without hope, she picked it up. "Hello."

"Jenny, this is Pastor Barstrom from Zion Lutheran. How have you been?"

"Very well, thank you."

"I hope Erich extended our sympathy at the loss of your baby. I wanted to visit you but he suggested I defer seeing you. Is Erich there?"

"No. He's away. I'm not sure when he'll be back."

"I see. Will you just remind him that our senior citizens center is almost complete? As the largest donor, I want to be sure he knows the dedication date is March tenth. He's a very generous man, Jenny."

"Yes. I'll tell him you called. Good night, Pastor."

The phone rang at quarter of two. She was lying in bed, a pile of books beside her, hoping that one of them would help her while away the night.

"Jenny."

"Yes." Was it Erich? He sounded different, high-pitched, tense.

"Jenny, who were you talking to on the phone?

Around eight o'clock. You smiled while you were talking."

"Around eight?" She tried to sound thoughtful, tried not to scream out the words, *Where are Beth and Tina?* "Let's see," she made a point of the delay. Sheriff Gunderson? Mark? She didn't dare mention either. Pastor Barstrom. "Erich, Pastor Barstrom phoned. He wanted to talk to you, to invite you to the opening of the senior citizens' hall." Her hands clammy, her mouth trembling, she waited for his comment. Keep him on the phone. That way they might be able to trace the call.

"Are you sure it was Pastor Barstrom?"

"Erich, why would I say that?" She bit her lips. "How are the girls?"

"They're fine."

"Let me talk to them."

"They're very tired. I put them to bed. You looked nice tonight, Jenny."

"I looked nice tonight." She felt herself begin to tremble.

"Yes, I was there. I was looking in the window. You should have guessed I was there. If you love me you would have guessed."

In the darkness Jenny watched the crystal bowl, eerie, green. "Why didn't you come in?"

"I didn't want to. I just wanted to make sure you were still there waiting for me."

"I am waiting for you, Erich, and I'm waiting for the girls. If you didn't want to be here, let me come and be with you."

"No . . . Not yet. Are you in bed now, Jenny?"

"Yes, of course."

"What nightgown have you got on?"

"The one you like. I wear it a lot."

"Maybe I should have stayed."

"Maybe you should. I wish you would."

There was a pause. In the background she could hear sounds of traffic. He must always call from the same phone. *He had been outside the window.*

"You didn't tell Pastor Barstrom that I'm mad at you."

"Of course not. He knows how much we love each other."

"Jenny, I tried to phone Mark but his line was busy. Were you talking to him?"

"No, I wasn't."

"You really were talking to Pastor Barstrom."

"Why don't you call and ask him?"

"No. I believe you. Jenny, I'll keep trying to get Mark. I just remembered. He has a book of mine. I want it back. It belongs on the third shelf of the library, the fourth from the right end." Erich's voice was changing, becoming whiny, fretful. There was something about it.

She was hearing it again. The high-pitched screaming that had nearly destroyed her with its accusations: "Is Mark your new boyfriend? Does he like to swim? Whore. Get out of Caroline's bed. Get out of it now."

There was a click. Then silence. Then the dial tone, a mild, impersonal buzz radiating from the receiver in her hand.

37

Sheriff Gunderson phoned twenty minutes later. "Jenny, the phone company partially traced the call. We have the area he dialed from. It's around Duluth."

Duluth. The northern part of the state. Nearly six hours driving from here. That meant if he was staying in that area he had started down in the midafternoon in order to have been looking in the window at eight o'clock.

Who had been with the children all the hours he'd been gone? Or had he left them alone? Or weren't they alive anymore? She hadn't spoken to them since the sixteenth, almost two weeks ago.

"He's coming apart," she said tonelessly. Sheriff Gunderson did not try to offer empty cheer. "Yes, I think he is."

"What can you do?"

"Do you want us to go public? Release the facts to television stations, newspapers?"

"God, no. That would be signing the girls' death certificates."

"Then we'll get a special squad combing the Duluth area. And we want to leave a detective in your house. Your own life may be in danger."

"Absolutely not. He'd know."

It was almost midnight. February 28 would become March 1. Jenny remembered the childhood superstition she had. If you fell asleep saying "hare, hare" on the last night of the month, and woke up in the morning the first day of the new month saying "rabbit, rabbit," you would get your wish. Nana and she used to make a game of it.

"Hare, hare," Jenny said aloud into the quiet room. She raised her voice: "Hare, hare." Shrieking, she screamed, "Hare, hare, I want my children, I want my children!" Sobbing, she collapsed back on the pillow. "I want Beth, I want Tina."

In the morning her eyes were so swollen she could barely see out of them. Somehow she got dressed, went downstairs, made coffee, rinsed off her cup and saucer. The thought of food sickened her and there was no use stacking the dishwasher with one lonely cup and saucer.

Slipping on her ski jacket she hurried outside and walked around to the window on the southern side of the house that looked into the family area of the kitchen. There were footsteps outlined in the snow below that window, footsteps that had come out of the woods, gone back to the woods. While she sat in that room, Erich had stood out here, his face pressed against the glass, watching her.

The sheriff phoned again at noon. "Jenny, I played that tape for Dr. Philstrom. He thinks we'd better take the chance of going public in search for the children. But it's your decision."

"Let me think on it." She wanted to ask Mark.

Rooney came over at two. "Want to sew a little?"

"I suppose so."

Placidly Rooney took a chair near the iron stove and got out the pieces she was working on.

"Well, we'll be seeing him soon," Rooney commented.

"Him?"

"Erich, of course. You know that promise Caroline made that she'd always be here on his birthday. Since she died twenty-six years ago, Erich has been on this place on his birthday. Pretty much like you saw him last year. Just kind of wandering around as though he's looking for something."

"And you believe he'll be here this year?"

"He never missed yet."

"Rooney, please help me, don't remind anyone. . . . Not Clyde or anyone about that."

Seemingly pleased to be treated as a conspirator, Rooney nodded eagerly. "We'll just wait for him, won't we, Jen?"

Jenny could not trust even Mark with the information. When he phoned to urge her to let the sheriff get help from the media, she declined. Finally she compromised. "Give it one week more, please, Mark."

The week would be up March 9. And Erich's birthday was March 8.

He would be here on the eighth. She was sure of it. If the sheriff and Mark suspected he was coming, they might insist on trying to hide some policemen around the farm. But Erich would know.

If the girls were still alive, this was her last chance to get them back. Erich was losing whatever grip he had on reality.

In the next week, Jenny moved in a near trance, her every thought a continuing prayer. *Oh, Lord in mercy, spare them.* She dug out the ivory case that held

Nana's rosary beads. Jenny closed her hand around the rosary. She could not concentrate on formal prayer. "Nana, come on, you say it for me."

The second . . . the third . . . the fourth . . . the fifth . . . the sixth . . . Don't let it snow again. Don't let the roads be impassable. The seventh. On the morning of the seventh the phone rang. A person-to-person call from New York.

It was Mr. Hartley. "Jenny, so long since I talked to you. How are you, the girls?"

"Fine, we're fine."

"Jenny, I'm sorry, we've got a terrible problem. The Wellington Trust, remember they bought *Minnesota Harvest* and *Spring on the Farm?* Paid a lot of money, Jenny."

"Yes."

"They were having the paintings cleaned. And, Jenny, I'm sorry to tell you this but Erich forged his name to them. There's another signature under his, *Caroline Bonardi.* I'm afraid there's going to be a terrible scandal, Jenny. The Wellington people are having an emergency board meeting tomorrow afternoon. They've called a news conference after it. By tomorrow evening there will be a big news story."

"Stop them! You have to stop them!"

"Stop them? Jenny, how can I? Art forgery is serious business. When you pay six figures for a new artist . . . When that artist wins the most prestigious awards in the field . . . You can't keep quiet about a forger, Jenny. I'm sorry. It's out of my hands. Right now they're investigating to find out who Caroline Bonardi is. In friendship I wanted you to know."

"I'll tell Erich. Thank you, Mr. Hartley." Long after she put the phone down, Jenny sat staring at the receiver. There was no way to stop the story. Reporters would be here looking to talk to Erich. It wouldn't take too much investigation to find that Caroline

324

Bonardi was the daughter of the painter Everett Bonardi and the mother of Erich Krueger. Once they started examining the paintings carefully they'd be able to determine that all of them were over twenty-five years old.

She went to bed early in the hope that Erich might be more likely to come in if the house was dark. She bathed as she had that first night, only this time she used a handful of pine crystals in the tub. The fragrance of the pine filled the room. She let her hair trail in the water so that it too absorbed the scent. Each morning she rinsed out the aqua gown. Now she put it on, slipped a dry cake of soap under the pillow and looked around the bedroom. Nothing must be out of place, nothing must disturb Erich's sense of orderliness. The closet doors were closed. She moved the brush of the silver dressing set a half-inch nearer the nail buffer. The shades were drawn exactly even. She folded the cranberry brocade spread over the lace-edged sheets.

At last she got into bed. The walkie-talkie the sheriff had given her that she carried in the pocket of her jeans made a outline under her pillow. She slipped it in the night-table drawer.

Hour by hour she listened as the clock chimed the night away. Please, Erich, come, she thought. She willed him to come. Surely if he were in the house, if he crept down this hallway, the scent of pine would draw him in.

But when the first light of the sun began to filter through the drawn shades, there was still no sign of his presence. Jenny stayed in bed until eight o'clock. The coming of the day only increased her terror. She had been so sure that during the night she would hear faint footsteps, that the door would start to move, that Erich would be there looking for her, looking for Caroline.

Now she had only the hours until the evening news broadcast.

The day was overcast, but when she turned on the radio, there was no forecast of snow. She was not sure how to dress. Erich was so suspicious. If he came upon her in anything other than slacks and a sweater, he might accuse her of expecting another man.

She barely bothered to look in the mirror anymore. This morning she studied herself, saw with shock the prominent cheekbones, the haunted, staring look in her eyes, the way her hair had grown past her shoulders. With a clip, she caught it at the nape of her neck. She recalled the night she had looked in this mirror and, as she wiped away the steam, had seen Erich's face, Erich's outstretched hands holding the aqua gown. Her instincts had warned her about him that night but she hadn't listened.

Downstairs she scrutinized every detail of every room. She washed the surfaces of the kitchen counters and appliances. She'd barely used the kitchen for more than a can of soup these past weeks but Erich wanted everything mirror-bright. In the library, she ran a dustcloth over the bookshelves and noticed that the third shelf, fourth from the end, did have a vacancy, as Erich had said.

How odd that she had resisted truth so long, refused to face the obvious, lost the baby and maybe the girls because she didn't want to know what Erich was!

Clouds darkened the house at noon; a wind began to blow at three, sending a moaning sound through the chimneys but driving the clouds back so that the late-afternoon sun burst out, shining on the snow-crusted fields, making them glisten as though with warmth. Jenny walked from window to window, watching the woods, watching the road that led to the riverbank, straining her eyes to see if anyone was lurking under the protective overhang of the barn.

At four she watched the hired men begin to leave, men she'd never really gotten to know. Erich never let them near the house. She never went near them in the fields. The experience with Joe had been enough.

At five o'clock she turned on the radio for the news. The briskly crisp voice of the commentator reported on new budget cuts, another summit meeting in Geneva, the attempted assassination of the new president of Iran. "And now here's an item just in. . . . The Wellington Trust Fund has just announced a stunning art forgery. Prominent Minnesota artist Erich Krueger, who has been hailed as the most important American painter since Andrew Wyeth, has been forging his name to the work he has been representing as his own. The true artist is Caroline Bonardi. It has been determined that Caroline Bonardi was the daughter of the late, well-known portrait painter, Everett Bonardi, and the mother of Erich Krueger."

Jenny turned off the radio. Any minute the phone would start to ring. Within hours reporters would be swarming here. Erich would see them, would perhaps hear the broadcast, would know it was over. And he would take his final revenge on Jenny, if he hadn't already.

Blindly she stumbled out of the kitchen. What could she do? What could she do? Without knowing where she was going, she walked into the parlor. The evening sun was streaming into the room, illuminating Caroline's portrait. A bleak pity for the woman who had known this same bewildering helplessness made her study the painting: Caroline sitting on the porch, that dark green cape wrapped around her, the tiny tendrils of hair brushing her forehead. The sun setting, the small figure of the boy Erich running toward her.

The figure running toward her. . . .

The sun rays were diffused throughout the room. It

would be a brilliant sunset, reds and oranges and purples and charcoal clouds streaked with diamond-tinted light.

The figure running toward her. . . .

Erich was out there somewhere in those woods. Jenny was sure of it. And there was only one way to force him to leave them.

The shawl Rooney had made for her. . . . No, it wasn't large enough, but if she wore something with it . . . The army blanket that had been Erich's father's in the cedar chest? That was almost the same color as Caroline's cape.

Racing up the two flights of stairs to the attic, she tore open the cedar chest, reached down into it, pushed aside the old World War Two uniforms. On the bottom was the army blanket, khaki-colored but not unlike the shade of the cape. A scissor? She had scissors in the sewing basket.

The sun was getting lower. In a few minutes it would begin to sink. . . .

Downstairs, with trembling hands she cut a hole in the middle of the blanket, a hole just large enough for her head, and drew it around her. Then she pulled the shawl over her shoulders. The blanket fell around her, draped capelike to the floor.

Her hair. It was longer than Caroline's now, but in the painting Caroline had it loosely drawn up into a Psyche knot. Jenny stood in front of the kitchen mirror, twisting her hair, curling small tendrils over her fingers, fastening it with the large barrette. Caroline inclined her head a little to one side; she held her hands in her lap, the right hand lying over the left. . . .

Jenny stood at the west door of the porch. I *am* Caroline, she thought. I will walk like Caroline, sit like her. I am going to watch the sunset as she always did. I am going to watch my little boy come running toward me.

She opened the door and unhurriedly stepped out into the sharp cold air. Closing the door she walked over to the swing, adjusted it so it directly faced the sunset and sat down.

She remembered to shake the shawl so that it folded over the left arm of the swing, as it had in the painting. She tilted her head so that it was at a slight angle to the right. She folded her hands in her lap until the right hand lay encased in the left palm. Then, slowly, very slowly, she began to rock the swing.

The sun slipped out from behind the last cloud. Now it was a fiery ball, low in the heavens, about to slip over the horizon, now it was going down, down, and the sky was diffused with color.

Jenny continued to rock.

Purples, and pinks and crimsons and oranges, and golds, and the occasional clouds billowing like gossamer, the wind just sharp enough to move the clouds, rustle the pines at the edge of the woods. . . .

Rock, back and forth. Study the sunset. All that matters is the sunset. The little boy will soon run out from the woods to join his mother. . . . Come, little boy. Come, Erich.

She heard a high wail, a wail that grew louder and shriller. "Aai . . . yee . . . devilll . . . devilll from the grave. . . . Go away. . . . Go away. . . ."

A figure was stumbling from the woods. A figure holding a rifle. A figure draped in a dark green cape, with long black hair that the wind blew in matted tangles, a figure with staring eyes and a face caught in a grimace of fear. . . .

Jenny stood up. The figure stopped, lifted the gun and aimed it.

"Erich, don't shoot!" She stumbled to the door, turned the handle. The door was locked. It had snapped locked behind her. Lifting the army blanket, trying not to stumble over its trailing ends, she began to run, zigzagging down the porch steps, across the field, while she heard the sound of shots following her. A burning sensation bit into her shoulder . . . warmth flooded her arm. She staggered, but there was no place to run.

The strange screaming was behind her. "Devilll, devilll . . ." The dairy barn loomed to the right. Erich had never gone in there, not since Caroline died. Frantically she wrenched the door open, the door that led into the anteroom where the vats of milk were stored.

He was close behind her. She rushed into the inner area, the barn itself. The cows were in from the pastures, had already been milked. They stood in their stalls, watching with mild interest, grazing at the straw in the troughs before them. She could hear footsteps close behind her.

Blindly she ran to the end of the barn, as far as she could go. The stock tank was there, the pen for the new calves. The tank was dry. She turned to face Erich.

He was only ten feet away. He stopped and began to laugh. He lifted the gun to his shoulder and took aim with the same precision he had shown when he shot Joe's puppy. They stared at each other, mirror images with the dark green capes, the long dark hair. His hair too had been clumsily pinned up in a knot; his own blond curls escaping from under the wig gave the impression of tendrils on the forehead.

"Devilll . . . devilll. . . ."

She closed her eyes. "Oh, God. . . ."

She heard the gun going off, then a shriek that gurgled into a moan. But not from her lips. She opened her eyes. It was Erich who was sinking to the ground, Erich who was bleeding from the nose and mouth, Erich whose eyes were glazing, whose wig was matted with blood.

Behind him Rooney lowered a shotgun. "That's for Arden," she said quietly.

Jenny sank on her knees. "Erich, the girls, are they alive?"

His eyes were dim but he nodded. "Yes. . . ."

"Is someone with them?"

"No. . . . Alone. . . ."

"Erich, where *are* they?"

His lips tried to form words. "They're . . ." He reached up for her hand, twisted his fingers around her thumb. . . . "I'm sorry, Mommy. I'm sorry, Mommy . . . I didn't mean . . . to . . . hurt . . . you."

His eyes closed. His body gave a last violent shudder and Jenny felt the pressure on her hand released.

38

The house was crowded but she saw everyone as vague shadows on a screen. Sheriff Gunderson, the people from the coroner's office who chalked the outline of Erich's body and took it away, the reporters who swarmed in after the news of the art forgery and stayed for the far bigger story. They'd arrived in time to snap pictures of Erich, the cape draped around him, the wig matted with blood, the curiously peaceful face of death.

They'd been allowed to go to the cabin, to photograph and film Caroline's beautiful paintings, Erich's tortured canvases. "The greater the sense of urgency we give to the search, the more people will try to help," Wendell Gunderson said.

Mark was there. It was he who cut away the blanket and her blouse, bathed the wound, disinfected it, bandaged it. "That will hold it for the present. It's only a flesh wound, thank God."

She shivered at the touch of those long, gentle

fingers through all the burning pain. If there was help possible it would come through Mark.

They found the car Erich had driven, found it hidden in one of the tractor paths on the farm. He'd rented the car in Duluth, six hours' drive away. He'd left the children at least thirteen hours ago. Left them where?

All through the evening the driveway was filled with cars. Maude and Joe Ekers came. Maude, her strong, capable bulk bending over Jenny. "I'm so sorry." A few minutes later Jenny heard her at the stove. And then the smell of perking coffee.

Pastor Barstrom came. "John Krueger worried so about Erich. But he never told me why. And then it seemed as though Erich was doing so well."

The weather report. "A storm is moving into Minnesota and the Dakotas." A storm. Oh, God, are the girls warm enough?

Clyde came to her. "Jenny, you gotta help me. They're talking about committing Rooney to the hospital again."

At last she was startled out of her lethargy. "She saved my life. If she hadn't shot Erich, he would have killed me."

"She told one of them reporters that she did it for Arden," Clyde said. "Jenny, help me. If they lock her up, Rooney can't take it. She needs me. I need her."

Jenny got up from the couch, steadied herself against the wall, went looking for the sheriff. He was on the phone. "Get more flyers. Tack them up in every supermarket, every gas station. Go over the border into Canada."

When he hung up, she said, "Sheriff, why are you trying to put Rooney in the hospital?"

His voice was soothing. "Jenny, try to understand. Rooney intended to kill Erich. She was out there with a gun waiting for him."

"She was trying to protect me. She knew the danger I was in. She saved my life."

"All right, Jenny. Let me see what I can do."

Wordlessly, Jenny put her arms around Rooney. Rooney had loved Erich from the moment he'd been born. No matter what she said, she had not shot him because of Arden. She had shot him to save Jenny's life. *I couldn't have killed him in cold blood,* she thought. *And neither could she.*

The night wore on. All the properties were being searched again. Dozens of false reports were coming in. Snow was starting to fall, swift, biting flakes.

Maude made sandwiches. Jenny could not swallow. Finally she sipped consommé. At midnight Clyde took Rooney home. Maude and Joe left. The sheriff said, "I'll be at my desk all night. I'll call you if we hear anything." Only Mark remained.

"You must be tired. Go on home."

He didn't answer her. Instead he went and got blankets and pillows. He made her lie down on the couch by the stove; he poked a new log on the fire. He stretched out on the big chair.

In the dim light she stared at the cradle filled with wood, beside the chair. She had refused to pray after the baby died. She didn't realize how bitter she'd been. *Now . . . I accept his loss. But please let me have my girls.*

Could you strike a bargain with God?

Sometime during the night she began to doze. But the throbbing in her shoulder kept her on the edge of wakefulness. She felt herself stirring restlessly, making soft hurting sounds. And then it eased, the pain and the restless tossing. After a while when she opened her eyes, she found herself leaning against Mark, his arm around her, the quilt tucked over her.

Something was teasing her. Something in her subconscious that kept trying to surface, something desperately important that was eluding her. It was something to do with that last canvas and Erich watching her, his face peering through the window at her.

At seven o'clock Mark said, "I'll fix some toast and coffee." Jenny went upstairs and showered, wincing as the stream of water struck the adhesive on her shoulder.

Rooney and Clyde were in the house when she came back down. They sipped coffee together as they watched the national news. The girls' pictures would be shown on the *Today* show and on *Good Morning America.*

Rooney had brought the patches. "Do you want to sew, Jenny?"

"No, I can't."

"It helps me. We're making these for the girls' beds," she explained to Mark. "The girls are going to be found."

"Rooney, please!" Clyde tried to quiet her.

"But they are. You see how nice and bright the colors are. No dark stuff in my quilts. Oh, look, here's the story."

They watched as Jane Pauley began the report: "A forgery that rocked the art world yesterday turned out to be only a very small part of a far more dramatic tale.

"Erich Krueger . . ." They watched as Erich's face came on the screen. The picture was the same as the one on the brochure in the gallery: his bronze-gold, tightly curled hair, his dark blue eyes, the half-smile. They had films of the farm, a shot of the body being carried away.

Now Tina and Beth smiled from the screen. "And this morning those two little girls are still missing,"

Jane Pauley said. "As he died, Erich Krueger told his wife that her children are still alive. But police are not certain he can be believed. The last canvas he painted seems to suggest Tina and Beth are dead."

The entire screen was filled with that last painting. Jenny looked at the limp puppet figures, her own tortured image staring, Erich looking in the window at them, laughing as he held back the curtain.

Mark jumped to turn off the set. "I told Gunderson not to let them take photographs in the cabin."

Rooney had jumped up too. "You should have showed me that painting!" she screamed. "You should have showed it to me. Don't you understand. The curtains . . . The blue curtains!"

The curtains! This was what had been gnawing at Jenny's memory. Rooney spilling the scraps onto the kitchen table, that dark blue material, the faint design visible in the painting.

"Rooney, where did he put them?" They were all shouting the same thing. *Where?*

Rooney, totally aware of the precious knowledge she held, tugged at Mark, excitedly crying, "Mark, *you* know. Your dad's fishing lodge. Erich always used to go there with you. You didn't have curtains in the guest room. He said it was too bright. I gave him those eight years ago."

"Mark, could they be there?" Jenny cried.

"It's possible. Dad and I haven't been at the lodge in over a year. Erich has a key."

"Where is the lodge?"

"It's . . . in the Duluth area. On a small island. It makes sense. It's just . . ."

"Just what?" She could hear the sound of snow slapping against the windows.

"The lodge doesn't have central heating."

Clyde vocalized the fear that was now in all of

336

them. "That place don't have central heating and you mean those kids may be alone in it now?"

Mark raced for the phone.

Thirty minutes later, the police chief from Hathaway Island returned their call.

"We've got 'em."

Agonized, Jenny listened to Mark's question. "Are they all right?"

She grabbed the phone to hear the answer.

"Yep, but just barely. Krueger had threatened to punish them if they ever tried to set foot out of the house. But he'd been gone so long and the place was freezing so the older girl decided to take a chance. She managed to unlock the door. They'd just left the house to hunt for Mommy when we found them. They wouldn't a lasted half an hour in this storm. Wait a minute."

Jenny heard the phone being moved and then two small voices were saying, "Hello, Mommy." Mark's arms held her tightly as she sobbed, "Mouse. Tinker Bell. I love you. I love you."

39

April broke over Minnesota like a godhead of plenty. The red haze haloed the trees as tiny buds began to form, waiting to burst into bloom. Deer ran from the woods; pheasants strutted on the roads; cattle wandered far into the pastures; the ground softened and snow melted down into the furrows, nourishing the spring crops as they pushed their way to the surface.

Beth and Tina began to ride again, Beth straight and careful, Tina always ready to give her pony a kick and send him racing. Jenny rode on Fire Maid beside Beth; Joe rode close to Tina.

Jenny could not get enough of being with the children: of being able to kiss the soft cheeks, hold the sturdy little hands, hear the prayers, answer the endless questions. Or listen to the frightened confidences. "Daddy scared me so much. He used to put his hands on my face like this. He looked so funny."

For so long she had wanted to go back to New York, to leave this place. Dr. Philstrom warned her against it. "Those ponies are the best therapy for the children."

"I cannot spend another night in this house."

Mark had provided the answer: the schoolhouse on the west end of his property that years before he'd converted for himself. "When Dad moved to Florida I took over the farmhouse and rented this place, but it's been empty for six months."

It was charming, with two bedrooms, a roomy kitchen, a quaint parlor, small enough that when Tina cried out in terror-filled dreams, Jenny could be at her side instantly. "I'm here, Tinker Bell. Go back to sleep."

She told Luke of her plans to turn over Krueger Farm to the Historical Society.

"Be sure, Jenny," he told her. "It's worth a fortune and God knows you earned the right to have it."

"There's plenty for me without it. And I could never live there again." She closed her eyes against the memory of the bassinette in the attic, the panel behind the headboard, the owl sculpture, the portrait of Caroline.

Rooney visited frequently, proudly driving the car Clyde had bought her, a contented Rooney who no longer needed to wait home in case Arden chose to return. "You can accept anything, Jenny, if you have to. Not knowing is the worst torture."

The people of Granite Place came calling. "It's about time we welcomed you here, Jenny." Most of them added: "We're so sorry, Jenny." They brought cuttings and seeds for her.

Her fingers in the soft, moist earth as she planted her garden.

The sound of the comfortably shabby station wagon in the driveway. The girls running to meet Uncle Mark. The joyful awareness that like the earth she too was ready for a new season, a new beginning.

**POCKET
BOOKS**

This book and other **Mary Higgins Clark** titles are available from your bookshop or can be ordered direct from the publisher.

Please send cheque or postal order for the value of the book, free postage and packing within the UK; OVERSEAS including Republic of Ireland £2 per book. **OR: Please debit this amount from my**

VISA/ACCESS/MASTERCARD ....

CARD NO ....

EXPIRY DATE..

AMOUNT £ ....

NAME..

ADDRESS...

....

SIGNATURE..

www.simonsays.co.uk

Send orders to: SIMON & SCHUSTER CASH SALES
PO Box 29, Douglas, Isle of Man, IM99 1BQ
Tel: 01624 677237, Fax 01624 670923
www.bookpost.co.uk
bookshop@enterprise.net

Please allow 14 days for delivery.
Prices and availability subject to change without notice